There was fire to h
and spark. It was
to love about her. Hold on. . .

Love?

That was a strong word to describe his feelings.

"I had a choice just like everyone else. Bad things happen to good people all the time and whatever happens in childhood isn't a child's fault," Alice said, and he already knew he was in trouble with her. "But the day I turned eighteen, I figured that I had a choice about my life. I could blame my rough situation on everyone else and be miserable. Or I could take charge of my life and find happiness. Not that I'm all that great about that last part. I make mistakes, but I'm giving my best effort."

Alice stood toe-to-toe with him now. What she lacked in height she made up for in spirit.

"You didn't answer my question," he said. Staring into those blue eyes was like looking straight into the sun. He was going to get burned. He just didn't know how badly yet.

ONE TOUGH TEXAN

BY
BARB HAN

Our policy is to use papers that are natural, renewable and recyclable
products and made from wood grown in sustainable forests. The
manufacturing processes conform to the legal environmental regulations of
the country of origin.

Printed and bound in Spain
by CPI, Barcelona

MILLS
BOON

First Published in Great Britain 2016
By Mills & Boon, an imprint of HarperCollins*Publishers*
1 London Bridge Street, London, SE1 9GF

© 2016 Barb Han

ISBN: 978-0-263-92851-8

46-0117

I feel hugely blessed to be a Harlequin author. Working with my editor, Allison Lyons, is truly better than any gift I've unwrapped during the holidays. The same rings true for my agent, Jill Marsal. Thank you both!

Merry Christmas to Brandon, Jacob and Tori. I love all three of you. I hope you always know how very much!

The best present in my life has been you, Babe. Thank you for always encouraging me to follow my dreams and enjoying every step of the way as much as I do. With you, every day feels like Christmas. I love you!

Chapter One

Joshua O'Brien eased his foot off the gas pedal. His Jeep shuddered before the power died. He was out of gas in a flash flood thirty miles from the family ranch in Bluff, Texas. He cursed his floating gas gauge as he pushed open the driver's side door. Running two towns over to Harlan to pick up a box of donations to be auctioned off at his family's annual Christmas Benefit wasn't exactly his idea of an exciting Friday night. When the Nelson widow had opened the door in her red silk bathrobe and then offered him a nightcap, he'd been even less thrilled. Drawing the short straw to make that pickup—and deal with the seventy-year-old Mrs. Nelson—was just one in a long list of reasons that Joshua wasn't cut out for the family business at the Longhorn Cattlemen Ranch and Rifleman's Club and it made him miss his job in law enforcement that much more. Could he make his temporary leave permanent in order to stay on at the ranch? The decision could wait.

He shook off his bad luck, grabbed a gas container from the back and trudged through the ankle-deep water. According to his phone's GPS, there should be a gas station a few blocks ahead. He figured he could walk there and back quicker than one of his brothers could drive into town from the ranch to get him so he set out on foot rather than make a call for help and admit his own stupidity.

It was the kind of pitch-black night outside that made it hard to see much past the end of his nose. His eyes would adjust in a few minutes. A bolt of lightning raced sideways across the sky, emphasizing layers of thick gray clouds as far as he could see. This storm wasn't passing anytime soon. Joshua checked his surroundings. He'd passed the quarter acre cul-de-sac lots and was now walking past a field with overgrown grass. The bad weather must be keeping everyone indoors because the roads were empty. That meant no chance of hitching a ride.

A flash flood alert had already buzzed on his cell. If he hadn't been distracted thinking about his parents' murder investigation then he would've filled up the tank sooner, instead of sloshing through water that was rapidly gathering on the roads and sidewalks while wearing his good boots.

He still couldn't think of a soul who'd want to harm his folks. His father, a self-made millionaire cattle rancher who'd owned a few thousand acres in Bluff, Texas, had built his business on handshakes and hard work. His mother, the matriarch of the family, was as kind as she was giving. Joshua and his five brothers had inherited the lion's share of the family business, which included a successful rifleman's club. A token share went to their aunt and uncle, same as it had been when his parents were alive. The brothers had voted to give a devoted worker a piece of the pie.

Joshua's investigation experience told him to look at those who were closest to his parents, the ones who had the most to gain. Skills honed by Denver PD told him to look for motive, means and opportunity. The only people who stood to benefit from his parents' murders were him and his brothers. None of his brothers had motive. Each was successful in his own right and the O'Briens had always been a loving, close-knit bunch. It couldn't be one of them, which led Joshua to believe that someone had a beef with his parents. It was the only thing that made sense. And he drew a blank there, too. There were no secret affairs, no emotional dramas with friends. His parents were exactly as they appeared on the surface. Generous. Kind. Loving.

The sheriff was checking every angle. He was a close family friend and Joshua knew he was taking the news just as hard.

A warm glow, most likely a streetlight in the distance, meant Joshua was getting closer to the station. At least it wasn't freezing cold outside like it had been recently. Christmas was three weeks away and weather this time of year was unpredictable.

Another bolt of lightning helped Joshua see that if he cut through the field he'd get to the station faster. He took a step onto the land and knee-deep grass. Heavy rain. Tall grass. Horrible luck. Looking down caused water to run off the rim of his Stetson, but he didn't care. His eyes were beginning to adjust to the darkness, which meant he'd been on foot for a solid fifteen minutes already. The station was ahead and he stepped up his pace through the field. As he made the clearing he noticed a teen, maybe sixteen years old based on her petite build, walking ahead of him. Was someone else stranded in this crazy weather?

She seemed a little young to be out walking on a night like this. He started to call out to her when a flash of lightning blazed across the sky and he caught sight of a man watching her intently from behind the trash bins of the gas station. Thunder rumbled in the distance and Joshua counted three seconds in between the flash and the noise. That meant lightning was right on top of them.

Joshua's pulse spiked as he spotted another man crouching at the edge of the field as the unsuspecting teen kept bebopping along. She must have no idea the amount of danger she was about to walk into. And Joshua didn't either because he counted a third man closing in on her from the east. How many others were there?

Based on the way she made the occasional stop to shake her arms or perform some other dance move, Joshua figured that she must be wearing earbuds. That wasn't her brightest move for a couple of reasons. For one, she didn't need to be wearing electronics in a storm. For another, it meant she wouldn't hear him even if he screamed at the top of his lungs. That would, however, alert the men bearing down on her like hunters closing in on a quarry.

Damn, his shotgun was locked inside his Jeep.

Dropping to crouching position, Joshua tried to make himself as small as possible—not exactly easy with his six-foot-four-inch frame—as he shifted all his attention to the teen. She kept her head down. She was wearing jeans that were plastered to her legs and a couple layers of tank tops slick from rain.

And she had no idea what was about to go down.

The big question was how Joshua was going to get her out of this mess. Staying low was his best chance of not being noticed. He palmed his cell, moving closer. Could he call his friend Tommy Johnson, the sheriff? Probably not without being seen. The light from his phone could give him away. If the men saw him, he had no idea what they were capable of doing to him and the girl. Then again, an ill-timed bolt of lightning would have the same effect.

His Jeep was too far away to run back and get his shotgun. The men would be long gone with the girl. He focused on the teen as he moved closer to the gas station. She had a tiny frame and hair for days that she was trying to wrangle into a ponytail. Even wet he could see how thick it was. With her back turned, Joshua couldn't see the details of her face, but the rest of her looked straight out of an Abercrombie & Fitch ad. Scanning the area, watching the men, Joshua knew that this was a coordinated kidnapping attempt. Outnumbered by at least three to one, Joshua calculated the odds of getting to her and they weren't good.

Could he use the darkness to cloak them both? One wrong move and he'd be exposed. She wouldn't have a chance on her own. He needed a plan and yet there was no time to make one. If the men got to her first it would be all over. No way could he handle three against one without a weapon of his own. He'd turned in his service weapon and had stopped carrying his backup since he spent most of his time with cattle on the ranch.

Joshua glanced down at the gas container in his hand, sloshing around what little leftover contents were at the bottom. There hadn't been enough to get him to the gas station, but there might be enough to create a diversion. Distract the men for a few seconds and grab the teen. If he could get her into the convenience store safely there'd be shelter and witnesses. That should scare these guys off. He hoped.

Joshua tucked away his cell and then fished his emergency lighter from the front pocket of his denim jacket. With all this water coming down everywhere, he needed something that he could use as a wick. Nothing was dry.

Lighting the plastic container on fire right next to him was too much of a risk. He cleared an area, poured a little of the gasoline out and then rolled several times until he was a few feet from the container.

Joshua flicked his lighter and then tossed it toward the spot. He didn't wait for it to light up, he bolted toward the teenager.

As the blaze ignited, Joshua wrapped an arm around her waist.

Maybe it was fear that had her frozen but he'd expected a fight. He noted that her struggle was weak at best. Shouldn't she be biting and kicking to get away? Other than a little squirming, she wasn't doing much to help herself. Joshua was even more grateful that he was there to help.

He sprinted toward the gas station. Lightning struck as he scrambled onto the lot, illuminating the man by the trash bins. Joshua could see the guy's face clearly and the dude was looking right at Joshua. Not only was his gaze fixed, but he made a move toward a weapon, a gun maybe, as Joshua barreled around the corner, memorizing the details of the guy's face in the light. He had black-as-night hair, and an oval-shaped face. His eyes were set wide and his nose prominent. His eyebrows were bushy, his forehead large and he had a decent amount of scruff on his chin. His face was familiar but Joshua couldn't place it.

Then he heard someone cussing at him, realized it was coming from the teen as she started actually fighting. Good for her.

"You're okay. I'm not going to hurt you," Joshua said, trying to reassure her. She must be confused and scared as he rounded the corner.

"I didn't think you were, jerk," she shot back.

What the...? Not the reaction he was expecting but then she was probably still in shock.

"Put me down," she demanded. Her voice was a study in calm.

"Not so fast," he said, scrambling inside the station.

Her response came in the form of twists and turns so quick he almost lost his grip around her tiny waist. Her elbow slammed into his ribs. Did she want to be taken by those scumbags?

"Call nine-one-one," Joshua managed to say to the attendant as he shot down an aisle, trying to recover from the blow and stay on his feet. His law enforcement training had kicked in and adrenaline was on full-tilt. He'd lock them in the bathroom until help arrived.

Joshua managed to open the door to the men's room even though the teen was fighting him like a wild banshee. Her freeze response sure made a wide turn into fight mode in a hurry.

"Cut it out. I'm trying to help, if you hadn't noticed," he said through heavy breaths. She wasn't making it easy, either.

He stuffed her inside the bathroom with him and then locked the door. "Those men weren't exactly trying to take you to prom."

Joshua heard a familiar noise and realized he shouldn't have turned his back on her. He whirled around. There she stood. A Glock aimed at the center of his chest.

Now didn't that just make this night even better?

"What do you think you're doing?" he asked, noticing how off his initial assessment of the teen, the woman, had been. Strips of hair clung to her neck even though most of her blond mane was in a ponytail. She had piercing crystal-blue eyes—eyes that shone like he was looking across the surface of Diamondhead Lake at first light—and she had thick, dark lashes. Her body had more curves than he'd initially realized; he'd felt those the second he'd picked her up. They were easier to ignore when he thought she was sixteen. She was closer to his age, so around thirty and his throat went dry despite water dripping from him everywhere.

She was soaked, crown to toe, and as much as Joshua didn't like it, he felt a surge of attraction. All of which was overridden by the anger coursing through him. Even though she put up a good fight, he disarmed her quickly and then wrestled her against the wall before she could make a dive for her weapon that he'd sent sprawling across the floor.

His body had that same irritating sexual reaction when it was pressed up against hers. He captured her wrist as she nailed him in the chest and then he caught her other as it rose up in a fist. He pinned both of her hands above her head. Big mistake, a) because the move caused her breasts to rise and press against his chest harder, and b) because her knee shot up quickly.

Joshua pinned her thigh with his before she could knee him where no man wanted to be kneed.

"What's your problem, lady?" he asked, staring into furious blue eyes.

"BACK OFF. YOU HAVE no idea what you've gotten yourself into," Alice Green said, fuming that this guy had disarmed her so quickly. She was exhausted and getting rusty now that she'd been off the job for the past six weeks, having dedicated herself solely to finding Isabel. "And let go of me."

The cowboy might be the epitome of tall, gorgeous and chivalrous but his good deed had just cost her the investigation. Alice cursed.

This was the closest she'd been to Marco Perez, aka The Ghost, in days. She'd spent long weeks before that researching crime rings to narrow it down this far, and had been abducted by two other criminal organizations. The last time she'd seen her boys was Thanksgiving Day. Since then, she'd been choked, punched and stabbed. And it had come down to The Ghost as her last chance to find Isabel.

Alice had put herself out there as bait, using her informant to plant the seed and set up the kidnapping. It had been difficult undercover work and had taken more patience than she realized she had. Perez's organization finally bit and this jerk had just messed up weeks of damn fine police work in sixty seconds. Well, if she'd still been on the force.

Alice was furious. And frustrated. And she could think of another word she'd like to drop when it came to the cowboy's actions but it wouldn't do any good. The fact that he was acting on goodwill was the only reason she didn't completely unleash hell on him.

"I have to go," she managed to get out through clenched teeth. If the task force found out what she was up to after being warned to stay away she'd lose everything, including her twin boys. "Thanks for going all Dudley Do-Right on me but I need to follow those men out there."

Tall, Dark and Cowboy cocked an eyebrow. "I'm sure

the police would be happy to help as soon as they get here."

"I don't have time to lose," she countered. "They're getting away as we speak."

"Then tell me what's going on and I'll consider letting up," he said, staring her straight in the eye.

She ignored the shiver racing up her arms, chalking up her goose bumps to being soaked to the bone in an air conditioned bathroom. Didn't the worker believe in turning on the heat?

Telling the truth wasn't an option. Fighting didn't help. She'd have to take another approach.

Alice relaxed her body against the strong cowboy, looking up at him with her most sincere expression as she prepared a lie. "I'm sorry. Thank you for helping me. I don't know what I would've done if you hadn't been there. That guy out there is my ex and I really need to know what he's up to for the sake of our boys."

Shock registered in the cowboy's eyes. He had a rare combination of green eyes and black hair—no, black wasn't a good enough word—it was more like onyx.

Water dripped from his thick black eyelashes and his tight curls. She could tell that he'd been wearing a hat, and in this part of the country that meant a Stetson. He was tall, six feet four inches would be her best guess. Based on the ripples running down his chest, she'd say the guy spent serious time at the gym. His hands were rough, which meant he worked outside. But not too rough, telling her that he hadn't been doing it for long.

"Are you telling me you know that guy?" he asked and she could tell he wasn't buying her story.

"Intimately." It was easy to sell that last part because it was the truth. Alice did know more details about Marco Perez's life than she ever wanted to about any criminal on the loose. He was the head of a large-scale kidnapping ring known for selling teenage girls or using them for baby farms. He was also most likely long gone by now. His ability to disappear and make every witness around him do the same had earned him The Ghost moniker.

Alice couldn't afford to explain herself to law enforcement. They'd run her name and she'd be discovered. She had to protect her identity.

"What's your name?" she asked. If she could bait this guy into casual conversation she had a chance at making it out of there before the cops arrived. With her arms hauled over her head the cowboy was in the power position.

"Joshua O'Brien," he said. "Now it's your turn."

It was a statement, not a question and she figured that she was grossly underestimating this guy.

"Will you let me go if I tell you, Joshua?" She'd used his name on purpose. Get him talking, get him comfortable and she could break out of his grasp.

"Maybe," he said.

"I'm Alice," she responded. The cops would be banging on that door in a matter of minutes in a best-case scenario…a matter of seconds in her worst nightmare. In no way could Alice allow that to happen. She'd be taken to jail and her reputation, as well as her career, would be over. As it was she could still return to the force after she located Isabel and brought her home safely.

Sirens wailed in the distance, which meant cops were getting closer. She needed to move faster with the cowboy in order to get away. Or distract him long enough to…

The chance presented itself, so she took it.

The cowboy had loosened his grip. Alice drew her knee up and tagged him as hard as she could in the groin.

She dropped and spun, breaking free from his grasp. A sweep of her right leg and he stumbled to catch himself.

He recovered quickly using the wall to redirect his weight, but he wasn't fast enough.

Alice pulled her backup weapon, a Glock G42 .380 pocket pistol, from her ankle holster. "Hands where I can see 'em, cowboy."

He righted himself and complied.

Now all she had to do was walk out that door and never look back. She made a move toward it and then stopped, a bout of conscience eating at her. It was her fault that the cowboy was in this mess. He'd seen Perez. Worse yet, The Ghost had seen the cowboy.

No one lived who could describe Perez. He was one of the most ruthless criminals in the country and he protected his identity with the ferocity of a starved lion.

But how could Alice protect her own identity and spare the cowboy's life?

Chapter Two

Alice's voice was high-pitched and had that listen-up-or-I'll-shoot quality. The attitude registered with Joshua as law enforcement. Was she on the job? Alice had that same swagger he'd seen in the officers he knew; granted hers was a heck of a lot sexier than theirs. Based on her reactions so far she was covering something—something big. She wasn't breaking the law, or at least not currently, so he was even more confused by the fact that she was adamant about not bringing in the police. He figured this wasn't the time to tell her about his law enforcement background or the fact that he had an application in at the FBI—a fact he hadn't shared with his brothers yet. He shoved the guilty feeling aside. He'd deal with that later.

"I'm running out of time. Word of advice. Forget what I look like," she barked. "And forget all the details about tonight."

Joshua put his hands up, palms flat, in surrender mode. "Sorry. Too late for that. But it's not for you. You haven't done anything wrong."

She shot him another look that told him he didn't have a clue.

"I'm serious about this next part so listen up. When

the law arrives, tell them that you're being hunted by Marco Perez. Do you hear me?" she asked with seriousness in her voice that left no room for question.

He nodded, keeping watch on her and the door while tamping down his reaction to the name she'd just thrown out. The name Marco Perez was on every watch list and that's why his face had looked familiar.

"Also, and I can't stress this next part enough, you need to surrender to protective custody. Tell the sheriff what I said about seeing Perez and he'll arrange everything."

"We can talk this through and get help for you." Joshua wasn't ready to tip his hand about his own background, especially since she hadn't figured him out.

She shook her head.

"This whole situation can be sorted out. You don't have to keep running. Nothing is as bad as it seems," he added, trying to stall. She was the one who needed protection and most likely a skilled attorney.

"I know he saw you," she said, backing toward the door, keeping her intense gaze on him. "And he'll come back for you. Mark my words. No one who has ever seen Perez in action has lived to tell about it."

"Whatever it is you think you need to do…don't," Joshua said. He didn't need to be reminded of that rumor about Perez. His gaze bounced from the gun that had been tossed onto the floor to her again. He'd protect himself from Perez. Who did she have?

She made a move to open the door, keeping a close eye on him.

Joshua had no plans to be shot in the men's room of a gas station. That wasn't even a good cliché.

"Hold on," he said, trying out that same authoritative voice she'd used on him a few minutes ago. It was his cop voice.

Her gaze kept bouncing from him to the door, and instincts honed from years of police work told him she was about to flee. Given that she was obviously in some kind of trouble, even though she seemed more concerned about him at the moment, he needed to act fast or she'd disappear and he couldn't help her. Joshua held out his wrists. "Fine. You win. Take me into protective custody."

She balked.

"You need someone in law enforcement to do that," she said in that crisp, do-as-I-say-and-don't-ask-why voice and he'd be darned if it didn't sound sexy coming from her. With everything going on around them he shouldn't even notice. Being turned on by a woman who'd pulled a gun on him twice now wasn't his brightest move.

Then again, she was beautiful and his body reacted with a mind of its own. Logic had nothing to do with it.

"You're right about that. I do need someone in law enforcement to put me in protective custody." He didn't budge. "And since your cover is blown, it might as well be you."

The only thing he couldn't figure out was why she wasn't coming clean about being on the job. Best he could figure she'd been on some kind of detail, which made more sense as to why she fought when she did earlier. Was she in the middle of an undercover operation? Then again, if she was wouldn't she want police protection now?

Not necessarily. If she was in deep, she'd want to stay that way. Before he could raise another argument, she slipped out the door. He immediately bolted toward it but she'd managed to secure it with something on the other side.

Joshua muttered a curse as he pulled out his cell. Explaining this whole scenario to his friend Tommy ensured that he'd be ribbed about this forever. He'd allowed himself to be locked inside a bathroom while the "teen" he'd been trying to save got away.

Best case scenario? Tommy was already pulling up in front of the gas station. The door opened at the same time Tommy's line rang.

"Turn that thing off." The mystery woman had returned. The business end of her gun pointed squarely at his chest. "And my name's Alice Green."

"If you're running from the law, it wasn't your best move to come back," Joshua said flatly.

"I know that. So, don't make me regret it." There was something else in her eyes this time. Fear?

Curious, Joshua ended the call. He didn't know what she'd gotten herself into but preferring a murderous criminal's company to the sheriff's didn't signal good things about her head being on straight.

"You have to decide right now," she said, her gaze bouncing from him to the hallway leading to the store as the sound of sirens moved closer.

He didn't budge.

"Please." There was a desperate quality in her eyes that tugged at his heart. She could've shot him twice now and hadn't so he figured she wasn't planning to hurt him. And he was more than mildly curious what she was really up to.

"Okay. But you're going to tell me what this is about," he said, bending over to retrieve the weapon they'd discarded earlier.

"Don't even think about it," she said as he made a motion to pick it up.

"I leave it here and they finger you immediately." If it was her service weapon then they could trace the serial number. Joshua at least wanted to hear what she had to say before he hauled her in to Tommy. He might even be able to convince her to turn herself in and that would make things a lot easier on her legally. But then, she would already know that.

"Where are we going?" he asked.

"Do you live nearby or have a ride anywhere around here?" She kept a brisk pace as round two of pouring rain flooded them.

"Yeah, my Jeep's a couple blocks away. But it won't do any good."

"Why not?" she asked, navigating them out of the dark parking lot as the sound of sirens neared.

Either she or Perez had shot the light out in back of the convenience store and his money was on her. "Out of gas."

She muttered a curse as she led him into the field.

"Stay low," she directed.

"You know that clerk can give the police our descriptions," Joshua hedged.

"He was too surprised to pay attention. He won't be able to give them anything more than a general idea. You're tall and that might mean something outside of Texas but all the men seem over six feet here. Plus, we rushed in and straight to the back without showing our faces. No way will that young kid be able to give them anything they can work with and any recording will be too grainy to make out," she responded matter-of-factly.

More proof that she knew a little too much about the process to hold up her claim of not being in law enforcement. Plus, he picked up on the fact that she was from out of state because of her height reference. No one in Texas really thought about whether or not six feet was tall.

"Why are you running?" Joshua asked.

"I'm not," she dismissed him.

"Maybe the appropriate question is, Who are you running from?" It couldn't be Perez since she was trying to be captured by him. She'd said they had boys together, another reason he should ignore any sexual current flowing between them. Once they were safe he'd ask her about her family situation.

"Stay down and be quiet if you want to get out of here alive," she said, irritation lining her tone.

Since Alice, if that was her name, was already belly down he figured he'd better do the same. She'd holstered her weapon and that reminded him of the fact she wore an ankle holster in the first place. No one did that outside law enforcement.

"Where are you from?" he asked.

"Tucson," she said.

"Why are you really here?" he asked, retrieving his hat.

"I already told you," she said. "My ex."

"You can drop the act," Joshua said, not bothering to hide the fact he was done with lies. Besides, the thought of her returning for an ex stirred a different reaction inside him—jealousy? "Nobody and especially not me believes you came all the way out here to be abducted by the father of your children."

He intended to find out what she was really up to and how much of what she'd said was the truth.

WAITING FOR OFFICERS to clear out of the gas station while lying belly down in two inches of water wasn't Alice's idea of a great Friday night. Then again, being dumped by the father of her twins two weeks before the babies had arrived hadn't been, either. Fridays were right up there with poking her eyes with hot sticks.

Soaked to the bone, she shivered as she waited for the cruiser to leave the gas station. The cold front that had been promised was moving in. Experience told her that the clerk hadn't actually witnessed a crime so there wouldn't be much to investigate. A deputy would take a statement, file a report and move on. Then, he or she would keep an eye out for anything suspicious in the area for the rest of the night.

The deputy left ten minutes after he'd arrived.

"Take my jacket," Joshua said, sitting up, water sloshing as it rolled off him and hit the puddle on the ground.

"It's okay. I can handle it," she said quickly. Being on the force, Alice had learned not to admit weakness. Officers depended on one another in life-threatening situations and being a woman she felt that she had to prove herself even more so than male officers. Men had a height and weight advantage, and they tended to be stronger. Alice wasn't the tallest person at five feet four inches and she'd been mistaken for a teenager by people approaching from behind more than once while wearing street clothes. She'd had to work hard to compensate for her size differential.

"Your teeth are chattering," the cowboy said. And his tone almost made her laugh out loud. He sounded almost offended that she hadn't accepted his chivalry.

A female cop coming off as needy or not being able to pull her weight killed her career before it got started. It was a certain way to make the officer next to her wonder if she could come through in a clutch and since lives were at stake everyone took that seriously. So, even if it made her look stupid or she caught the death of a cold later she couldn't accept his jacket.

"Believe it or not, I can take care of myself and I have been for a long time. I don't need your charity," she quipped defensively. Spending time with this cowboy was going to be fun. If by fun she meant stabbing her fingers with a serrated knife.

"Suit yourself," came out about as flat as her pancakes.

Hey, it was the twenty-first century. Women weren't slaves to the kitchen anymore. And that was pretty much how she defended her lack of cooking skills. She could, however, make one mean pot of coffee. And wasn't that more important anyway? "The gas container you used to create a diversion earlier should be around here somewhere."

"Yep."

Great, now they were at one-word answers. She'd spent enough time around the opposite sex to know that she'd offended him, didn't have time to care. He was alive. He could thank her later. "Think you can find it?"

"Of course."

At least he was up to two words now.

Maybe she should've left him back at the station. Except that she was responsible for getting him into this mess in the first place and she couldn't let him get himself killed given that he was genuinely trying to help her. And stupidity could be deadly.

Joshua was a liability.

She needed to convince him just how much danger he was in and that he needed to turn himself in. There was a reason she'd saved Perez's organization for last.

People didn't walk away after they saw him. He had no qualms about erasing a threat, real or perceived. Precisely the reason he was considered one of, if not *the* most ruthless criminal in the United States.

It was getting late. The trail was a dead end now. Alice was starving and she needed to get back to her motel room to bunk down for the night while she came up with plan B. She also needed to touch base with her informant and let him know everything had gone south.

Pushing up to her feet proved more of a challenge than she expected. She landed down on her bottom pretty darn quick with a splash.

The cowboy was by her side in a half second, helping her to her feet.

"I haven't slept in a few days," she said quickly and a little too sharply.

"Yeah? Even Superwoman needs rest."

She didn't say anything and the cowboy didn't budge.

"When was the last time you had a decent meal?" he asked, standing so close that her body was aware of his every breath.

"It's been a while. I got distracted tracking this lead," she quipped. Exhaustion was taking a toll and she couldn't help herself. Her tone tended toward being harsh in a situation like this. "Thanks for the hand up, by the way."

"No problem. You don't have to sound like I broke your arm."

What? Did she? Okay, that did make her feel bad. She wasn't trying to be a jerk.

The cowboy chuckled as he turned and walked away.

Oh, so he had a sense of humor. Under different circumstances, Alice might actually laugh. Searching for

Isabel nonstop for the past six weeks had brought her to the brink of exhaustion. Then there were the twins. Two baby boys who had one speed…blazing. She missed her boys so fiercely it had physically hurt since she'd left home three weeks ago on a hot tip.

Isabel Guillermo had disappeared two months before her sixteenth birthday. And it was Alice's fault. Before that, Isabel had been placed into the foster care system. Also Alice's fault. Because Alice had had a bad day at work, Isabel's parents were dead. Again, Alice's fault.

A sweet and innocent teen's world had shattered because a criminal got one over on Alice. Her mistake had cost Sal and Patsy Guillermo their lives. Alice should've been more aware.

She shook off the reverie, focusing on the cowboy instead. Not only had he already located the canister, but he was standing perfectly still, studying her.

Alice pulled out her cell, grateful the downpour should provide enough of a curtain between them to mask her true emotions, and covered it with her free hand to shield it from the rain.

"We need to find another gas station," was all she managed to say. Thinking about Isabel's case, about the past few weeks, had her missing her boys. Her heart ached and she wanted to be with them. But what kind of mother could she ever be to them if she didn't find Isabel?

"Anyone expecting you at home?" Alice asked the cowboy as he took his seat in the Jeep after hiking for what felt like half the night to get gas. She needed to know if she'd just put a family in danger and that's the reason she told herself she asked. His ride wasn't tricked out for mudding so she figured it was his commute vehicle.

"No."

Why did that one word make her heart flutter?

Ignoring it, Alice thought about her next move. Going back to get him had been impulsive and dangerous. She couldn't afford to take unnecessary risks or rack up collateral damage. The cowboy would have to go with her to her motel room. She hoped that he remained cooperative so she could talk sense into him.

"Where to?" He turned the key in the ignition and the engine came to life.

"Take Highway 287 out of town," she said, rubbing her temples.

"Mind if I stop for food first? There won't be anything once we leave town and it's not like you can order pizza from The Bluff Motel."

"How did you know where we were going?" She snapped her head to the left to get a good look at him.

"Not a lot of options around here."

Okay. Fine. He had her on that point.

"There a drive-thru nearby?" She needed something to eat and she could always hide in the backseat so no one saw her. Perez had eyes everywhere and she didn't want to risk anyone seeing the two of them together. No one should be looking for her, Perez or otherwise, at least not officially. Her SO had been texting for her return to work and to make sure she wasn't interfering with a federal investigation. She hadn't exactly broken any laws unless she counted unauthorized tampering with the National Crime Information Center—NCIC—database. As far as technicalities went, she wasn't exactly hacking into the system. She was just doing a little side research project.

Her stomach rumbled from hunger and her side ached. She needed to re-dress her stab wound, a gift from the last crime ring she'd infiltrated.

"We can zip through the line in a few minutes," he said, pulling into a burger stand parking lot.

"Okay." Eat. Rest. Talk the cowboy into witness protection. How hard could it be to convince someone to give up the only life they knew because of a perceived threat from a stranger?

"And then you'll come clean with why you're tracking one of the most dangerous criminal organizations in the country," the cowboy said with law enforcement authority.

Chapter Three

The motel room was basic but comfortable. There were two full-size beds with a nightstand in between, a small table with two chairs near a picture window, and a dresser with an old-fashioned TV. Joshua would bet money there was a bible in the top drawer. The floral pattern in this room was bluebonnets, a nod to the state flower, and they were on the curtain and both bedspreads. The floor was tiled in a neutral shade.

One of the bedspreads was rumpled and the other bed was being used as a makeshift office. Papers were spread out across the comforter and there was a laptop along with a couple of cell phones and a small technological device that Joshua figured was for surveillance.

"Let's talk about your options," Alice said after she'd finished the last bite of her burger and drained her Coke. She wadded up the wrapper and tossed it in the trash. They'd toweled off and she'd changed into dry clothes.

Joshua couldn't remember the last time he'd seen someone wolf down food so fast, and that was saying a lot given that he had five brothers.

"Or you could tell me what's really going on. Why you're on the run from the police," he countered, motioning toward the second bed, not ready to tip his own hand.

"I'm not—"

He put a hand up to stop her. "If you don't want to tell me why you're in this mess we'll bunk down for the night and I'll leave you alone in the morning. I have no interest in playing games."

The woman needed rest and the only reason he stuck around was because he figured she'd be crazy enough to follow him if he left her alone. Or so he lied to himself. There was more to it than that. He wasn't ready to acknowledge whatever "it" was because she mostly frustrated him.

She slipped off her shoes, settled against the headboard on the second bed and pinched her nose like she was trying to stem a headache. "I'm trying to find a young girl. It's my fault she's missing and, therefore, my responsibility to get her back."

Joshua turned his chair around to face her and clasped his hands, resting his elbows on his knees.

"She disappeared six weeks ago and I've been searching for her ever since. With each passing day, her odds crash…" There was so much anguish in her voice that Joshua had to fight the urge to cross the room and pull her into his arms to comfort her. She'd probably poke him in the eyes if he did, he thought dryly, remembering how unwelcomed his attempts to make her feel better had been so far. She'd been clear on where she stood when it came to accepting help or being pitied. She'd taken a zero-tolerance stance.

"How old is she?"

Alice's eyes were closed now and distress was written all over her features. "Almost sixteen."

He couldn't even go there mentally…a place where one of his family members had disappeared. Two of his grown brothers had had brushes with death in recent months and that was enough to keep Joshua on full alert. They were adults capable of handling themselves. But a sixteen-year-old?

He flexed his fingers to keep his hands from fisting.

"I'm sorry," he said and meant it. Her admission explained a lot about why she'd be staying in an out-of-town motel, alone. "What happened?"

"She was around one day and then not the next." She opened her eyes and fixed her gaze on the wall directly in front of her. "You asked about me being on the job before. I used to be until this happened."

"You left to investigate this girl's disappearance?" he asked, thinking there were at least a half dozen scenarios where he would've done exactly the same thing.

She nodded.

"Why not do both?"

"We weren't getting anywhere on the investigation and my boss wanted my full attention on the job. I agreed, but on my own time I had to do everything I could to find her. The longer she was gone…well, let's just stay statistics weren't—*aren't* on her side. After three weeks of red tape and netting zero following procedure, I figured I could get a lot further my own way."

As a cop she'd have to follow procedure to a T when all she really wanted to do was find the girl and bring her home. She wasn't interested in prosecution and laws would get in the way.

"Did you quit the force?"

"Took an extended leave," she said. "But I have no idea if I'll have a job when I return. The chief threatened me and told me not to interfere with an ongoing investigation."

"Bet you've covered a lot more distance than they have," Joshua said. A flicker crossed her features. Regret? Anxiety?

What was she holding back?

"I wouldn't know," she said, some of the tension leaving her shoulders. She bit back a yawn. "This guy I've been tracking is the real deal. He is going to come looking for you. It's not a matter of if, but when."

"He won't find me tonight," Joshua said. "He's probably still looking for the cute blond teenage girl who got away."

She laughed but her amusement disappeared too quickly. She zeroed in on him. "I'm serious. This guy is nothing to joke about. He's ruthless and no one has lived after catching him in action."

Joshua balked. "And you were trying to get him to take you so you could investigate this girl's disappearance?"

"Yes."

"That makes you either stupid or brave. I can't decide which." He admired her dedication. He also noted that it would take a whole lot of guilt to make a cop walk away from her job. "How many other organizations have you done this with?"

"Several."

"And that led you to Perez's group?"

She fixed her gaze on the ceiling. "He's my last hope of finding her and I tracked down a lead that says he's the one who took her."

"I'm guessing you saved him for last on purpose based on how dangerous he is." Joshua wasn't worried about being exposed to Perez. He wouldn't be sticking around in Bluff for long anyway. He'd been searching for the right time to tell his family that he had no plans to live out his life on the cattle ranch. Granted, he loved the land but he'd applied for a job in the FBI and had every intention of picking up his life where he'd left off once things were settled. A cranky little voice in the back of his mind asked, *Then why haven't you told anyone yet?*

The truth? He resented everyone's assumption that he'd drop everything and change his life. His older brothers might be fine with doing that, hell, they'd all spread out and made their own millions with success-ful businesses. They'd proven their worth as men. But Joshua was just getting going on his future. To have that stripped away just as it was getting good wasn't in the plans. As much as he loved his brothers, they wouldn't understand. His only regret—and it kept him awake at night—had been that he hadn't stepped up and told his father before he was gone.

Joshua had known on some level that his father wouldn't have liked his plan so he kept on living a lie, thinking that the right time to bring up the subject would magically present itself. The worst part was that the old man would never have expressed his disapproval. He was a good father. There was no way he'd make Joshua feel obligated. But Joshua had seen the look of excitement in his father's eyes last year when he'd told the boys about the plan to have them work the land he loved so much. He'd built a small empire for his sons from nothing. Re-jecting his father's offer would make Joshua feel a lot like he was rejecting the man, his legacy.

Selfish as it might have been, Joshua hadn't wanted to see disappointment in his father's eyes. Now it was too late and he felt trapped.

"I thought I was alone with Perez and his men in that location. Never saw you coming," Alice admitted.

"How'd you know he'd be there?" he asked, redirecting his thoughts to something he could fix.

"I'd tracked him to the area based on a meeting he'd set up to talk to someone about a new transportation route and so I used an informant to plant a tip. I knew that if he could get me on Perez's radar that I'd have a good chance of becoming his target. My informant had already told me that Perez had a buyer for a sixteen-year-old blonde, so he set me up."

She'd fit the clean-cut American teenager to a T. Even now with her blue-striped pajama pants and white tank, she looked years younger. Her hair was drying and the rubber band looked barely able to contain her waves.

"And then you came along and…" She didn't say that he'd ruined it but he could tell based on her expression that's exactly what she was thinking.

"If I interrupted your plan to be kidnapped by one of the most dangerous men in the country, then I'm glad I came along when I did," Joshua said. He pointed to her right side below her armpit where blood flowered. "How bad is that?"

She glanced down and panic flitted across her face as she hopped up. "Oh."

"Don't move. You'll only make it worse." He glanced around the small room looking for some kind of emergency kit. "You have first aid supplies?"

"Not much. I meant to pick some up."

"Hold on." He ran out to the Jeep and retrieved his, shivering in the cold. The temperature must've dropped fifteen degrees in the last hour alone. On the ranch, he never knew when he'd need first aid so he'd gotten in the habit of keeping supplies on hand wherever he went.

The thunder had eased and the rain was coming down in a steady beat. He planned to head out at first light as soon as he knew she'd be okay.

Joshua returned to the room a few minutes later and found Alice as he'd left her. Head against the headboard with her eyes shut. Since her hand was closed around her Glock, he didn't want to startle her.

He moved closer so that he could disarm her if need be. He didn't take her skills lightly. She was good with a weapon but he was better. Couple that with the fact that exhaustion was slowing her reaction time and he had the edge he needed.

Her eyes snapped open the second the bed dipped under his weight.

"It's me," he said, his hand covering hers on the weapon as she brought it up. Physical contact sent a different kind of heat through him. A sexual attraction wasn't appropriate or wanted, especially under the circumstances.

She apologized and then shook her head.

"How long has it been since you've had a good night's sleep?" he asked. There were other more pressing questions he needed to ask, but he reminded himself not to get too personal with someone he would never see again after tonight. Because he had every intention of helping her and then getting back to the ranch to deal with his own problems.

"A while, I guess."

"What else do you know about Perez?" he asked to distract her as he lifted her shirt enough to see where the blood came from. He was worried about Alice. He peeled back the bloody bandage to reveal a two-inch gash three inches below her armpit.

"Most of these criminal rings take girls from places where huge crowds are gathered, like the Super Bowl. Not Perez. He searches for just the right one, looks for a certain kind and mostly prefers all-American types. He seems to have a particular affinity for blondes although Isabel—" she flashed her eyes at him as he cleaned the blood off the cut and then she continued "—that's her name, is a brunette. I can see why he'd take her, though, because she's a beautiful girl."

There was probably no way he could convince Alice to follow him to the ranch until he could dig deeper into the situation and things settled down. Her eyes were pure blue steel and determination and she'd left behind a job she loved to track down this girl. This was the closest she'd been to getting answers and he highly doubted he could convince her to slow down.

"Innocent girls and blondes fetch a higher price. His target age range is twelve to sixteen years old." She winced.

He apologized as he finished cleaning her wound, warning her that the next part might hurt more. "I'd be happy to take you to the ER."

Her head was already shaking before he could finish his sentence.

"Those are practically babies," Joshua ground out, thinking about what she said about the girls. Anger bit through his normally easygoing nature.

She nodded. "He likes to target places where there won't be a lot of extra security or cameras. Remote spots in small towns like this."

Joshua blotted her wound with fresh antibiotic ointment on a clean piece of gauze.

"Then, he sells them to various jerks or uses them to farm babies for high-profit adoptions," she said.

Didn't this conversation just spike Joshua's blood pressure in two seconds flat? No matter how many years he spent on the job he'd never get used to people who hurt children. He shook his head as he placed a new bandage over her cut.

"I learned that several of his girls have been used for the sole purpose of being impregnated and then held captive through multiple pregnancies," she continued.

Joshua knew all about those sickening operations. He'd get more information out of Alice if she believed he was a civilian. He pretended to be hearing this for the first time even though he didn't feel right deceiving her. "Do I want to know what Perez does once he… *uses* the girls?"

"Dumps the bodies once he's made enough from the babies and the girls start to become liabilities," she said with an involuntary shudder. "And that's just one of the things they could be doing with her. Perez has been known to sell them to a high bidder, which is why he likes a specific look. He knows the market and what his customers like. He gets a sense for their taste and then snatches a few girls to give a 'client' options."

Joshua had learned even more about illegal adoption rings when his oldest brother Dallas got involved with a woman whose baby was almost abducted before Halloween. Thankfully, Kate and baby Jackson were doing fine and Joshua figured a wedding announcement would be coming soon since Dallas and Kate had fallen in love during the process.

"I can't imagine the kind of monster it would take to do something like this to children," Joshua said, and then apologized as soon as he realized that Isabel was most likely in the hands of someone like that. By now, she could be pregnant, abused or dead. And that explained the worry lines etched in Alice's forehead. Being on the job, she would know firsthand what a deviant like Perez would do. And Joshua hated seeing her go through something like this when she should be home with Isabel, doing normal stuff girls do this time of year like holiday shopping.

"No need to be sorry," she said. "Believe me, it won't help Isabel."

"How do you know she didn't run away? Maybe she needed a change of scenery and she's somewhere safe in another city," he offered.

"We're close and I stay in touch with her foster parents and caseworker. She's a good girl and she loves my twins."

Joshua hadn't thought about the fact that Alice could be married with kids. She'd mentioned her boys earlier but he thought that was part of the lie she was making up about a relationship with Perez. He glanced at her ring finger and stifled the relief that came when he didn't see a band. But then she wouldn't wear one while on a case like this. "You're married?"

"No," she said.

He didn't want to admit the relief he felt with her answer. "You have twins?"

"Yeah. Why? You got something against twins?" Her eyebrow spiked.

"Nope. Not me." Joshua couldn't help but laugh given

that he was a twin. His brother was the oldest by two minutes.

"It's not funny. I love them with all my heart but those two can be holy terrors."

"I'm sure they are." He smiled wryly thinking of all the misadventures he and Ryder had had. He was pretty certain his mother would've used that same term to describe the two of them.

"You have kids?" she asked.

"Nope."

"Then you have no idea what twins are like," she said so matter-of-factly that he laughed again. "What's so funny?"

"It's nothing." He wondered if his mother would have had the same exacerbation in her voice when describing him and his brother. The fact that she'd had six boys, the last of which were twins, made him certain she would.

THE COWBOY PUSHED off the bed. He'd done a nice job of dressing her wound.

"Mind if I grab a shower?" he asked.

"Not at all. I'll clean off the other bed for you," she said but he waved her off.

"I can manage. I'd rather you get some sleep." His jacket was already draped over the back of the second dining chair. He tugged his T-shirt up and over his head and then fanned it out to dry on the dresser.

Alice shouldn't let herself notice the ripples of muscles cascading down his back. He obviously spent some serious time at the gym. Then again, he'd mentioned something about a ranch. Working outside would give a man a body like his.

Tiredness pervaded every one of Alice's bones. There

was no amount of caffeine that could keep her eyes open for much longer but she was so used to fighting sleep that she tossed and turned instead of giving in.

The fact that the cowboy was in the next room cleaning up shouldn't edge into her thoughts. Or that his body looked made of steel. It had to be the fact that she was overwrought with hormones combined with severe lack of sleep that had her thinking about the water rolling down the ripples in his chest that gave way to a solid six-pack stomach. She'd felt just how strong and masculine he was when her body had been pressed against his at the gas station. A place deep inside stirred, a need she'd felt too many times recently. She wished he could wrap those steel arms around her and make her feel safe.

How tired was she that her mind could wander to such a place given the circumstances? She forced her thoughts to the case and a sense of despair washed over her. It had been weeks since she'd seen her boys and that was probably the reason tears threatened so heavily this time. Or maybe it was the fact that the last lead to find Isabel had disappeared in front of her eyes. Perez wouldn't be looking for Alice, but if he ever saw her again her cover would be immediately blown. He'd been her last hope to find Isabel. She fingered the pendant on the necklace around her neck, half a heart. The other half belonged to Isabel. When put together they read Best Friends. Isabel had scrimped and saved to purchase the necklaces over the summer. Tears threatened as Alice thought about the gift she'd been planning to give Isabel.

Alice had planned to tell Isabel about her plans to file for adoption. She wanted to be more than a big sister to Isabel. She wanted to be family.

A dark sadness blanketed her like a thick fog rolling in. The clock was ticking, time was running out and Alice didn't know how much longer she could abandon her boys to chase down clues. Christmas was in three weeks and they deserved to have their mother home with them, too.

Alice hadn't been completely honest with the cowboy earlier. She'd kept to herself the fact that she'd been forced to step down from the case because she'd gotten too close to an existing investigation with the FBI. Tears spilled and a sob released as she thought about her options.

Alice hated her weakness, but she could no longer hold back the onslaught of emotions bearing down on her, suffocating her.

Chapter Four

Joshua hoped he'd get back to the motel before Alice woke. He'd slipped out to pick up breakfast supplies. Outside the local coffee shop, Dark Roast, he called his twin brother. Ryder picked up on the second ring.

"What's going on at the ranch today?" Joshua asked.

"Where are you?" Even though the sun wasn't up Ryder sounded wide awake, typical hours for a rancher. Joshua had always been more of a night owl. In fact, he'd done little more than doze off for a few minutes here and there in the past few hours. His seniority at the Denver PD had given him the right to choose his shift. Unlike his peers who worked the day shift, he'd picked evenings. Even though he'd been home for weeks, his internal clock hadn't made the adjustment.

"I'm in town at the coffee shop." It wasn't a lie.

"Don't tell me you have a hot date this early?" Ryder joked.

"Nothing like that. Just needed to make a run into town."

"How'd it go last night with the Nelson widow?" Ryder asked. He must've picked up on Joshua's tone and figured she was to blame.

"As well as can be expected when she opened the front door in a silk bathrobe." Joshua hadn't been thrilled.

Ryder laughed and that didn't help Joshua's mood.

"How'd you manage to get out of that one without hurting her feelings?" His brother must've known the widow would pull something. She always did.

"I pretended not to notice."

Ryder roared with laughter. "And she let you get away with that?"

"No, she let her robe fall open at one point," Joshua said, still not enthused. "I almost told her to go put on a turtleneck."

"That would have sent her into the other room crying," Ryder said defensively. "She's a little out there, lonely, but she's harmless."

"I didn't actually say that even though someone should. If you wanted diplomatic you should've sent Tyler." Joshua didn't hide his irritation. Their older brother was known for his ability to navigate sticky situations, evaluate all sides and come up with a solution everyone could live with. No doubt he would've handled the Nelson widow with ease.

"You don't have to bite my head off, man. I'm just here to shovel cow patties in the barn," Ryder shot back. "Besides, you're the one who drew the short straw at the family meeting last week."

That didn't cover the half of it. Joshua didn't mean to be terse with his brother. The two had always been close. Keeping his secret about applying to the FBI was eating at his conscience, especially as he moved through the rounds. Then there was the woman sleeping in the motel room twenty minutes away. "I haven't had my morning coffee yet. I don't mean to be a jerk."

"You're fine. Besides, the Nelson widow can have

that effect on people," he teased, lightening the mood. "What's she donating this year?"

"A bronze statue called *Horse and Rider*. It's actually nice," Joshua said, thinking that an expensive piece of art like that needed to be out of the back of his Jeep before someone figured it was there and helped themselves to it.

"Sounds heavy," Ryder joked. "And classy."

"Should help with our fund-raising goal this year at the silent auction." He had no idea what that ultimate number was but he was sure a few of his brothers did, and rightfully so. They seemed like naturals when it came to stepping in for their parents.

"We ever going to talk about what's really been bugging you, because I know it's not the Nelson widow?" Leave it to Ryder to come right out with something on his mind. Then again, his twin would be the first to pick up on his underlying mood.

"It's just not the same without them at the ranch," Joshua said quietly, referring to their parents and that was 100 percent the truth. It was hard to think about being home without them there. And yet, that wasn't what was really bothering him. He hoped his brother would buy the excuse or give him a pass without digging further.

"I miss them, too." Ryder's tone said he was giving Joshua a pass. This conversation wasn't finished but would be saved for a later time.

"How's everything going this morning?" Joshua asked, ready to change the subject.

"Fine. Dallas and Tyler are out checking fences. Austin and Tyler are in the office today. Austin said something about being up to his neck in financials and Tyler is negotiating next year's supplier contracts. Are you coming in today? Uncle Ezra called last night and re-quested a family meeting," Ryder said.

"What's that about?" Joshua asked, distracted. He didn't feel good about leaving Alice alone. He checked his watch, 5:40. It'd been less than twelve hours since their first encounter with The Ghost. Perez could be anywhere. Based on his reputation he was most likely searching for Joshua, not Alice. Joshua still didn't like it. He scanned the parking lot aware that he had to watch his back a little more carefully until this whole situa-tion blew over.

"I'm guessing he's fighting with Aunt Bea again and wants us on his side," Ryder said.

"Maybe he has another 'opportunity' for the family to invest in," Joshua quipped.

"Yea, like his others have been so successful." Ryder laughed.

Joshua tucked his free hand inside the front pocket of his jeans, staving off the morning chill. "What time's the meeting?"

"Said he'll come around suppertime. Think you can make it or do you need me to cover and then fill you in later?" Ryder asked.

"I'll do my best to be there. Can I text you later when I know for sure?" Joshua had missed three of the last four family meetings and he was starting to feel guilty. No matter what else he decided he would always need to be involved in the family business on some level. As for his life, he needed to set his priorities and work from there.

"Of course. I better get back to it. These cows don't clean up after themselves," Ryder said.

Joshua resisted making a snappy comeback as he

ended the call. His next was to his friend, Sheriff Tommy Johnson.

"We got trouble in town," Joshua said after exchanging greetings.

"What happened?" Tommy asked, sounding half asleep.

"Did I wake you?" His friend was normally up and running by now.

"Not really. I've been working a case and didn't get much sleep last night. What's going on?" Tommy didn't say it but Joshua knew that his friend was staying up late working on his parents' case. He'd been poring over the guest list at the art auction the night before their deaths.

"Marco Perez was sighted last night at the gas station off Highway 287 near Harlan and he may be coming to Bluff next," Joshua said.

"What makes you think he'll come here?" Tommy asked.

"Me."

"Okay, back up and tell me everything." Tommy sounded wide awake now as ruffling noises came through the line.

Joshua relayed the details from last night up to the point of Alice taking him to her motel room. Even though it felt like he was betraying her, Tommy needed to know about any threats to the area. Joshua couldn't have innocent people being caught in the crossfire if Perez was on a hunting mission—the prey he was after might be Joshua. "Can you check out Alice Green? She's tracking these guys and she's a cop out of Tucson."

"Green. Got it," Tommy said. "I'll run her through the system."

"Would you mind keeping this quiet instead? Do you

know anyone out west you could contact and ask unofficially?" Joshua didn't want to alert her boss to her whereabouts.

"I can't think of anyone offhand but I'll ask my deputies and see what we can come up with," Tommy replied after a thoughtful few seconds of silence.

"I'll owe you one." Joshua figured that line pretty much covered his morning, and his life ever since he'd clocked out the last time with Denver PD and returned to the ranch. He loved the land, there was no question about that, but living the life of a rancher was for his father, his brothers, not him. So, his twin had been doing nothing but covering for him. And Joshua couldn't keep up the charade much longer.

A SUDDEN NOISE woke Alice with a start. Heart thumping, she shot up and fumbled around for her Glock. The room was cast in darkness. Her heart raced at the sound of the door closing and the snick of the lock.

"It's just me," the familiar voice, the cowboy, said as a reading light clicked on. "And I brought coffee."

Alice sank onto the bed, trying to shake the feeling of heavy limbs that came with suddenly waking in the middle of a deep sleep. "Coffee sounds like heaven right now."

"How do you take yours?" he asked.

"Black works for me."

He handed over a cup and the warmth was amazing against her cold fingers.

"Okay if I turn on another light?" he asked.

"Sure." She took a sip, enjoying the dark roast taste and the burn in her throat.

"Mind if I join you?" He motioned toward the foot of the bed.

"Not at all." It was nice to have company for a change. She'd basically spent the past three weeks alone aside from being kidnapped, stabbed and burned. In all fairness, the burn was an accident. She missed her boys, home, her job. Even though she couldn't tell the cowboy everything about herself, she didn't have to pretend to be a sixteen-year-old with him.

Alice glanced around the room. "Someone around here is into bluebonnets."

"It's the state flower."

"I know that." She took another sip. "I'm not an idiot."

"Never said you were." He arched his eyebrow.

Okay, she was probably being too defensive. She needed to tone down her attitude. "Thanks for the coffee, by the way. I appreciate it."

He nodded and half smiled. "How's your side?"

"No fresh blood. That's a good sign." She lifted her shirt enough to get a good look at the bandage.

"We'll need to clean up the wound this morning to make sure infection doesn't set in."

"Hold on a second, cowboy. *We* don't need to do anything. I've got this." Her defenses were set to high gear again.

He shot her a disgusted look that she didn't want to overanalyze.

"Of course you do," he said.

Well at least he took a hint. Or so she thought. Until he got up, moved to the bathroom and then returned with the first aid kit he'd stashed there last night.

"I'm not the most agreeable person before coffee and I think we've gotten off on the wrong foot this morn-

ing," she started but he interrupted her. He was trying
to help and, although that grated on her, she also realized how nice it was to have a friend.

"Letting me clean and bandage your wound doesn't
make you dependent on me, or weak." He spoke slowly
as though he didn't want to leave any question about
his intentions. There was also a sharp edge to his voice.

"I never said it did," she protested but he was already
by her side, kneeling down. And if it wasn't for those intense green eyes of his she'd stop him right there.

"Then lift up your shirt and quit being a baby about
it," he dared.

Alice did and then took a sip of coffee, realizing for
the first time in weeks just how tired she was. Her still-
foggy brain wasn't helping with her disposition. The caffeine was starting to make headway toward clearing it.
As it was, she'd been running on power bars and adrenaline, and even though she'd slept like a champ last night
she knew it barely scratched the surface of what she really needed. Careful not to hurt her already aching side,
she tried to stretch the kinks out of her arms and legs.

"I need to come up with a new plan," she said on a
heavy sigh, not sure why she was confiding in the cowboy.

"Since I have no confidence in your plan-making
abilities, I'm willing to offer my services," he said with
a smile.

"Great. Thanks for the confidence," she said and then
laughed. The cowboy had a point. And a great smile. "I
guess I can see where I might look a little crazy from
someone else's point of view."

"Desperate or determined are probably better words.
I just don't want you to get yourself killed in the pro-

cess," he said. Maybe it was too early in the morning and Alice's brain hadn't fully engaged but the deep timbre of his voice sent sensual shivers down her back. "Why don't you tell me what you've done and where you've been so far? We can go from there."

Alice took another sip of coffee and then leaned her head against the headboard. She took in a deep breath and closed her eyes. "Okay. Let's see. Isabel went missing six weeks ago."

"And we've already determined that she's not a disappear-with-a-band type," he said with another endearing half smile.

"She's more of a Taylor Swift person," Alice said, wishing she could return the smile. Just talking about Isabel made her heart ache.

"When did you realize she was gone?" He said the last word quietly and his reverence was duly noted and appreciated.

"We were supposed to meet at Lucky Joe's Café right after school. She didn't show." Alice took another sip and opened her eyes.

"Is that when you realized something was wrong?"

"No. Not right away. I called her first and her phone went straight into voice mail. I thought maybe she got tied up with a teacher. She'd been stressing over her upcoming exams and didn't feel prepared. The whole semester had been stressful. I thought maybe she was biting off more than she could chew. She's a motivated student and she signed up for AP World History, Pre-AP Chemistry, Pre-AP English, and Pre-AP Algebra 2. Even though she speaks fluent Spanish, she signed up for AP French."

"Sounds like an intense load," he said. "I think I took one AP class before graduating."

"Times have changed. Kids push themselves harder these days. Isabel wanted to get a college scholarship and she had no athletic ability."

"So, she had to push herself that hard?" His dark brow arched.

"She thought she did. Her parents didn't leave her any money and she didn't have any other family in the US. The rest of her family is poor and live in Mexico. Conditions are worse there. She wanted to stay in the States and make a better life."

"Why don't you sound convinced?"

"Part of it was true. I do think she wanted to make a better life for herself but I also believe she was pushing herself so hard because she wanted to keep busy. Not deal with the fact that her parents were gone or that her foster parents didn't care. She and her parents were close-knit and I could see how much she missed them." An emotion passed behind the cowboy's eyes that she couldn't quite put her finger on. He didn't say anything, so she kept going. "She'd been spending a lot of extra time at school, going to tutoring early in the mornings and staying late so I figured she forgot about our plans."

"And you're sure that's all she was doing?" the cowboy asked.

Alice shot him a look.

"Whoa. Don't get mad at me. I have to ask and you know it." He put his hands up in the surrender position, still gripping his coffee with his right. "Don't mind me. I'm just a rancher."

Alice noted that he seemed to be pretty darn good at asking questions for someone claiming to work on a ranch. A simple life sounded damn amazing to her at this point. Was there a place she could get away with Isabel and the twins? Away from the world and all the stressors it contained? Or did a place like that even exist? Alice was anxious and that was the only reason she was thinking about escaping. The truth was that she loved everything about her job except for the guilt that came with making a critical mistake. When she had a bad day, someone could die.

The thought sat bitterly on her chest.

"Isabel didn't have a lot of friends. Her school counselor said she'd always been a shy, bookish girl. She never got into trouble."

"Did she have *any* friends?"

"No one close. She liked school and turned all her homework in on time."

"You mentioned that she was feeling overwhelmed with her studies," he said.

"Well, yeah, wouldn't you? She was pushing herself too hard and I told her that I thought she should lighten her load," Alice said.

"How did she respond?"

"She agreed with me. But the school wouldn't let her change out of her Pre-AP classes until the end of the semester. She was worried about her GPA dropping in the meantime, so she started going to all available tutoring sessions," Alice defended.

"Which is the reason you didn't think too much about her blowing off a meeting with you?" he asked.

"I should've realized she was in trouble or that something had happened right then. She was dependable. I should've known that she would've shown if she'd been able to." Alice couldn't hold back the tears threatening any more than she could stop the heavy feeling pressing down on her chest. "I should've sounded the alarm right then and maybe we would've found her before she was taken out of town."

"Hold on there a second," the cowboy said. "Had she ever missed a meeting with you before?"

"Well, yes. Once or twice at midterms," she supplied, trying to tamp down her guilt before it overwhelmed her and tears flooded.

"So, this time was no different than before. Experience had taught you that when Isabel got stressed she could get distracted like any normal human being, let alone a fifteen-year-old." His words stemmed the flow of tears burning the backs of her eyes.

"I guess you're right. I just keep replaying that day over and over again in my mind trying to figure out what I could've done to stop all this from happening in the first place," she admitted, unsure why she was dumping the truth on a complete stranger. Maybe it was easier to confess her sins to someone she didn't know and would never see again once she left Bluff, Texas.

"Unless you have some kind of crystal ball that's not possible." His tone was matter-of-fact.

She took a minute to let those words sink in.

The cowboy spoke first. "When did you realize she was missing?"

"Not until the next morning when her foster parents called, Kelly and Bill Hardings. Kelly assumed that she'd gone home with me to spend the night. When the school called the next morning to say she didn't show up, they called to find out what was going on."

"Sounds like they cared about her," he said and she

could tell he was reaching for something positive out of the situation.

"I think they were more worried about them looking bad to the state. They'd already talked to her caseworker about having her removed from their house and replaced with someone younger," she said, frustration rising.

"Why would they do that? She sounds like the perfect foster kid. Studied hard. Got good grades."

"She's also fifteen, which pretty much means moody and self-absorbed. Don't get me wrong, she's a great kid. But teenagers aren't exactly the easiest people to deal with. Plus, Isabel still hadn't gotten over missing her parents so she didn't really open up to them like they'd hoped."

"Why take her on in the first place? They had to know what they were getting into."

"I'm not sure they did. They were new. After reading her file I think they thought she'd be a good way to get their feet wet with foster care. And then when she didn't bond with them right away they got discouraged." Alice knew that scene a little too well.

"I don't understand that thinking. I mean, either you want to help or you don't. These are human beings we're talking about not pieces of furniture." She appreciated the outrage in his tone because she felt the same way.

"The caseworker said the couple is asking for someone quite a bit younger next time." Alice bit back her anger. "Isabel is a good kid and she doesn't deserve any of this."

The look of compassion in the cowboy's eyes was like comforting arms around her. Alice needed to change the subject and get back on track. She didn't deserve to feel at ease until Isabel was home. "Fast forward to that next morning after I got the call from the Hardings. After contacting Isabel's caseworker and confirming she hadn't heard from her, I pleaded with my boss to issue an AMBER Alert. The Hardings filed the paperwork, so he did. At that point, we had to assume it was a stranger abduction since she had no relatives near."

"And you already knew something was very wrong by that point," he said.

She nodded before taking another sip of coffee.

"What did you do next?" he asked.

"I started investigating right away. Went to the school and talked to the last person who saw her, her AP World History teacher. He didn't notice anything unusual that day. Neither did her other teachers. I already said she didn't have a lot of friends but the few she had didn't notice anything strange."

"How far was Lucky Joe's from her school and how was she planning to get there?" he asked.

"It's across town. She had to take two city buses, which I didn't like. I volunteered to pick her up from school but she insisted on taking the bus. Said it was good practice for when she left for college and that she needed to learn how to get around on her own. She was almost sixteen and most people were already driving. I think she was worried about me being in the car instead of spending time with the boys. I work the evening shift and that means I don't get home until the boys are already in bed most days."

"I already know you spoke to the bus drivers. What did they say?" he asked.

"Isabel never made it on to the second one. There's a half hour wait in between buses. Again, I didn't like it but she said it gave her a chance to get ahead on her homework so she could focus on me and the boys during our visit." Those words were getting harder and harder to choke out. Isabel's connection to Alice also made it harder for her to bond with the foster family. Alice would've stepped aside if she'd believed that was best for Isabel but she never did fully trust that Kelly and Bill had Isabel's best interests at heart. So, she'd interceded and bonded with Isabel, which most likely messed up her foster situation. Alice had messed that up for Isabel, too.

Chapter Five

"I already know you canvassed the area, so I'm guessing no one claims to have seen her," Joshua said. Alice bore the weight of the world on her shoulders and he found himself wishing there was something he could do to ease her burden.

She cocked her head to the side and stared at him for a long moment before answering. Joshua needed to be more careful or his cover would be blown and she'd stop talking.

"Either that or no one wanted to admit to seeing something, which doesn't surprise me since I've narrowed down the possibilities to The Ghost. He's powerful in the small area of town we live in, in the southeast of Tucson. The locals wouldn't dare go up against him. They fear him too much. There are other criminal groups there, too. The people in small towns off Interstate 10 know to look the other way if they want to keep their own families safe. Everyone is aware of human trafficking and prays that it never happens to one of their own," she said.

"Sounds like a great place for criminals to thrive."

Alice nodded. "There are three main groups with

strong footing there—the Santos, the Giselles and Perez."

"You've already ruled out the first two." He motioned toward the stab wound on her side, trying to keep her focused on something besides putting the pieces together that he was in law enforcement. Her exhaustion worked in his favor.

Alice may be bone-tired but she was still smart. *And beautiful*, an annoying little voice in his head added.

"That's right. I'm down to Perez," she said. Her forehead crinkled when she was frustrated.

"You already mentioned that your informant set you up."

"That's right," she said. "In fact, I need to touch base with him this morning. I meant to do that last night."

"Sounds like he was taking his life in his hands in order to help," Joshua said. The pieces of what Alice had been through were starting to fit together and he was beginning to understand the depth of her guilt.

"It was that or go to jail for the rest of his life," she said quickly. "I gave him an out if he'd help me."

"What about Isabel's cell phone records?" he asked.

Alice motioned toward the other bed. "Whoever got to her must've taken away her phone and destroyed it. I couldn't trace her using the GPS I'd downloaded. You can look at the log if you want. It's over in that stack of papers. Basically, she didn't make any calls all day while she was in school. Me and her foster parents were the last people calling her cell."

"At least they cared enough about her to try to track her down," he offered, trying to ease some of her remorse.

"Really? Check the records. They phoned all of once

at nine o'clock at night, which was the time she was sup-posed to be home. They went to sleep and got up the next morning not concerned enough about her to call me to make sure she made it in the first place," she said.

"What about since then? It's been six weeks, surely they've had some reaction to all this," he said. Now that her cover was blown with Perez she needed to come up with another plan that didn't include being abducted by the most dangerous criminal in America. And if she had to go after Perez, it would be best to gather evidence and present it to a law enforcement agency who could then go in for the bust. He had a strong feeling she'd never go for this idea.

"I haven't spoken to them since the first week." Alice absently toyed with the lid to her now-empty coffee cup.

"And how did they act then?" he asked.

"Shocked and grieved at first. Maybe a little relieved, too. Like a problem had been solved."

"Have you ruled them out as suspects?" he asked. He didn't like to think someone who had been trusted with a child could do anything horrible, but his experience in Denver had shown him otherwise. "They would've known the route she was taking that day."

"True. Everyone was a suspect in my mind at first. I had my boss interview them because a) I was biased and b) it was a conflict of interest given our relation-ship. They met up with friends for dinner and a movie. I checked into their financials in case they benefitted financially from her disappearance and there was noth-ing."

"You got access to their financial records that quickly?" It was too fast for her to have gone through proper channels.

She shrugged, kept on talking, "None of their actions so far have indicated they were involved. There'd be a trail. They had no financial difficulty other than the usual things like still paying off student loan debt. His job is stable and she works part-time at a bank. Neither has bought a new car and they haven't taken an expensive vacation. I've looked at every possible angle and they came up clean."

"What about Isabel's caseworker?" he asked.

"Michelle Grant? She's actually decent. I'd spoken to her about Isabel's file a few times and she listened to my concerns. She was keeping an eye on Kelly and Bill, and their relationship with Isabel based on my concerns."

"When was the last time you spoke with her?"

"Three, maybe four weeks ago. Why?"

Hearing Alice's thoughts on the investigation and the people involved helped Joshua put a picture together. Based on what she'd told him so far, she was a solid investigator. "I can tell that you're depriving yourself of sleep and you've been doing all this on your own. Thought it might help to talk through your leads so far."

"I've dotted all the *i*'s and crossed all the *t*'s. I'm convinced this has to be Perez's group."

"And what if it's not? Plus, you can't exactly go waltzing back in there now. If he sees you he'll figure you out right away."

Suddenly her cup of empty coffee became the most interesting thing in the room based on how intensely she studied it. Was he getting through?

"If we go back and retrace your steps we have a better chance at finding her," he said, trying to drive home his point.

Alice sat motionless for a few minutes that stretched out before nodding her head. "You're right."

She struggled to bite down a yawn.

A wave of relief rippled through him. Joshua wasn't sure how he'd come to care so much in such a short time about a stranger—maybe he could relate to her determination to do the right thing and her sense of guilt—but he wanted to help Alice. No one should carry a burden like hers alone.

"That pretty much highlights what I've done. What's our next step, cowboy?" she asked, sounding resigned and maybe a little hopeful. "It's good to get fresh eyes on the investigation."

"I can take a few days off from the ranch." He didn't even want to touch the thought of how easily that statement rolled off his tongue. "It won't take long to travel to Arizona. We can leave tonight."

"Good idea." She nodded her head. "Arizona is the last place Perez would be expecting to see either of us."

"If what you said is true he'll stick around here a few days trying to find me. It would be smart to change our appearances."

"Right again." She smiled and maybe it was the spark of hope in her eyes that stirred something dormant in his chest.

Joshua didn't want to think about that. He was just glad that something moved in there. Since taking leave from the force, he could admit to feeling empty inside. He should have an interview or a rejection from the FBI coming soon. In the case of a job offer, he'd have to find a way to tell his brothers that he had no plans to return to the ranch. How in the hell was he supposed to do that? They were counting on him to do his part. As for his father's disappointment…he couldn't even go there right now.

If the FBI offered, he had every intention of accepting on the spot even though he knew it'd be a couple of months before he could officially start. The agency would need to complete a background check and he'd have to pass the physical—no problem there because he kept up his training. Other than his brothers, there wasn't anyone special in his life that he'd need to talk over the decision with. And why did that fact suddenly make his life feel like it was missing something? Or, more appropriately, *someone*. Being alone had never bothered him before. What had suddenly changed? *Hold on there, O'Brien.* Joshua wasn't touching that one, either. He refocused his thoughts on the investigation. He wanted to talk to the Hardings himself and get a feel for them. Years of training and experience had honed his instincts into a fine-tuned machine and he'd get an accurate feel for them after one good conversation. He trusted Alice's instincts, too. He also couldn't ignore her bias toward the couple.

Also, he wanted to talk to Alice's supervising officer to see if he had any new information on the case. If this case was important to Alice, it would be important to everyone she knew at work. Cops operated that way, like more of a family than coworkers. Hopefully, Tommy could help with the connection since Joshua didn't know anyone in Tucson.

"You hungry?" he asked after poring over the intel she'd gathered. All of which led to the same conclusion—Perez. Her source had believed a teenager with Isabel's description had been a target. But then the guy was a two-time loser heroin addict going for a get-out-of-jail-free card. Alice was so hungry and desperate to find Isabel she would have been willing to take just about anyone's word at face value. Her judgment was blinded and that's why it's never a good idea for an officer to work on a case too close to his or her heart. It's the reason doing so was considered a conflict of interest. She'd want to see something so desperately that she could miss real clues. Of course, mentioning the possibility to her would most likely get him a boot out the door. In her defensive state, she wouldn't appreciate having her judgment questioned.

"Do you happen to have any food stashed in your Jeep outside?" She stretched again, winced and he could tell she was holding in just how much movement hurt.

"I can do better than that. I'll pick up breakfast burritos. Bacon or sausage?" he asked.

"Bacon," she said with a slight smile, easing off the bed. "I'll clean up while you're gone."

Joshua took the last drink of coffee before tossing the cup. He'd offer to help her walk to the bathroom but figured that would just get him another look and he didn't want to do anything to jeopardize the progress he'd made so far in gaining her trust. Instead, he walked out to his Jeep, shivering in the cold morning air.

The breakfast run was going to take a few minutes more than Joshua had anticipated because the line in the drive-thru extended to the street. He'd forgotten all about the fact that it was a weekend. He also thought about the expensive piece of art in the back. He'd need to swing by the ranch before heading out of town or have one of his brothers meet him somewhere to make the exchange. It would be about a fifteen-hour drive to Tucson or they could cut the time dramatically if they flew. It'd be easy enough to arrange a car to be waiting at a private airport if they decided to fly and that would keep them off the highways where Perez and his men could be waiting, watching. The air might be their safest bet and especially since he could control how many people knew about the trip.

He'd paid and moved to the second window of the Burrito Barn when his cell buzzed. It was Tommy, so he used Bluetooth to answer as he took the food bags from the smiling redheaded attendant and thanked her.

"I have news on the name you gave me," Tommy started right in.

"Good or bad?" Joshua didn't like his friend's tone as he rolled up his window and pulled out of the drive-thru lane.

"She's in trouble with her employer in Tucson. How well do you know this person?" Tommy asked.

"What kind of trouble?" Joshua dodged the question.

"I've been advised to bring her in for her own good or have her stay put so someone can pick her up."

"She's wanted for questioning?" Sure, she'd dodged a few rules going out on her own to investigate this case. Joshua understood that her SO would probably be angry if she wasn't following the law to the letter. That was most likely the reason she'd gone off the rails in the first place. She needed answers, not red tape, and especially since a little girl's life hung in the balance—a girl Alice felt responsible for.

"It's worse than that. She disappeared in the midst of a Professional Standards Department investigation."

"What did the Professional Standards Department want with her?" he asked, but he already suspected that he knew the answer to that question based on his earlier discussion with her.

"To talk to her about charges of tampering with evidence in a federal investigation," Tommy said.

"Whoa. Hold on there. A federal investigation?" Joshua asked, not liking the sound of those words. If his involvement with Alice came to light, his application, his future could be ruined.

"Yes. And her SO said that if she didn't get herself back to the station soon there'll be nothing he can do to protect her. He's already covered for her as much as he can without jeopardizing his own job."

Damn.

"We're heading to Tucson tonight." Joshua trusted Tommy with his life but he didn't want to give his friend any specific details that might put him in an awkward position. Sharing the information that they'd be on a plane tonight would constitute prior knowledge and Tommy couldn't lie in court about it. "I'll convince her to go in and clear this whole ordeal up with Professional Standards."

"Good. I have everyone on alert for Perez. I'm guessing these two are connected in some way."

"It's best to hang up now," Joshua said, again thinking about how his friend might have to testify in court and that it would be best if Tommy didn't know everything.

"You sure about that?" Tommy asked.

"Keep eyes out for Perez. I'll give you a call after I get Alice to her station house."

Tommy agreed to the last part, so Joshua didn't argue. He was pulling into the parking lot of The Bluff Motel and his stomach was reacting to the smell of the burritos. There'd be no time to stop off at the ranch. Joshua owed a call to one of his brothers to give them the statue. He decided to text his twin brother, Ryder, instead. He picked a location near town and set the time. Ryder confirmed a few seconds later.

At least the rain had let up from last night. The sun was out but a cold front had moved in overnight just as promised and the temperature was hovering a bit above freezing.

Joshua wondered if Alice had brought any warm clothes with her. At least his had dried out. The door to the motel room would be locked, so he knocked and waited.

Was she still in the bathroom? Surely she wasn't showering longer than forty-five minutes. She might've dozed off again while she waited for him. She looked more than exhausted earlier and he figured that was half the reason she hadn't pegged him for a cop yet. He had no plans to tell her about his background even though it felt like a deception, and those were mounting. Keeping things from the people he was closest to was beginning to be a habit, he thought as he knocked louder this time.

Still no answer and that fact spiked his blood pressure. What if Perez had found her?

Don't do that, O'Brien. Don't make assumptions.

Joshua made a quick dash toward the motel's front office.

A bell chimed as he opened the door and the attendant looked up from the newspaper spread out on the counter in front of him. The older man smiled to acknowledge Joshua. He was leaned forward over the paper and must've been sitting on a stool. He had on a mint-green button-down shirt that looked a size too big.

"Something I can help you with this morning?" he asked.

"I'm visiting a friend in room 115 and she's not answering the door." He heard how that sounded the minute it came out of his mouth. He held up the food bag. "She called and asked if I'd bring over something to eat. Said she wasn't feeling well last night. Stomach bug or something but now she was starving."

"I have the key right here. I'd be happy to check on her." The idea someone might've messed up the room etched a frown line across his forehead.

"I'd appreciate it."

"Hold on. You want to take a seat?" the man asked.

Joshua introduced himself.

"I'm Sherman." The old man took the hand being offered.

"Any chance I can follow you, Sherman? She didn't sound good this morning when I talked to her and I want to see for myself that she's okay," Joshua pressed.

"As long as you stay outside the room," Sherman said. "I reckon' it'll be all right if you take a peek."

Joshua didn't want to touch how poorly that spoke to security at The Bluff Motel as he followed Sherman out the front door. He waited as Sherman posted the out of the office sign before locking the door.

"Let's see here." Sherman held the key up as he shuffled his feet, moving forward at a hair faster than a snail's pace. "You said room 115."

"Yes." Joshua shouldn't be impatient with the older man but his danger instincts kicked up, telling him something was wrong.

Sherman paused in front of the door and it was all Joshua could do not to take the key and open the door himself.

"Here we go," Sherman said, opening the door and

stepping aside. His nose wrinkled like he expected to be hit with the stench of vomit.

Joshua stepped inside the doorjamb ahead of Sherman. There was nothing. No smell. No mess. No Alice. Worst of all, there was no sign she'd ever been there, either. The secondary bed had been cleaned off and there wasn't so much as a scrap of paper lying around.

"Where could she have gone?" Joshua asked out loud, forgetting that he had company.

"Maybe she got to feeling better and took off."

"Would you mind checking the bathroom? Just to make sure it's clear?" Joshua asked, stepping aside to allow Sherman access.

"Sure thing," Sherman said but the tone of his voice said he didn't expect to find anything.

Joshua turned and leaned against one side of the doorjamb while he waited for the old man to shuffle across the room.

"No sign of her in here, either. Looks like she left in a hurry, though," he said.

A thought dawned on Joshua. He hadn't questioned the fact that Alice had asked if he had a vehicle last night. It hadn't occurred to him that she would have one of her own. And by taking his, the question of what she drove never even came up. He had no idea what to look for on the road.

Basically, she could've driven right past him on his way back to the motel and he never would've realized.

ALICE CROUCHED DOWN low in the field next to the trailer another half hour from The Bluff Motel off Highway 287 going west. Her informant had texted her last night about Perez's whereabouts and she hadn't checked her phone until the cowboy had gone for breakfast.

Even if Dale hadn't sent that text she'd been prepared to walk away from Joshua. His investigation skills were a little too highly honed for him to be a simple rancher and he didn't seem to be inclined to share his background with her. He'd gone with the rancher cover and she'd pretended to believe it, all the while plotting her escape. She'd tricked him. Mission accomplished. So, why did she feel like such a jerk? It wasn't like she really knew the guy.

Alice tried to shrug off the feeling. The truth was that she was an honest person. No one hated lies more than Alice. Had she been doing her fair share lately? Yes, she thought with a sharp sigh. Her back was against the wall when it came to Isabel and she was bending rules she knew better than to break, none of which made her feel comfortable. Then there was the internal investigation she had ducked out of back at the precinct. No matter how pure her reasons were, Alice knew there'd be a price to pay for her actions.

She mentally shook off her reverie and refocused on the 1990s single-wide Palm Harbor trailer in front of her. Her body was already soaked from lying in the still-wet grass and she was thinking about that warm cup of coffee she'd had earlier in an attempt to stave off the shivers rocking her. Being from Arizona, she didn't exactly own a winter coat and the light jacket she had on did little to brace her against the cold, unforgiving earth.

Isabel had to be Alice's priority right now. Nothing else mattered, she tried to lie to herself. She missed her boys. The thought of being away from her babies for their first Christmas ripped up her insides and yet how could she enjoy the season while Isabel's future was so uncertain?

The boys were too young to know what day it was. If she missed Christmas with them, she'd put up a tree anyway and make her own day. If her worst fears came true she wouldn't have a job to go back to anyway. Meaning she'd have a lot of free time while she figured out her next move.

A part of her she didn't want to acknowledge missed the cowboy, too. And that was as productive as packing herself in ice to stay warm.

Holidays or not, handsome cowboy or not, Alice had to stay focused.

She glanced at her watch. She'd already been staking out the place four hours and not one person had come or gone.

A station wagon drove up the gravel lane fifty yards away from her by the time she looked up. There wasn't another trailer for a couple of miles. Alice watched as the white station wagon pulled in front of the trailer. There were two guys in the front who exited the vehicle simultaneously.

This was her first real break since blowing the setup last night. If she could get a good look, she could ID the guys, maybe even snap a picture. Her hands were stiff from cold. She flexed her fingers a few times to warm them up.

Alice pulled binoculars out of her backpack, trying to erase thoughts of Joshua O'Brien out of her mind… which would be a lot easier if she didn't see him, unconscious, being hauled out of the backseat of the station wagon and up the pair of wooden steps into the trailer.

Chapter Six

Alice needed a plan, like, right now. Otherwise all her efforts to save the cowboy last night would be for nothing. Okay, what would she do if she was Perez or one of his men?

First she'd interview the cowboy to find out what he knew and/or if he'd told others about the operation to determine if there was additional threat. Perez would also want to know why he'd shown up the other night to help her. There was no way Joshua O'Brien was going to give him or his men anything, which would leave Perez with no choice but to try to torture the information out of him.

Again, she couldn't see a scenario in which the cowboy would talk. So Perez or one of his men would kill Joshua. She couldn't stand by and let that happen.

So, if Perez wasn't there, his men would need a direct order to dispose of the cowboy. There was no way they'd act without permission. They'd need to check in with their boss first, which introduced a variable since Perez might not be available right away. That could buy Alice precious time. Even a few minutes could mean the difference between life and death for Joshua.

One thing was certain, the cowboy wouldn't talk and they would kill him.

There was another important variable she had to consider. She had no idea how many men she was up against. The station wagon was the only vehicle parked out front but that didn't mean there weren't others inside or on their way. There was no time for recon and she couldn't take the risk of getting close to the trailer and being caught anyway.

This seemed like a good time to curse the fact that she'd been waiting for it to get dark outside before she tried to get closer to the trailer, which was hours away on a bitterly cold day. That fact also fell into the category of Things She Could Not Fix. So, she moved on.

Other factors that she didn't like included the idea that she had no clue how many or what kind of weapons Perez's men had inside those walls. For all she knew, this could be where they kept an arsenal. And then there was the fact that she wasn't familiar with the layout of the trailer, although she could formulate a decent guess based on the year it was built and her experience having carried out busts in several other trailers over the course of her law enforcement career.

The front door, which she currently had eyes on, would lead straight into the living room, based on its position to the right of center. On the immediate right would be a hallway with a couple of secondary bedrooms and a bath. To the left would be the kitchen and the master bedroom with an en suite. The back door would most likely be off the kitchen. She closed her eyes and envisioned the layout, recalling all the details of the last trailer she was in, walking through it in her mind.

Joshua could be anywhere inside. Going in blitzkrieg style without knowing how many men she was up against could end up getting them both killed. She needed to create a diversion and get them outside so she could count them.

Alice willed her hands to stop shaking, a combination of cold and adrenaline, as she fumbled with the zipper on her backpack. What could she use? Papers? Maps? GPS device? She mentally shook her head. None of those were useful as of now.

An idea sparked as she pulled out matches and then quickly died as she examined them. They were soaking wet and therefore no use to her. However, could she figure out a way to light a fire somewhere like the cowboy had in the field?

Her mind zipped through the possibilities of setting a blaze to the field, the trailer—catch the trailer on fire and Joshua might burn with it—or the station wagon. Hold on. That last thought might work. Best she could tell it was the only vehicle around and that would mean their only form of transportation. Surely that would draw the men out since they'd need to put out the fire or risk it catching the trailer, as close as it was parked. In fact, if the car exploded, the windows of the trailer might blow out and cause injury to someone inside.

She palmed her cell. She'd downloaded an app that had scrambled her location in the event her co-workers or boss, or the feds, decided to take matters into their own hands and look for her. It would come in handy now because she would need to call 9-1-1. On the off chance the fire wasn't enough to clear the place, sirens would make criminals scatter faster than deer catching the scent of a hunter.

The fact that the men would have no transportation would make it easier for the police to catch them.

Okay, so, burn the station wagon and call 9-1-1 was the plan, adding arson to her growing list of felonies.

Now, what could she use to start a fire since her matches were soaked?

The soggy packet in the palm of her hand mocked her. Since they would do no good she tossed them inside her backpack.

Maybe there was something closer to the trailer. Alice shouldered her backpack, stuffed her cell in her front pocket and then belly-crawled across the slick grass. She climbed under the wood slats in the fence and then circled the perimeter to check out the backyard, giving the trailer a wide berth and keeping with the tree line.

When she was within twenty yards of the place, the back door opened so hard it smacked against the wall. She suppressed a yelp and froze, praying she was camouflaged against the landscape.

A man hopped down the couple of stairs with a lit cigarette hanging out of the side of his mouth. She may have just found her fire source.

Alice scarcely breathed while waiting for the stocky guy in his early- to mid-twenties to finish his smoke. She was losing precious minutes and the feeling of being stuck there doing nothing while God only knew what was happening to Joshua was like heavy weights pressing on her shoulders. Her teeth chattered from the cold and being on the frigid, wet ground sent chills through her body.

The smoker finally took the last drag off his cigarette after what felt like an eternity and then flicked it onto the ground. He hopped up the couple of steps and disappeared into what she figured was the kitchen area.

As she neared the trailer, the silence was deafening.

She tried not to think about what might be going on inside as she surveyed the area. In order to reach the butt—which she could only pray was still burning—she'd have to get within ten feet of the back door. A risky move.

While she was still out of earshot, Alice fished her cell from her front pocket and called 9-1-1. In barely a whisper, she reported a car fire, gave an address and then ended the call. That way, if she was caught while retrieving the cigarette butt law enforcement would arrive soon enough and that would give her and Joshua a fighting chance. The call was basically backup insurance. This being a rural location, she figured it would take at least fifteen minutes, maybe more, for a deputy to show. And that also meant she needed to kick her bottom into high gear because a deputy would be expecting a car fire.

Belly down, Alice crawled toward the spot where she estimated the smoker had flicked the butt. She should see smoke by now. Maybe she'd miscalculated. She double-checked her positioning against the back door.

Alice searched the ground. This should be near the spot but she saw nothing. A mild breeze was blowing and that could be the problem. She prayed the wind was the culprit because she was running short on ideas, had waterlogged matches in her backpack and Joshua was in trouble.

Besides, there was no way on earth she could be at the trailer when the sheriff or one of his deputies arrived. Time was ticking and the cigarette butt was hiding.

There, she caught sight of a sliver of brown less than an inch long. That had to be it. She crawled closer, praying this would be the break she needed.

There was no fire. The wet earth must've put it out. Damn. Damn. Damn.

Desperation made her arms hard to lift as she rolled onto the ground on her side. A loud masculine grunt came from inside the trailer, kicking another wave of adrenaline coursing through her. *Joshua!* She pushed up onto all fours and scurried around the other side of the trailer determined to find something she could use to ignite a flame.

Rocks battered her knees and cut her palms as she navigated onto the makeshift driveway. She didn't dare raise to her full height, even though the trailer was positioned on cinder blocks making the windows high. But she couldn't stay on all fours, either. She forced herself into a crouching position, keenly aware that she'd aggravated the cut on her side, causing it to bleed again. She could deal with the fallout from that later. For now, all she could focus on was getting Joshua out of that trailer and to safety. It was the least she could do after the way he'd put his life on the line to save her. In fact, it was her fault he was in this position in the first place.

There was nothing obvious out front that she could use to light a fire, so hopes of finding something inside the station wagon were her last resort. The door was unlocked and that was the first break she'd gotten all day. The second came when she found a half-empty pack of cigarettes on the dashboard. The smoker. He would have multiple sources of fire. Since bad news came in threes, she prayed the same was true for the opposite. She smoothed her hand across the seats and deep into the joint where the bottom met the backrest. She scanned the floorboards and ran her hands under the seats. Surely, there were matches or a lighter in there somewhere. The station wagon was too new to have a built-in lighter.

There was a Google Maps printout folded and tucked between the driver's seat and the console. She grabbed it with her left hand, continuing to search with her right.

Her fingers stopped on a small plastic piece. Could it be? She closed her fingers around it and pulled it out…a lighter.

Alice dropped her right shoulder, causing the backpack to tumble to the ground. She fumbled with the zipper, wincing as pain ripped through her side, and tucked the page into the side pocket. She pulled out a few of her own papers and twisted several together before locating the release latch for the gas container.

Somehow, she was supposed to set this baby ablaze without injuring herself and then get around the back of the trailer to the rear door unseen. She planned to slip inside, find Joshua and free him before the bad guys came back in—provided they all left in the first place—and then get the heck out of Dodge before anyone from law enforcement arrived.

There were more holes in her plan than a piece of aged cheese and her good luck had already run out. And just to make things a little more interesting, Alice heard the faint roar of sirens in the distance.

Alice zipped her backpack and shouldered it. She moved toward the rear driver's side of the vehicle and to the gas line. The door was already open so she removed the cap. She lit one end of the paper, said a quick prayer and then stuffed the dry end of the paper into the gas line. Fumes blew out a burst of fire, catching her right forearm before she could pull her hand back fast enough. She immediately dropped to her knees to get out of the way.

The station wagon was about to go *boom*.

Her fight, freeze or flight response kicked in from there as she ignored the pain piercing her side. She scampered to the side of the trailer, located the biggest rock she could find and then tossed it toward the vehicle. The alarm system engaged, piercing the air with shrill beeps.

One and then two men burst out of the front door, the ones from earlier. Alice cleared the back of the trailer at the same instant a loud *boom* sounded. She instinctively dropped to her knees and located her Glock, palming it.

The sheriff or some other law enforcement official was nearing and Joshua was still trapped in there with those jerks. Talk about a plan unraveling. The worst part was that she might've just made it worse for him. Part of her feared she'd hear a gunshot. And then there was the fresh burn that wrapped around her forearm. It was already red and looked angry. She figured shock was the only thing keeping the pain away. For now, at least.

Then she heard voices out front as the sounds of the fire ravaged the rest of the vehicle. She raced to the couple of steps at the back door away from the voices, anxious to find Joshua and get out of there.

The back door was unlocked. Thankfully. So she took a risk, opened it, and bolted inside letting her Glock lead the way.

Alice stopped in the kitchen, quickly scanning the area. The living room was next. Something was wrong. Why was there so much smoke inside the trailer? She coughed, taking in a lungful of thick gray air. Her eyes started to burn. She needed to find the cowboy and get out of there.

The kitchen was clear. She moved to the living room and beyond the couch that had been blocking her view. A man was rolled up on his side, unconscious. "Joshua."

Sirens grew louder as Alice cleared the hallway, the bedrooms, and then returned to the cowboy. She couldn't risk putting her gun away and helping him until she knew it would be safe. Running to an injured person without clearing a crime scene would be a rookie mistake. She tucked her Glock inside her backpack and dragged the cowboy across the carpet and then the laminate flooring to the back door. Smoke filled the room and she had no idea if there'd be another blast. All she knew for certain was that they had to go.

Her lungs felt like they would seize as she gasped for fresh air. He was a solid mass and dragging him was taking all her strength. It was all she could do to get him out the door and to the tree line, hoping they'd be able to disappear there long enough to catch her breath and get a second wind.

As it was, her head was dizzy, her vision blurred and pain ricocheted through her body. She wasn't sure what hurt more, her side, her burned arm or her lungs. Two steps inside the tall grass and safety of the trees, Alice collapsed onto the ground next to the cowboy. She faintly registered that he looked different but then she'd never seen him unconscious before, either.

No matter how hard she tried to fight, exhaustion wrapped long-lean fingers around the edges of her consciousness. There was no way she'd be able to keep it at bay much longer.

Footsteps registered, not from the direction of the trailer but the trees behind it. That couldn't be a good sign, she thought, as she gave in to the darkness.

THERE WERE TWO bodies slumped over in the woods twenty feet ahead of Joshua. He immediately called Tommy and briefed him. Even though this wasn't his jurisdiction, he could call in favors should Joshua get into trouble. As he closed the distance between him and the bodies, he made them out to be Alice and his twin brother, Ryder. Guilt was a hot brand searing his heart because this was his fault. He'd been on his way to meet Ryder at the Tastee Freez Old Fashioned Ice Cream stand and hand over the bronze statue when he'd witnessed the entire scene. Two men in their early- to mid-twenties driving a late-model white station wagon had pulled in next to Ryder, who'd parked in the back lot away from other cars. Ryder had been staring down at his phone, no doubt texting Joshua to see how close he was to their meet-up point. The red light at the intersection had detained him.

The first man had exited his vehicle and stretched. Ryder had glanced up but didn't think twice about it and neither had Joshua at first. The second, the one closest to Ryder, had exited next but his brother had already dismissed any threat, his eyes glued to the device in his hand.

Joshua hadn't thought much of that either, figuring his years of police work had him overly paranoid when he started committing their descriptions to memory. What could he say? Old habits might die hard for others but not for Joshua. He was law enforcement through and through.

Even so, the entire situation had seemed nonthreatening until guy number two, the short and stocky one, pulled a gun and pointed it directly at Ryder's forehead and forced him inside the station wagon. It had taken every ounce of self-discipline for Joshua not to stomp the gas pedal and roar into the parking lot. His training had kicked in, overriding his adrenaline rush, so he'd forced himself to breathe slower and take measured action instead of blindly reacting to the situation playing out in front of him. One wrong step and they could both end up kidnapped or killed.

Because Joshua was late, his brother had been abducted. Now, he lay wounded and unconscious in the woods in rural Texas. Joshua had tracked those jerks who'd taken his brother, making sure he wasn't detected and then he'd been making his way through the thick mesquites for half an hour trying to find the damn trailer from the back side of the property. If only he'd arrived ten minutes sooner and not ended up lost in the damn trees.

The explosion followed by flames had jump-started his adrenaline again. His heart had stopped for a few seconds until he coughed to force it into action and started running toward the smoke.

Guilt seared him. He'd deal with the fallout from his emotions later. Right now, he had two unconscious—at least he hoped like hell they were unconscious because that would mean they were still breathing—and injured people to get to safety. He dropped to his knees next to the bodies, watching their chests, praying for movement. Ryder was facedown in the wet weeds and Alice was curled on her side, her skin pale. Her lips were blue. Both she and Ryder were still breathing, and that was the first time Joshua released the breath he'd been holding since initially identifying them.

There was a flurry of activity at the trailer and law enforcement would descend on these woods at any moment. Getting the two of them out of there undetected became his number one priority.

Retracing his steps would be easier now that he'd gotten his bearings. His Jeep was fifteen minutes away by foot. He needed to assess their injuries and figure out how he could get them out of there.

Carefully, he examined their injuries. Ryder had a serious gash in his forehead that needed to be dealt with and between the pair of them Alice looked to be in worse shape. The cut on her side was bleeding, her shirt soaked red. She'd picked up second degree burns on her right forearm that would need medical treatment. He rolled up a shirt from her backpack and put pressure on her cut to stem the bleeding. He had a few supplies in the Jeep. No. He didn't. He'd taken them into her motel room last night. Speaking of which, given what he knew about her circumstances, turning her in or taking her to the hospital would ensure her losing her job in law enforcement. He instantly regretted calling Tommy.

There were more pressing things than jobs right now, like, getting these two the hell out of these woods. In a few minutes, the trailer, woods and beyond would be crawling with deputies and Joshua didn't want to lie to law enforcement. Besides, he had two unconscious people to tend to and both needed medical attention.

He pulled water from Alice's pack and poured a little over Ryder's forehead to get a good look at the cut. It was a flesh wound, so that was a relief, despite the amount of blood dripping down his face. Forehead cuts were known for their bleeding. Ryder's eyes blinked open. And that was the second relief.

"Thank…God, you're awake," Joshua said, praying his brother would keep his eyes open.

Ryder looked around, seemed to be trying to get his bearings. "What happened?"

"There's a pretty good cut on your forehead," Joshua said, scanning his brother for any other injuries. From the looks of it, he'd taken a few shots to the face and there could be trauma. "Do you know who I am?"

"The less good-looking of a set of twins," Ryder quipped, his hand coming up to his forehead. "What happened? My head hurts like hell."

"You don't want to touch that," Joshua warned, thankful his brother wasn't showing signs of a concussion. He'd keep an eye on him, though. "The cut isn't too deep but it's bloody."

"Figures," Ryder said with a smirk. "I'm all show and no substance."

And that was the second bit of good news. If Ryder's sense of humor was intact he was going to be fine.

"Who jumped me?" he asked, making a move to sit up, wincing with pain.

"Go slow there, buddy," Joshua said, grateful his brother would be okay. Seeing him lying there on the ground hadn't done great things to Joshua's blood pressure.

Ryder glanced toward the trailer. "I can rest later. We gotta get the hell out of here."

"Think you can walk?" Joshua asked.

"I plan to." His brother's resolve was one of the many things Joshua appreciated about his twin. "What's the deal with her?"

"I'm guessing she's the one who pulled you out of that trailer," Joshua said.

"Like that?" Ryder's voice showed his shock as he motioned toward her injuries.

Joshua nodded. "Let's get her to safety and treat both of your injuries then figure out what happened."

"That's the best plan I've heard all day," Ryder agreed, accepting help up from Joshua to stand.

Next, Joshua picked up Alice. Even though she was fierce and he knew how much she insisted on taking care of herself she seemed small and soft cradled in his arms. Being a cop, he understood her thinking but he also needed to teach her that accepting help from him wasn't a sign of weakness. "My Jeep isn't far. Lean on me and we'll get there faster."

"I can walk on my own. Your hands are full with her," Ryder said, wincing and sucking in a burst of air when he put weight on his right leg.

His brother didn't know the half of it.

Chapter Seven

"What happened?" Alice gasped as she bolted upright. Of course, her mind would snap to the last thing she remembered.

"Hold on there. You're okay, you're safe," Joshua tried to soothe her. He could see confusion in her wide blue eyes and she was disoriented, which he'd expected. It was the middle of night, pitch-black outside. His eyes had long ago adjusted to the dark while he stayed by Alice's side, not wanting her to wake up scared or alone after the ordeal she'd endured to save his brother. "Lie back down and try to relax."

She reached up to tug on her oxygen mask.

"Doc said you could take that off once you woke. You breathed in a lot of smoke and she mumbled something about oxygen levels and preferring to take you to the ER," he said as he moved to her side and then sat on the edge of the bed. He did his level best to calm her panic as he helped her adjust the oxygen mask so she could talk.

"Where am I?" she asked. "Wait a minute. You were hurt. I dragged you from a trailer in the woods. There was blood all over your face. Your forehead was covered in it."

"I'm fine," he said and a place deep in his heart stirred

at seeing how concerned she was about him. "That was my twin brother you saved. His name is Ryder and we both owe you for what you did. You're at Dr. McConnell's house. She's a family friend, taking care of you at her home on a favor, and only agreed to treat you here because I gave my word you'd stick around until she said you were well enough to leave."

Confusion knitted her brow.

He'd given her a lot to digest at one time. He wished there was more he could do to take the fear out of her eyes.

"Hold on a second. You're a twin?" Her look of shock tugged at his heart. He hadn't exactly deceived her and yet the feeling was the same.

"Yes." He'd planned to tell her at some point but there hadn't exactly been a good time.

"Why didn't you tell me that before?"

"We didn't get around to talking about it," he said, which netted a cross look from Alice. "I didn't tell you before because there's a girl out there who needs our help." That part was true enough. "And as long as we're confessing our sins…why did you disappear on me?"

Alice shifted her position, looking uncomfortable. "What branch of law enforcement did you work in?"

"You didn't answer my question," he said, moving to adjust the pillows so she could sit more comfortably. "Is that better?"

She nodded and didn't meet his gaze. "I left the motel because I had a tip from my informant."

"It couldn't wait until I got back?" he asked. "In case you're still wondering, I'm on your side."

"How could I know that for sure? I kept you around because I thought you might end up getting hurt if I left you alone. The reason you got yourself into trouble was because you were trying to help me. Once I realized you were in law enforcement I knew you could take care of yourself, so I took off to follow a lead."

"Your informant told you about the trailer?" Joshua asked. He'd been wondering how she knew about that location.

"Yes. I thought maybe they were holding girls there since it was out in the sticks."

"And you hoped that either Isabel was there or one of the girls would know where she'd been taken?" It was more statement than question.

She nodded.

"Want me to turn on the light?" he asked.

"Yes. Please. What time is it?"

"Two twenty-five in the morning," he said, flipping the switch on the soft light next to the bed. The warm glow brightened the room and he could see her anguish clearly on her face. "What can I get for you? Water? Food?"

"Nothing, no, wait. Water," she said, examining the bandage covering her right forearm.

He made a move to get up but her hand stopped him and he did his level best to ignore the jolt of electricity spreading through him from the point of contact.

"Hold on. First of all, thank you for saving me. I owe you one," she said.

"Best as I can figure, we're even," he said with a half smile.

"Tell me what happened before you go. How'd I get this?" She motioned toward the extra-large white bandage covering her arm wrist to elbow.

"I'm not sure. I found you with these injuries, so I'm

guessing this happened while you were trying to save my brother." He repositioned the pillows behind her so she could sit up more easily, thinking about the fact that she'd put herself in harm's way again trying to save the person she believed to be him.

"My cut was bleeding. Did you stop it?" She pushed the covers down to expose her side. "Wait. How'd I get into pajamas?"

"That was me and the doctor I told you about." He tried to push the images of the soft curve of her hip and the long lines of her legs out of his mind. He'd been a gentleman and looked away as soon as he could.

"She treated your cut and your burns, most of which are second-degree. We have a salve to put on twice a day and we have to keep the burns dressed, especially once they blister."

"And you arranged all this?" she asked suspiciously as she glanced around the room.

"You saved my brother. For that, I owed you." He was grateful to have Dr. McConnell as a friend. The woman was country to the core from wearing jeans and boots underneath her lab coat to the rustic Southwest feel of her home. The queen-size bed was positioned as the focal point of the room. The headboard and footboard were each made of a single large pine log with log side rails. A thick burgundy bedspread contrasted with the light-colored wood. The walls were painted a light gray shade that reminded him of a chilly, winter sky—the kind that made him want to throw a few logs onto the fireplace and stay in, stay warm. "You lost a lot of blood. Doc groaned a little bit about me not taking you to the ER, but I asked her to treat you here instead." He could only imagine how weird it would be to wake up in a strange bed next to a man she barely knew after sustaining the kind of injuries she had. "I should wake the doc, so she can check on you while I get you that water."

Her fingers touched his forearm again. She pulled back when he stared like she'd just touched him with a branding iron.

"The other night at the motel was the first night I've really slept in a long time," she said.

Joshua didn't want to give away his real reaction to her, especially since his attraction was completely out of place under the circumstances.

"How's your brother?" she asked.

"I've had better days," Ryder said from his position in the doorway.

"How long have you been up?" Joshua asked, turning toward his brother's voice. He stood and then covered the distance between them in a few short strides to embrace his brother in a bear hug.

"Half an hour maybe," Ryder responded. He looked tons better than he had a few hours ago.

McConnell had insisted that he stay with her, too. Joshua had seconded her argument, preferring to keep watch on his brother while he healed.

"Take a seat." Joshua pointed toward the side chair. "You shouldn't be walking around yet."

"I made it out of the woods," Ryder quipped and they both chuckled at his bad pun.

"Even so, I'd feel better if you took a load off," Joshua said with a wry grin.

Ryder nodded, but stopped short of letting Joshua help him walk to the chair.

"This is my brother Ryder," Joshua said to Alice as she studied his brother's features.

After a thoughtful pause, she said, "No wonder I thought he was you. You two look almost identical."

"Yeah, but I'm the better-looking twin," Ryder teased.

"Still holding on to that dream?" Joshua shot back.

"I have a mirror. I know what I see. Then I look at you. Doesn't take a rocket scientist to figure it out."

"You also have a head injury," Joshua pointed out with a smirk.

"Shots fired. Looks like I'm taking aggressive action," Ryder kept the joke going, shooting a pleading look toward Alice, who smiled back.

Joshua loved all of his brothers but he and his twin had always had a special bond, the kind that made long explanations unnecessary. Which made keeping a secret from him feel even worse and especially one as big as he was holding on to.

The two used to joke that they knew what the other one was thinking without needing to say the words. Most of the time, Joshua enjoyed their special bond. But when it came to his career move and Alice, he'd rather keep his brother in the dark a little while longer.

Especially where it applied to Alice. He had yet to figure that one out for himself.

ALICE COULDN'T HELP but notice the ease with which Joshua and his brother spoke to each other, the obvious love they had for one other. They shared the kind of relationship she wanted and hoped for her own boys.

In her job, she saw the bad side of people. Families at odds. Husbands hurting their wives. Abuse. Being witness to too much of the dark side of humanity had tainted her view, if not extinguished all hope there was something better, something more to people and relationships. There was still a spark in her that believed in people who did the right things for the sake of honesty. Men who loved their wives, families, and didn't hurt their children. Even if her personal experience had mirrored more of her professional experience.

"Do you have any siblings?" Ryder asked Alice.

The question caught her off guard.

"No. It was just me," Alice answered, hating the lonely edge to her voice when she said the words out loud. Now that she'd started down that slippery slope she figured she might as well go all in. "My dad disappeared before my first birthday and my mom was killed on her way to work a few years later."

The look of surprise and compassion on both men's faces brought stinging tears to the backs of her eyes as both offered apologies. This wasn't the sort of thing she ever talked about with people. In fact, she'd been holding it all inside so long. Looking at Joshua, seeing sympathy and not condemnation, gave her the strength to power on. "I'd started kindergarten by the time I had to be moved from my first foster family. They were religious zealots and believed in hitting first and asking questions later."

Joshua returned to his seat on the bed and she could felt the mattress dip under his weight. The concern in his eyes turned darker, like clouds as a storm brewed. His eyes were how she could tell the difference between the brothers. Joshua's were so green, almost like clear emeralds, whereas his brother's were more hazel. Both of the men had black hair—Joshua's was darker and a little curlier—and she wondered if dark hair was an O'Brien trademark.

Joshua also had a freckle by his left ear. She told herself it was the cop in her needing to memorize every detail and not the woman.

"The second and fourth foster families weren't bad. Neither had bet on a long-term assignment when they'd taken me into their homes. They were emergency relief when a placement went wrong." She didn't want to think about the nonemergency families having spent the better part of her life trying to block those out. Her experiences varied from people who wanted money from the state and "free" help around the house to "fathers" who wanted easy prey. Alice had stabbed one with kitchen scissors; he lived. She simply ran away after fighting off the next one, figuring she'd fare better on her own. "By the time I was a teenager, I figured I'd do better on my own. Figured it might be easier than fighting off some of my male guardians. Got caught after two weeks, which turned out to be a good thing. I was placed with a retired sheriff and his wife. They were kind and I was able to bring up my grades enough in high school to get into a local college." She looked up at the brothers and realized she'd been a little too chatty. Her cheeks flamed. "Sorry. I don't usually tell my life story to strangers."

"Don't be," Joshua said quickly.

The room was suddenly too quiet and Alice could hear her own breathing. Had she shared too much? Looking at Joshua made her heart race and especially seeing the intense look on his face that said he could read between the lines of what she was saying.

"Are you feeling better?" Alice asked Ryder, trying to change the subject and calm her racing pulse.

Joshua covered her hand with his; that little bit of contact spread warmth through her.

Ryder smiled sympathetically before nodding. "I owe

you for saving my hide. If you hadn't been *there*…I wouldn't be *here* right now."

"We both owe you," Joshua said and there was an emotion in his voice she couldn't quite put her finger on. Regret? But that didn't make sense, did it?

"I have a feeling both of you would've done the same thing for me," she countered. "One of you already has."

A gray-haired no-nonsense-looking middle-aged woman with rounded shoulders stepped into the room. Her hair was cut short, just above her ears and to the collar in back.

"What's my patient doing out of bed in the middle of the night?" she asked, staring at Ryder.

"I was getting a drink before going to the bathroom, ma'am," he said, the utmost respect in his voice as he grinned at his brother like he was about to be sent to the principal's office.

Joshua made a move to help his brother up, but Ryder wasn't having it. He waved off his twin as he grimaced. "I'm getting out of here in the morning and heading back to the ranch."

"We'll see about that," Dr. McConnell said.

"If you get the green light, I'll call to make arrangements for you to be transported safely." Joshua was all business when it came to his brother's life. "You'll need to lay low until we catch this son of a—"

"Not with a lady in the house," the doctor interrupted, clucking her tongue.

Alice suppressed a chuckle. Besides, it hurt to laugh.

"My apologies, ma'am. I didn't mean to offend." Joshua tipped an imaginary hat toward Alice.

"Apology accepted." She winked, grateful for the lighter conversation.

Joshua moved from his spot presumably to give the doctor better access. He walked a step behind Ryder with his hands up, ready, in case his brother needed him but without Ryder even knowing he was doing it. Witnessing the two of them together stirred her heart in so many ways. Their parents had done something right in raising these men and she hoped to do half as well with her own boys despite the seeds of doubt that reminded her she had no idea what she was doing in the parenting department. She absently fingered the half-heart charm necklace resting on her chest as the doctor pulled a stethoscope from around her neck.

The exam didn't take more than a few minutes and the doctor gave her a stern warning about movement. "If you need to go to the bathroom, ask for help."

Alice glanced from Joshua to the doctor and must've blushed because the doctor quickly added, "He'll help you to the door and wait outside until you say it's okay if I'm not around."

McConnell reinforced her recommendations of hydration and bed rest before turning off the light.

"It's good that your brother is going to be okay," Alice said in the dark once the doc had gone. She was still thinking about the close bond between the two men.

"Thanks to you." There was that edge in his voice, like earlier. Then it dawned on her why. Joshua blamed himself.

"It's not your fault," she said.

"You don't want to go down that road," he said quietly. There was a warning in his tone but no real threat.

"Which one?" She wasn't ready to move on from the topic and maybe it was because she recognized guilt when she heard it, saw it. Leaving a teenager to ride the bus on her own and not immediately sounding an alarm when she didn't show was a good reason to be guilty. Looking too much like your twin was not.

"I know what you're trying to do here, but leave it alone," he said.

"It's not your fault, Joshua."

"I put him in harm's way. I may as well have tossed him to Perez and his men on a platter."

"You had no idea any of this would happen," she countered, not ready to let him take all the blame. "If you remember correctly you were just trying to save me and that's what got you into this mess in the first place. You were doing the right thing in helping what you thought was a teenager in trouble. That's how Perez spotted you. That's why his men are after you. And all that is because I tried to do undercover work that I wasn't authorized to do. If anyone's to blame, it's me."

"Not so easy. I make my own choices and I take responsibility for them. You didn't ask for my help and I think we both know you wouldn't have. I still have the bruise on my left arm from you being frustrated about that one. He's my brother. I didn't warn him about Perez. This is on me. Besides, you don't get to corner the market on all the guilt."

Was that true? Had she been making herself responsible for everyone around her? Always turning every situation that went sour into her fault? Yeah, the cowboy was probably right. Didn't change the fact that neither O'Brien would be on the run or hurt if it hadn't been for her carelessness.

"I should've known better. Perez was after me and I didn't connect the dots that my own twin brother might be in danger. How stupid does that make me?"

"From my point of view?" she asked but it was rhe-
torical. "You're always trying to put others first. That's
the whole reason you intervened in the field. And you've
been trying to keep me out of trouble ever since. If anyone's taking the blame for Ryder being jumped, it's me.
I never should have taken off like that without telling
you."

If he really believed what he was saying about himself what did he think of her? She'd messed up big time
with Isabel. Did the cowboy blame Alice as much as
she blamed herself?

The room went quiet and she could tell he was turning over what she'd said in his mind.

"You didn't say what happened to your mom," Joshua
whispered after several silent beats had passed. "Is it
okay to ask about her?"

"Yeah, sure. It happened a long time ago. Her body
was found exactly two months after the day she disappeared. She'd been strangled and then dumped on the
side of the highway. The case was never solved," Alice
said with as much detachment as she could muster. The
truth was that she would never stop wondering what
had happened to her mother and how different her own
life might have turned out if she hadn't been shuffled
into the system. Would she be able to trust? Because not
trusting anyone, ever, and always expecting the worst,
was exhausting.

"That the reason you went into law enforcement?
Needing answers in your mother's case?"

"Probably. At least part of it."

"The sheriff must've made a good impression,"
Joshua said after another thoughtful pause.

"I admired him for how much he cared about people,

strangers." Her own father hadn't cared enough to stick around but there was no use sinking into that self-pity hole. Feeling sorry for herself didn't change her situation and only made her bitter.

"For what it's worth, I'm sorry about everything you've been through," Joshua said. She could tell that he meant every word and there was something about hearing it that eased her burden. "No one and especially not a kid should have had to endure any of it."

"It's not your fault, but I appreciate what you're sayin'." It was pitch-black in the room and she couldn't see a hand in front of her face if she wanted to and yet she felt comforted while talking to Joshua. What was it about darkness that made it seem safe to spill secrets? Or was it the cowboy's presence that made her feel that way?

"It wasn't yours, either," he said quietly.

She let that thought hang in the air, waiting for her eyes to adjust.

"I know that you don't want to lose momentum in the investigation, so I'm planning on going out tomorrow to recheck the site. I need to know what all you've gotten yourself into," he said matter-of-factly.

"Sharing won't be a problem for me. I won't hold anything back as soon as you tell me which branch of law enforcement you work for," she said.

Joshua sat there, silent, as her eyes were beginning to adjust to the dark. She could make out his basic form if not the details of his face. She wished she could see his expression so she'd know if he was about to lie.

"I'm on leave from my job as a cop in Denver, trying to decide my next move." His steady, even tone said he was telling the truth.

"Why would you leave the force for a cattle ranch?" she asked, quickly adding, "Not that cattle are bad. It just seems like a drastic change."

"My parents died and I inherited part of the family property. It was always assumed that I'd come back and take my rightful place with my brothers to help run things," he said.

She picked up on the way he'd said *assumed*, like he had no say in the decision. Joshua O'Brien didn't strike her as the kind of man who would roll over on something as important as the work he did. Before she could ask, he stood.

"I'm going to check on my brother. Do you need anything while I'm up?" he asked, the topic clearly closed.

"No. Thanks. I'm fine."

He stopped at the doorway. "Are you really?"

"I will be when I get Isabel back."

MORNING CAME AND the smell of fresh-cooked eggs and bacon streamed through the hallway and into Alice's room. She eased to a sitting position, trying not to think about how much movement hurt. She needed to get back on track with the investigation but there was no way she could do anything in her present condition.

Joshua appeared in the doorway with a tray of what smelled like heaven on earth. "I thought you might be hungry."

"Starving." She figured it was a peace offering after the way things ended last night.

"Doc said that would be a good sign. She's doing rounds at the hospital this morning and said she'd drop by on her lunch hour to check on her favorite patient."

"Me?"

"I know she wasn't talking about my brother." He laughed as he set the tray on her lap.

"How is he, by the way?" she asked, taking the mug of coffee first.

"Sleeping. Better. He'll be fine. He didn't sustain a serious enough blow to worry the doc. She wants him to stay until she gets here and then she figures she'll cut him loose." Joshua took his seat, clasped his hands together and rested his elbows on his knees.

That wasn't a good sign because his body language said he was closing up on her.

"What is it?" she asked.

"I have something to say and you're not going to like it."

She took another sip to clear her mind.

"I spoke to the sheriff this morning."

She started to protest but he cut her off.

"Before you get riled up, hear me out."

She picked up the fork and toyed with the eggs, staring intently at them.

"Here's the deal. You already know about my law enforcement background and that's why I know how important it is to follow protocol if you ever want your job back. I also know about the situation with Professional Standards—"

She tried to cut him off again with similar results.

"Maybe you don't want to work in law enforcement again, and that's fine. Either way, I want to give you the option."

"You have my attention." She dug into a chunk of scrambled egg and pushed it into her mouth. It was probably too late to save her job but it would be helpful in trying to raise the twins if she wasn't in jail for obstruction. The thought of doing something that could separate her from her boys, and especially with no father in the picture, threatened to eat away at what was left of her stomach lining.

"I know the feds are involved and you've ignored everyone's warnings to butt out of this case. Tommy is a friend of mine and he wants to speak to you as a witness," he said. "You don't have to worry. He isn't planning on arresting you or giving up your location to your SO."

Alice chewed the eggs.

"Before you tell me what a bad idea all this is I'd like to point out that you're in no condition to do any of this on your own," he added. "You need me at the very least and I need to bring in help to do this the right way and avoid anyone else getting hurt."

That much was true. She wouldn't argue there.

"You have strict instructions to rest and I've been told to apply salve to your burns and redress them twice a day," Joshua seemed to add that part to further his point of her needing to accept help.

"Is that why my burns don't hurt? Some miracle salve?" she asked, considering his proposition. She thought about lighting the station wagon on fire, the blaze...and then remembered the printout she'd taken from in between the driver's seat and console a few moments before she lit the paper and stuffed it in the gas line.

"Where's my backpack?" She frantically scanned the room. The piece of paper could mean nothing more than a family gathering or restaurant location but she'd seen cases blown wide open with less.

"It's in the kitchen." He didn't ask if she wanted him

to get it. He seemed to sense the importance of it as he cleared the room and returned a few seconds later. "What am I looking for and where?"

"In the front compartment."

Joshua pulled out the Google map, shooting Alice a warning look. "No. We're not going to investigate this ourselves. You're going to finish your breakfast and I'm going to send for the sheriff."

"But—"

"Nothing. You're in no shape to confront these guys and they most likely assume I'm dead."

"They'll know you're alive when they read the news and learn there were no bodies in the trailer."

"Details about the incident are being suppressed," he said.

"Your sheriff has that much power?"

"Here locally, yes. But that's not why."

Alice knew what he was going to say before he said it.

"You already know the feds are involved because they told you if you didn't leave this alone they'd haul you to jail on obstruction charges," he said.

"So you already know," she said. "They'll do it anyway as soon as I surface. They have to know I've been involved."

"Not necessarily. Tommy's working on your behalf. Giving him this map will help prove that you're willing to step aside and let them do their jobs. You act otherwise and none of us will be able to help you or keep you out of jail."

"They would still be clueless if it weren't for me. I'm getting further than they are on my own and they'll mess everything up for me if I let them in," she countered, knowing full well they didn't care about her or Isabel. All they wanted was Perez.

"I understand where you're coming from and I have to think that they do, too, on some level." Joshua's tone had softened. "So, I'm not asking you to do this for them. I'm asking you to do it so you can be around this Christmas for your boys. They need you. Isabel needs you. And we have to do this the right way or you could lose everything."

The weight of those last four words sat heavy on her chest.

Everything the cowboy said made sense. She knew in her heart that he was looking out for her best interests and so was her SO. She could give it another chance with the sheriff's support. The feds couldn't be trusted. They'd been clear that they were willing to sacrifice Isabel for a bigger conviction. Granted, she wanted Perez or whoever had Isabel to go to jail for the rest of his life but Isabel would always come first. If Alice had the chance to swoop in and get Isabel away from Perez's operation she wouldn't think twice even if it meant jeopardizing the bigger case.

"Call your friend. I'll tell him everything I know about Perez's operation and what I've found out so far if he promises me to put Isabel first," she said.

"Deal. He'll do the right thing. You can trust him," Joshua seemed to read her worried thoughts.

Show her a cop with blind faith in people and she'd expose the real Santa Claus.

Chapter Eight

"Thanks for coming on such short notice," Joshua said to Tommy at the front door.

"I'm not sure how you convinced her to talk to me." Tommy glanced around the living room.

"We want the same things," Joshua responded. "Trust is going to be an issue for her."

"She's a cop, so I figured as much," Tommy said.

"It's more than that. Her dad abandoned her at a young age. Her mother was murdered. Then she was shuffled around the system." Her fierce determination to protect Isabel made even more sense to him now. Because of a mistake she felt that she'd condemned a young girl to the same fate as her own—a fate that hadn't been kind.

"I'm guessing that didn't work out too well for her," Tommy said.

"Not until a retired sheriff and his wife stepped up to the plate. She was in high school by then." Joshua also figured it was the only reason she'd agreed to speak to another sheriff instead of one of her own. He could also see the attraction in becoming an officer because cops were all about the camaraderie, about being a family. Her earlier defensiveness about needing to feel like she was pulling her own weight made more sense to him now, too. He was slowly breaking down that wall and, he hoped, gaining her trust in the process.

"I see," Tommy said with a frown. He would understand the implications of her life better than anyone. "She sounds like a strong woman."

Joshua nodded. On the outside? She was tough. But she'd constructed a fortress around her heart. It took a lot of strength to walk away from her boys in order to throw everything she had into finding Isabel and he could see that decision hadn't come lightly by the depths in her blue eyes. It took sheer determination and grit to do what she was doing. And that was one of the many reasons he wanted to do everything he could to help. "We better not keep her waiting."

Joshua led Tommy into the guest room where Alice waited. Her hands were clasped, resting on her lap. The bandage wrapped in gauze covered her entire right forearm.

"Thank you for agreeing to see me, Ms. Green," Tommy said after introductions.

"Call me Alice." Her body language, clasped hands and tension lines creasing her forehead, said that she was not at ease.

Ryder appeared in the doorway. "Whatever's going on, I want in."

Joshua would remind his brother that he was in no condition to help catch a guy like Perez if it would do any good. It wouldn't. So, he said, "I'll get another chair."

By the time he returned, Tommy was sitting in the guest chair, leaned slightly forward with his torso angled toward Alice. Joshua set the kitchen chair down next to Tommy and then sat on the foot of the bed.

"First off, I wanted to thank you for what you did on-site," Tommy began.

"Anyone in this room would do the same for me," she countered with a glance toward Ryder.

Joshua had noticed she didn't like receiving compliments. He needed to change that. She should know how brave everyone thought she was. And strong. *And beautiful*, that annoying little voice in the back of his head said again. Annoying or not, the voice was right. Even banged up and defensive she was beautiful.

"I'd take you on my team any day," Tommy said, the comment making the tension lines bracketing her mouth ease. That was the best compliment a cop could receive.

"Thank you, Sheriff," she said and then changed the subject. "Have you figured out what that map is about?"

"We can talk about the map in a second. I appreciate what you did for Ryder. He's more like a brother to me than a friend so I owe you. I was also thanking you for making the call to the sheriff before you set the station wagon on fire," he said.

"I don't know what you're talking about." Alice moved her right arm to her side as though shielding it from Tommy's view would make him not notice it. And that's exactly how Joshua knew she was guilty. He'd been so grateful that she'd helped Ryder that he hadn't really thought about much else.

Tommy leaned closer. "I'm not condemning you for setting the fire. I might've done the same thing given what you were up against if I'd thought of it. In case I haven't made myself clear, I'm grateful that you did whatever was necessary to save my friend."

Alice had believed it was Joshua in there and from the looks of it she'd been willing to sacrifice herself to save him. He shouldn't be surprised. She'd been doing the same thing for Isabel even though she was putting herself in grave danger doing so and she'd done it for him when she realized Perez would be after him. He'd find a way to convince her to stay on the sidelines and let law enforcement do their jobs. Or he'd do it himself. No way was he allowing her to risk her life anymore.

"What makes you so sure it was me who made the call?" She wasn't exactly denying it.

"Because dispatch received an anonymous call before the fire was set based on the preliminary report from the fire marshal. He chalked it up to a computer glitch or human error, thinking the time stamp was wrong on the call. You know what I think?"

Alice didn't respond but she suddenly became very interested in a patch of blanket on her lap.

Joshua put his hand on her leg to offer some measure of reassurance.

"You phoned it in right before you lit that fire," Tommy continued. "I'm guessing you were already injured and you figured you might not have time to call once everything was in motion."

"They had Joshua, or so I thought, and it was only a matter of time before Perez's men killed him," she admitted. "I didn't know how long that would take. They'd try to get information out of him first and I knew for certain he wasn't about to give them any, which would anger them and probably speed up the whole process. I couldn't live with his blood on my hands since he got into this mess trying to help me in the first place."

Ryder pushed up to his feet, walked to the bed, and hugged her. "Thank for saving me but especially because you thought you were saving my brother."

Alice awkwardly hugged him back with her one good arm before bowing her head and wiping her eye. Joshua was pretty certain she'd just tried to hide tears. He gently squeezed her calf where his fingers rested, ignoring the electricity pulsing up his arm from contact.

She glanced at him and he was pretty certain her cheeks flushed and that didn't exactly help with his inappropriate attraction to her.

"So what now?" she asked, clearly needing to change the subject.

"I made contact with the task force and offered my resources to the team," Tommy said, throwing her a lifeline.

One that sank to the ocean floor instead of floating.

"That's all?" Her stress levels had just spiked based on the anger thinning her lips and her tense expression.

"You of all people know that I have to follow protocol. The good news is that after looking at the property on the map and realizing it's in my county we have a good chance they'll take me up on my offer," he added quickly.

That seemed to strike a chord with Alice although she stopped short of relaxing. Joshua already knew how much she distrusted the task force. He also knew they'd warned her to stay out of their investigation and he didn't want to think about the fact that he might be killing his own chances for a job with the FBI by associating with this case.

"Until we know what's inside that house, I can't do much of anything," Tommy said honestly.

"Do you know the area very well?" she asked.

"Yes. Most of the folks are decent and like to keep to themselves. That's why they buy an acre of land because they want space between themselves and their neighbors," Tommy said. "The house itself is small but there are several barns on the site and that could be used to hold victims."

"Have you sent a deputy to canvass the neighbors yet?" she asked.

"That's the easiest way to get myself excluded from the investigation, so the answer is no."

Alice blew out a breath and she looked completely at a loss. "What's the next step then?"

"Wait until I hear back from the leader of the task force. Get myself included in the process."

"Isabel could be long gone by the time they act," Alice said, more than a hint of hopelessness in her voice.

"We won't give up until we find her," Joshua said and Ryder quickly chimed in with his pledge.

"I'm going to pretend I didn't hear that," Tommy said on a harsh sigh. "I know this is asking a lot but I need a commitment from all three of you to give this a little time."

"There's no—"

"What? Time to do this the right way?" Tommy stopped her. "Let me put it this way. You may rush in and save Isabel but what then? Perez is still on the loose. All three of you are constantly looking over your shoulder and I already know that you're going to tell me that's okay. You don't mind making the sacrifice to find someone you obviously love so much. But here's the kicker. Perez is still out there because the entire operation was botched. Other girls are still being taken, girls like Isabel. They're being ripped from their lives and their families destroyed all because you ran out of patience."

Tears streamed down Alice's cheeks but she didn't

make a move to clear them or speak. Tommy's words were obviously scoring a direct hit.

"I don't mean to sound harsh, or maybe I do. There's a big picture here that we can't lose sight of even though I understand your reasoning one hundred percent. Perez has to be stopped because he is ruining lives. And if that means I have to shout from the rooftops or remind you every day, I will. If I have to get down on my knees and beg you to take a step back, I'll do it. He's a monster and he belongs behind bars where he can't hurt any more girls." Tommy stood and started pacing. "I don't even have to remind you guys that if anyone tied to this case sees Alice so much as park her car on the same block as a stakeout she'll be arrested on the spot, which will do Isabel absolutely no good."

No one spoke for several long minutes that stretched on, even though Joshua knew that his friend was right. Joshua moved to the window, and cracked open the curtain, flooding the room with natural light.

"You won't get any interference from me," Alice finally said. "But I want your word that you'll keep me posted every step of the way. Anything happens, even something you think means nothing, I want to know about it."

"Deal," Tommy said without hesitation, which seemed to ease some of Alice's anxiety. "And since I know you won't be able to walk away completely, I want the same courtesy."

"I'll touch base with my informant and see if I can squeeze him for more information about possible routes or what the compound might be used for," she said motioning toward her cell. "I'll let you know if I get anything out of him."

"Sounds like a plan." Tommy glanced from Ryder to Joshua. "Are we good?"

"We're all on the same side," Joshua said as Ryder nodded. "We want to put an end to Perez's operation."

"I'll text the minute I hear from the task force," Tommy said, and then moved toward the door.

"I'll walk him out," Ryder said, pushing to his feet.

"We need to fix up that arm," Joshua said to Alice, moving the tray table filled with supplies next to the bed.

She was already picking at the tape holding her gauze together with her left hand.

"I can do that," Joshua said quickly.

When she looked up, there were tears streaming down her face.

"What is it? What's wrong?" he asked, taking a seat on the bed next to her. He leaned to the right placing his weight on his fisted hands on either side of her thighs. "You can talk to me."

She turned to face the opposite wall. "I'm just frustrated that's all."

There was more to it than that. He could read her pretty well by now. But she still seemed determined not to let him in.

ALICE'S BOYS WERE in Tucson, safe. Isabel was out there somewhere, in trouble. Alice was stuck in a bed, wounded. This wasn't the life she'd envisioned for the people she loved. And the worst part about the whole situation was how helpless she felt. She picked at the corner of the medical tape. It didn't budge. She yanked at it, ripping the gauze instead of the tape. *Great.* She couldn't even do that right.

"Let me help," Joshua soothed. His masculine tone offered more comfort than she knew better to take.

"I need to make the call to my informant that I promised the sheriff," she countered, reaching for her cell on the nightstand next to the bed.

"It can wait until I'm finished." He shot her a look that begged the question of why she was being so difficult.

Relaxing and being "helped" wasn't exactly her forte. She'd never been a spa-day girl. She'd rather poke her eyes out than get a massage although Joshua's hands on her felt pretty damn good. Her body hummed with awareness every time he got close enough to reach out and touch. So, she did reach out for him just to see what it did to her body.

With her left hand she grabbed a fistful of his black V-neck and pulled him toward her. Her arm might be burned and her side stabbed but there was nothing wrong with her lips and right now she wanted to kiss the cowboy more than she wanted to breathe. She pressed her mouth against his, briefly, and then pulled back to check his reaction.

Big mistake looking into those deep green eyes this close. They opened slowly and a flash of primal need registered before he spoke.

"This a good idea?" he asked, that spark growing into something more flaming.

"Probably not but I don't care." She pressed her lips to his again, need rising from low in her belly and sending warmth to that feminine spot between her thighs.

The cowboy's tongue surged inside her mouth and she parted her lips, ready for more.

His fingers cradled the base of her neck and she lost herself in the moment. His mouth moving against hers, their tongues tangled, and all she could think about was how much she wanted more.

And then he pulled back. He stared into her eyes daring her to speak.

She didn't.

"I need to change your bandage," he said.

"Did I do something wrong?" Her heart pounded against her ribs and her breathing had become a little frantic in those few seconds their mouths fused.

"We don't need this distraction right now."

Was that how he classified what was simmering between them since they'd met? *A distraction.* At least she knew where she stood with Joshua O'Brien.

Alice stuck out her burned arm and looked the other way while he grabbed the container of salve that looked like white cupcake frosting and then smoothed the cream over her blistered skin. When he was finished dressing her wound, he handed her a pair of ibuprofen and a glass of water.

"You can take more than two of these according to the doc," he said and his voice was low and gravelly.

She tried to ignore that fact.

"Two's fine," she said, thinking how much she needed to check on her twins, to hear their little coos. As soon as Joshua left the room, she'd make the call. In the meantime, she took the pills from his opened palm, ignoring the fissures of heat the contact brought. Lot of good those did her. Apparently, the need to act on their attraction was one-sided.

"If you need anything, I'll be in the shower," he said, adding, "a very cold shower."

Alice couldn't hold back a smile as she watched him

walk out of the room, checking out the ripple of muscles down his back through his T-shirt.

Maybe it was out-of-control hormones or the fact that she hadn't had sex in longer than she cared to admit, but Joshua O'Brien was probably the sexiest man she'd ever met.

Once he cleared the room she phoned her neighbor who was watching the boys. Marla picked up on the first ring.

"How are my babies?" Alice asked, forcing cheer in her voice she didn't feel.

"Wonderful. Let me round them up and I'll put them on," Marla said.

Alice ignored the stab of pain in her chest that had nothing to do with her injuries and everything to do with missing her boys. She could hear sounds of them laughing in the background and an image of Marla chasing them around the living room instead of her doing it sent another shard of pain through her chest. Their given names might be Alex and Andrew but she should've named them Rowdy and Rambunctious, and she missed everything about them both.

"Hel-low?" Rambunctious, aka Andrew, got on the line first.

"Hi, baby," Alice said, loving the sound of his little voice.

"M-m-momma!" he exclaimed.

"Are you being a good boy for Miss Marla?" she asked, knowing full well her boys were energetic angels. Having a retired school teacher as a neighbor had been a godsend. Marla's only child had a job overseas and her husband's health was failing, so she'd needed to stick close to home. She'd offered to take care of the boys to help Alice, but also because she missed her own grandchildren.

"Uh-huh," Rambunctious said. His heavy breaths from crawling around coupled with his sheer excitement vibrated across the line.

"I love you, Andrew," she said, fighting tears, figuring she'd held his attention about as long as he could.

Rowdy popped on to the line next and she could hear shuffling noises, and bare feet on Marla's tile floors as Rambunctious belly-laughed in the background. Was he walking? No, she didn't want to know. It did no good to know what she was missing out on. Knowing wouldn't bring Isabel back faster.

Alice sighed. She missed those belly laughs.

"Momma?" he said in his adorable baby talk.

"That's right, baby. It's me."

His burst of excitement nearly crushed her heart. She heard something that sounded like the phone being dropped before Marla's voice returned to the line.

"All is well here," she said, recovering quickly.

Alice needed that. She desperately needed to know that her boys were okay. She needed someone else, too, as scary as it was to admit that fact. He was currently in a cold shower in the other room and she'd probably just ruined their friendship by kissing him.

"How are you?" Marla asked.

"I'll be better when this whole ordeal is over and I can come home," she said on a sigh.

After chatting about bedtimes and activities for several minutes, Alice ended the call having safely avoided the topic of how she was really doing. With two boys less than a year old in tow, Marla didn't have time for lengthy conversations and Alice was grateful for that fact. She'd broken down in tears enough in the past twenty-four hours to last a lifetime and she'd never been much of a crier.

Next, she called Dale, hoping her informant might know something about the address on the map. She was getting restless sitting in bed while everyone else worked on the case. Doing nothing, being alone with her thoughts was the worst feeling. She needed to keep her mind busy.

The call rolled straight into voice mail.

ALL THINGS CONSIDERED, Joshua figured the meeting with Tommy had gone well. After dressing Alice's burns like the doc had trained him to do he decided to return to the trailer site so he could survey the area. At least that was the excuse he used to get out of the house. Being with Alice 24/7 was messing with his mind. He needed to get some fresh air to clear his head, but his thoughts kept winding back to that kiss. The softness of her lips. How much he wanted to kiss that little dimple on the corner of her mouth to the left.

He dismissed it as dangerous. Joshua couldn't afford the slightest slip right now. Too much was on the line with people he cared about, not to mention his own life. He could chalk this attraction up to primal need in a life-and-death situation but it was more than that. There was so much more to Alice than a physical attraction and that stirred his heart in ways he didn't want to think about while he was about to make a serious life change. Momentarily being trapped in a life he didn't want wasn't the best time to let his emotions run wild. The best thing he could do for both of them was redirect his thoughts to the case.

It played to Joshua's hand that Perez believed he was dead. Even so, he planned to have a conversation with Ryder about staying at the ranch until Perez was safely out of town. In the meantime both needed to keep a low profile, which was why Joshua had borrowed Dr. McConnell's pickup truck rather than take his own Jeep. In this part of the country, there were more pickups and SUVs than sedans on the road, so it was the best way to blend in.

A cold front had blown through and it was too chilly outside for Joshua's taste. One of the best parts about leaving Colorado for Texas was gaining sunshine and warmth. Nature wasn't cooperating with his plans today. He buttoned up his denim jacket, tucked his chin to his chest and adjusted his gray Stetson low on his forehead as he made his way through the brush, retracing his steps from yesterday. There could be feds on-site or staking out the place to see if one of the criminals returned so he needed to stay alert.

While he'd expected crime scene tape cordoning off the place, he didn't anticipate seeing deputies and feds crawling everywhere. He couldn't risk getting closer to the single wide, so he retreated and placed a call to Tommy once he was back in McConnell's pickup.

"Did you connect with the task force?" he asked as soon as Tommy answered, hoping there was some good news to come out of this.

"I just sent over the map and Ms. Green's statement," he replied with a questioning overtone to his voice. "Do I need to ask why?"

"You didn't reveal her identity, did you?" Joshua asked.

"It's best that they know she's cooperating. They'll go easier on her," Tommy said.

He was right so Joshua let it go.

"I'm at the crime scene and the place is crawling with law enforcement. You have any idea what that's about?" Joshua asked, trying not to think about just how badly he could be blowing his chances at ever working for the FBI if he was caught interfering with a federal investigation.

"No, I don't." Tommy paused for a beat. "I don't have to tell you not to stick around, do I?"

"I'm on my way back to McConnell's," Joshua said, turning the key over in the ignition. "Think you can find out what's going on?"

"Can't make any promises they'll tell me, but it never hurts to ask."

The call from Tommy came a few minutes before McConnell was due back for lunch. Ryder joined Joshua in Alice's room as he put the call on speaker.

"I have bad news so I'll cut to the chase," Tommy said. "A body was found inside the trailer."

Being able to identify one of Perez's men could go a long way toward cracking this case open. There were a few knowns, so Joshua hoped this wasn't a no-lead. "I'm guessing it's too early to have a positive ID on the body."

"No. We got it."

"How is that possible?" Joshua asked. "I figured with the fire—"

"Because he wasn't burned at all. He was stabbed through the throat and his tongue had been cut off," Tommy said wearily. "He was found in the living room with his wallet in his pocket. Does the name Dale Sanders mean anything?"

Alice's face paled. "He's my informant."

Joshua could almost read Alice's thoughts because they would be similar to his own if roles were reversed. Dale might've been tangled up with criminals and dependent on drugs but no one deserved to die and especially not like this. Dale had to have had a mother or someone who loved him—even if it was misguided love which was often the case with people who lived outside the law—out there somewhere and her heart would be broken with the news.

"This is obviously an attempt to shut Alice up or warn her to back off," Joshua said. Stabbing someone was incredibly personal and a bigger message couldn't be sent than by cutting someone's tongue out. The crime was violent and meant to show just how betrayed Perez felt by Sanders.

"It's his signature," Alice said, all color draining from her face. "It's what he does to men in his organization who turn on him. I've seen this same scenario with one of his top lieutenants who also happened to be his nephew."

"Damn," Joshua said. The word was followed by silence. "I'm sorry this happened to your informant. And I know it's a blow to the investigation but we can recover. The feds are most likely working the other angle, right, Tommy?"

It seemed coldhearted to focus attention on the investigation but that's what he needed to do. Processing Dale's death would take time.

"They're setting up a raid as we speak, figuring they need to move fast. If Perez thinks his operation has a hole in it they fear he might clean out the compound."

"So they're going in tonight?" Alice asked with as

hopeful a voice as Joshua figured she could muster under the circumstances.

"It might take a couple of days to coordinate and organize but they don't want to wait any longer than they have to since the guys tried to set fire to the trailer to erase evidence. We know they'll do the same thing to the compound if they realize there could be a threat to that location. Also, a print was lifted at the scene. It belonged to Perez so we can link him to the crimes committed there now."

"About time we got some good news in this case," Joshua said. "Also good that the feds are moving quickly. If Isabel's there, they'll find her."

Joshua knew full well that the teen could be anywhere by now. Six weeks was a long time to be missing with a man like Perez.

"I'll let you know everything as it unfolds," Tommy said. "I know this is difficult but sit tight a little longer. We're getting close."

Joshua thanked Tommy before ending the call.

"I'll join you in the kitchen to make a fresh pot of coffee in a minute," Joshua said to Ryder. His brother took the hint and moved out of the room.

"What is it, Alice? What are you thinking?" he asked, moving to her side and then taking her left hand in his. This wasn't the time to think about how small hers seemed by comparison. Or how much contact with her brought warmth to his chest like he'd never known.

She blinked and a few tears rolled down her cheeks.

"What is it?" Joshua asked, and then it dawned on him.

"If they tortured Dale, and I'm sure they did, he probably told them about me looking for Isabel…"

"And blew your cover," Joshua added.

"Worse than that, he just signed her death warrant."

Chapter Nine

Alice pushed the plate of food to the back of the tray and focused on the glass of iced tea, tracing the rim with her left index finger. It had been three nights since they'd heard word from Tommy and she was tired of everyone reminding her that was a good thing. Experience had taught her that just because they hadn't found a body—and she meant Isabel's—didn't mean they wouldn't. Her mind snapped to the past, to her mother. She couldn't think about the fact that she was putting her life in danger, which could leave the twins without a mother or father, in order to help someone else. A new person had taken over the task force at the FBI. She needed to press Tommy for a name. He wasn't giving any other details.

"You planning to eat any of that or just stare it down all night?" Joshua asked from the doorway, startling her.

Ever since that kiss and the awkwardness that had followed she was unnerved by his presence.

"How long have you been standing there?" she asked, forking a piece of broccoli.

"Long enough to know that your food is getting cold." He leaned against the doorjamb, filling the frame. "Mind if I come in? It's time to replace your bandage."

Alice nodded, not especially thrilled about the prospect of slathering more of that silver sulfadiazine onto her skin. The first couple of days it had been manna from heaven, somehow magically pulling out the heat from the burn while soothing her patches of varying shades of red. The blisters came on day two, popped on day three and now large parts of her skin alternately oozed and bled. The cream burned when a new coat was put on and her ibuprofen barely touched the pain but she needed a clear head so she refused to take more than two pills at a time. She'd finally agreed to a cold compress and that had given her a few hours of sleep last night. Dr. McConnell had offered reassurances that Alice was healing beautifully. She would have to take the good doctor's word for it.

The mattress dipped under Joshua's weight as he positioned the folding tray with supplies next to him. It didn't help that he'd avoided spending time in her room since the kiss and she wondered if he regretted ever getting mixed up with her. Alice was like a virus, dangerous to everyone including the host.

Wow. What was up with the self-pity, Green?

She winced as the cowboy pulled the nonstick pad away from her arm.

"Sorry," she said quickly.

"Don't be." His calm voice was a welcome change to silence. "I hate that I'm hurting you."

"Only way to make it better, right?" She said, forcing a laugh. There were about five shades of red on her arm. The first-degree burns were starting to heal thanks to the magic cream. Those were pale pink. The area where the two-by-two-inch blister had popped was level five red. So red, in fact, it almost looked burgundy.

"I spoke to Tommy a few minutes ago," he said.

"Oh, yeah? Any news?" she asked, grateful to have something to focus on besides the pain. In times like these she reminded herself that it could be so much worse.

"They've had the compound under surveillance long enough to assess the situation."

"And that is?" Impatience edged her tone.

"The place is being used as a holding cell. The horse barns are where they believe girls are being held and possibly drugged, although no one knows the last part for sure," he added. "No one has tried to escape so they're bound by something."

"So the place is a major component of their overall operation," she said, grateful for progress.

"Yes, and the feds believe there's evidence there that can tie Perez to the location."

"Like what?" she asked.

"Computer entries. They received a tip from one of their informants that Perez keeps an 'inventory' log and likes to be updated daily about his 'cargo.'" He smoothed the frosting-like cream over her burns.

"I don't care what the informant thinks. Perez is smart enough to cover his tracks," she said and she couldn't help but think about Dale.

"All they need is a link to an IP for one of his devices and they can tie him to the crimes," he said. "He also has a lieutenant in his operation who is questioning tactics, according to another source. The feds think they can get him to turn on Perez by offering witness protection."

"If that's the case then prosecutors will have enough to work with." She didn't ask about where this would leave Isabel. If Alice could get ahold of those records, she could find out for herself. Getting to know the leader of the task force was even more important now.

"They were able to get enough intel to get a warrant to search the place. Illegal activity is occurring on that site and that can't be denied. Seizing the computers should give us the data needed to link the operation to Perez and nail his coffin closed for a lot of years," Joshua said.

"*If* everything goes according to plan." She knew a man like Perez would most likely have a fail-safe in place and that was the reason he was still at large, kidnapping girls and getting away with it among other heinous crimes. He knew how to be involved in day-to-day operations while keeping a safe distance. But if there was a chance she could get Isabel back she wouldn't argue and she sure didn't want the task force to wait. "How do they know about the girls in the barn?"

"They were able to use a drone to obtain footage of a truckload of girls being carried out of the back of a semi and into the main barn."

"Did they get a positive ID on any of the girls?" she asked, a spark of hope lighting up inside her chest. She quickly suppressed it, afraid to give the emotion too much credence. Hope could be more dangerous than fear.

"Yes, there's a positive ID on one of the girls, Erin Daily. She was reported missing from a wealthy Dallas suburb two days ago," he said. "One of the girls being carried inside fit her description down to the clothes she was wearing at the time of her disappearance."

She didn't ask about Isabel because if Joshua had news he would've come right out with it.

"When is the raid?" she asked.

"Tommy couldn't say for sure. The team doesn't want to risk a leak so they're being tight-lipped about it. He did guess that they'd be going sometime tomorrow and possibly at first light."

Once Joshua applied a thick layer of salve and a fresh bandage covered by gauze, he made a move to get up.

"Can I ask another question?" Alice was trying to build her courage, which was faltering at the moment.

"Okay."

"In your professional opinion, what are the chances Isabel is there?" she asked.

"I wish I had a number, but I don't." He moved toward the door. "You need an extra blanket tonight? The cold front isn't planning to let up and they say it might freeze."

"No. I'm good." She pushed off her covers.

"Where are you headed?" he asked.

"I was just going to put the tray up. I'm not hungry right now," she said.

"I'll do that for you." He waved her off before taking the tray and disappearing down the hall.

Alice leaned against the headboard and pulled her knees up, trying to push the raid from her thoughts. If Isabel had come through the compound there was a good chance that she had already been moved to another location.

A GUST OF cold wind blasted, causing branches to scrape against the window outside Alice's bedroom. Restless, she pushed off the covers. Sleep was as close as summer and she was about to give up hope when a figure appeared in her doorway.

"You okay?" Joshua asked.

She hugged her knees into her chest, not exactly sure how to answer that question. Physically, she was fine, healing. Mentally, she was sick with worry. Instead of a real answer, she mumbled that she'd get over it.

She expected Joshua to turn and walk away, like he had been doing. But he walked toward her, sat next to her on the bed, and covered her hands with his.

"Waiting stinks. Not knowing what's going on when you're used to being in the action is even worse," he said, his masculine voice warming her. "I can't even begin to imagine what it must be like to be away from your boys this long. And then to be uncertain about what is happening with Isabel on top of it all is pretty rough."

He nailed her frustration and feelings of inadequacy, leaving out the part about what was going on between them adding extra confusion into the mix.

"I'm sorry about what happened to Dale," he added. "I know that must be bugging you, too."

She couldn't even begin to process the thought of being responsible for his death.

"You're going through a lot and your injuries have you sidelined," he said, pretty much nailing it again.

"No one will ever accuse me of having too much patience," she joked, trying to lighten the tension. But it was true. "The truth is that all this worry is driving me insane."

"What can I do to help?" he asked.

She could see well enough in the darkness to know he was being sincere based on his expression. She surprised herself when she said, "I know that you're not… *interested*…in starting anything and that's fine. I agree that it's not a good idea. It's just… I don't want to be alone right now. Stay with me tonight."

The long pause he issued made her think twice about

her request. If he really didn't want to be around her that much she shouldn't push him.

"Okay," he said and she noticed how gruff his voice had become.

Alice curled up on her side under the covers, facing the opposite wall as he climbed in next to her. The next thing she knew he pulled her toward him and repositioned her so that her head was on his chest and she rested in the crook of his arm. For the first time in a long time, she relaxed against a strong, muscled body with warm, soft skin pressed against hers.

Alice closed her eyes and fell into a deep sleep.

Sunlight filled the room as Alice blinked awake. Her legs were entwined with Joshua's and she could hear his even breathing, feel the rhythm of his heartbeat as it matched hers.

Neither had moved much from last night and she wasn't sure how long she'd been awake when he surprised her by tightening his arms around her. He pulled her in close and pressed a kiss to her forehead so fluidly it was like he'd done the same thing every morning for their entire lives.

And then he seemed to catch himself because his grip loosened and he cleared his throat.

"How long have you been awake?" he asked.

"Not long." She hadn't exactly checked the clock. She'd been content to lie there in his arms, which should freak her out. Somehow, it calmed her instead. She reasoned that with everything going on it could've been anyone in that bed next to her and she would've felt reassured. It was a lie. She gave herself a free pass in the honesty department this morning.

"You must be hungry. You barely touched your dinner

last night." He eased his arm out from underneath her and then sat up, rubbing his eyes. She tried not to stare at the ripples of muscles on his back visible through the white T-shirt he wore.

There was no way she was embarrassing herself by throwing herself at him again even though she wanted to do just that.

"I can get breakfast," she said, tossing the covers aside.

"Hold on there." His hand on her calf stopped her and it also sent a current rippling up her leg.

He didn't immediately speak even though it seemed like there was something on his mind.

Before he could make some lame excuse as to why last night couldn't happen again, she said, "Thanks for... you know...everything. I haven't slept that well in a long time."

Getting too comfortable with Joshua O'Brien would be a mistake. Alice didn't have to be a rocket scientist to figure out that as soon as this case was over she would go back to her normal life in Tucson with Isabel—she prayed—and her boys, and he would go back to life on his family's ranch.

"Me, either," he said, and that shocked her. What problems did he have to keep him awake at night? "I'll put on a pot of coffee."

He didn't immediately make a move to get up.

"Are you okay?" she asked, concerned.

"I need a few minutes. Waking up with a beautiful woman in your arms does...*something* to a man."

Alice's cheeks flushed and heat washed over her. All she could say was, "Oh."

"Go ahead and start without me," he said. "I'll be there in a minute."

Alice couldn't think of a snappy comeback, so she moved into the bathroom to brush her teeth before heading into the kitchen. She pulled a carton of fresh eggs from the fridge at about the same time she heard the shower turn on in the other room. Her lips curled into a smile knowing the effect she'd had on him. It felt good to know that she was still considered an attractive woman and he wasn't completely immune to her.

There wasn't much she could make in the way of breakfast food except for a mean omelet and toast. She went to her go-to meal, stirring milk into the beaten eggs. She chopped an onion and cut a green bell pepper, tossing both in the pan with the eggs. Moments before the omelet was perfect she added shredded cheddar cheese just long enough to melt it.

"What smells so good?" he asked, entering the room as the toaster popped.

Another smile broke on Alice's face, a rare occurrence since Isabel's disappearance.

He walked over, placed his hand on her hip and a kiss on her forehead. "How are you really holding up?"

"I can use a little extra glue to be honest. I'm scared," she admitted as she turned off the heat and set the pan off the red coils.

ALICE'S ADMISSION SURPRISED JOSHUA. Something—and he still wasn't sure what—had changed between them in the past three days that had allowed Alice to lower her guard. He didn't want to get too inside his head about the transformation, or admit how much he liked it.

She leaned into him, and he could feel her trembling—not from fear but from something else—as he pulled her into his arms.

Much more of this and he'd need another cold shower.

"I don't know about you but I could use a strong cup of coffee." The feelings he was beginning to have for Alice were a distraction he couldn't afford no matter how much his body said otherwise. One call from the FBI and he'd be out of there. It would take a little while to finish his application so he could see this case through, which most likely wouldn't be too much longer after the big break they'd received when Alice had found that address. But then, he didn't need to get ahead of himself with the FBI. It was a lengthy process and he hadn't been called in for an interview yet.

"Sounds like a plan," she said, turning to plate the eggs.

The smell of bacon replaced the scent of her shampoo, a mix of citrus, flowers and the sun. As much as he loved bacon, and he did love bacon, her scent was so much better.

He made coffee before fishing his cell from his pocket and placing it on the table alongside two steaming mugs.

"What do we do now?" She plunged her fork into her omelet.

"We eat."

Chapter Ten

Joshua's cell phone buzzed and Alice's heart jumped into her throat. She glanced at the clock. It was half past one and they'd just sat down to lunch, which she had no appetite for.

"It's Tommy," he said, glancing up from the screen.

Alice set her glass of water on the table as he answered the call.

"I'm putting you on speaker with me and Alice," Joshua said into the receiver.

After perfunctory greetings, Tommy said, "I'll share everything I know. The raid went down two hours ago after the task force received a tip that an empty semi was on its way to the compound for a pickup. The team mobilized quickly into their white minivan two miles from the site. A chopper full of feds took to the air. The plan was to drop in from above while ground troops engaged. There were a dozen law enforcement officers on scene, two of which were my deputies and another pair from our neighbors in Hampstead County. There were four agents from the Bureau of Alcohol, Tobacco, Firearms and Explosives, and another four from the FBI."

"Sounds like they brought enough firepower to the fight," Joshua said as Alice held her breath waiting for the news she desperately wanted to hear. Alice also thought about the fact that so much could go wrong when officers from varying agencies pulled together so quickly without time to rehearse and get to know each other's habits when going on a raid. It was a fact that could prove fatal when the pressure was on. Knowing each other intimately, who went right and who went left on instinct could mean the difference between walking out alive and mistakes being made, critical mistakes like an officer being shot by another officer. It was always a risk with task forces but especially ones that didn't have a chance to get to know each other and rehearse. Yes, there were fail-safes in place with plans made accordingly, but under pressure people tended to revert to their comfort zone.

"Eighteen girls with an estimated age range of twelve to sixteen years old were found inside the residence and the primary barn. Ziploc bags containing pills or a powdery material were also discovered and the substance inside is believed to be ketamine."

Alice's heart pounded against her ribs and sadness pushed through. So many lives affected. So much innocence lost. In order to be able to deal with situations like this and still do her job well, Alice had learned to compartmentalize her emotions, to hold them at bay. She'd learned to deal with them after her adrenaline spike was a distant memory and she was alone in her bed. The avalanche came when the rest of the world was quiet. And, sometimes, the weight was crushing.

Rather than allow herself to be sucked under, she refocused her energy on the girls, on Isabel, and how all of them needed everyone in law enforcement to keep a clear head. "Do any of the girls match Isabel's description?"

There was a pause, which pretty much gave Alice her answer.

"I'm sorry," Tommy said quietly.

Joshua was already standing behind her. His hands on her shoulders were the only things keeping her from unraveling.

"What about the computers? Surely, they can track her if the records were kept up to date like you said before." She couldn't suppress the panicked feelings engulfing her so she didn't try. Instead, she channeled them into crystal-clear thinking and pure determination. Perez would pay. She didn't know how or when, but he would not be allowed to hurt other innocent children.

"That's the hope," Tommy said and she could tell he was trying not to get her hopes up in case the files were too encrypted. "The FBI has them on a plane to Quantico, but then you already know that."

"And Perez? Any chance he was around during the raid?" Joshua asked.

"He disappeared without a trace, but the feds have a couple of his men," Tommy said. "Garcia got a visual on Perez. There was heavy gunfire and he disappeared in the chaos."

"Were any of our guys hurt?" Alice immediately asked.

"An agent and one of my deputies volunteered to go in first. Both were injured in the hailstorm. They've been taken to Bluff General Hospital for treatment."

"I'm sorry to hear that," Joshua said and Alice was about to say the same thing. Again, her heart hurt but she couldn't allow the emotions to take center stage. Not with so many other lives at stake.

"Garcia is in critical but stable condition for now. The federal officer was treated and released," Tommy said.

There was a moment of silence on the line in a show of respect.

Hopelessness was settling over Alice. Two good men were down, her informant was gone, and Perez was free. Isabel was still out there and most likely had been sold given that she wasn't at the compound. Of course, this might not be the only holding place. Although, given the number of girls being kept there it probably was. Finding Isabel just got a thousand times more complicated.

"What about Hammond? Did you get him?" Alice asked, praying they picked up the guy who was believed to be ready to roll on Perez.

Tommy's delay in answering was another blow.

"He was shot."

"Fatally?" she asked.

"I don't want to give you false hope. He's still in surgery and the doctor won't have answers until he's out."

So, no Perez. No Isabel. And the only person the feds had a decent chance of rolling might not make it out of surgery.

"What else?" Joshua said when Alice was unable to keep probing.

"That's all the bad news, and it's a lot," Tommy said. "Here's some good news. Teams are combing the site and they have all been briefed on what Isabel looks like."

Not exactly good news but Alice would take what she could get. At least law enforcement was working on her side again.

"I offered my interrogation room and holding cells for the few men who were placed under arrest. And the task force is taking me up on it," Tommy added.

That was better. At least Tommy would be in the loop now. And Alice had every intention of being in the adjoining room, staring through that one-way mirror during those interviews.

Joshua squeezed her shoulders so he must've been thinking the same thing.

"And the best news is that we have two still-sedated but coherent girls who have been treated and who are being brought in for questioning. Again, I offered my private office."

Alice jumped to her feet and shot a look at Joshua that said she was going down to that station no matter who tried to stop her.

He nodded.

"We'll be right there, Sheriff," Alice said.

"That's not advi—"

"Either way, I'm coming," she said matter-of-factly. He could argue until the cows came home but she was going to be in that room.

"Perez is still out there," Tommy started.

"I'll bring her, Tommy. I can get her there safely," Joshua said.

"Need I remind you that he and his men will shoot both of you on sight?" There was genuine concern in Tommy's voice and Alice appreciated there being two people she could count on to have her back. She missed the camaraderie since going out on her own.

"He won't get anywhere near the town right now," Joshua reasoned. "Not with all this heat."

"Normally, I'd agree with you but this guy is trouble. It would be exactly like him to set up near the station just to make sure his guys don't talk," Tommy said. "I have all my people on extra alert but you need to stay put and wait for me to get back to you. Plus, I don't have a guarantee the feds won't arrest Alice for obstruction. I'm working on it."

"I understand," Alice acquiesced, ignoring the what-the-heck look from Joshua.

"Good. Thank you. I'm not looking to make any of this worse. I'll share everything that I can from the interviews," Tommy said.

Joshua thanked his friend before ending the call. He turned his full attention to Alice. "You want to tell me what the heck that was about?"

She was already starting toward the bedroom to get dressed. "There's no use arguing with a man whose mind is already made up. Plus, I can't be sure his phone lines are secure. It's best if no one expects us, especially Perez."

"What about the possibility of being arrested?" Joshua asked.

"There's only one way to find out."

"WHAT ARE YOU doing here?" Tommy asked as Joshua ushered Alice through the metal detector in the lobby area of the sheriff's office.

Joshua knew the layout well given that Tommy was like family and all the brothers had spent considerable time with their friend around town and visiting him in his office.

"I didn't want to explain myself over the phone but I've been tracking this case exclusively for more than six weeks now and I might be able to shed light on comments the girls make during the interview process," Alice explained. Her jaw was set and determination sparked in her eyes. "I'm here to offer my expertise as a professional consultant, that's all. You can take or leave my thoughts but I deserve to see what's going on for myself."

One of the federal agents stepped into the hallway and into view. He was short with a sturdy build. His red hair was combed to one side and almost too perfectly parted. His gaze shifted from Alice back to Joshua before narrowing. "That won't be necessary, Alice."

Joshua noted the man's posture change as he crossed his arms over his puffed-out chest. At least he wasn't reaching for handcuffs.

"I can see that you still undervalue the presence of a woman, Special Agent Fischer," Alice shot back. "What the hell are you doing here?"

What was that all about? Joshua gathered that the two already knew each other but this seemed personal. Tommy must've picked up on the animosity, too, because he excused himself to get a cup of coffee.

"This is my investigation now," Fischer said with another glance toward Joshua, and it was really more like a glare. He focused on Alice. "I need to speak to you in the other room."

"I'm here as an off-duty cop. The only people I want to listen to are beyond those walls." Alice motioned toward the back of the building where Tommy's office would be, standing her ground as she crossed her arms.

"Do I need to remind you that you aren't supposed to be involved in this investigation?" Fischer asked, his temper flaring. "All I have to do is make one phone call and you're out of a job and in jail."

"You want to arrest me? Then do it," Alice shot back as she put her arms out, taking a page from his book. Joshua hid his smirk.

"Would you excuse us?" Fischer said to Joshua.

Before Joshua could answer, which was going to be negative unless Alice said otherwise, she was already shaking her head.

"This is not a good time, Fischer," Alice said. "We can play catch-up later. Right now, all I care about is finding out what happened to those girls."

Alice brushed past him and stalked down the hall.

"You got a problem with me?" Joshua asked Fischer directly as the man stared him down. Joshua always was one to face forward and take the bull by the horns.

"Should I?" Fischer countered.

"I don't have an issue with you unless you give me a reason," Joshua said, holding his position. Fischer had tensed and Joshua would be ready should the guy decide to throw a punch.

"You'll never be as important to her life as I will," Fischer said.

If that was true Joshua had to believe he would've known by now. And yet, her initial reaction to Fischer and their exchange sat like hot nails in Joshua's stomach. As far as Joshua could tell Fischer had no designs on Alice. Her reaction said there'd been something more than work between them. Joshua didn't like it even though he had no right to be jealous.

"That may well be but she actually wants to talk to me." Joshua walked past Fischer and straight to Tommy's office where Alice sat across from the victims. One was huddled in the other's arms with her head down. The other teen glanced up at him and immediately tensed, so he took a seat near the door as Alice offered reassurances.

Erin looked like she hadn't had a shower in days.

Her long blond hair clung together in clumps against her neck, her pale blue eyes wide and frightened. She sat hunched over, avoiding eye contact with any of the males in the room. Her clothes were dirty and smelled exactly like she'd been in a barn for days. Fischer strode in still strapped to his High Horse. He stood at his full height next to where Alice sat, which was maybe five foot ten inches.

"Can you describe the men who kept you captive?" Fischer asked without a hint of empathy in his voice.

Erin's gaze dropped to the floor. She was closing up and that wasn't good. Maybe Fischer had skipped the day in witness interview techniques where they taught compassion because he was going about this all wrong. Anyone could see that Erin was intimidated by every male presence in the room, so standing over her was likely to have the exact opposite of the desired result. She closed up on his first question and he didn't seem to notice when he repeated it, louder and slower.

Then again, maybe the man wasn't thinking clearly after Alice's rebuke. Joshua got Tommy's attention and motioned for him to meet in the hallway.

"This guy isn't going to get anywhere with his tactics and he's going to hurt the investigation," Joshua started but Tommy's hand immediately came up.

"I can't interfere if that's what you're about to ask. This case belongs to the feds and if I stick my nose in they'll only cut me out." Tommy had a point.

"Granted. I know you're right but did you see her? The girl went silent the minute he stood in front of her with his chest puffed out. I don't care what's going on between him and Alice. This interview is too important to let personal…*entanglements*, for lack of a better word, taint it."

"You're right and I agree with you one hundred percent," Tommy said. "And yet my hands are still tied."

"Well, mine aren't," Joshua said, stepping into the doorway fully aware that he was most likely about to kill his own career prospects. Seeing Erin about to cry was more than he could stand by and watch. "Special Agent Fischer, I need to speak to you in the hallway. Now."

Fischer whirled around. "If you can't see, I'm in the middle of something…"

Alice stood and placed her body in between Fischer and the girls. "I think that's a great idea. I believe the rest of these men could use a break as well. Gentlemen…"

The look Fischer shot Joshua could've covered the Sahara in a thick blanket of ice. After a quick glance at Alice, Fischer stalked toward the hall, crashing his shoulder into Joshua as he walked by. His men filed out behind him, two of whom thanked Joshua quietly on the way out. As it turned out not everyone had missed sensitivity training.

Fischer, on the other hand, was all fire and fury as he whirled around. "You pull another stunt like that and I'll make sure your SO has a full incident report for your jacket."

Joshua didn't want to think about what this might do to his current application. Even though he didn't need someone with the FBI on a hunt for his blood while he was trying to get a job with the agency, Erin didn't deserve to be placed in the middle of a different fight. Shutting the door to give Alice and the girls privacy was probably another nail in his coffin but Joshua decided to go *all in* at this point.

Agents and officers lined the walls of the hallway. The two who had thanked Joshua were the only ones standing on the same side.

Twenty minutes later, Alice emerged. "I need to go to the site."

Chapter Eleven

"There's no way I'm letting you stomp all over my crime scene," Fischer said, blocking her path. Alice was not thrilled at seeing the father of her twins. "You got your way with my witnesses now I expect a full debriefing."

"Then you can ask me anything you want at the compound because that's where I'm going," she said before turning to Tommy. "Thank you for the use of your office. The girls are exhausted so I told them to curl up on your couch and get some rest. They need to be with a woman until their parents arrive."

"I'll take care of them," an older woman with a kind face said as she stepped into the hallway. "I'm Abigail and I work for Tommy."

"I'm Alice." She quickly found herself on the receiving end of a warm hug.

"I know," Abigail said with a quick smile.

"The girls are fragile right now. They need someone like you by their side," Alice said to Abigail. She straightened her shoulders to address the men again. "Someone called both of their parents, right?"

"It was the first thing I did after we positively ID'd each of them," Tommy said.

Alice didn't want to get into why it wasn't Fischer

who'd made the calls but she figured it was pretty typical of him. He didn't "do" family stuff. Isn't that what he'd told her after he all but accused her of getting pregnant on purpose to derail his promotion?

Yeah, that's exactly what she'd wanted…to have her birth control fail after the two of them had been dating for all of six weeks because she didn't know that antibiotics made the pill temporarily ineffective. The long distance so-called relationship they'd had during her pregnancy was almost as big of a joke. And then, that Friday night had happened…the crowned jewel of all ways to kick off a weekend, when he'd told her that she couldn't stick around.

"Good." She lowered her voice and softened her tone when she turned to Joshua. "Will you give me a ride to the compound?"

He nodded as he fished the keys to his Jeep out of his pocket and led her toward the door before anyone could put up an argument.

Joshua didn't ask questions when he started the engine, or when Fischer immediately hopped into his silver sedan and followed. Alice didn't like the silence or the tension sitting between them.

"We dated." That wasn't the half of it, but those were the words that blurted out of her mouth when the GPS device said they'd reached the halfway mark to their destination.

"I gathered as much," Joshua said and his tone was even, unreadable. "Is it over?"

"Yes," she said with a little more enthusiasm than she'd planned.

"He doesn't seem to realize that fact." There was a hint of jealousy in his voice now and it was confusing.

"Well, it is," she said frankly.

"Is it?" His gaze zeroed in on the stretch of road in front of them.

"For me? Absolutely," she said. "But you should know that he's technically the father of my twins."

Joshua's grip tightened on the steering wheel and his stare intensified but he didn't say a word.

ALICE COULDN'T GET a good read on Joshua since he'd been dead silent for the rest of the drive. Then there were her own stirred-up emotions to deal with about her relationship with Joshua. Sleeping in the same bed last night, the comfort she felt in his arms, only added to her confusion. Feelings between her and Joshua complicated an already complex life. The attraction between them was strong, even he couldn't deny that now, and yet he seemed just as determined as ever not to act on it. He was smart. Alice was allowing her heart to take over common sense. She cursed her weakness and stuffed her emotions down deep, secure in the knowledge that it would never work between them.

As it was, she was lucky that she hadn't been arrested for obstruction of justice and she was pretty sure the reason Fischer had imposed himself on this case was so he could control her future. She chalked his act of chivalry up to guilt for abandoning her and the boys. As far as anything else happening between them? Fischer needed to move on. She had. Besides, how could she ever trust a man who'd walked out on her when she was at her most vulnerable?

Alice pinched the bridge of her nose trying to stem the raging headache threatening. This was going to be one red-letter day. It was also the closest she'd been to

Isabel in more than six weeks. She was like a hound that'd caught a scent and she planned to follow it through to its conclusion—no matter what that meant. Erin had shared a few startling details about the way the girls had been treated. Hailey, who'd been at the compound for more than thirty terrifying days, didn't make eye contact, couldn't. Alice's heart felt ripped from her chest at seeing that girl—no older than her when she'd gone to live with the sheriff and his wife—after she'd lived through what had to have been her worst nightmare.

If that wasn't bad enough, Alice had had the added bonus of seeing Fischer again. Although, maybe she should've known he'd eventually show if only for curiosity's sake. In the first few weeks following the breakup, he'd sent checks that she'd torn up. He was only doing it out of guilt and she was determined to take care of her boys on her own, financially and otherwise. Fischer must've gotten the hint because money stopped coming a few months later and he never tried to contact her.

She had nothing to say to the man. There were no words that could smooth over the fact that he'd walked out on her when she'd needed a shoulder to lean on. The unexpected pregnancy hadn't only shaken up his world. She'd been more than shocked. And where had he been since? Her boys were about to reach their first birthday without their father. What had suddenly given Fischer a bout of conscience? If he'd wanted to see his sons he would've done it by now. Granted, if he honestly wanted to get to know his boys she wouldn't stop him. The boys deserved to know their father. But if he wanted to use them to get to her, as she suspected, he was barking up the wrong tree. Experience had taught Alice that people couldn't be trusted. Besides, her life was a confusing mess and it wouldn't be long before Joshua figured that out and disappeared, too.

The crime scene was alive with activity when Alice and Joshua arrived twenty minutes later. Neighbors in the acre lot cul-de-sac lingered at their mailboxes, heads shaking as they spoke in hushed tones. Trees lined the property as well as shrubs, making it difficult to see the house and barn from the street or neighboring houses.

"What did Erin say to you that had you needing to come here?" Joshua finally asked after parking, cutting through her heavy thoughts.

She got out and he handed her a pair of gloves and then placed a pair on his own hands. Then, he pulled a few evidence bags from the dashboard of his Jeep.

"Someone who fit Isabel's description was here when she was first brought to this place two days ago," Alice said, grateful for the change in subject. All that personal drama was making her crazy anyway.

"How certain is she?" Joshua asked. She couldn't get a good read on his emotions.

"There weren't a lot of dark-haired girls, so Isabel stood out. I asked about the birthmark on the back of her left hand. It's almost the shape of a shamrock and Erin could've sworn that she remembered something like that. She'd been so scared when she was thrown into a stall in the barn. There were men watching over the girls in shifts. They'd walk back and forth in front of the stall, checking each one, making sure the girls didn't interact or try to run," Alice said, anger rising in her chest. She knew that she should remain detached during an investigation but that was impossible in some cases and especially this one. She glanced to her right and saw a burly-looking officer removing evidence from the house while he wiped away what she figured were tears. Another had punched a board that had been nailed to a tree and used for games of darts.

Even the strongest person had a breaking point, an Achilles' heel. Heinous crimes against children were right up there at the top of the list for most officers. And especially since many of these officers were parents. The ones with daughters would be especially affected. It would be impossible for them to completely shut out their frustration and anger. "She said that the girls were ordered to stick to their assigned corner. Erin was crying and she couldn't stop, which was drawing attention. The guards had already threatened her once, saying that if she didn't cut it out they'd pull her out and shut her up. She was afraid they'd do other things to her, too. But Isabel crawled over and held Erin until she stopped crying. She told her they would get out of there together and not to be afraid."

"Isabel sounds strong," Joshua said after a thoughtful moment and Alice was grateful they were talking again. He fell in step beside her as she walked toward the barn situated behind the ranch-style house, which teemed with law enforcement officers.

"She is. And smart. She told Erin that her mother was a cop and wouldn't stop looking until she found her." Alice's voice broke. "She was right. I won't give up until she's home."

"Neither will I," Joshua said so quietly she almost thought she'd imagined hearing it.

The barn was large enough to house a dozen horses if each were given a private stall. White paint had faded and chipped on the doors. There was straw scattered inside the individual stalls on the ground and now-empty buckets the girls had been forced to use in place of a bathroom. Erin had told Alice about all those things, the horrors of being treated worse than animals. They'd even been branded with a small capital *P* on their left hip so that buyers would know they were getting authentic Perez "product." It was sickening and Alice wanted to see the man rot in a cell for the rest of his life.

"Isabel was bought the day after Erin arrived," she finally told Joshua as they scanned the makeshift cells to either side of them. Alice pushed open the door to her right. "Erin said that when someone had been purchased they were moved into the main house to be prepared for the delivery."

Alice could tell Joshua's reaction mirrored hers by the way he ground his back teeth.

"How long would that process take?" he finally asked.

"She wasn't sure because she'd only heard rumors. She guessed it could take anywhere from a couple of days to a few weeks. They got to shower daily, eat better and were taught how to dress and wear makeup." The last word came out with disgust.

"What if they rejected the help?" Joshua asked.

"Then they were punished in front of the other girls to make sure the next one complied." She pointed at the corner where a water hose snaked around a bale of hay. "Some were stripped and then blasted with water."

"That water would be freezing this time of year," he ground out.

Alice nodded. "If that didn't work, they were beaten."

Something very dark passed behind Joshua's eyes and he didn't immediately speak. "I'm guessing the stubborn ones were used for the baby farms."

"They'd keep a couple on hand, locked inside the house." Alice wasn't sure she could handle seeing what was inside there being a mother herself but she would force herself to if it meant finding Isabel.

"No drugs for impregnated ones because that would damage the babies," he deduced.

Alice nodded. That's what Erin had said.

"This is the stall Erin said she was in with Isabel," Alice said, standing in front of the second stall to the right.

"You want me to check it for you?" Joshua asked.

Alice shook her head as she stepped inside the open door. "Come with me?"

He nodded and followed her inside.

She dropped to all fours, skimming the ground, moving pieces of hay out of the way.

"What are we looking for?" he asked.

"I know Erin has good intentions and I don't think she would lie," Alice started.

"But she'd been drugged and we can't exactly rely on her information to be accurate," he finished.

"I need something more, some evidence she was here in the first place." She touched the half-heart pendant hanging from a silver chain around her neck. "Isabel always wore the other half to this."

"I wondered about that," he said.

"Erin didn't remember seeing it but Isabel never took it off." Neither did Alice.

"It could've been hidden under her shirt," Joshua said.

"I was thinking the same thing." Alice's hand ran over a small object in the corner. She brushed hay out of the way to get a closer look, praying it was the other half to her necklace. No such luck. She tossed the small stick aside. Just as she started to tell Joshua to look for the chain, commotion from behind stopped her.

"You shouldn't be here alone," Fischer's voice boomed.

Joshua was already to his feet, blocking Fischer's view of Alice. "She isn't."

"Last I checked, neither of you had authority to investigate this case," Fischer said.

"Then it's a good thing you're here," Joshua shot back, unmoved. The man was steel under pressure.

"You wanted to talk to me about Erin?" Alice asked, redirecting the conversation as she stepped beside Joshua. The thought of all those scared girls huddling in their corners filled her with new resolve. At least this group would be home for the holidays with their families. Yes, broken and damaged, but alive. The healing could begin. It wasn't exactly a great situation for anyone involved, make no mistake about it, but it was a start and more than Isabel had.

Fischer nodded and then led them out of the barn to a shaded area under an oak tree with a picnic table underneath. She noticed that he stood rather than sit and then propped his left foot on the bench. That was no subtle reminder that he was the one in a position of authority. She'd been attracted to his arrogance when they'd first met, confusing it for confidence. Maybe having the boys had changed her because she much preferred Joshua's quiet strength.

Alice shivered as the frigid air cut through her light jacket. Joshua, cool as ever, seemed unfazed by the weather and especially by Fischer as he leaned against the oak's thick trunk, arms folded. The two men couldn't be more opposite. Fischer was territorial and quick to anger whereas the calm cowboy kept a level head under all conditions.

She'd wondered what she'd say to Fischer when she saw him again. As it turned out, she felt sorry for him. He was the one missing out on the two greatest boys in the world. It was his loss.

"Erin said the girls were given a glass of water and told to drink it all so they could sleep on the first night. She doesn't remember much after that, so it was obviously laced with some kind of drug. I'm guessing ketamine because she felt aware of what was happening to her but she couldn't move," Alice said.

"Could've been GHB or Rohypnol. Did she say if the water tasted different? Salty?" Fischer's lips thinned and his tone was clipped.

Alice was already shaking her head. "She couldn't tell a difference. Said that she felt like she was in a dream and she had trouble remembering even simple things. Her arms and legs felt numb and she remembered the odd feeling that she couldn't control her body. When she woke the next morning all her personal belongings including the clothes off her back were gone and she was given jeans that were too big and a baggy T-shirt to wear. She had makeup on that she had never worn before and was thrown into the shower and told to clean herself up. She overheard a few of the men talking and realized that first night she was photographed."

"So, either Perez has the pictures sent directly to his clients or there will be a website," Joshua said, a spark of hope in his voice.

"I've got tech guys working on it right now," Fischer said. "I know you're hoping to find information about Isabel."

"Yes."

"We'll do everything we can to locate her," Fischer said and she hated how perfunctory it sounded. She wasn't a random civilian who had no idea the odds of finding Isabel at this point. Yes, the probability increased exponentially having both her and Joshua on the case. Fischer most likely would throw extra resources in the mix, too. And none of that guaranteed a good outcome.

Alice pushed aside her despair in order to fill Fischer in on the rest of the details as evidence was carefully removed from the scene. With any luck, the tech gurus would unearth information that would put all the pieces of the operation together and then arrest warrants could be issued. In a worst case, they wouldn't get anything more than they already had. Fingerprints from the trailer were a good start. A good prosecutor could work with that if they could find Perez.

It's more than we had yesterday. She would grip that thought with both hands.

"Who do you have back at the sheriff's office interviewing the men who were picked up?" Alice finally asked Fischer.

"I'll be talking to them myself. Right now, I'm sweating them a little bit. Giving them a chance to think about how little their boss actually cares for them now that they've been arrested. I've already planted the seed that the girls are talking and that the guys should've been more careful around them. Then, I gave implicit instructions to my team to leave both of them alone until I return. I want to oversee every aspect of the interrogation," he said. It was just like Fischer to want to control every detail. He planned everything to a T. Her pregnancy was one of the curveballs he couldn't handle but in this case she was relieved. He would be thorough.

"Thank you," she said quietly. "Will you ask about Isabel?"

"Yes," he said.

"What else can I do?" she asked, trying not to sound as helpless as she felt.

Fischer took a step closer to her and lowered his voice. "You could go out to dinner with me."

"Not a good idea," she said a little more emphatically than she'd planned.

"You're welcome to hang out at the sheriff's office where we're setting up camp. The sheriff has also arranged for us to take over a house nearby. We plan to stick around in town until we see this through."

"I want access to the house," she said, nodding toward the small ranch-style on the property.

"As soon as my men finish processing it," Fischer said, glancing at his watch. "Give me a couple more hours."

Alice didn't want to think about the evidence that might be bagged up—evidence that might lead her to Isabel—walking out of there. She needed a quiet place to think this through. The cold was starting to get to her and she tried not to think about how little the girls were given to keep warm in that barn.

"I can drive you wherever you want to go," Fischer said.

"Thanks for the offer, but—"

"Are you ready?" Joshua asked Alice, stepping away from the tree.

Fischer shot him a look that could freeze alcohol.

"Yes," she said to Joshua. Even with the few good hours of sleep last night, she could feel her bones ache for more.

An agent wearing cargo pants and a dark jacket jogged over to Fischer before she had a chance to get up. "Sir."

Fischer introduced him as Special Agent Lund.

"We found that item we discussed," Lund said, holding out an evidence bag with his gloved hand.

Fischer put on a pair of latexes and reached into the bag, pulling out the other half of Alice's necklace.

"That belongs to Isabel." Alice produced hers.

"I know," Fischer said. "I read about it in the file."

Tears stung the backs of her eyes as she processed what seeing the necklace meant. Isabel had been here. She'd been in that house.

And now she was gone.

"WHEN YOU SAID you owned a ranch, I thought you meant like a couple of acres and a one-story house with a barn in back," Alice said, staring at the grand colonial two-story with black shutters bracketing the windows, grateful for the distraction from churning over the same dark thoughts about what might've happened—might still be happening—to Isabel. Alice needed to stay positive and there wasn't much else she could do until Fischer let her know it was safe to go inside the ranch at the compound. She refocused on the house in front of her, trying to lift her mood. This place oozed holiday and family and love. Equally grand were the white columns adorned with thick strings of holly. Christmas-red ribbon twined throughout the greenery. Despite her heavy mood she couldn't help but feel the spirit of the holiday looking at the house and wonder how much her boys' faces would light up seeing a place like this. "Those French doors are gorgeous."

Joshua smiled.

From each window—and Alice counted fourteen including the French doors—a massive wreath hung complete with a red bow on top and a candle in the center. The porch stretched easily to match the width of the house, although *house* seemed like such a small word for this grand place. Large pots of holly with red ornaments flanked the couple of stairs to the veranda where pairs of white rocking chairs were grouped together on both sides.

"Do you own this place?" she asked, feeling suddenly out of her element. The amount of time she'd known the cowboy could be reduced to days but in her heart she felt like she'd known him so much longer. So, this was a shock. This was another side to him that she had no idea. Besides, he acted nothing like the kind of wealthy man he'd have to be to own this place. Once again, he shattered all her preconceived notions about Texas cowboys.

"A piece of it," he said and he sounded a little awkward about it. "My brothers own the rest."

"I'm sorry. Is that a sensitive subject?" she asked as he parked, remembering that his parents had died.

"Not really," he said and then shrugged. Not exactly convincing.

"I feel like you know everything there is to know about me, so I'm not going inside until you bring me up to date on you," she said, not making a move to unbuckle.

"There's not much to tell," he said.

She rolled her eyes.

"Okay, my parents grew a successful cattle ranch. Dad built the business from scratch, slowly buying the land around us. Then, he started a rifleman's club and, together, my parents made more money than they could give us or spend, so my mother threw herself into charity work."

"They sound like good people," Alice said.

"They were."

"I'm really sorry for your loss," she said, and meant it. Sitting in front of the house they'd built, on their land, she felt an unexplainable connection to them.

"Thank you."

"I can tell that you loved them very much. So, forgive me for asking but why did you go into law enforcement? Don't you like it here?"

"I love this land," he said so defensively that it almost sounded like he was trying to convince himself, too.

"I wasn't trying to question your devotion to your family," she said, wishing she had better words to express herself.

"This is where I grew up and it holds a lot of great memories. I love my brothers and being close to them is the biggest bonus to being here," he stared.

"But—"

"I never signed on in life to be a rancher. This path was chosen for me and I've always been expected to take my rightful place beside my family. I figured that I'd come to terms with that someday or convince my parents otherwise but then suddenly everything changed when they died and it felt selfish to chase my own dreams. So, I've done what was necessary to fulfil my role. I figured that I would *want* to at some point in my life after I'd gotten other things out of my system. I just never expected to come back this soon," he said and she appreciated his honesty.

Alice touched his arm, ignoring the electricity pulsing through her fingertips, wishing a few words of comfort would come to mind. They didn't.

"So, you gave up your job and moved back here?" she asked.

"Sort of. I'm on leave. My parents had homes built for each of their sons at various spots on the land. My place is on the northwest side of the property, next to Diamondhead Lake." He took the key out of the ignition, unbuckled his seatbelt and opened the driver's side door.

Alice met him in front of the Jeep.

"I miss being on the job. It's part of who I am. So I understand what you're saying." Alice fell in step beside him. "Who lives here now?"

"A wing was opened up years ago for club guests and there are offices on the other side. Janis lives in the main house."

A stab of jealousy shot through Alice. "Janis?"

"She worked with the family for years before my brothers and I voted to give her a share of the property. She's like family," he said, stopping at the front door.

"That was kind."

"It was the right thing to do," he said.

"You always do the right thing?" she teased, trying to infuse a little humor to break up the otherwise heavy mood.

Joshua turned to face her, wrapped his arms around her waist and pulled her flush against his body. His lips were so close to hers, she could breathe in the scent of coffee. "No."

He closed those intense green eyes. And then he kissed her.

Chapter Twelve

Kissing Alice wasn't in the plan. Then again, most of Joshua's ideas about his life had been turned upside down in recent months. Why should this be any different?

Pulling on all of his strength, he took a step back. She felt a little too right in his arms, fit him a little too well and he wasn't sure what to do with that.

"Are you attracted to me?" she asked, lips full and pink. He tried not to stare at them.

"Without a doubt."

"Then what's the problem?" she asked with a flush to her cheeks that nearly did him in.

"If the timing was different," he started but she waved him off.

"Don't say it. I know," she said. She was beautiful, no question. There was so much more that attracted him. She was smart and funny. He wasn't much of a talker but conversation with her came easy and he actually liked it. There was something about the way her curves fit him when he held her while they slept. And for all her exterior toughness, he could see just how vulnerable she was inside—that was especially the part that drew him in. She was determined and could be a little reckless but only with herself. She was careful to protect people she loved and anyone she believed to be innocent.

Alice was pretty much everything that had been missing in the women he'd dated up to now. But she needed to be off-limits. As soon as the FBI called for an interview, he'd be gone and she needed someone who could stick around in her life. Be there for her and her boys. A stable force for Isabel. Besides, the father of her twins had just walked back into her life. There was no stronger bond than family and he had to give Fischer a fair chance at winning her back.

So that kiss pretty much went against everything Joshua believed in. And yet he still couldn't help himself. No matter how powerful a pull his attraction to Alice Green became, Joshua needed to "man up" and be stronger. For her sake and that of her family. He'd never forgive himself for getting in the way of a family. Plus, he had nothing to give to her. His own situation was a mystery and he'd be gone the second the feds offered a job. If that didn't happen, he needed time to reconcile his life. To make his brothers understand that he wasn't abandoning their parents by choosing a different path. *Whoa.* Was that really how he felt?

If he was being honest? Yes.

What could he give her if he felt trapped in his own situation?

Against his better judgment, Joshua twined their fingers together and led Alice into the house.

Overanalyzing the kiss was a big mistake. It only led to more questions with no easy answers.

"The inside of this place is even more beautiful than the outside, if that's even possible," Alice said, motioning toward the dual staircase and he tried not to focus on how much he liked the sound of her voice. Or how right it felt for her to be there in his family home.

For the time being, he wanted to take her mind off her problems and get some food in her so she could keep up her strength. He tried to tell himself that was the only reason he'd opened up to her about his personal circumstance and not because of his growing feelings for her or that part of him wanted her to know the real him before she walked out of his life.

"Now that's a table," she said, blue eyes wide, as they walked into the kitchen. "I bet you could seat fifteen people if you needed to."

"Janis always teases us that we have no manners but the truth is we all like eating in here better than the formal dining area. Always have. I guess we figured that room was meant for holidays and guests," he said with a chuckle.

"What is he accusing me of now?" Janis rushed in, wearing her full holiday gear.

"Being a great cook," Alice said quickly. "My boys would love being at a place like this. The decorations are beyond amazing."

Janis was short, little more than five feet and she had those grandmotherly soft features and a figure that could best be described as round.

Joshua introduced the two of them with a half smile. "Janis goes all out this time of year through New Year's. She keeps this place running and has been helping my family most of my life. Would you care for some cider?"

"Forgive the outfit." Janis motioned toward her black pants, white shirt and red apron. Her head of white hair had been fixed in a loose bun. She could be a dead ringer for Mrs. Claus in that getup.

"I think it looks fantastic," Alice said and her face lit up. "It would be a huge hit with my boys."

"Where are they?" She looked around.

"I'm from Tucson. They're home with a sitter while I investigate a missing teenager," Alice said.

"Must be hard to be away from them this time of year," Janis said and then embraced Alice in one of her warm hugs.

Joshua had squirmed out of that grip more than once as a teen, reluctant to show just how much he'd needed it at the time. He blamed teen hormones and all that came with them. He gave the two women a private moment while he scooped out two cups of cider that was mulling on the six-burner.

By the time he set them on the wood table, Alice and Janis joined him.

"The Nelson widow really outdid herself this year," Janis said.

Joshua almost laughed out loud. "Does she normally wear her red silk robe to greet guests?"

"I was talking about the bronze," Janis said on a laugh, shaking her head. "That must've been a strange sight."

An emotion crossed Alice's features that looked a lot like jealousy. She had no idea.

"Awkward is a better word," Joshua said.

"I'm sure it was. A woman her age." Janis made a tsk-tsk noise.

"How old is the Nelson widow?" Alice asked.

"She must be going on seventy by now," Janis responded.

Alice's tense expression broke into a wide smile. And

then she laughed. The sound filled the air and brightened everything it touched.

"Sure, it's funny to you," he quipped. And then he laughed, too.

"I better change out of these old clothes," Janis said on that note, turning to Alice. "It was nice meeting you."

"She's a wonderful person," Alice said when Janis disappeared down the hall.

"Yeah? Don't let her hear you say that. She'll never be able to walk through the door again for how big her head'll get," he teased, enjoying a relaxed moment with Alice. There was so much trouble brewing around them, he liked being her temporary shelter.

"I heard that," Janis quipped from the hallway.

"Good. That's why I said it so loud," Joshua said with a wink toward Alice.

Her smile was better than a string of a thousand sparkling lights. He'd given himself another problem because his thoughts kept rounding back to that kiss.

After warming up with a hearty bowl of vegetable soup, Alice's expression turned serious.

"I feel like I'm so close to breaking this case open but answers are just out of reach." She absently fingered the half-heart necklace. "Now that I know Isabel was there, I hope I can find something to give me a direction at the ranch house."

"Sometimes, it helps to think about something else for a little while," he said, glancing up at the wall clock after hearing the whop-whop-whop of chopper blades. Good. His delivery would be right on time.

"I probably shouldn't ask this but I hear a helicopter outside. Does it belong to you?" Alice asked.

"It's my brother's but we all use it when needed."

She leaned back in her seat as the text he'd been waiting for arrived. He palmed his cell and sent back their location in the kitchen.

"This is crazy. I mean, you don't seem like a rich man and I thought all ranches struggled to make ends meet," she said.

"Some of the smaller ranches have been affected by the economy but we've been fortunate over the years. This is a large place. We sell beef from longhorn, breed them with Hereford and sell that, and then there's the Rifleman's Club, although our members call it the Cattlemen Crime Club because they like to sit around and discuss crimes. I'd like to show you the property sometime." One of the things Joshua loved—loved? Maybe appreciated was more the right word—about Alice was her strength. Her determination was a close second. Being in law enforcement suited her and that was fine. But when she came home, she deserved a place like this, a place he knew she'd be safe where she wasn't constantly putting herself in harm's way. Maybe the package he was about to deliver would make her think twice before she jumped into another dangerous situation.

"I'm sure your brothers need you around here and I've been taking up all your time," she said. "If you want to drop me off at the station I can catch rides with some of the guys."

"You asked me about law enforcement work before and I never really answered. The truth is that I do miss it. So, stop trying to kick me off the team," he said, revealing another truth about himself he hadn't planned on.

The conversation was about to change dramatically, he thought, as the back door opened and Ryder burst through.

"Everything okay?" Alice said with one look at him.

He was healing fine and that's not what she was talking about. It was the distraught look on his face.

"Not really," he admitted with a laugh. "I just spent two hours in a helicopter with a pair of twins. I don't know how in the hell our parents survived our childhoods."

An older woman walked in with a twin on each hip.

For the second time, Alice's face lit up. "How on earth did you get here?"

A chorus of "Mama!" followed the twins' entry.

Their bodies started twisting and turning as she hurried to them. Joshua noticed that she winced as she took them, so he moved to her side and helped get her to a chair. She sat, one on each knee, and must've kissed each of them a good twenty times. Her smile, that amazing smile lighting her face, was the best he'd ever seen.

The pint-size boys were the spitting image of their mother, both blonds but their hair was short and curly. Joshua could see their blue eyes from across the kitchen when they first came through the door on their babysitter's hip. Darn cute kids.

"Hedi-copter," one of the twins said, babbling in a language only his brother could understand.

"Was that fun?" Alice asked with the biggest smile Joshua had seen on her face yet. And there was something right about him being the one who put it there.

INTRODUCTIONS HAD BEEN made and the twins were finally settled for a nap in one of the guest rooms on the ground floor. Marla decided to rest with them, saying she could use a few minutes of downtime after the exciting helicopter ride.

Alice couldn't remember the last time she'd been this happy. The boys loved crawling around the house and being outside in the backyard, and she enjoyed every minute of playing with them. She strolled into the kitchen as relaxed and happy as she could be under the circumstances.

"Thank you," she said to Joshua. "How on earth did you arrange this?"

"I thought you could use a morale boost," he said, offering a cup of coffee. "And I have my ways."

"People say that laughter is the best medicine," she said, taking the warm mug. "But I'd say those people must not have kids because one kiss from those pudgy faces and my mood is up here." She held her free hand as high above her head as she could reach.

"Good. I'm glad my plan worked without repercussion. I wondered if you'd chew me out for putting your boys in a helicopter with my brother at the gears," he teased.

"Are you kidding? I missed them too much to care how they got here. As long as they made it safely, you won't hear a complaint from me," she said, taking a sip and enjoying the liquid as it warmed her throat. "Fair warning. I don't think I'll be able to convince them to leave without taking Denali home with us." She referred to the family's Labrador retriever.

"He's a good sport and especially loves children. I don't think he's played that hard or licked so many faces since he was a pup," Joshua said.

The twelve-year-old chocolate Lab had let her boys follow him around and laid still while they climbed all over him and tugged at his ears. Alice had been quick to make sure they didn't do anything to hurt Denali.

"He's beautiful," she said. "Fits in perfectly with this place, which is filled with—" she was at a loss for the right word so she settled on "—magic."

"It's a good place," he agreed and there was an emotion behind his eyes that she couldn't quite put her finger on. "I have a family meeting to attend in about an hour. Want to go for that walk I promised you now?"

With Marla settled in with the boys Alice didn't have to worry about hovering over them. Plus, this place had better security than Fort Knox.

"Why not." She emptied her mug and set it on the counter, energized from the caffeine, sure, but mostly from seeing her boys, hugging them. There really was something magic about baby hugs.

Joshua stopped at the door and offered his arm. She took it and he ushered her out the door and into the crisp late afternoon air. The sun was shining, warming everything it touched.

"Which direction is your house?" she asked as they walked to the white wooden fence around the yard.

"That way." He pointed northwest. "I'll take you there sometime."

"How about right now? Is it far?" She glanced at the house where her boys were sleeping. She'd been content to watch them sleep but didn't want to take a chance of disturbing them. Her two energy-fueled boys needed their rest and she didn't even want to think about the consequences of them not getting it.

"It's too far to walk. We'd have to grab a golf cart."

"Maybe we should wait until the twins wake. I don't want to miss a second of them with their eyes open."

"They're great boys," he said.

"For all my jokes about never sleeping and never

sitting down since they were born I wouldn't change a thing, except maybe to make them grow up a little slower," she said. "Find a 'pause' button somewhere."

"Time speeds by," he agreed. "Even without having little guys around to remind you just how fast."

"And it can change just like that." She snapped her fingers.

Joshua's gaze dropped and his jaw clenched. She was referring to Isabel's kidnapping but she'd struck a nerve with him. He had his own investigation going on. "Are you really okay?"

"Yeah, sure." She didn't want to give away her emotions, emotions that left her feeling overwhelmed and running on empty. Seeing her boys and being with Joshua were the only two positive things in her life right now.

"A lot has gone on in the past few days. It's a lot to process."

"I'm one of these people who's calm in the moment and then it hits later." When she was alone in bed. How many nights had she cried herself to sleep in her lifetime? More than she cared to count or admit.

"I know you like to play tough guy and you put on a good show. Do people who really know you believe it?" he asked.

"Yeah, they have to. My job and my life depend on it. I don't have to tell you how important it is for fellow officers to trust that you can do your job," she said, wishing she could let down her guard a little more.

"You don't have to be like that with me," he said, his voice a low rumble. "I'm not a threat."

She couldn't let his words affect her, so she took a

step back to put some distance between them. "That's where you're wrong."

Joshua gazed out onto the expansive property looking like he was letting her words sink in.

Alice needed to change the subject because that conversation wasn't going to lead where she wanted it to go and should know better than to want.

"You said before that your parents were murdered. Do you want me to take a look at the file and give my professional opinion?" she offered, wishing there was something she could do to repay him for everything he'd done for her. "Sometimes it helps to have a second set of eyes."

Before Joshua could answer, the sound of gravel crunching underneath tires caught both of their attention. A brand new dual-cab Ford F-150 pulled down the lane.

"That's my Uncle Ezra," Joshua said as he checked his watch. "He's early."

Alice watched Joshua walked away, thinking that she wasn't the only one who'd mastered the tough-guy routine.

"I WOULDN'T HAVE called this meeting if it wasn't important," Uncle Ezra began and Joshua wondered if there'd ever been a time when Ezra didn't think that what he had to say was worthy of everyone's immediate attention.

His brother Tyler was the best negotiator, so he sat to Ezra's left at their father's conference table. Ezra had been given the right-hand seat to their father, his chair now empty and a constant reminder of the loss the brothers felt, as a gesture but he wasn't given any real responsibility. To the right of Tyler were Uncle Ezra and

Aunt Bea's spots. The next empty seat, directly opposite of Dad's at the long oak conference table, belonged to their mother. To her left were Janis, Ryder, Colin, Joshua, Austin and Dallas. Dallas's seat was directly opposite Uncle Ezra.

"We need to address—"

Dallas put up his hand to stop Uncle Ezra. "Not everyone's here yet."

Uncle Ezra stood in a huff. "Who else is invited?"

"We can't have an official family meeting without everyone present, Uncle Ezra. We're still waiting on Aunt Bea," Tyler, ever the calm negotiator, said.

"But I specifically asked for a meeting with the brothers only," Uncle Ezra complained, his hands planted on the oak table.

"That's against policy and you know it. You wouldn't like it if someone tried to exclude you from important family business," Tyler continued.

"Which is why I'll never understand why she's here." He motioned toward Janis as she picked imaginary lint off her sleeve with a here-he-goes-again look on her face.

"Everyone's clear on your vote to keep Janis out of the family's interests. The rest of us disagreed and majority vote ruled," Tyler continued. "Can we put this discussion to rest or do we need to readdress bylaws every time we meet?"

Uncle Ezra blew out a puff of air and then moved to the coffee tray set up near the door.

Ryder leaned toward Joshua. "For someone whose vote literally counts for nothing in our business this guy sure calls a lot of meetings."

"And he sure is full of a lot of hot air," Janis whispered, leaning toward them both.

Joshua and his twin brother smirked.

"Well, I'm glad *he* decided to join the meeting this time," Uncle Ezra said. His gaze locked on to Joshua.

Before Joshua could respond, Aunt Bea rushed in.

"Apologies to keep everyone waiting," she said in her best sugary-sweet voice. Joshua wasn't sure whether she spoke like that just to get on Uncle Ezra's nerves or if she was being true to herself. The two matched about as well as a rose petal and a cactus, both personalities multiplied in the presence of one another. That's not where their differences ended. Where Uncle Ezra was thin and wiry, Aunt Bea made up for it in girth. Despite her hearty size she was inclined toward floral dresses and matching hats with ribbons, and she always dressed like she was on her way to Sunday service. The brother and sister had a long history of being at odds that ran deeper than their physical appearances.

"It's kind of you to finally show, Bea," Uncle Ezra countered, ever the gentleman.

"Let's get to business," Dallas said. Even though all brothers had equal share of the ranch, they'd voted Dallas in charge due to his natural leadership tendencies and the fact that he was willing to take on the job no one else wanted. "You requested this meeting, Uncle Ezra. What would you like to discuss?"

"Since my brother passed, God rest his soul, I think the burden of running this place has been a lot to put on you boys as you straighten up your affairs," Uncle Ezra said.

"You've said that before and we appreciate your willingness to help," Dallas said.

Aunt Bea made a disgruntled noise.

"As I've said before the division of the family business—"

"Of our father's business you mean?" Joshua couldn't help himself. Uncle Ezra was always trying to make it seem like he'd contributed to the success of the ranch and club even though he hadn't lifted a finger.

Uncle Ezra shot him a look that almost made him laugh out loud.

"At least some of us are willing to pitch in during times of crisis," Uncle Ezra continued, another dig toward Joshua.

Instead of responding, Joshua leaned back in his chair. His phone buzzed in his pocket. He fished it out, didn't recognize the number. He excused himself and took the call in the hallway.

"Mr. O'Brien, this is Rupert Grinnell with the personnel department of the Federal Bureau of Investigation," the male voice said.

"This is an honor, sir. I've been looking forward to this call," Joshua said, hoping this meant what he thought it did, an interview.

"We're impressed with your background, Mr. O'Brien. We'd like to bring you in to talk to a few people," Grinnell continued.

"I'd like that very much," Joshua said.

"Are you available in two days for an interview?" Grinnell asked.

"Yes, sir," Joshua said with a pang of guilt that he might be walking away from Alice when she needed him. His brain kicked into high gear. He'd be gone a day at best. He could leave early and might even be able to make it home in time for dinner. They were getting close to blowing the Perez case wide open and surely they'd find something concrete on the computer that would help them locate Isabel. They were in a holding pattern for now anyway.

"My admin will contact you with the details," Grinnell said. "I should tell you that there haven't been a lot of applicants we've been this interested in for a while."

"I appreciate the confidence, sir. I look forward to the meeting," Joshua responded.

He ended the call and then reclaimed his seat in the conference room. He should feel elated and yet he couldn't deny feeling like he was sneaking around, doing something wrong. He chalked it up to abandoning his brothers and the fact that he felt like he was letting his father down in some way, feelings he'd felt his entire life.

The next time his phone buzzed, it was a message from Tommy. The crime scene was clear and he and Alice were free to examine it themselves.

"Which brings me to my dilemma." Uncle Ezra didn't miss a beat. Joshua would have to ask Ryder if he missed anything important in the last few minutes. Somehow, he doubted he had. "I'd like to do more. Given the recent...*news*...about your parents I'm sure you'll want to put all your extra resources into helping solve the investigation." Making a play for more power while their heads were still spinning about the fact that their parents had been murdered was right up there with one of the slimiest things he'd ever proposed.

"I'm not saying that any of us agree to this, but I'm guessing you have something specific in mind," Dallas said and Joshua knew his brother was digging around to find Ezra's real motivation behind the proposal.

"Given that I'm always willing to pitch in when needed whereas Bea is content to collect a check, I feel that it's only fair that I receive a larger piece of the responsibility." He should've said what he really meant… a larger piece of the *pie*.

This wasn't his first play for more so no one freaked out but Bea did make that grunting noise again.

"As you know, we can't give more to you without taking away from others," Dallas said, impatience edging his tone. "And Dad's instructions were pretty clear as to how he wanted the place divided. If he'd wanted you to have more, he'd have given it to you."

"It's not necessary to be so formal," Uncle Ezra hedged. "We can deal with the legalese later. I'm talking about something temporary and unofficial here. I've had my lawyer draw up papers so everyone's on the same page." Uncle Ezra opened the folder he'd brought with him and pulled out what looked like a contract.

"For a document that isn't supposed to be official, he sure went to a lot of trouble," Joshua whispered to Ryder, who lifted an eyebrow and smirked.

"All of those in favor of considering this request, raise your hand," Dallas said, obviously getting impatient with this conversation.

No hands went up, save for Ezra's.

"All against," Dallas said, his hand was the first to jut into the air. "Motion declined. This meeting is—"

"Now, just a minute," Uncle Ezra interrupted. "You didn't hear me out."

"I think we're clear on where you stand. So I'll be clear on where we do. Making demands isn't going to get you where you think you should be. Neither is trying to slip a legally binding document under the radar. So, back off or we'll exercise our legal right to have you removed from this company." Their father had given them a way out. All they had to do was unanimously vote to remove Uncle Ezra. No one would go against Dad's wishes, though, unless his brother got out of control.

"That would be a long and costly process," Uncle Ezra said.

"I sure hope that wasn't a threat," Dallas countered.

Uncle Ezra's phone buzzed. He was probably looking for a distraction when he answered the call. He turned his back to the group and lowered his voice enough that Joshua couldn't hear what he said. Uncle Ezra ended the call a few seconds later. When he turned around, he looked a little pale.

"Who was that?" Dallas asked.

"The Johnson boy," Uncle Ezra supplied, quickly regaining his disgruntled demeanor.

"What does Tommy want?" Dallas asked the question on the tip of everyone's tongue.

Uncle Ezra stuffed the pages inside the folder and tucked it under his arm. "I'm sure it's nothing. Said he wants me to come down to the station to answer a few routine questions to help him out with my brother's case."

"I HOPE THIS doesn't become a theme between us," Joshua said to Uncle Ezra, following him outside after the meeting. He'd scanned the kitchen for Alice, figured she was somewhere with her boys when he didn't see her.

"What's that supposed to mean?" Uncle Ezra seemed committed to playing dumb. His uncle looked a little more rattled than usual.

"The jabs back there." Joshua wasn't one to mince words.

Uncle Ezra whirled around just before reaching his

truck. "You and the others are blind to what's going on around you. I see this situation for what it is." He thumped his chest and his voice was sounding a little hysterical.

"Easy there, Uncle Ezra. You don't need to have a heart attack," Joshua said.

"It wouldn't surprise me if I did," was all Uncle Ezra said back. He turned, opened the door to his truck and then slammed it after climbing inside the cab.

What was that supposed to mean?

"Think he's going to give us a problem?" Joshua asked Dallas as he returned to the kitchen and told him about their exchange.

"Yeah, he'll be a pain in our backside for the rest of his life," Dallas quipped.

"About what he said earlier about me, I know—"

"No need to worry about what that old coot thinks," Dallas said. "We all have previous business to take care of before we can fully devote to the ranch. That's why we work together to ease the load."

Joshua wanted to tell his brother that he had no plans to stick around if the FBI offered him a job. He'd pretty much decided that he wouldn't anyway. There were other branches of law enforcement that he could work for and his former chief had placed him on temporary leave rather than process his paperwork, reminding him how tough it could be to get back into law enforcement once he left voluntarily. Keeping the secret was eating at him. Telling his brothers was the only fair thing to do.

What if he didn't get the job at the FBI? He could always change his mind and decide to stay at the ranch. After all, nothing was out of the question and there was a big part of him that started feeling at home there recently. Maybe he could settle into a role?

Alice walked into the kitchen with a baby on her hip and froze. He could tell by her reaction that she was overwhelmed by all the O'Briens in one place. He crossed the room to her and she relaxed the minute she made eye contact with him.

"Alex is hungry," she said.

"What do you need me to get?" Joshua was ready to roll up his sleeves. He also needed to tell her that she could have access to the whole crime scene now.

"Marla said she left the formula and bottles in the diaper bag under the table." She scanned the room.

Everyone kept right on talking as if she wasn't there, a fact she seemed to appreciate. They were used to strangers being in the main house. Janis was there, too, and she seemed to know on instinct what Alice needed, bringing over the bag.

"I'm happy to help make a bottle," she offered.

"That would be great actually," Alice said trying to hold the baby and navigate the contents of the bag. She looked happy, really happy. Joshua didn't want it to end and he knew it would as soon as he told her.

"You want me to take him?" Joshua offered, unsure of how to hold a baby or toddler, whatever this little guy was. He held his arms out and the little boy leaned toward him. Joshua took that as a good sign. "Come here, buddy."

Surprisingly, Alex didn't scream. Joshua bounced up and down anyway for good measure.

"Who have you got there?" Dallas asked, turning his attention toward the little boy. His brother had had a crash course in parenting after meeting and falling in love with a single mother. He and Kate were now proud parents of a little boy by the name of Jackson who she'd adopted before meeting Dallas. He had already declared his intention to officially become Jackson's father after the wedding. Joshua may not have been around the ranch as much as he felt he should be, but he'd been around enough to witness the changes in his older brother, the happiness and peace having a family of his own brought.

"This is Alex," Joshua said, and then introduced Alice. He'd barely noticed that the room had gone silent and everyone's attention shifted to Alice and the baby. "There's another one just like him in the other room named Andrew."

"Twins?" Dallas asked as their brothers took turns welcoming the newcomers.

Joshua nodded.

"I'm not touching that one." Dallas's hands came up in the surrender position.

In that moment, in that room, Joshua felt like he belonged right where he was.

"Bottle's ready," Janis announced. "Can I do the honors?"

Alice smiled and said, "Yes."

Which was probably a good thing because Marla walked in a few seconds later with Andrew and Alice had to get busy making another bottle. Once Marla was settled with Andrew, feeding his bottle, Joshua handed Alice a fresh cup of coffee.

Everyone sat at the table together for the first time in weeks. And also for the first time, Joshua felt like he was right where he was supposed to be. A moment like this was rare and like snow on the ground in Texas, it wouldn't last. He'd get restless and need to get back on the job.

Speaking of which, he turned to Alice. "We're clear to examine the crime scene."

Chapter Thirteen

The air was cold, the sky a foreboding shade of gray. Alice shivered to stave off the chill.

"Tommy hasn't shared any information from the crime scene with you, has he?" she asked Joshua as they pulled up.

"They've picked up a lot of prints and other DNA evidence," he said, which could tell them which rooms Isabel had been in. Alice already knew she'd been there based on the necklace find.

"Hopefully, they'll be able to link these crimes to Perez," she said, holding on to the thought that all wasn't lost. Bad men had been taken off the streets. Eighteen girls had been rescued and were beginning a journey toward healing.

"Since they tried to torch the trailer, he's checking the database to see if he can get a hit on similar crimes in the Southwest," Joshua said.

"Maybe they'll find other locations," she said. It was a smart move and something she would've done in order to learn everything about the man she was pursuing. The more she knew, the easier it would be to anticipate his movements. Perez was still out there, somewhere. She scanned the cul-de-sac as she exited the Jeep. And he knew where Isabel was.

The sun hid behind the clouds, lights were out inside the ranch-style house, giving it an eerie quality.

Alice pulled her jacket closed tightly in an attempt to keep the biting wind from penetrating as she ducked under crime scene tape and crossed the yard. It was day five of her burn and her nerve endings were waking up. Her forearm hurt and she refused to take anything stronger than an ibuprofen, needing a clear head.

The lack of activity, the quiet, was a stark contrast to her earlier visit. Walking inside the house made chills run up her spine. She'd been to dozens of crime scenes in her career and this one was right up there with the worst of them. Places like this had their own feel, as if the horrors carried out there imprinted the air, the walls. It was as though terror and desperation had a physical manifestation that couldn't be cleared out by opening the windows and airing the place out.

Alice stepped inside the too dark living room. Neither she nor Joshua would open the curtains. Both would tread lightly at the scene on the off chance investigators needed to return. The room had an old brown plaid sofa, something that looked left over from the seventies, off to one side. There was a card table and chairs. All the laptops had been confiscated, the data being pored over by technical experts.

The place had a filthy half frat, half junkyard feel. Stacks of newspapers were on the floor and the center of the table. She shuffled into the kitchen where there was a coffee maker and a microwave. Dirty dishes filled the sink along with a few cigarette butts and there were a couple of flies buzzing around the empty pizza boxes on top of the counter. The place looked and smelled like it hadn't been cleaned in months. She doubted it had ever truly been scrubbed. She had an urge to throw on plastic gloves, grab a bucket and some soapy water and scour the place clean. The dirt could be wiped off; those were temporary marks. Her urge had so much more to do with what lay beneath the surface, what a bucket of soap and water couldn't erase.

"Looks like the team swept the place pretty well," Joshua said. He was taking the scene in for himself and Alice could feel his eyes watching her for a reaction, maybe a breakdown. He stood beside her in the otherwise empty room.

The tremors started slowly and from a place deep inside her. Thoughts of Isabel in this horrible scene assaulted her. These were exactly the kinds of weaknesses she'd suppress if she stood there with anyone else. But this was Joshua. He was so tall, so muscled, and yet all of his strength came from within, like he had a bottomless well to draw on.

Alice turned to face him. He didn't seem to need her to spell it out. He just held her. His arms circled her waist as she buried her face in his chest. She didn't know if the holidays had her feeling vulnerable or the fact that this crime scene hit her right at home, but she needed him in a way she'd never allowed herself to need anyone.

The scene they'd walked into was something out of a horror show and her personal connection to it had her rattled to the core. And yet, standing there with Joshua, his arms around her, leaning into his towering strength, Alice finally knew what it was to feel safe. Isabel had had her family. She'd gone to sleep with this feeling every night. And Alice needed to return that feeling to Isabel.

The ranch had three bedrooms and no basement thanks to the shifty clay soil in Texas. It was a similar deal in Arizona. Using her phone's flashlight, Alice walked into each room. All were similar, a bed with a tether, blankets scattered on the floor and those damn buckets that had probably been taken outside and rinsed out once a day. There were cosmetics in the bathrooms and bindings in the showers so that the girls could be tied up and left alone. A few nice outfits hung in the closet of the master. The others had been boarded up. There was very little in the way of furniture. Pillows, blankets and towels scattered across the filthy gray carpet. Alice wouldn't let an animal live there, let alone a young girl. Another wave of gratitude hit her at the thought of eighteen girls going home. There was so much heat on Perez he wouldn't strike again anytime soon. For the moment, his operation was on lockdown. That fact brought another wave of thankfulness.

Alice studied the beds, the walls of each room. Inside the bedroom farthest from the main living quarters, she dropped to her knees beside the bed and searched for any clues. Beside some of the beds were notches in the floorboards. What did they mean? The obvious answer was a girl marking the days she spent in that room. There were other scratches, too. At least one was a set of initials. The marks in the last bedroom were different from the other two. Instead of straight up and down marks like ticks, they had more of a pattern. Alice snapped a picture so she could study it later. Her phone buzzed in her hand, startling her.

"I need to see you," Fischer said before she had a chance to utter a greeting.

"What is it, Fischer?" she asked, the urgency in his tone not exactly a welcomed sign.

"In person or no deal," he practically grunted. More of his manipulation tactics. Well, no thanks.

"Tell me on the phone or not at all," she said, not willing to play games.

A sharp sigh issued through the line.

"There was only one set of prints on the necklace and they belong to your friend," he finally said. At least he'd cut to the chase.

"She was here. I had no doubt it belonged to her." No one had stripped the necklace from Isabel and that was the first positive thought. So, had Isabel taken off the piece of jewelry in hopes that Alice would find it? She'd be smart enough to realize leaving a trail would help Alice find her. *Keep hoping, sweetie.*

"This isn't the right time but I need to talk to you about our boys," Fischer said.

"Okay." She'd received confirmation that she was on the right track in looking for Isabel. She was close. For the first time in a long time she felt a very real sense of hope, like this might not end with her finding a body. Everything else could be recovered from. Alice was living proof. She glanced up at Joshua. He was a comforting presence. And for the first time, she saw a future.

"When?" Fischer asked.

"Now."

"Like right now?" he asked.

"There's never going to be a good time for me to talk to you," she said. "So, tell me what's on your mind."

"I should see them," he said low into the phone.

"That's probably a good idea." She'd be more enthusiastic if Fischer hadn't used the one word that made it seem like he was only asking out of obligation...*should.* More confirmation that she and Fischer would never be on the same page in life. His job would always be more important, would always come first. Alice was career minded. She understood devotion to the job. This was something different. It was more like hiding from real life in a career.

"You didn't cash the checks," he said.

"No." She didn't owe him an explanation.

"I've been saving the money anyway," he said. "Didn't feel right about keeping it."

"How about I let you put them through college?" she asked, letting him off the hook from the day-to-day.

"Deal." There was a lot of relief in that one word. "Alice. Be careful with this investigation. I'm doing everything I can to help you but there's only so much I can do and my superior is pushing me to arrest you."

She ended the call, stood and asked Joshua to take her home.

JOSHUA OPENED THE door to his place—a place he'd basically avoided moving into save for his bed—and navigated through stacked boxes to his kitchen. All the basics were there for making coffee. He ate most of his meals on the go or at the main house. And he noticed how embarrassingly little he had in the way of real supplies. Up to now, a microwave and a basic plate would've covered all his needs. He wished he'd done a better job of making the place presentable now that Alice was there.

His house could best be described as a rustic log house. It had four bedrooms, which he'd protested at the time it was built, only one of which was furnished. Before meeting Alice, four had seemed like overkill. Now, he wished he'd furnished them all so she and the kids could stay over instead of at the main house.

Furniture was sparse. There was a sofa in the middle of the living room. He'd positioned it to take advantage of the fireplace. There were a few bar chairs huddled under the granite island. His mother had spared no expense with the finishes and Joshua suspected she'd done that to entice him to move home sooner.

Now that Joshua really thought about it, his apartment in Denver had had a similar unfinished feel, barely any furniture and not enough kitchen supplies to cook up a decent meal. He'd worked evenings and ate out most meals. He'd kept a decent coffee maker, and a guest room with a bed in case one of his brothers came through town.

"I love this place," Alice said as she took in the tall beamed ceilings in the living room.

"I'd like to say that I had a hand in building it but that would be a lie. My mother oversaw all the details," he admitted.

"It fits your personality to a T," she said, walking into the kitchen, eyeing the chestnut cabinets and stainless steel appliances. She smoothed her hand across the island. "And this granite is just…perfect."

"Thank you." It shouldn't matter so much that a stranger liked the place. "You want a cup of coffee?"

She nodded as she settled into a seat at the island. He could see in her expression there was a lot rolling around in her mind.

"It might be helpful to go over what we already know," he said, handing her a fresh cup, ignoring the thought that having her at his place made it feel more like home. He chalked it up to this year being odd without his parents and that was true enough but there was so much more he didn't want to analyze. His life had other complications. He still hadn't figured out how he was going to tell his brothers about the call he'd received from the FBI that afternoon asking him to come in for an interview.

It's just an interview, he told himself like there would be any discussion if they offered a job. He had every intention of taking it on the spot. He'd wanted to be with the FBI since he was old enough to know what the letters stood for. Even so, he felt like a liar for not telling his brothers. *Or Alice,* a voice reminded.

Alice took a sip of the fresh brew. "I keep thinking where she could be and come up empty."

"What about the picture you took at the crime scene? Any thoughts pop into your mind as to what those marks are about?" he asked.

"They aren't consistent with the ones in the other rooms and that makes me think they're significant. Or maybe hope's the right word." She shrugged. "Fischer said Isabel's necklace was found in the same room."

Otherwise, the trail to Isabel had gone cold and Alice was becoming discouraged.

"How about the piece of jewelry?" he asked.

"The necklace didn't have any prints other than hers, so that leads me to believe she was the one who took it off. I have to think that was on purpose, especially since the necklace is intact."

"Agreed," Joshua said, taking a seat next to her at the counter.

"Which leaves us with the fact that we know she was

there but we have no idea what happened to her next."
There was so much pain in Alice's eyes, so much tension outlined in the brackets around her mouth. "I'm not sure I like this part better."

"It might take the tech guys a few days to figure out what's going on, but they're the best and I have every hope they'll find what we need," he said.

"And that should be reassuring except that there could be unimaginable horrors happening to her right now and I can't stop it." Alice's shoulders deflated as despair sank heavy.

Joshua gripped his mug.

"I know I shouldn't obsess over it and I should stay positive, but how can I not?" she asked, frustration rising. "This is the closest I've been to her in weeks and I can feel it in my bones. I'm missing something and if I can put that final piece together, I can find her."

"Everything that can be done is happening right now," Joshua said in an effort to soothe her. His words seemed to have the opposite effect.

Alice smacked her flat palm on the granite. "If that were true, she'd be home right now."

ALICE KNEW FOR certain that if she were a better detective Isabel would be safe right now. There was nothing the cowboy could say to convince her otherwise. "I know you're trying to be helpful but I have to face facts."

"And those are?" He folded his arms and leaned against the counter.

"Being here isn't helping find Isabel," she said flatly. The reality was that she couldn't get too comfortable, not while Isabel was still out there missing. "I appreciate everything you've done for me. Being with my boys brought me back from a dark place and I'm grateful for that."

"But?"

"You've done everything you can and the rest is up to me. You've helped me get this far but my arm is improving and I need to get out there on my own."

"If he gets to you, it's game over," Joshua said. "You know that, right?"

"I can't care about that right now." That wasn't entirely true. Alice twisted her hands together. She had two boys in the main house who desperately needed her. It wasn't like there was a father around. She was all they had, for better or worse.

"Then what about Alex and Andrew? Stay here for them," Joshua said.

"And what? Be the kind of mother who can't look herself in the mirror?" She took a deep breath to ease her tension. Didn't work. "That's exactly how it will be if I don't find her."

"I get that," he said, his voice calm. And that probably angered her even more. He was too calm when she wanted to scream.

"No, you don't. You've never caused a child to lose both of her parents and then be pushed into the foster care system," she said a little too loudly.

"I'm sorry," he said quietly.

"Words can't take away the pain," she fired at him, anger building inside her like an out-of-control storm. Talking about the past wasn't something she'd ever done with anyone, not even the sheriff and his wife. They'd accepted her for who she was and taken her in, showed her kindness. But they'd never forced her to speak of the horrors she'd experienced. Now that she was older

she realized there had to have been a file on her somewhere and she was certain that both the sheriff and his
wife had read it. Maybe that's why they hadn't forced
her to speak about her past.

"No, they can't and I won't pretend to understand
what you've gone through," he said in that infuriatingly
calm voice of his.

"People have been through worse," she said because
that was the only mantra she knew. The one that had
gotten her through several beatings and two attempted
sexual assaults before the age of fifteen. Foster care
could be great. She'd seen it work with the sheriff and
his wife. And it could be the worst possible hell. She'd
seen that side, too.

"Worse than what?" he pushed. "Being locked in a
closet?"

"Those were good days at some places," she said,
anger a rising tide inside her.

"Being hit?" His calm voice barely breaking over the
whoosh-sound thrashing in her ears.

"You're getting closer," she said. "Try being whipped
with a cord but only in places that can't be seen so you
wouldn't have to miss school the next day."

"I'm sorry." His words were quiet but he'd broken the
seal on that topic.

"And then there was the time my 'uncle' Ralph forced
himself on top of me while I was trying to do homework
on my bed." Her pace picked up. "I stabbed him with
my pencil and he beat me to within an inch of my life."

"I'm so sorry." Those calm words broke through the
anguish in her mind.

"Or how about the time I dropped the bowl of mashed
potatoes on Thanksgiving so I was forced to pick my

switch from the tree outside and then I was beaten before being locked in my room with no food." She couldn't stop now that those floodgates had been opened.

"You shouldn't have had to go through that," the calm voice said.

JOSHUA DIDN'T LIKE pushing her but there was so much she was keeping inside, burying. He knew exactly what that could do to a person. He'd lied to both his parents, said everything was fine when they were laying out their grand plans for the future, plans that he'd agreed to even though everything inside his body said no. He'd sat at the same conference table he had earlier with his family and let his future be laid out for him. And now he couldn't take any of it back.

"People go through worse. Every single day," she shot back. "There's nothing special about me."

"There's where you're wrong," he countered.

"I'm not." She stopped in front of him, her glare daring him to argue. Her shoulders were tensed, her hands flexing and releasing and there was panic in her eyes. Maybe she was afraid to feel special.

"Do you ever do anything to make yourself happy?" he asked.

"What's that supposed to mean?"

"It's a simple question. I'll rephrase it. When was the last time you did something for yourself?" he asked.

"Why is that important?"

"Because it's important for me to know," he said as calmly as he could. The truth was that with her so close his heart was thumping in his chest. It was taking pretty much all the willpower he had to stand there, a foot apart, without touching her. There was anger in her eyes but there was something else, too. Trust.

"To be honest, I don't really think about myself much."

"Do you think other people are like that? That every person looks out for others in the way that you do?"

"I don't know." She shrugged. "I guess not."

"You know they don't. You've seen it firsthand. You've been bounced around, mostly to places that were a living hell. I'm amazed that you dedicated your life to upholding the law because one look at the statistics says you should be on the wrong side." He'd seen enough of that side through the charity work his mother was involved in and the stats were downright depressing. Most kids brought up in an unstable environment ended up unstable adults. It was like bad seed planting bad seed, perpetuating itself all over again.

There was fire to her eyes now. Fire and spark. It was what he'd come to love about her. Hold on...

Love?

That was a strong word to describe his feelings.

"I had a choice just like everyone else. Bad things happen to good people all the time and whatever happens in childhood isn't a child's fault," Alice said and he already knew he was in trouble with her. "But the day I turned eighteen I figured that I had a choice about my life. I could blame my rough situation on everyone else and be miserable. Or I could take charge of my life and find happiness. Not that I'm all that great about that last part. I make mistakes, but I'm giving my best effort."

Alice stood toe-to-toe with him now. What she lacked in height she made up for in spirit.

"You didn't answer my question," he said. Staring into those blue eyes was like looking straight into the sun. He was going to get burned. He just didn't know to what degree.

"I didn't want to but I'll tell you what scares me," she said.

"Okay," he said, arms folded, feet positioned in an athletic stance.

"I'm scared to death that I'll mess up my kids. Or worse, they'll end up in the system because their father didn't want anything to do with them and I land myself in jail because I do something stupid," she said.

"You're doing better than you think," Joshua said. "Your boys are amazing, happy."

"Rambunctious," she added and he had to smile.

"I wouldn't have it any other way." It was true enough. The pair of them were lively. But they were also like a sunny day after months of cold, hard winter. "You won't go to jail. I'll see to that."

"And what if you're not around?" she asked.

It was a good point.

"Where am I going?" he asked. He had every intention of making sure she was okay.

"There are two times when I'm truly happy," she said and her words came out like a dare.

"Okay." He readied himself for pretty much anything.

"One is when I'm with my twins and we have the whole day together with nothing to do but hang out and play," she said and her entire demeanor softened.

"And the other?" he asked.

"Right now. When I'm with you."

Chapter Fourteen

Joshua knew that he was going to pay for this later, but he hauled Alice against his chest anyway. Her scent, fresh flowers and clean, filled his senses. He'd memorize that scent for when she disappeared into her own life in Tucson and he spent lonely hours on the job. A flash of his apartment in Denver invaded his thoughts. There'd been very little furniture, only the necessities for day-to-day living. There'd been months on end of cold, gray skies. Looking back, it seemed so…empty.

Instead of wallowing in that thought, he buried his face in her hair. Her hands were on either side of his face now and she was guiding him to her lips.

They'd need to take it easy and that was going against everything inside Joshua's body. Strung taut, his muscles vibrated with tension that begged for release. He would have to take it slow, careful. Counter every primal urge inside him because he wanted to go fast and hard and lose himself inside her.

When their lips touched, electricity hummed inside his body searching for an outlet.

His arms were already around her waist as he bent down and scooped her up, her legs wrapping around his midsection. His erection was already painfully stiff, pressing against the denim of his jeans, and he'd never wanted a woman like he wanted Alice. Her skin was soft, silky against his.

"Take me to bed," she said and his feet were already moving, their breath quickening. His heart was a hammer against his rib cage.

"I don't want to hurt you." He eased her down on the floor at the foot of the bed.

She grabbed the hem of her shirt and pulled it over her head. He watched for any signs of pain that movement caused and was relieved when there were none. Any indication and he'd force himself to stop, somehow.

"You can't," she said with a look in her eyes that said he couldn't physically hurt her anyway. Emotionally, well, he didn't even want to go there. He was already in too deep.

Joshua had another problem. He needed to slow their frantic pace or this whole thing would be over before it had a chance to get good. He smirked. "You're beautiful, Alice."

"No, I'm not." She blushed, her cheeks flush in the light from outside his window.

He ran his finger along her lacy bra before unsnapping it in the front. She shrugged out of it and her full breasts felt silky and hot against his palm. Her nipple beaded and he groaned. "Then you don't see what I see."

Her hands were already tugging at his shirt, so he discarded it on the floor next to her pile of clothes. His jeans and boxers followed a half second later and he stood there, naked, just as she was. Her body shone in the moonlight and it was about the sexiest thing he'd ever set eyes on.

He started with her shoulder and kissed her, tenderly.

He moved down to the stab wound on her side and feathered a kiss above the bandaging. Moving slowly, his lips grazed her ribs until he could easily access her bare breast.

Alice mumbled something he didn't pick up with a little moan as he took her nipple in his mouth.

And then his lips trailed down across her firm belly. His movements were fluid, careful. The next second, she was on the bed, positioned at the edge, her legs apart.

He pulled a condom from his bedside table and fumbled as he rolled it over the tip of his erection, hands shaky with need…a need for Alice. And then he was inside her, her hands around his midsection, urging, as he drove deeper.

The sound of pleasure that tore from her throat egged him on. He pulled back and then thrust again. She joined his movements, slow and precise at first, that built to a frantic pace as both struggled to breathe, needing release.

Her muscles tensed and her breath held, so he drove faster and harder until she shattered around him. A single thrust and he detonated inside her in an explosion that rocked his core.

For a long moment, neither moved, frozen in time, neither wanting it to end.

Until they repositioned onto his bed, under the covers, their arms and legs tangled, warm bodies together in the chilly evening.

Joshua held on until he could feel her even breathing, her sweet sounds of sleep.

And then he let go, too, full of the knowledge that he was in serious trouble with her in his arms.

THE NEXT MORNING, Joshua stretched, untangled his limbs and then forced himself out of bed to make coffee. He could lie there all day with Alice, her warm smooth skin pressed to his.

Okay, he'd better cut it out before he created a problem that couldn't be fixed while she was sleeping. He finished his first cup and opened email on his laptop. His itinerary was there. He'd leave tomorrow morning on an early o'clock flight. He needed a ride to the airport.

Ryder would be up since it was already light outside so Joshua called his brother's cell.

"Did you hear about the meeting tomorrow morning?" Ryder asked. "Eight a.m."

"No." Joshua scanned emails until he found one from Dallas. He quickly read it. "What does Uncle Ezra want now?"

"Same thing as always, I guess. Our land," Ryder said.

Joshua had no interest in fighting the same battle over and over again. It was already time to let go and move on.

"I need a favor," he hedged.

"Okay."

"I need a lift to Houston Hobby early tomorrow morning."

"Where are you headed?" Ryder asked.

"Just some business I need to take care of." Joshua tried to sound casual.

"We have that meeting," Ryder said.

"You'll be back in time to make it. I'll call in from the airport," he said, felling another bite of guilt because they both knew he wouldn't.

"Where are you headed?" Ryder asked, leaving it alone. Joshua was grateful.

"Up north. Have to talk to someone there. I'll be back

tomorrow night and I'm hoping to get another ride," he said, giving his brother the details. "You can fill me in on the Uncle Ezra situation."

"Sounds like a plan," Ryder said and Joshua was pretty sure he picked up on a hint of disappointment in his brother's voice.

He hated feeling like he was letting his family down.

"Thanks, bro. See you tomorrow morning," he said. He moved to pour his second cup of coffee as Alice entered the kitchen.

"What was that all about?" she asked and he wondered how much she'd heard.

"I have a meeting tomorrow out of town. It'll be an in-and-out trip." It wasn't a lie and yet it sure burned like one. Joshua moved to her, kissed her. She looked amazing wearing the flannel shirt he'd left out for her. "How about a cup of coffee?"

She didn't immediately respond, just bit her lower lip and then nodded.

Joshua poured two cups and handed one over.

"I can't stop thinking about those marks." She picked up her cell phone and located the picture she'd taken last night of the floorboard at the compound. She set the phone down in between them, studying it while she sipped her coffee.

Joshua was grateful for the change in subject. He didn't want to lie to her, *couldn't* lie to her. And yet he wasn't ready to tell her, either. He was stuck in a weird space not knowing what he really wanted. Ask him yesterday morning or the days leading up to it and he would've answered that he wanted that job more than anything else. Last night had changed things. Now, with her in his house, he wasn't so sure. He'd go to the interview and see how he felt after. He'd know one way or the other once the job was offered, *if* the job was offered.

The rest of the morning was quiet. He picked up breakfast from the main house after seeing her twins off with Marla back to Tucson. Joshua had another one of those weird feelings in his chest, a stir from somewhere deep, as he buckled them into their seats on the helicopter.

Alice spent the balance of the morning online trying to figure out what the scratches in the picture meant—I III II B V I-I—and came up empty.

Joshua had had a few food supplies delivered so he fixed sandwiches for lunch and made her promise to rest on the couch. Curled up with his laptop, she looked right at home there. And a very big part of him was ready to claim her as his. But then there was something else on Joshua's mind. Something that had been eating away at the back of his mind and he needed to talk to her about it because he was falling down a rabbit hole with his emotions and he needed to know if this, whatever *this* was, was a good idea.

"When you were talking about Fischer the other day, you said he's 'technically' the father of your twins." Joshua paused for a beat. "What does 'technically' mean? He either is or he isn't."

"The only tie he has to my boys is shared DNA," she responded and her voice was even, indicating no deception.

"That is the substance that binds a person together," he countered. "It's what makes families and that's powerful if you ask me. Not something that can be shoved aside or ignored."

"True. If he wants a relationship with the boys, I

would never stand in his way. They have a right to know their father as much as he has a right to know them. As for anything between the two of us, well, that possibility died when he walked out two weeks before they were delivered. I gave it a chance before and nothing has changed since. We spoke the other day and I let him off the hook with helping care for the boys. He sounded more relieved than anything else."

"It's pretty clear that the man still has feelings for you," Joshua said.

"Yeah, well, me and my boys are a packaged deal," she said quickly. "As for Fischer and me, I'm done."

Joshua took a sip of his coffee. He wanted to think over what she was saying. He couldn't imagine not knowing his own sons. First of all, the twins were pretty darn cute. They had personalities to match. What if Fischer spent time with them and decided he wanted to play Dad? Would it be right for Joshua to stand in the way of a family?

Knowing how important sharing the O'Brien name with his brothers meant to him, she would easily be able to understand why he'd see this issue more as blank and white. But then, she had to have figured out that no O'Brien would walk away from his own child.

"Besides, there are stronger and more important forces in the world than shared genes," she said after a thoughtful pause and he realized that she'd been staring at him the whole time.

"Yeah, like what?" Joshua asked.

"Love."

Chapter Fifteen

By the time Alice woke the next morning, Joshua was gone. The bed felt too big without him and she lay there an extra few minutes breathing in his unique masculine scent—clean and spicy—that lingered on the pillow and sheets.

Alice threw the covers off and her feet over the side of the bed keenly aware of the fact that it was Friday. She stretched, amazed at how fast her burn was healing. Her stab wound was better, too. She'd have to remember to send Dr. McConnell flowers when this whole ordeal was all said and done. Alice shuffled her feet into the kitchen and then made a fresh pot of coffee. It was her second favorite scent, next to Joshua's. Speaking of which, he'd said that he'd call once he landed in…wherever he'd said he was going. Or did he?

She probably forgot. Her mind had been preoccupied with the case.

After a few glorious sips of coffee, she phoned Marla to check on the boys. Her sitter didn't have anything new to report except how excited they'd been at riding in the helicopter again. Marla admitted to being thrilled about that fact herself.

After hearing an earful of baby talk, Alice ended the

call and refocused on Isabel, desperately needing to redirect her attention or risk crumbling into a ball for how much she missed her family.

Alice had considered every angle she could think of for the marks. There was something familiar about the pattern but she couldn't figure it out. Could it spell out a name? It was a stretch and a fairly long one. Isabel would be smart enough to make it difficult for the men in the next room to be able to tell what she was doing and that could account for the fact that the markings were different. Alice spent a good two hours skimming every document that came up with no luck. Her stomach growled, convincing her to get up so she could eat.

Isabel's birthday loomed. The boys' birthdays were early into the New Year. No way did Alice want to make it through the holidays without Isabel home. *Where are you?*

Glancing around Joshua's place, she noticed that he didn't have a tree or much of anything else for that matter be it Christmas or otherwise. Pretty typical of a man's house, she thought. Except for the fact that there were unopened boxes stacked in almost every room. She thought he'd said that he came back there to live but another thought struck. Was he planning to stick around? From the looks of the place the answer to that question was no.

JOSHUA SHOULD BE the happiest guy in the world, he thought as he unlocked the door to his home. The house was dark, which meant Alice was already asleep. It was good to be back. He stepped inside and punched his security code into the pad near the back door. He rearmed the alarm before quietly setting down the paper he'd carried with him. The interview had gone well. Better than well. He'd been offered his dream job—a job that would be waiting after a few more steps in the process. So, why did he tell the director he needed time to think it over?

On the trip home, he'd told himself that he wanted to run it by his brothers before he accepted. He didn't want to acknowledge the real reason was that he wanted to talk it over with Alice. His feelings confused the hell out of him but nothing in his world felt right without her.

After a shower, he slid under the covers and Alice, still asleep, rolled over and curled around him. There were other problems stewing in the back of his mind. Isabel was first and foremost and then there was trouble brewing between Aunt Bea and Uncle Ezra. According to Ryder, the two of them were fighting worse than usual. Joshua chalked it up to the fact that his father had been the one to keep things settled between them. Ezra was making moves to push her out, but then he wanted Janis out as well. The two of them were known for fighting but was something else going on between them besides sibling rivalry?

Aunt Bea was getting flustered and the boys were quick to jump to her defense. Everyone dismissed Ezra as harmless, saying he was a sentimental old fool. But was he?

He'd been using his ranch money to finance other projects, unsuccessful ones. But that wasn't the most disturbing news. Dad would roll in his grave if he knew that Uncle Ezra was involved with the McCabe family, their father's rival.

After the meeting, they'd resolved to keep Uncle Ezra in check and start digging around in his personal affairs to make sure he wasn't in over his head somewhere.

Joshua tossed and turned, unable to give over to sleep. Was it really family business keeping him awake or was it something more? His guilty conscience?

All he needed was a few hours of sleep to get through a day. He checked the clock as his phone buzzed.

"I shouldn't be making this call," Tommy whispered and he sounded anguished.

"What is it?" Joshua shot up. Alice was already up and hopping into a pair of jeans that had been laid out on the dresser.

"Perez has been seen in town. The informant said to watch out for a white van. He's on a mission and Fischer thinks he's back to take you down. He's sending someone your way to intercept Perez. Keep your guard up," Tommy said. "I have to get back in my office so the task force can see me. They've been keeping close watch on my every move."

"Do you have a general vicinity for Perez?" Joshua asked, already half-dressed.

"He's outside the city limits, heading east." A shuffling noise came through the line before Tommy ended the call. He was smart enough to handle his end, so Joshua wouldn't worry about that.

"What did he say?" Alice asked, already buttoning up her shirt.

"Perez is here." From the time of the call to sitting in the Jeep was less than a minute-and-a-half. He could fill her in on the road.

"THE HEAT IS ON. Looks like Perez is making a run for me. I'm guessing that also means he's cashing out his interests in this area and about to disappear for a while,"

Joshua said to Alice as soon as they were on the two-lane highway outside the ranch.

He cursed.

"What is it?" she asked.

"I need gas," he said.

Alice's thoughts raced. Perez could not get away. A cold chill trickled down her spine. She didn't want to hope that Isabel could be with him because that would be too much of a coincidence and, frankly, Alice wouldn't be that lucky. He could give answers, though. He would know where she'd been sold. She could force him to talk. He was finally within reach and she couldn't allow this chance to slip through her fingers.

"There's a shotgun tucked behind your seat," Joshua said, eyes on the road, pedal to the metal. "My Glock's in the glove box. Which one do you want?"

"I'll take the shotgun," she said, figuring she could get a wider spray that way in case she had to give chase. "But I need Perez alive."

"I know we do." Joshua's focus stayed on the patch of road ahead. He slowed as he approached a gas station and then turned in.

At the second pump, there was a white van.

"He's here." She expected him to say they should call it in and wait. The man at the pump was pushing on the van, shaking it, holding the dispenser in his hand while trying to squeeze out that last little bit of air in the tank. Another few seconds and it would be too late.

Joshua pulled in front of the van, blocking it, like he was getting in line for the pump. His headlights would keep the driver from getting a good visual on them.

Pump Man glanced around, caught on to what was going on, and fiddled with the lever on the dispenser.

Alice realized the guy was engaging the lock mechanism that would keep gas pumping before he tossed it
toward the Jeep and then hopped into the van. The engine hummed and he must've put the gear shift in Reverse. Gravel spewed toward them as the van peeled out
and then spun backward.

Joshua ran toward it, took aim and nailed the front
tire. The van turned so hard it tilted to one side and Alice
was half afraid it would roll over. She had no idea who
might be in the back or how many people but she knew
in her heart that innocent girls were in there.

She ran into the stretch of highway that would put her
directly into the line of the van.

All it would take would be one shot, she thought, as
the van's headlights stared her down.

The driver could gun it, and he might do just that, so
she spread her feet in an athletic stance and took aim,
her finger hovering over the trigger mechanism.

If she went down, she was taking the driver with her.

The shell was engaged in the chamber and she was
good to go. She could get off a shot and, hopefully, roll
out of the way into the ditch before the van hit her. Unlike in Hollywood movies, a man who'd been hit didn't
immediately drop. There was only one shot capable of
instant death and it was nearly impossible to pull off
even for a trained sniper. That was a bullet straight to
the brain stem.

No way were her boys becoming orphans.

Alice was a decent marksman, especially for a cop.
But she wasn't *that* good. Almost no one was. And she
didn't exactly feel lucky. Besides, if she believed in luck
she figured she'd used all hers to get to this point.

No, the kind of shot she could get off was different.

With a direct hit, it would take a while for Pump Man's brain to catch up with the news that he was hit, and essentially already dead. He'd keep on doing whatever it was he'd been doing before the shot had been fired. In this case, that meant he'd floor the pedal while locked on to her. Buckshot would spread and Alice could end up killing innocent girls in the back of the van.

Staring at the white van, she realized what seemed so familiar about the markings in the picture... Isabel was giving her a license plate number. Roman numerals I, III, II, so 132. And then the others B V I-I, BVH. The license plate was 132 BVH.

The engine revved, threatening her. This whole scene had been reduced to a game of chicken.

If her plan worked she'd be safe. Her boys would have a mother. Alice thought about that as the van kicked toward her. It took a few seconds for the wheels to grab the blacktop.

Alice couldn't risk killing anyone else inside the van, so she jumped toward the ditch and rolled, came up with the shotgun so she could shoot the driver at closer range as he blew past.

As it turned out, she didn't have to. The cowboy took a shot from the gas station side of the street and pegged the driver, who wasn't Perez. He never saw it coming because he was too busy looking at Alice with his foot on the brake.

There was no one in the passenger seat. If Perez was inside that van, he was in the back.

Alice darted around the side of the vehicle just as Perez rounded it. The shotgun barrel was too long and it was too easy for Perez to knock it out of her hands. He was strong, aided by adrenaline. He swung his right fist, connecting with her left cheekbone. Alice's head shot right and she felt warm liquid in her mouth—blood.

His elbow came up to her throat and he slammed her into the van. She coughed, her lungs clawing for oxygen.

No way was he getting away. Not this time.

Perez was stronger than her, no doubt at it. Trying to overpower him physically would be a mistake and possibly cost her life. Alice dropped to the ground and swept her left foot, catching his legs as he attempted to flee. She twisted her legs around his ankles in a scissor-like grip and then rolled like an alligator. He bit the dirt hard, trying to wrangle his way out of her grasp.

Too bad, jerk.

She folded forward, reared her fist back and then fired a punch, connecting with his stomach before he knocked her out of the way. She threw another punch, determined to inflict as much pain as she could and hopefully wear him out enough to cuff him. This scumbag was going to jail.

Just as he managed to wriggle away, she caught the butt of the shotgun with her hand. She gripped it with both hands and then pumped the handle. And then a thought dawned on her. Shoot him and Isabel could be lost forever.

Perez spat in her direction, those snakelike eyes bearing down on her. Chicken. He was daring her to shoot.

And then, Joshua whirled around the van and tackled Perez.

Alice pushed up to her feet in a swift motion, shotgun in hand. Joshua had Perez on the ground in front of her. She fired off a kick, connecting with Perez's thigh as he writhed on the ground underneath the bigger man's heft. She tossed the shotgun aside and pulled zip cuffs from her hip pocket.

Joshua shifted position enough to allow her access. She jammed her knee into Perez's back and hauled his arms behind his back. He spat and cursed as she zip cuffed him. When the dust settled, he was going to have a nasty headache. And he was going to spend the rest of his life in jail.

"I'll be right back," Joshua said and she knew he'd be securing the driver and checking for additional threat inside the van.

"Where is she?" Alice asked, forcing Perez onto his knees.

"You think I'm telling you, bitch?" Perez spat.

Alice walked around to face him, needing to look into his eyes. Then she remembered the license plate number and she knew in her heart that she would find Isabel. "You don't need to."

"I have three girls in the back of the van," Joshua shouted.

There was a faint wail of sirens in the distance. She picked up the shotgun and aimed the barrel at a spot on Perez's forehead. "Give me a reason to shoot."

THE SUN WAS rising and the forecast said the cold front would break later that morning. Warmer weather was on its way.

Fischer had run the license and produced an address. The address belonged to a middle-aged dentist.

Perez and his men were in the minivan in front of Joshua's Jeep as they blazed toward the home of the dentist across town.

"We're bringing her home today," Joshua said quietly, his gaze focused on the road ahead.

She wanted to believe those five words so badly her heart ached.

"I sent Ryder for the boys," he added.

"There are no words to thank you for everything you've done for me," Alice said and she meant it.

"She'll want to see them and your family deserves to be together." He turned right behind the minivan.

The street was quiet and in the part of town with expansive front yards and large two-story houses. Disgust rippled through Alice as she thought about the horrors going on behind the doors of at least one perfect-looking house with a manicured lawn.

"I need to tell you something," he said.

"Okay."

"I've been offered a job at the FBI."

"Is that why you went out of town? To interview?" she asked.

"Yes."

"Why didn't you tell me before?" she asked, trying to block the hurt that came with him keeping a secret.

"Before I met you that was my dream job. Now, I'm not so sure." Red brake lights illuminated in front of them as the minivan stopped in front of a huge house with white siding and black shutters. There was a large concrete porch. Everything looked so peaceful, so suburban.

Men exited the minivan and circled the house as Alice jumped out of the passenger seat of Joshua's Jeep. She barely heard him say something about them talking later over the sound of her hammering heart. For one, Joshua could be leaving soon for a new job. Her heart didn't even want to go there. And then there was the obvious anxiety that came with a bust.

The dentist was about to go down.

Fischer stopped Alice before she walked onto the property.

"Let me go in," she pleaded.

"I'm not here to stop you. I'm here to thank you," he said.

She bit back her shock. "Okay."

"I mean it," Fischer said. "The devotion you have toward this girl who you obviously love tells me that you're an amazing mother to the boys."

"Thank you," she said, noticing he hadn't said *our* boys. And it was just as well. Her heart belonged to another man anyway.

"If you ever need anything, you know where to find me. Now it's my job to warn you to stay back," he said and then turned toward the house.

She understood what he was really saying. He couldn't technically allow her to be part of what was about to go down but he could look the other way.

Alice stalked around the porch, trying to get a view of the layout of the house. Joshua was right behind her, his calming presence keeping her from losing it. This was it. Isabel was here. And she was taking her home. Only where was that now? Her heart said with Joshua.

Bam. Bam. Bam. The sound of an agent banging on the front door echoed in the crisp morning air. The sun warmed her back as she heard the door open.

A man cried out as agents stormed the place, pushing past him, searching for Isabel. One of the men stayed back to deal with the dentist.

Alice was supposed to wait, but she couldn't. With

Joshua's steadying force behind her, she flew toward the front door.

The dentist was already on his knees, his hands clasped on top of his head, and it took everything inside Alice not to hurt him the way he hurt others. He looked like someone she'd see at the library browsing, not a child molester. But then, experience had taught her that there was no type.

"I never meant to hurt her," he repeated over and over again as he must've realized his life was going to be spent behind bars.

Isabel might be in one of the bedrooms and all those would most likely be upstairs, so Alice darted toward the staircase. As she ran up the first stair, she saw her and froze. Isabel looked frightened and weak next to the agent helping her at the top of the stairs. But when she spotted Alice, her face changed.

They met in the middle of the stairwell and embraced.

"You're safe now," Alice said, tears streaming down her face as she held Isabel in her arms.

"I knew you'd find me," Isabel said softly, crying.

"You're coming home."

With those words, the teen sobbed.

JOSHUA WANTED EVERYTHING to be perfect for Alice, Isabel and the boys. He called ahead to the ranch and made arrangements for everyone to stay there a few days while waiting outside the hospital room.

Isabel needed to be examined by a doctor for forensic evidence purposes and there was a counselor on hand to begin the process of guiding her toward recovering from the horrible ordeal she'd endured. She was strong and that girl deserved to have the world at her fingertips. He would do everything in his power to ensure she got it.

Then there was Alice. Also strong and so tough on the exterior with such heart and tenderness on the inside. He'd never met a woman like her before and his heart said he never would again. Which was why he was determined to keep her in his life one way or the other.

The flurry of activity in her room had slowed and a nurse finally exited, saying she was ready to leave.

He stepped inside Isabel's room. She was smiling through tears and talking quietly with Alice, who had introduced them earlier.

"Are you ladies ready to go home?" he asked, and he meant his home—a home he wanted to share with them.

"Yes," Alice said as Isabel nodded.

THE STEAKS ON the grill smelled amazing. It was Sunday supper at the O'Brien ranch and the whole clan had turned out to send Alice and the kids off as they prepared to go back to Tucson the next morning.

Fingerprints and DNA found at the ranch matched Perez and his men and all were facing spending the rest of their lives in jail.

Joshua had spent the past week getting to know Isabel and he'd developed fatherly instincts he didn't know had existed before. He'd finally taken the time to unpack boxes at his place on the ranch and Alice and Isabel seemed to enjoy decorating together. Even Denali had made fast friends with Isabel, but then she really was a sweet teenager.

He glanced across the lawn and his heart was full. Tommy was there and he'd offered Alice a job if she ever wanted to come back to Bluff.

Alice had practically forced Joshua to take the job at the FBI and he'd be heading to Quantico for twenty weeks of training next week.

And yet, his heart knew he would never set foot on that plane.

He located Alice, who was standing next to his favorite tree and made a beeline toward her. She glanced up, saw him coming and her smile eased some of his overwrought nerves.

Taking her in his arms, he whispered three words he'd been needing say all morning, "I love you."

There was a pause before Alice said, "I love you, Joshua O'Brien."

That was all he needed to hear.

"I don't know how I'll survive being so far away," she said.

"Then, don't leave."

She pulled back and examined his face. It seemed like she was checking to see if she could believe her ears. "I want to stay. But it's complicated with the kids."

"It doesn't have to be." He bent down on one knee and produced a little red box from his pocket. He opened it and the diamond sparkled as though he'd captured Christmas in a box. "If you'll have me, Alice Green, I'd like to marry you."

She looked directly into his eyes. "No one has ever made me feel the way you do. I can't imagine loving anyone more but—"

"Don't say anything else until you hear me out."

She nodded.

"I love you, Alice. I've never felt this way before about another person. I love our boys and Isabel, this ranch. You and the kids are what have been missing here for me. And I want to spend the rest of our lives together, on this land, bringing up our children. There's a lot to figure out but we have all the time we need. Will you do me the honor of being my wife?"

She kissed him and they both glanced over at Isabel who was already nodding her head. The half-heart necklace she wore sparkled in the sunlight, made whole by the one around Alice's neck.

Alice turned back to Joshua. "With everything in my heart, yes. You, this place, have felt like home from day one. I can't wait to make a life together here."

The rest of his brothers crowded around, celebration in the air.

And for the first time in his life, Joshua felt like he was home.

* * * * *

Look for more books in
USA TODAY *bestselling author Barb Han's*
series CATTLEMEN CRIME CLUB
throughout 2017.

You'll find them wherever
Mills & Boon Intrigue books are sold!

Steve did something he hadn't done in twenty years of law enforcement: lowered his weapon in shock.

"Rosalyn?"

She reached up and lowered the hood of her windbreaker as she turned completely around.

It was her. Beautiful black hair, gorgeous blue eyes. Even the splattering of freckles over her nose. Rosalyn was alive.

Which was impossible because he'd just ID'd her dead body a few hours ago. Steve didn't care. By whatever miracle she was here—and he would get her to explain it all, no doubt—he would take it.

He holstered his weapon and pulled her into his arms. Then yanked her back immediately, looking closer at the rest of her body.

Rosalyn was here. She was alive.

And unless he was very, very wrong, she was definitely pregnant.

BATTLE TESTED

BY
JANIE CROUCH

MILLS & BOON

First Published in Great Britain 2016
By Mills & Boon, an imprint of HarperCollins*Publishers*
1 London Bridge Street, London, SE1 9GF

© 2016 Janie Crouch

ISBN: 978-0-263-92851-8

46-0117

Our policy is to use papers that are natural, renewable and recyclable products and made from wood grown in sustainable forests. The logging and manufacturing processes conform to the legal environmental regulations of the country of origin.

Printed and bound in Spain
by CPI, Barcelona

Janie Crouch has loved to read romance her whole life. The award-winning author cut her teeth on Mills & Boon Romance novels as a preteen, then moved on to a passion for romantic suspense as an adult. Janie lives with her husband and four children overseas. She enjoys traveling, long-distance running, movie watching, knitting and adventure/ obstacle racing. You can find out more about her at www.janiecrouch.com.

This book is dedicated to my aunt Donna. You are a blessing to me and so many others. Thank you for all the times you brushed my hair (because goodness knows I didn't do it) and loved me like a second mother. And for teaching me that romance books are the best books.

Chapter One

Rosalyn Mellinger had reached her breaking point.

She was exhausted, frightened and about to run out of money.

Sitting in a diner in Pensacola, Florida, one she'd chosen because she could see both the front customer door and the rear employee entrance from her corner booth, she huddled around the third cup of coffee she'd had with her meager meal, stretching out her stay here as long as possible.

Although sitting with her back to the wall didn't help when she had no idea what the person who stalked her looked like. She tensed every time the tiny bell chimed signaling someone new had come through the door, like it had just now.

The couple in their mid-eighties, entering and shuffling slowly to a table, were definitely not the Watcher.

But she knew he was around. She knew because she would get a note later tonight—or an email or a text or a phone call—that would say something about her meal here. About what she'd eaten or the name of her waitress or how she'd used sweetener in her coffee rather than sugar.

Some sort of frightening detail that let her know the Watcher had been nearby. Just like he had been for the last five months. She scanned faces of other patrons to see who might be studying her but couldn't find anyone who looked like they were paying her any attention.

It always seemed to be that way. But still the Watcher would know details as if he had been sitting here at the booth with Rosalyn. And would mention the details in a message to her, usually a note slid under her door in the middle of the night.

Rosalyn clutched her coffee cup, trying to get her breathing under control.

Or maybe the Watcher wouldn't say anything about the diner at all. Maybe he wouldn't contact her for days. That happened sometimes too. Rosalyn never knew what to expect and it kept her on the precipice of hysteria.

All she knew for certain was the constant acid of fear burning in her gut.

Her waitress, Jessie, who couldn't have been more than eighteen or nineteen years old, wiped the table next to Rosalyn's, then came to stand by her booth. The kid looked decidedly uncomfortable.

"I'm sorry, ma'am, but my manager said I would have to ask you to leave if you're not going to order anything else. The dinner crowd is coming in."

The burn in Rosalyn's belly grew at the thought of leaving the diner, although she didn't know why. She was no safer from the Watcher in here than she was somewhere else.

He'd found her again last night. Rosalyn had been in Pensacola for four days, staying at a different run-down hotel each night. Three nights had passed with no message, no notes, and she'd let just the slightest bit of hope enter her heart that she had lost the Watcher permanently.

Heaven knew she had driven around enough times to get rid of anyone who followed. Hours' worth of circles and sudden turns around town to lose any tails. Then she had parked at a hotel before sneaking across strip malls and a small park to *another* hotel about a mile away just in case there was some sort of tracker on her car. It seemed to have worked for three nights.

Rosalyn thought maybe she had figured it out. That the Watcher had been tracking her car and that's how he always found her. She would gladly leave the car rotting in the wrong hotel parking lot if it meant she could get away from the man who stalked her.

But then last night a note had been slipped under the hotel door as she slept.

When she saw the envelope lying so deceptively innocently on the floor of her hotel by the door as she woke up this morning, she promptly vomited into the trash can by the bed.

She finally found the strength to get up and open the unsealed envelope and read the note. Handwritten, like them all.

Sorry I haven't been around for a few days. I know you must have missed me. I missed you.

She almost vomited again, but there was nothing left in her stomach.

She took the note and put it in the cardboard box where she kept all the other notes. Then she meticulously put the box back inside her large duffel bag. From her smaller tote bag, the one she always kept with her, she took out her notebook. With shaky hands she logged the date and time she found the note, and its contents.

She'd taken her bags and gone back to her car—a tracker there obviously wasn't the problem—and driven toward the beach and ended up at this diner. She needed to get on the move again. But she didn't know how—her savings from when she'd had a decent-paying job as an accountant were gone. And she didn't know where she would go even if she had had money.

The Watcher found her no matter where she went.

Sometimes she was convinced he was in her head since he seemed to know everything she did and thought. But that would mean she was crazy.

An idea that was becoming more and more acceptable.

Rosalyn rubbed her eyes. Exhaustion weighed every muscle in her body.

"Ma'am?"

None of this was her waitress's fault. She turned to the girl, who seemed so much younger even though she was probably only five or six years less than Rosalyn's twenty-four. "Of course. I'm sorry, Jessie. Just let me pay my bill and get my stuff together."

Jessie shuffled her feet. "No need to pay anything. I already took care of that for you. Pay it forward and all that."

Rosalyn wanted to argue. Jessie had been working hard the three hours Rosalyn had been in the booth. The girl was probably saving up for college and needed the money.

But the truth was, Rosalyn was down to her last twenty dollars. Not having to pay six dollars for her meal would help a lot.

Being able to live a normal life and return to a regular job would help a lot more, but Jessie's gesture was still touching.

"Thank you," Rosalyn whispered to the girl. "I truly appreciate it."

"I can probably hold my manager off for another thirty minutes if that will help you. I'm sorry I can't do more."

"No. I'll be fine. Thanks."

The girl nodded and walked away.

Rosalyn wondered if she would read about her conversation with Jessie later tonight in the note the Watcher left her. Or even worse, if Jessie would end up dead. That had happened three months ago with the detective in Shreveport, Louisiana, when she'd passed through. Rosalyn had taken a chance and told him what was happening and found, to her surprise, that he believed her. Detective Johnson was the one who suggested she keep all the notes and take photos of any texts and try to record any phone messages. He was the one who got her the notebook and told her to write down everything that happened.

The relief to find someone who believed her, who didn't think she was just out for attention like her family had, was overwhelming. Finally the feeling of not being utterly alone.

Unfortunately, Detective Johnson—a healthy fifty-year-old man—suddenly died of a heart attack two days after meeting with Rosalyn. He was found in his bed. Natural causes, the newspaper said. Rosalyn was heartbroken that she'd so unfortunately lost the one person who had listened and believed her.

Until she received an anonymous email the next day with a link to a drug called succinylcholine. A drug that in a large enough dose caused heart attacks but was virtually untraceable in a victim's system.

Detective Johnson's death had been no accident.

Neither had the mechanic's—a man named Shawn who had been super nice and repaired Rosalyn's car at a deeply discounted rate a month ago in Memphis. She mentioned to him that she was on the run. Didn't want to say more than that, but he asked. Shawn's sister had an ex who had turned violent and terrorized her. Shawn recognized some of the same symptoms in Rosalyn. He pressed and Rosalyn gave him some details. Not all of them, but enough. He invited her to his mother's house for dinner, explaining the importance of not going through something like this alone.

Rosalyn, almost desperate for a friend, agreed. When she came back to the shop that night, she found the place surrounded by cops.

Shawn had been a victim of a "random act of violence" as he was closing up his garage. He was dead.

She still had the newspaper clipping that had been slipped under her door the next morning.

Rosalyn rubbed her stomach against the burn. She hadn't spoken to a single person about the Watcher since that day. She'd just kept on the run, trying to stay ahead of him.

He'd found her again. Pensacola was the sixth town she'd moved to in five months. He always found her. She wasn't sure how.

Exhaustion flooded her as she grabbed her tote bag and walked toward the door. Jessie gave her a small wave from behind the servers' station and Rosalyn smiled as best she could. She was almost to the entrance when she stopped and turned around, walking back to Jessie.

The girl looked concerned. For Rosalyn or *because* of her, Rosalyn couldn't tell. Rosalyn took six dollars out of her bag.

"Here." She handed the money to Jessie. "Paying for my meal was very kind and I'm sure it will get you karma points. But I know you're working hard, so I'll pay for my own meal."

"Are you sure?"

No, she wasn't sure. All she knew was that she couldn't take a chance that something would happen to this pretty young woman because she'd spotted Rosalyn six dollars' worth of salad and chicken.

"Yes." She pressed the money into Jessie's hand. "Thanks again, though."

Rosalyn turned and walked out the door feeling more lonely than she had in…ever.

She couldn't do this anymore.

What good was it to run if the Watcher was just going

to find her again? What good did it do to talk to people if any ties she made were just going to get them hurt?

And at what point would the Watcher stop toying with her and just finish her off? Rosalyn had no doubt her death was his endgame. She just didn't know when or how.

Maybe she should just save him the trouble and do it herself. At least then she would have some measure of control.

She looked down the block toward the beach. She would go sit there. Think things through. Try to figure out a plan.

Even if that plan meant taking her own life. That had to be better than allowing innocent people to die because of her. Or living in constant fear with no end in sight.

She began walking toward the beach. She would sit on the sand, watch the sunset. Because damn it, if this was going to be her last day on earth—either by her own hand or the Watcher's—she wanted to feel the sun on her face one last time.

Beyond that, she had no idea what to do.

Chapter Two

Steve Drackett, director of the Omega Sector Critical Response Division, was doing nothing. He couldn't remember the last time that had happened.

And even more so, he was doing nothing in a tiki-themed bar on the Florida Panhandle. In *flip-flops*.

He was damn certain that had *never* happened.

It was his first real vacation in ten years. After his wife died twelve years ago, there hadn't been much point in them. Then he'd become director of the Critical Response Division of Omega—an elite law enforcement agency made up of the best agents the country had to offer—and there hadn't been time.

But here he was on the Florida Panhandle, two days into a weeklong vacation for which his team had pitched in and gotten for him. Celebrating his twenty years of being in law enforcement.

And to provide him with a little R & R after he was almost blown up last month by a psychopath intent on burning everything and everyone around her.

Either way, he'd take it. Home in Colorado Springs could still be pretty cold, even in May. Pensacola was already edging toward hot. Thus the flip-flops.

Steve sat at the far end of the bar, back to the wall, where he had a nice view of both the baseball game on TV and the sunset over the ocean, along with an early-evening thundershower that was coming in, through the windows at the front of the bar. It also gave him direct line of sight of the entrance, probably not necessary here but an occupational hazard nonetheless.

The cold beer in his hands and an order of wings next to him on the bar had Steve just about remembering how to unwind. Nothing here demanded his attention. The bar was beginning to fill up but everyone seemed relaxed for the most part. The hum of voices, laughter, glasses clinking was enjoyable.

As someone whose job on most days was literally saving the world, the tiki bar was a nice change.

Then the woman walked through the door.

He glanced at her—as did just about every pair of male eyes in the bar—when she rushed in trying to get out of the sudden Florida storm. Another couple entered right behind her for the same reason, but Steve paid them little attention.

She was small. Maybe five-four to his six-one. Wavy black hair that fell well past her shoulders. Slender to the point of being too skinny. Mid-twenties.

Gorgeous.

Steve forced his eyes away, although his body stayed attuned to her.

She didn't belong here—he had already summed that up in just a few moments. Not here in a tiki bar where the patrons were either on vacation or trying to just relax on a Sunday evening.

She wasn't wearing some flirty skirt or shorts and tank top or any of the modes of dress that bespoke enjoying herself on a Florida beach in mid-May. Not that there was anything wrong with how she was dressed: khaki pants and a blue button-down shirt. No flip-flops for this black-haired beauty, or any other type of sandals. Instead she wore athletic shoes. Plain. White.

Her bag was also too large for a casual outing or catching a couple of beers for an hour or two. And clutched too tightly to her.

This woman looked ready to run. From what or to what, Steve had no idea.

Steve had been out of active agent duty for the last ten years. His job now was behind a desk on most days. A big desk, an important one. But a desk nonetheless. He didn't need to be an agent in the field to know the most important thing about the woman who'd just walked into the bar: she was trouble.

Since trouble was the very thing he was trying to get away from here in flip-flop Florida, Steve turned back to his beer and wings. Back to the game.

But as he finished his food, he found his eyes floating back to her.

She was obviously over twenty-one, so it was legal for her to be here. If she wanted to take off in a hurry—with her oversize tote-type bag—as long as she wasn't doing anything illegal, it was her own business.

She didn't want to buy a drink—he noticed that first. But as the storm lingered, then grew worse, she obviously knew she'd have to or else go back out in it. She ordered a soda.

She sat with her back to the wall.

She tried not to draw attention to herself in any way.

She was scared.

Steve finished one beer and started another. He flexed his flip-flop-enclosed toes.

Not his monkeys. Not his circus.

This woman was not his problem, but he still couldn't stop glancing her way every once in a while. She barely moved. Unfortunately, Steve wasn't the only one whose attention she had caught. Just about every guy in the place was aware of her presence.

At first men waited and watched. Was she meeting

someone? A husband? Boyfriend? When it became obvious she wasn't, they slowly began circling. Maybe not literally but definitely in their minds.

Then some began circling literally.

A couple of local boys who had been here since before Steve arrived—and had been tossing beers back the whole time—worked their nerve up to go sit next to the woman. She didn't give much indication that she was interested, but that didn't deter them.

Since the baseball game was over, someone turned on the jukebox and a few couples were dancing to some Jimmy Buffett song. One of the guys stood and asked the woman to dance but she shook her head no. He reached down and grabbed her hands and tried to pull her to a standing position, obviously thinking she was playing hard to get.

Steve could read her tension from all the way across the bar, but the guys talking to her obviously couldn't.

He should leave now. He knew he should just walk away. The boys weren't going to get too out of hand. As soon as the woman put them down hard, they would leave her alone.

She was trouble. He knew it. He should go.

He sighed as he put money on the bar for his meal and began to walk toward the woman and the two men who were now both trying to get her to dance. He hadn't become the director of one of the most elite law enforcement groups in the country by walking away from trouble.

He stepped close to the first local guy, deliberately invading his space. The way the guy was invading the woman's.

"Excuse me, fellas. The lady doesn't want to dance."

"How do you know?" The other guy snickered. "Are you her dad?"

The woman's eyes—a beautiful shade of blue that stood

out in sharp juxtaposition against her dark hair—flew to
Steve's. She winced in apology at the crack about his age.

Steve was probably fifteen years older than the woman.
Not quite old enough to be her father, but probably too old
to be anything else to her.

"No, not her father. Just someone old enough and sober
enough to realize when a woman is uncomfortable."

"She's not—" The guy stopped and really looked at the
woman then—the way she was clutching her bag, discom-
fiture clear on her face.

"The lady doesn't want to dance," Steve said again.

The local guy and his buddy released the woman, murmuring apologies. Steve stepped back relieved he wasn't
going to have to make some show of strength. He could've.
Could've had both men unconscious on the ground before
they were even aware what sort of trouble they were facing. But the guys hadn't meant any harm.

Steve nodded at the woman as the locals walked away.
He didn't step any closer or try to talk to her. His flirting
skills were rusty at best and this lady obviously wasn't here
to scope out men. Steve turned to make his way back to
his seat only to find someone had already taken his place.

Looked like it was time to go.

That was fine. It wasn't like Steve had any grand plans
for his evening here in the tiki bar. He began walking toward the door.

"Thank you."

He heard her soft voice as the black-haired beauty's
hand touched his arm. Steve stopped and turned toward
her.

He smiled. It felt a little unpracticed. "I don't think they
meant any harm, but it was no problem."

"There was a time I would've let them both have it, but
I just don't seem to have it in me lately." She looked a little
surprised that she was even talking to him.

She was skittish, scared. She'd been that way since the moment she'd walked in. It made him want to wrap an arm around her, pull her close and tell her to take a breath. He'd protect her from whatever demons she was trying to fight.

It surprised him a little that he felt that way. His entire life had been spent helping people, first as an FBI agent, then as he was recruited into Omega Sector. But usually he was more at a distance, less personal.

He already felt personal with this woman and he didn't even know her name.

"I'm sure you could've handled them. I just was doing my fatherly duty."

She snorted and humor lit her blue eyes. "Father, my ass. You're what? Thirty-nine? Forty?"

"Forty-one."

"Oh. Well, he should've said *grandfather*, then."

Her smile was breathtaking. Steve couldn't stop himself from taking a step toward her. "I'm Steve Drackett."

She shook his outstretched hand. He knew the thought that a flash of heat hit them both as their skin touched was both melodramatic and sentimental. Steve was neither of those things.

But he still felt the heat.

"I'm Rosalyn."

No last name. He didn't press. It was just another sign she was trouble, but Steve somehow couldn't bring himself to care.

"Can an old man buy you a drink or something?"

She studied him hard as they finally released hands. They were halfway between the bar and the door. He honestly wasn't sure which way she'd choose. To stay with him or to leave.

She ended up choosing both.

"May I ask you something?" She slid her tote more fully onto her shoulder. She had to step a little closer so they could hear each other over the noise in the bar. He found himself thankful for the chaos around them.

"Sure."

"Are you some sort of psycho? A killer or deranged stalker or both?"

She asked the question so seriously Steve couldn't help but laugh. "Nope. Scout's honor." He held up his hand in what he was sure was an incorrect Scout salute. "I'm an upstanding member of society. Although you know if I was a crazy killer, I probably wouldn't answer that question honestly."

She shrugged, her eyes back to being haunted. "I know. I guess I just wanted you to tell me so I could see if I would believe you."

"Do you?"

She smiled so sadly it damn near broke his heart. "I think so. Or maybe I just don't care anymore. And to answer your question, yes, you can buy me a drink. But let's get out of here."

Chapter Three

Rosalyn knew her actions bordered on reckless. Even if she hadn't known she had a deranged stalker following her every move, leaving a bar with a man she'd just met would still have been pretty stupid.

He'd laughed—in a kind way, but still obviously thinking she was joking—when she'd asked if he was a killer or crazy. But like he'd said, no true villain would give her an honest answer about that.

Actually, she believed the Watcher would. If she ever met him face-to-face and asked him outright if he was her stalker, she believed he might actually tell her.

Steve Drackett wasn't the Watcher. He might be an ordinary garden-variety psycho, but he wasn't the psycho she was desperately attempting to escape right now.

And in that case, she was willing to take her chances with him.

She looked up at him as he led her to the door. He had joked about being a grandpa but that couldn't have been further from the truth. His brown hair might be graying just the slightest bit at the temples, but that was the only sign whatsoever that he wasn't a man fifteen years younger. His green eyes seemed kind, at least to her, but the rest of his face was hard and unforgiving. Stark cheekbones, strong chin. Definitely not a pretty face but very much a handsome one.

His body was well honed—the black T-shirt Steve wore left no doubt he was in excellent physical shape. His khaki shorts were quite appropriate for a bar in Florida on a May evening, but she doubted it was what he normally wore. She was positive the flip-flops weren't.

"If you're not a psychopath, what do you do, Steve?" she asked as they walked out the door. Humid air from the coast blasted them. The storm had moved out to sea, but dampness still hovered everywhere, a sure sign another storm would be coming.

"Present occupation is beach bum. I'm here on vacation from Colorado."

They walked down the steps. "Mountains. Nice. I've never been there. Are you a bum there, too?"

He hesitated slightly before he smiled. "Worse. Management."

He didn't want to tell her what he did for a living. Okay, fair enough. She hadn't told him her last name.

Of course, she was doing it for his own safety.

"Are you from around here?" Steve asked. "Do you have a bar you'd suggest?"

She didn't want to go to a bar. Not somewhere the Watcher could hear them, see them.

"How about a six-pack and walk on the beach?"

He smiled down at her. "That might break some open-beverage-container laws, but I'm willing to risk it."

Rosalyn didn't know exactly what she'd been expecting when she'd left the bar with Steve, but the next few hours were not it.

They bought their beers and sat alone, where no one—not even the Watcher—could possibly hear them.

And they talked. About everything and nothing.

He told her about his wife—his high school sweetheart—who had died in a car accident twelve years ago. About places he'd traveled. Even a little bit about his job, that he was a manager in some sort of division office and how he sometimes felt more like he was babysitting than anything else.

Rosalyn was vague without being dishonest. She told him she had a mother and sister but wasn't close to either—an understatement. She told him a little about her college years and her job as an accountant. When he made a joke about the size of her bag, she told him she never went anywhere without it. Told him she was taking some time off, traveling around a little bit, trying to "find herself."

She somehow managed not to laugh hysterically as she said it.

Steve was a good listener, a friendly talker. He never made a move on her or made her feel uncomfortable. He seemed to be both completely at ease but at the same time completely surprised at their continued, comfortable conversation.

He obviously didn't spend a lot of time picking up strangers at a bar.

At some point deep in the night—it had to have been nearly four o'clock but Rosalyn wasn't sure—it began to rain again, gently, but enough that they couldn't stay here on the beach any longer.

It looked like her reprieve was over. She needed to make her way back to her car. Maybe she'd catch a couple hours of sleep in it—the thought of being out in the open like that made her skin crawl, but what choice did she have? She was out of money. A hotel, even a cheap one, was no longer an option.

She stood and Steve got up beside her, helping her. She smiled at him. "Thanks for hanging with me. It was nice to have a peaceful night."

"Been a long time since you had one?"

She was tempted to tell him about the Watcher. To share while they had complete privacy. But knew she couldn't.

Some middle-management guy from some business in Colorado couldn't remedy this situation.

"Seems like it," she said instead.

"Anything I can help with?"

She looked up at him. He was a nice guy. A nice, hot, utterly delectable guy. For the hundredth time that evening she wished she had met Steve under different circumstances.

"I'm fine. But thank you for asking." She smiled, trying to make it as authentic as possible. Trying not to think about the darkness that hovered all around them that she would have to face alone in just a few minutes.

As if the weather could hear her thoughts, it started raining a little harder.

He touched her gently near her elbow. "I need to tell you something I probably should've mentioned earlier but couldn't figure out how to do it without coming across like a jerk."

She braced herself for bad news. "Okay."

"My beach bungalow is about two hundred yards that way." He pointed up the beach. "It's a ridiculous room. Some sort of romance package. My colleagues at work chipped in and got it for me."

She didn't know what she'd expected him to say, but that wasn't it. "Oh."

"You're welcome to come in. Get out of the rain. No expectations or anything like that." He shrugged, the awkwardness on his tense face adorable. He obviously didn't want her to feel pressured. "The peaceful night doesn't have to end right now."

Rosalyn looked out at the darkness again. She knew what waited for her there. Fear. Isolation. Panic.

Steve reached up and tucked a damp strand of her hair behind her ear. He didn't say anything. Didn't try to talk her into it or put pressure on her in any way. Just stood silently, letting her know he was there if she wanted to go with him but he was fine if she didn't.

The lack of pressure, more than anything, helped her make the decision.

"Okay, just for tonight."

She couldn't take a chance and let the Watcher find her again. Find Steve.

He smiled and took her hand. They began to run through the sand toward his room. Like he'd said, it wasn't far.

The oceanside bungalow was nice inside: sort of what one would expect for the romance package on the beach. A king-size bed with a teal bedspread and canopy roof. A couch and chair over in the reading-nook section.

And a huge heart-shaped Jacuzzi tub in the far corner.

Rosalyn looked over at Steve, who grinned sheepishly.

"You failed to mention the giant heart-shaped Jacuzzi in the middle of your room."

Steve laughed. "I wasn't sure if it would work in my favor or against me."

"Are you sure you weren't supposed to be on your honeymoon here or something?"

Steve laughed again, crossing to the bathroom to grab them both a towel to dry off from the rain. Rosalyn set her tote bag down on the chair in the sitting area.

"Honestly, I just booked a normal room in the hotel section. When I got here, I found out I had gotten an upgrade—thanks to my colleagues chipping in. I'm sure they scoped out pictures and knew exactly what they were getting for me. Including the huge roll of condoms." He rolled his eyes, gesturing to the sparkling box on the nightstand. Rosalyn couldn't help but laugh.

"It's nice that they like you so much."

Steve shrugged. "They like to get rid of me for a week, that's for sure. And a not-so-subtle hint to come back more relaxed."

She had no doubt Steve was well respected, a good man. Guilt over the danger she was putting him in washed over her.

"Hey, what's going on?" He saw her face and walked over so he was standing in front of her. He put his thumb under her chin when she wouldn't look at him. "Do you regret coming here? Feel uncomfortable? If so, I can give you a ride wherever you need to go."

She didn't regret coming. She wanted to stay. Wanted more than just the safe haven Steve was offering.

She wanted him.

He looked so big standing in front of her. So able to take care of himself. Not someone who could be taken by surprise by someone else.

But she knew the Watcher didn't play fair. He'd taught her that.

"No, I'm not uncomfortable with you. The opposite, in fact. I just—" She stopped, not knowing what to say. She couldn't explain. Couldn't take the chance.

"What?" he asked gently.

"It's not good for you to be here with me, Steve. I'm afraid I'll only bring heartache for you." Or worse.

"Are you married?" he asked.

"No." She shook her head. "Never have been."

He took a step closer. She could smell his damp skin, the saltiness of the sea air and something that was distinctly male. She breathed in deeply.

"Are you running from the law?"

"No," she whispered as he moved closer again, his body now so close to hers she could feel the heat. She leaned closer, unable to stop herself.

"Then I don't think there's any reason at all for you to leave this room if you don't want to."

His lips closed the inches between them and she couldn't

think of any response even if there'd been a good one anyway. Instead she just gave herself over to the kiss.

If she was going to lose everything, she was going to have this one night with this gorgeous, strong man first. Tomorrow be damned.

The heat all but consumed them both. Her arms reached up to wrap around his shoulders, then his neck. She clutched at his hair, too impassioned to be gentle.

Steve didn't mind at all. His arms circled her waist, then reached lower to cup her hips and pull her up and into him.

Both of them gasped.

He took possession of her mouth. There was no other word for it. *Possession.* His tongue stroked against hers and fire licked at them both. Her fingers linked behind his neck to capture him. Not that he seemed interested in being anywhere but pressed up against her.

"Rosalyn." Her name was reverent on his lips.

She began walking forward, causing him to move backward toward the bed. His arms were still wrapped around her hips making sure they were fully pressed together. When his knees finally hit the bed and he fell backward, he lifted her—as if she weighed nothing at all—and pulled her on top of him.

"Are you sure this is what you want?" he murmured. "It's still okay if you just want to be here. Nothing has to happen."

He would say that while she was lying flat on top of him? They weren't undressed yet, but Rosalyn had no doubt they would be soon. In her experience most guys would call her a tease—or much worse—if she decided to call a halt to everything at this point.

"You would stop now if I asked you to?"

He threaded his hands in her hair and pulled her back so he could see her more clearly.

"Of course. Is that what you want?"

"No. Just most guys would give a woman a hard time if she decided to change her mind now."

"Honey, a real man accepts that a woman can change her mind at any time and respects the word *no* if he hears it."

Was it possible to fall a little bit in love with someone you'd known for only a few hours?

Rosalyn sat up, her legs straddling Steve's hips. She unbuttoned her shirt and slowly peeled it over her shoulders. "Well, thanks for asking, but I have no desire to stop." She pulled her sneakers and socks off and threw them over the side of the bed.

Steve crossed his arms under his head and just watched her. "Thank goodness. I would've stopped, but I sure as hell didn't want to."

She gasped as he sat up suddenly, forcing them even closer together. He spun and scooted them farther on the bed before dropping her down so he was now on top. She helped him discard his shirt, then pulled him back down to her.

His lips met hers again. No, she wasn't interested in stopping. She was already coming apart inside. She held on to Steve and let his lovemaking chase away the demons that weren't far outside the door.

THEY DIDN'T LEAVE the bungalow the entire next day, which was fine with Rosalyn. Who needed the beach? Especially on a cloudy, dreary day. Instead they made use of the bed and the couch and very good use of the heart-shaped hot tub. Steve ordered room service for every meal.

Steve's colleagues might have meant the room as a joke—and heaven knew it wasn't tasteful in its decorating—but Rosalyn loved every bit of it.

It was her own hideaway. The Watcher obviously didn't

know she was here. And as long as she stayed inside, there was no way he would find her.

She wondered if she could talk Steve into staying in the room forever. She looked over at him sleeping in the bed next to her right now, so late at night. His sexy face relaxed in sleep. It hadn't always been that way. She'd seen his face tensed in passion or smiling as he talked to her and told her a story from his past. She'd also seen the concern when she caught him studying her when he thought she wasn't paying attention.

He was worried about her.

If he knew about the Watcher, he'd be less concerned about her well-being and more concerned with his own. Might even ask her to leave right away.

Every person she'd told about the Watcher who believed her had wound up dead. She wouldn't take that chance with Steve. She'd just live in this little bungalow of fantasy until it didn't exist anymore. Then she would go.

But she knew she'd be leaving a little part of her heart behind when she did. She rolled onto her side so she could study him more fully. She reached out and stroked his hair by his ear, drawing her fingers down his cheek. He turned his face toward her, seeking her touch even in his sleep.

She should sleep now too. It had been a pleasurable but exhausting day and now it was late. Who knew what tomorrow would bring.

Her eyes were drifting closed when she heard the sound.

It didn't wake Steve. Why would he? It was just the barest whisper of a noise. If her body and mind hadn't already been programmed to listen for it—to fear it above all else—Rosalyn wouldn't have heard it either.

The sound of an envelope being slid under the door.

Her heart stopped and her breathing became ragged. The acid that burned in her stomach—blessedly missing

for the last day—returned with a force that caused Rosalyn to ball up on the bed.

She bit her fist, tears streaming down her face. She
didn't want to awaken Steve. If she did, she'd never be
able to keep this a secret from him.

The Watcher had found her again.

Rosalyn lay on the bed for what seemed like forever
trying to get herself under control. She finally managed
to crawl off, dropping silently to the floor, and stumbled
over to where the envelope lay.

With shaking hands she picked it up and pulled out the
paper from inside.

> If you like Steve so much, I guess I'll need to meet
> him soon.

She swallowed the sob in her throat. No. She couldn't
allow the Watcher to come after Steve. The thought gal-
vanized her into action.

Within minutes she had silently dressed and grabbed
her bag. Steve had rolled over toward her side of the bed,
as if he was seeking her missing form, but Rosalyn refused to let herself think about it. If she did, she would
never make it out.

And she had to concentrate on where she was going to
go. The time with Steve had given her the strength not to
give up her battle against the Watcher. To keep fighting.
But it hadn't given her a course of action with which to
do that. She didn't have any money and she had no plan.

She spotted Steve's wallet on the dresser. He'd used it
each time he'd paid for the food that had been delivered.
Food he wouldn't even consider letting her help pay for—
good, considering how broke she was.

Shame beat down on Rosalyn as she opened his wallet and took out the cash. One hundred and eighty-three dollars.

She didn't know how far it would get her, but at least it would get her away from here. Get the Watcher away from Steve.

She looked down at his naked back, his hips and legs tangled in the sheets. He'd never know how much he'd meant to her. What he'd given her in a time she'd needed so much.

He'd just remember her as a one-and-a-half-night stand and the woman who stole his cash. She'd become a cocktail story for him. A joking warning to his friends.

The tears leaked out of her eyes. This time she didn't even try to stop them.

Thinking about her would be distasteful for Steve.

But at least he would be alive.

Chapter Four

Six months later

"Would it be okay for us to see Steve now or should we make an appointment?" Brandon Han, Omega's top profiler, asked one of Steve's assistants in the outer office.

"Yeah, maybe we should make an appointment. For around eighteen months from now." That was Liam Goetz, leader of the hostage rescue team. "When hopefully Steve is in a better mood."

Cynthia, the assistant who kept his entire office running, laughed. "I think it's safe now."

Steve winced. Obviously nobody realized the door to his office was cracked and he could hear everything they were saying.

"Should we remove our weapons?" Liam asked.

"Why? Are you afraid you might shoot him?" Cynthia's gentle laughter didn't make Steve feel better.

"Are you kidding? I'm afraid he might take them and shoot *us*."

The topic moved on to more neutral ground: Liam's twins and Tallinn, the little girl he and his wife had adopted. Liam had pictures. Steve stopped listening.

Liam's jokes didn't bother him—Liam was always making jokes—but Brandon's initial question did. These men were an important part of the Critical Response Division's inner team. Steve's team. Moreover, they were his friends. They didn't need an appointment to see him.

But evidently they thought so given Steve's behavior over the last few months.

Rosalyn.

He ran a hand over his eyes, then turned his chair so he was facing the Rocky Mountains out the window.

When he'd awakened as the sun began to rise in Pensacola and found her gone, he'd at first thought she'd decided to walk on the beach or run out to get donuts or something. Heaven knew they hadn't left the room in a day and a half. Maybe she'd needed some air.

Then he realized all her stuff, including that giant catch-all bag she carried, was gone.

Going against his nature, Steve still gave her the benefit of the doubt. She was scared of something, he knew. He'd hoped to convince her to tell him what it was, to let him help.

Every time he'd considered broaching the subject—telling her he worked in law enforcement and could help her with whatever had her so afraid—they'd ended up making love instead.

Not that Steve had minded that. The only time he didn't see shadows floating in Rosalyn's eyes was when they were filled with passion. He had hoped to convince her to stay the rest of the week with him and during that time get her to tell him what was really going on with her. To share whatever burdens she carried. And the secrets she was obviously keeping.

Starting with her last name.

But it soon became obvious Rosalyn wasn't out to grab coffee or go for a jog. Steve had known that from the beginning, although he hadn't wanted to face it. Someone who looked over her shoulder as much as Rosalyn, who'd been so willing to stay inside the bungalow even when there was a gorgeous beach right outside, wouldn't be going out for a casual walk.

Checking his wallet confirmed it. She'd taken every bit of his cash.

She'd played him.

Even now, six months later, the thought sat heavily in his gut. The time they'd spent together hadn't meant anything to Rosalyn. He was just a means to an end.

Steve had packed up his stuff that afternoon and returned to Colorado Springs. He'd been in a bad mood ever since. Obviously something everyone was aware of, from the conversation that had just occurred outside his door.

The thing was, he would've given Rosalyn the money—more if she'd needed it—if she had let him know what was going on. Would've done it without her having sex with him or waiting until he was asleep to steal it.

But she hadn't. She'd found him to be an easy mark and taken off.

Steve stood and walked over to the plastic evidence bag on his windowsill and picked it up. It held a glass inside. One from the bungalow that he knew contained Rosalyn's fingerprints.

Steve had brought it back with him like it was some damn souvenir or something.

"Hey, boss."

Steve put the bag back down quickly. "Brandon, hi."

"Liam is showing Cynthia pictures of the twins."

Steve rolled his eyes. "Who would've thought the great womanizer would become such a family man."

Brandon joined Steve at the window. "Just takes the right woman."

Brandon had found the right woman a couple of months ago—Omega behavioral analyst Andrea Gordon—and Steve couldn't argue the change it had brought about in the man. The peace it had brought both Brandon and Andrea.

"You brought that home from Florida, right?" Brandon asked, pointing to the evidence bag. "Prints, I'm assuming. But you've never run them."

Steve shrugged. Brandon was a certified genius and a profiler. Not much got past him.

"I'm assuming something happened with a woman down there. If I had to guess, I would say a one-night stand."

Sometimes Han was spooky good at his job. Steve shrugged again. "It was Florida. And you guys did pitch in to get me the romance package."

"Then I'm assuming she took off suddenly, probably while you were unaware."

"Why do you say that?" Steve crossed back over to his desk chair.

Brandon leaned a shoulder against the wall. "You sure you want me to go into this? I didn't come here to profile you, Steve."

"No, please. Continue." Brandon was rarely wrong and Steve needed to hear what the man thought of his behavior.

"Okay, you met a woman. You were extremely interested in her. I would assume the relationship became intimate, but you didn't and still don't know much about her."

All right so far. Steve gestured for Brandon to continue.

"Something happened. Something not good. The fact that you have an evidence bag with a glass with her prints suggests that you want to know more about her. Who she is. But the fact that you haven't run them suggests that she hurt you personally in some way rather than actually committing a crime against you, in which case you would try to find and arrest her. She hurt your pride."

Actually, Rosalyn had done both, committed a crime and hurt his pride.

"And you're mad at yourself."

Steve's eyes narrowed. "Why do you say that?"

"You keep that bag in the center of the windowsill. You look out that window at least a dozen times a day. Every time you do, you're reminded of the woman who got the best of you. Who got past your guard, then hurt you. You want to remind yourself never to be weak like that again."

Steve leaned back in his chair. "I'm glad you're on our side, Han."

Brandon walked over to Steve's desk. "It's okay to want to check on her, Steve. To see if she's okay. To be concerned about her even after she did whatever she did."

Now he was getting further off course. "You getting that from an evidence bag too?"

"No. I can tell that from knowing you for so many years. Nobody just gets the drop on you. You let this woman close to you for a reason—more than just a physical one. No matter how it all ended, you're still a little concerned about her."

A picture of Rosalyn's haunted blue eyes jumped into Steve's mind but he pushed it away. Rosalyn was a consummate actress. She'd faked passion with him, then stolen his money. She was lucky he wasn't running her prints—he was sure she'd end up in the system somewhere—and having her arrested.

He told himself it was because stealing less than $200 wasn't worth the taxpayers' money needed to have her arrested and put in jail for a few months.

It had nothing to do with being concerned for her.

"Well, most of your profile of me and this situation is correct, except for the last part. I don't have any concern about her." Steve smiled, but it was stiff, as if it had been so long the muscles seemed to have forgotten how. "Just want the reminder not to be a jackass again."

"Oh man, are we profiling Steve?" Liam asked from the doorway. "I missed all the good stuff."

Liam would probably make the worst profiler ever. The

man didn't care how people thought, just wanted to understand the best way to bring down bad guys.

"Don't worry, Liam, I'll try to control myself and not
use your own weapon against you."

Liam at least had the good grace to look sheepish.
"Sorry about that, boss. I know I—"

"Don't worry about it." Steve cut him off. "I know I
haven't been the easiest person to be around for the last
few months."

"Are you kidding me? I have a wife trying to nurse newborn twins. She hasn't gotten a decent night's sleep since
they were born. You are not the grumpiest person I know."

Steve snickered. "Glad to hear I at least beat out an exhausted new mother."

"Yeah, well, I keep my weapons away from her too."
Liam grinned.

The two men took a seat. It was good to feel something
besides anger. Listening to Brandon's profile had helped
Steve realize it was time to let it all go.

Yeah, he'd been a fool and had gotten played. But now
it was time to move on.

STEVE LEFT LATE that night and was back in the office early
the next morning, as per his usual habits. Like always,
Cynthia was in the office before Steve got there.

"Morning, Steve." She handed him a stack of papers
as he came in. "I've got your overnight Washington, DC,
briefings, your weekly Omega Division Directors' update
and your Pensacola police briefings."

Steve took the papers from her. "Thanks."

As he got to the door to his office, he turned back. It
was time. Past time.

"You can stop the Pensacola PD briefings. I don't need
those anymore."

He didn't even know why he had started them in the

first place. Well, actually, he did. He figured Rosalyn would probably be arrested at some point. If she was a small-time crook preying on traveling salesmen, she would probably get arrested eventually.

What he really didn't know was what the hell he planned to do if her name came across his desk in an arrest report. Press charges himself? Or go get her released and keep her with him and make sure she never did anything that stupid again?

He shook his head, irritated with himself for his thoughts. He walked over to the evidence bag with the glass. He picked it up and carried it to the trash can by his desk. He hesitated just the briefest of moments before tossing it in.

It was time.

Steve set the division updates—the weekly reports that allowed all the directors to know what was happening in the different sectors of Omega—in one pile. He grabbed the Pensacola police reports and prepared to throw them in the trash.

A picture from that group caught his attention and brought him up short. A Jane Doe the Pensacola police hadn't been able to identify.

It was Rosalyn. She looked like she was sleeping peacefully.

But the picture was from the county morgue.

Rosalyn was dead.

Chapter Five

Steve caught the first flight he could get to Pensacola. Sadness and guilt weighed on him the entire time.

The prints on the glass in his office—immediately fished out of the trash—were being run right now. If Rosalyn was in any law enforcement system, Steve would have the full results by the time he met with the Pensacola police.

Damn it, he should have run them earlier. Should've gotten her information and gone after Rosalyn himself. Okay, maybe she might have had to do a short stint in prison for theft, but at least she would be alive.

Steve had known something was wrong, known Rosalyn was in serious trouble, but he hadn't been able to look past his wounded pride to see she got the help she needed.

And now it was too late.

He got the information about the prints via email as he was getting off the plane in Pensacola.

Rosalyn Mellinger.

Twenty-four years old from Mobile, Alabama.

Her prints actually weren't in any of the law enforcement databases; that's why the Pensacola PD hadn't been able to identify her. Cynthia had been able to identify Rosalyn from something to do with her juvenile record. She couldn't access the full record but had been able to link the print from the glass to the record.

Steve drove straight to the police department, which also housed the coroner's office. It was midafternoon but Steve was determined to identify Rosalyn's body today. Somehow he couldn't stand the thought of her sitting another night unidentified in the morgue.

The Pensacola county sheriff and the coroner were both waiting for Steve when he walked in.

"Agent Drackett." The sheriff, a portly man in his fifties, extended his hand for shaking. "Is agent the right title? I'm Sheriff Harvey Palmer."

"Just call me Steve." He shook the man's hand.

"This is Dwayne Prase, our county coroner." Steve shook his hand too.

They began walking down the hallway to the morgue.

"We really appreciate you coming all the way from Colorado," Sheriff Palmer said. "I have to be honest—I didn't expect your call."

"I don't know the victim in any official capacity. I met her when I was on vacation here six months ago. We spent a few days together. I recognized her immediately when the Jane Doe picture came across my desk."

"I see." The sheriff nodded and thankfully didn't ask why Steve would be getting police reports from Pensacola. "No one here has missed her at all. No missing-persons report or anyone asking about her. Her prints didn't show up in any of our computers."

Steve nodded. If he hadn't had access to the Omega databases, he wouldn't have known anything about Rosalyn either.

"She was definitely murdered?"

Palmer nodded. "Yes, strangled. In her car in a parking lot."

"She'd been dead for hours before anyone found her," the coroner chimed in. "And has been here unidentified for nearly thirty-six hours."

Steve brought his fingers up to the bridge of his nose. There was so much he wished he'd done differently.

They reached the cold chamber of the morgue, where the body was being kept to reduce decomposition. Steve entered with the two men and saw the body was already on the table ready to be identified.

Prase pulled the sheet slowly off the body's face.

Steve hadn't realized how much he'd been praying there had been some type of mistake, that it wasn't really Rosalyn, but looking at her now, he couldn't deny it.

"That's her. That's Rosalyn Mellinger."

STEVE SPENT THE next couple of hours with Sheriff Palmer, filling out some paperwork. He'd asked the sheriff if his men would mind if Steve stuck around for a couple of days and helped in any way he could with the investigation. Thankfully, Palmer hadn't felt threatened by the offer and readily agreed.

He'd called back into Omega and let them know he'd be out for a few days. One thing about having a team as good as his: they could continue to function without him when necessary.

Steve planned to find Rosalyn's killer. It was the least he could do.

But not tonight. Tonight he was going to go back to the tiki bar where he'd met her and have a drink in her memory.

Steve decided to stay at the same hotel he'd used before. Not the romance package, but still a nice place. It was only a few blocks from the station. He checked in and unloaded his overnight bag. He took off his suit and changed into jeans and a T-shirt. No shorts and flip-flops this time.

He decided to walk to the tiki bar from his room even though it was through sand. He stopped for a minute as he reached the area where he and Rosalyn had sat and talked for so long that first night, partially because he wanted to take a moment to remember that place.

But also because Steve could feel eyes on him.

Someone was watching him.

As inconspicuously as he could manage, Steve turned. He didn't see anything to his left. He knelt down into the sand as if he'd found some great shell and spun to the right. No one there either.

Maybe this feeling was just a result of stress. God knew today had been stressful enough.

He stood back up and began walking to the bar.

It was a Wednesday now, not a Sunday like when he'd been here before. The TVs had some basketball games on, and the place wasn't nearly as full.

No Jimmy Buffett playing on the jukebox, no storm driving in beautiful women from outside.

Steve didn't plan to be here long so didn't get his seat at the end of the bar. Instead just sat at the first seat he came to and ordered a beer.

He was only a few sips into it when he felt eyes on him again. Steve quietly paid the bartender in case he had to leave in a hurry but then sat back and eased himself casually around in the barstool.

No one seemed to be paying him much mind, but he'd been in law enforcement too long to ignore a gut feeling twice in one hour.

Somebody was following him. Probably had been since he left the police station.

Maybe it was the killer trying to see who had identified his victim. Or maybe hoping to make another victim out of Steve.

Steve felt adrenaline pump through him. Bring it on. There was nothing he'd like better than a physical altercation with Rosalyn's killer before arresting him. They would have to send the perp to the hospital before taking him to a holding cell.

Steve took a sip of his beer and allowed his vision to become slightly unfocused so he could better see everything happening in the room at once. After just a few moments he caught what he was looking for.

Someone out on the deck in a hooded jacket watching him through the window. The figure ducked as soon as Steve glanced his way.

Steve moved immediately but had to go out the side door to make it to the deck, losing valuable moments. The guy had already headed down the outer stairs and was moving quickly toward the closest set of hotels. Picking out his black jacket and hood was difficult in the darkening sky.

But Steve had no plan to let him get away.

Steve looked forward to the hotel buildings where the man obviously planned to go—his car was probably parked there. Then he ran down the back stairs, jumping down the last few. He began running up the path to the hotel also, but on a different path so the guy wouldn't look back and think Steve was following him and move faster.

Steve was going to come around the other side of the building and cut him off.

It was a risky plan, dependent on the perp not changing course, but Steve didn't dwell on it. He put all his effort into getting around the other side of the building before the person got there.

Racing through sand wasn't easy but Steve knew he was gaining ground. From the corner of his eye Steve could see the perp was slowing down. Probably because he didn't see Steve behind him. Or maybe he was trying to blend in with some other tourists now that he was closer to the hotel.

Steve didn't slow down as sand gave way to a sidewalk, then to the asphalt surrounding the hotel. Glancing over, he saw the hooded figure slip down a slim walkway between two buildings. This was his chance.

Steve forced another burst of speed out of his body. He had to make it around the corner and to the walkway before the guy got through and made it into the parking lot. Steve wouldn't have much chance of finding him then.

Steve barreled around the corner ready to make a flying tackle if necessary, but the guy wasn't there. He immediately scanned the parking lot but saw only one group of teenage girls getting into their car and two parents removing kids from car seats in another.

No hooded man. Damn it.

Steve squinted in the fading light. He could be hiding behind a vehicle. Or had made it around the corner and run the other way.

Something caught his attention away from the parking lot. About halfway down the corridor he'd been expecting the perp to run through, a head stuck out, looking the other way. It was the guy, looking for Steve but looking the wrong way.

Steve flattened himself against the wall and began making his way toward the man. He pulled out his weapon, although he kept it low and pointed to the ground. He didn't want to cause any panic for vacationers who might alert the suspect that Steve was coming up behind him.

Quickly but silently, Steve approached the hooded figure, who still watched the other way.

"I'm armed law enforcement," Steve said as he made his last few steps and pointed his Glock directly at the man. "Very slowly put your hands behind your head."

Steve saw the guy stiffen and stepped closer in case he tried to run again or fight. He was small, but Steve had seen plenty of small people who could do a lot of damage. Hell, he'd helped train some of the best himself.

Steve didn't have cuffs with him, so he'd have to call Sheriff Palmer to come make the arrest.

"Just stay right there," he said as he pulled his phone out of his pocket.

The guy began to turn around.

"Hey, did you hear me?" Steve poked him in the back with his weapon. "Just stay right where you are."

"Steve." The voice was soft. Almost a whisper, but it sent a bolt of electricity through him.

Steve did something he hadn't done in twenty years of law enforcement: lowered his weapon in shock.

This wasn't a man at all. It was a woman.

"Rosalyn?"

She reached up and lowered the hood of her Windbreaker as she turned completely around.

It was her. Beautiful black hair, gorgeous blue eyes. Even the splattering of freckles over her nose. Rosalyn was alive.

Which was impossible because he'd just ID'd her dead body a few hours ago. Steve didn't care. By whatever miracle she was here—and he would get her to explain it all, no doubt—he would take it.

He holstered his weapon and pulled her into his arms. Then yanked her back immediately, looking closer at the rest of her body.

Rosalyn was here. She was alive.

And unless he was very, very wrong, she was definitely pregnant.

Chapter Six

Steve stared down at her belly for a long time. He finally looked up at her face again.

There were so many questions in his eyes she hardly knew how to start answering them all.

His hand gently touched her stomach, so that's where she started.

"Yes, I'm pregnant. Six months."

It wasn't terribly difficult math, so she let him work out for himself that the baby was his. She didn't want to say it outright, because she wasn't sure if he would even believe her. They hadn't parted on the greatest of terms, after all.

He studied her for a long time without saying anything. Rosalyn just stood there. She was as surprised to see him as he was to see her.

"I just identified your dead body," he finally said.

Okay, maybe not *quite* as surprised.

"My twin sister," she whispered. "Lindsey Rose. I didn't know she was dead until today. I was coming into the police department when I saw you leaving."

She'd been skeptical about going to the police station anyway, knowing the Watcher would probably be waiting for her there. When she saw Steve exit the building, she'd been totally thrown.

What was he doing there?

Steve was the last person Rosalyn expected to see. His presence had to have something to do with Lindsey's death. Why else would he be here from Colorado?

"Have you been following me from the police station?"

"Yes."

Steve's eyes narrowed. "Why? To tell me about the baby? Why did you run when I saw you at the bar?"

He fired off the questions faster than she could answer them. Not that she knew how to answer them anyway.

She hadn't expected to see Steve. She'd been about to cross the street into the police station, knowing her sister was dead and the Watcher had found her again.

She was six months pregnant, alone, frightened and grieving. She'd pushed back the terror, so her only thought had been identifying her sister so Lindsey could have a proper burial.

Then Steve had walked out the door. He'd looked so strong. So capable of handling anything life threw at him.

Rosalyn had gotten in her car and followed him without even meaning to. When she saw he was going to the same hotel and then the same bar where they'd met, she'd felt a little hope inside.

Maybe he didn't hate her.

Maybe she could tell him about the baby.

Maybe she could tell him about the Watcher and everything that had happened.

She needed help.

But when his eyes had flown to her at the bar, obviously suspecting trouble, she'd panicked. She'd run—well, run as fast as her body would let her—to get away.

But she hadn't gotten away. He'd caught her and said—

He was law enforcement?

"You're a *cop*?"

He took a step closer, obviously trying to use his size to intimidate her. "You didn't answer my questions."

She couldn't get into the entire story now. They were too out in the open. "I will answer your questions, but not out here. You told me you were in management before."

Steve shrugged. "I never said what sort of management I was in. And I want answers to my questions before I arrest you."

"Arrest me for what?"

"How about the theft of nearly $200 six months ago?"

Rosalyn's face heated. "I'm sorry about that. I didn't have any other choice. I was desperate. My whole time with you I was pretty desperate."

That wasn't the right word, or at least she should've phrased it differently, she realized when he stiffened and stepped back. She hadn't meant that she'd spent time with him because she was desperate, but he'd obviously taken it that way.

"I guess your little souvenir from our time together—" he gestured at her belly "—wasn't what you wanted, then. Is the baby even mine?"

"Yes." She took a step toward him without even meaning to. "I know you probably don't believe me, but you're the only man I've been with for a long time." The only man she'd allowed herself to trust in a long time.

"Yeah, well, once the kid is born, there are paternity tests that are probably in our best interests to complete."

Rosalyn knew she shouldn't be hurt given what had happened between them but she couldn't help it. "Of course. I don't expect you to just believe me."

Now that the Watcher had found her again, she needed Steve's help whether he believed her or not. She had more than just herself to look out for. Steve didn't know the entire situation but at least she knew she could trust him.

Steve ran a hand through his hair. "Look, I'm not trying to be an ass. You've caught me off guard on multiple levels here. But I need some answers."

"Okay. I have a room at a hotel a few miles from here. Let's go there."

ROSALYN WAS ALIVE.

Rosalyn was alive *and* pregnant. Steve could hardly get his head around the first part, much less the second.

She was sitting right in front of him in a pretty scary run-down hotel room they'd driven to in her car, eating a packet of crackers. He was sitting in the desk chair that he'd pulled over and placed right in front of the bed just watching her. Like her eating crackers was the most interesting thing he'd ever seen.

Did she need more food than that? Was she taking care of herself? Had she been seeing a doctor throughout her pregnancy to make sure everything was okay?

Was the baby honestly his? They had used protection. But he knew accidents still happened.

He wanted to believe her when she'd said yes. She'd taken off her jacket and he could more clearly see the outline of her stomach under the T-shirt she wore. There was very definitely a baby bump. Not one that had her waddling or anything like that, but very definitely pregnant. Someone as petite as Rosalyn couldn't hide it.

He wanted to ask her all sorts of questions about her pregnancy but had so many other questions to ask that those got pushed to the back burner.

Steve sorted through important information for a living, made decisions on where Omega's Critical Response team would go and what they would do, based on his reading of a situation. Knowing what questions to ask to get the information he needed was his *job*. And lives depended on his ability to do it well.

But damned if he knew where to start with Rosalyn.

The dead body seemed the most reasonable place.

"So the woman I identified in the morgue—"

"Like I said, my identical twin, Lindsey Rose Mellinger. My mom—in a fit of soberness—thought it was quite clever."

Rosalyn and Lindsey Rose. "The reversal of each other. Well, almost."

She nodded. "Yeah. And it ended up being true in just about everything. We were twins, but we were complete opposites. Very different from each other except for how we looked."

"When was the last time you saw your sister alive?"

Tears came to Rosalyn's eyes, but she brushed them away. "At least a year and a half ago. We've never been close but grew even further apart as adults. Lindsey was in and out of drug rehab all the time. She still lived in Mobile."

"And that's where you're from?" Steve already knew the answer to that but wondered if she would lie.

"Yes, but I haven't lived there for nearly a year."

Steve wondered where she'd been for the past six months, but he'd get to that.

"Do you know anything about your sister's death?"

She shook her head. "No, but she was murdered, wasn't she?"

"What makes you say that?"

This time the tears overflowed before Rosalyn could wipe them away. "Lindsey was in Pensacola because I asked her to meet me. We were supposed to meet at a restaurant a few blocks from here two days ago, but she never showed up."

She gave him the name and address of a local café. Lindsey's body had been found inside her car very close to that area.

"Lindsey's pretty flighty," Rosalyn continued. "I thought she'd just gotten the day or time wrong. Or that she was high again. I didn't know she was dead until a waiter showed me a tiny section of the local paper that stated the police were looking for information about a deceased Jane Doe who looked exactly like me."

Rosalyn stood up and grabbed a tissue from the box on the small desk. "I was coming by this afternoon to identify the body when I saw you."

"You said she did drugs a lot, so what makes you think she was murdered? Don't you think it's more likely something happened with her drug abuse?"

"Normally, yes." She sat back down. "But I suspect foul play because she was meeting me."

"I don't understand."

Rosalyn's blue eyes bore into him. "You saw her body, right?"

Steve nodded.

"I'll answer your questions, I promise. But first please tell me, was she murdered?"

Steve couldn't see any good in lying to her. "Yes, I'm sorry. She was strangled in her car."

Rosalyn began to cry quietly, holding her face in her hands. Steve moved to sit next to her. No matter what had happened between the two of them, he would never deny comfort to someone who had lost a family member.

"I had hoped you would tell me something different. That it was related to drugs," she finally said.

"I don't understand why you don't think it would've been." In Steve's experience, when regular people heard a family member had died, they did not assume it was murder. And if Lindsey had been involved in illegal drugs, Steve didn't know why Rosalyn didn't assume the murder wasn't centered around that.

Because Rosalyn knew something. Something she wasn't telling him.

"Rosalyn." He tilted a finger under her chin so she was looking directly at him. "Tell me. Whatever is going on, I need you to tell me."

She tried to look away, but he wouldn't let her.

"I can't." Another tear slid silently down her cheek. "I can't risk you too."

Steve stared at the tiny woman—tiny, *pregnant* woman—determined to protect him. Why would she care about him if he was just someone she had scammed and robbed? Either way, he was getting to the bottom of all this.

"I can take care of myself, Rosalyn. Just tell me what's going on."

At first he didn't think she was going to answer, but finally she did.

"For the past year someone has been stalking me."

Steve sat up straighter. "Stalking you how?"

"Mostly he leaves notes. Ones he slides under my door while I'm sleeping at night." She shuddered. "Although on occasion he has emailed, texted or called me."

He'd been in law enforcement long enough to take stalkers very seriously. Especially ones who were close enough to leave notes under doors. That meant they were close and probably deadly. "What types of messages?"

"Never anything threatening. Not even 'We'll be together forever' stuff. Usually just little comments about something that has happened in my day."

Odd for a stalker, making it about her rather than about him. Stalkers were usually caught up in their own fantasy world and tried to make their victims a part of that.

"And you reported it?"

"Yes. I told my family first about a year ago. They just accused me of wanting attention. I decided to move across town, just to get rid of the weirdo, hoping that would stop it all."

"But it didn't?"

"The first night I moved into my new apartment, someone slid a note under my door."

Steve frowned. The guy had been following her closely. "Did you go to the local police?"

"Yes, I talked to them in Mobile, but I had thrown a lot of the letters away, so they didn't believe it was anyone wishing to do me harm."

It was easy to be frustrated with the Mobile police for doing nothing to help Rosalyn, but the truth was, funds were always limited in local departments. If the notes weren't threatening Rosalyn in any way, it would be easy to not give them or her much attention.

She stood up and began walking back and forth.

"It got so bad that after about a month I chose to just leave town. I had a pretty big savings account, so I quit my job and decided to go somewhere different. Anywhere different. I didn't have a moving truck, didn't grab a bunch of suitcases—I just got in my car one morning and left."

She stopped walking for a minute.

"I ended up in Dallas. Thought it would be a cool town to vacation in while I was losing my annoying little follower. Thought I had done it too, until the second night. Another note under my door mentioning the crème brûlée I had eaten at dinner."

She wasn't looking at him, but he could hear the fear in her voice.

"I left just minutes later. Drove all around to make sure no one was following me. Ended up in Shreveport. I went straight to the police station."

It wasn't the best of plans, since nothing had happened in their jurisdiction, but Steve didn't tell Rosalyn that. She would've been better off going to the Dallas police.

But a note that mentioned a dessert probably wouldn't have been taken seriously there either.

"Nobody wanted to listen to me, but this one detective, Johnson, offered to meet me after he got off his shift. I told him everything, and he helped me. Or he tried."

"What did he do?"

She began rubbing her hands on her legs, a nervous gesture he didn't think she was aware of.

"I showed him what notes I had kept. He told me to keep them all, and any I got from now on, in a box. And he gave me a notebook and showed me how to keep track of everything that the Watcher did."

He reached over and grabbed her hands so she would stop the rubbing. "The Watcher?"

"Yeah, that's what I call him. I've kept everything since Detective Johnson showed me what to do."

"And did he do anything with it? Did it go any further?"

"Unfortunately, he died of a heart attack the next day."

Steve's head snapped up. "Was he old?"

"Maybe fifty. And in pretty good shape."

"That's a damn unfortunate coincidence." And probably a devastating blow for Rosalyn, to have found someone who wanted to help, then died.

"I thought so too until I got an anonymous email the next day about a drug that caused heart attacks."

"What?"

"The Watcher killed Detective Johnson. He's killed everyone I've told about him. I'm afraid you'll be next."

Chapter Seven

Steve didn't believe her.

He wasn't overt in his disbelief, didn't mock her or anything like that. But she could tell he didn't think the Watcher was actually a credible threat. He thought Detective Johnson, a fifty-year-old policeman, had died of a heart attack.

It certainly happened all the time. Police work was stressful.

Her sister was also dead, but she'd been a drug addict. That happened all the time too.

She didn't tell him about Shawn, the mechanic, who'd also died after she'd told him about the Watcher. Because she could already tell Steve thought she was exaggerating.

She'd recognized the placating look. The attempt to figure out how to convince her of reason without offending her. He didn't want to add to her stress, but he also didn't think there was anything sinister to her story.

Not to mention he was still pretty shocked about her reappearance and pregnancy. So she should probably cut him a little slack.

She hadn't planned to drag him into this. Because whether he wanted to believe her or not, she knew it was true: the Watcher would try to kill him next.

Rosalyn wanted to run, to try to keep Steve safe. But she couldn't anymore. She had to face the fact that soon it wouldn't just be her. She'd have the baby. She couldn't go back on the run with a child in tow.

She'd had six months of relative peace. Although she'd lived in fear every single night of the Watcher contacting her, he hadn't. Rosalyn didn't know why. She'd thought he'd given up, decided to leave her alone.

She'd made a huge error, she realized now, contacting her sister. It had not only cost Lindsey her life, but put Rosalyn back on the Watcher's radar.

She knew she wouldn't escape him again. Not without help.

Steve turned to her. "Look, let's just sleep on everything tonight. We can discuss this more in the morning."

She nodded. Maybe if she showed him the notes, he'd take her more seriously. Plus, she knew the questioning was nowhere near done on either side.

He was a cop and had deliberately withheld that information from her. She wasn't mad, but it changed some things. Maybe he could help protect her from the Watcher.

Of course, Detective Johnson had been in law enforcement too, and the Watcher had killed him. But that had been before she had realized how far the Watcher would go. Until Johnson's death Rosalyn had assumed only she would be his victim. She knew better now. When they met tomorrow, she would have to make sure Steve understood the danger he was in.

"Okay, what time do you want to meet tomorrow?"

Steve looked at her like she'd lost her mind. "I'm not leaving you here. You're coming with me."

She hadn't been expecting that. "Why?"

"Multiple reasons. One, I don't trust that you're not going to be gone again in the morning."

Rosalyn felt her face heat but didn't say anything.

"Two, by your very own account you have a stalker and possibly a murderer after you. I'm not sure what all the facts are in this case, but I intend to find out. You can believe I won't be leaving you alone as I do it, especially not if you're carrying my child."

Rosalyn felt relief wash through her. Steve might not believe her completely but at least he was willing to look into it. And help protect her and the baby.

"Now, I will stay in this fleabag motel if you really insist on remaining here. But I would prefer we go to my hotel." He glanced around in distaste, then looked straight at her. "Either way, you can plan on spending tonight— every night until we figure out this stalker situation and the baby is born—with me."

He obviously didn't necessarily believe the baby was his, but at least he was willing to try to keep Rosalyn safe until he knew for sure. She wasn't sure whether to be thankful or offended.

But to stay here when he had a nicer place would just be foolish.

"Okay. Just let me get my stuff."

He took her duffel bag and walked her to her car. He took the key from her and put her bag in the trunk. "Have you been going from town to town for the last six months?"

Rosalyn bit her lip. Telling him the truth, that the Watcher hadn't contacted her since she'd last been in Pensacola, wasn't going to help him believe her about how dangerous her stalker was.

She didn't know why the Watcher hadn't contacted her while she'd been hidden at the Ammonses' home in Georgia, had lived in constant fear that he would, but she'd been thankful for the reprieve.

"Let me go pay for the room. You stay here," he said.

"No, I'll pay. I can afford it."

One of his eyebrows raised. "I don't even want to know how you got the money."

"I didn't steal it, all right? That was a one-time thing and only because I was desperate."

He still didn't look like he believed it.

"You stay here with the car and I'll go pay." She gave him the evilest glare she could.

Which only made him smile. "Fine, you pay. I'll be here."

The motel office was at the other end of the parking lot, close to the main street. Rosalyn was aware she was marching off in a huff and had neither the size nor stature to pull that off with any authority, especially when she looked like she'd swallowed half a basketball. She knew Steve was probably laughing at her, but she didn't care.

At least if he was laughing at her, he wasn't threatening to arrest her. Not that she really thought he planned to.

She went inside and paid her bill, a little mad that they still charged her for two nights even though she'd stayed only one. Regardless, she wasn't going to let Steve pay. At least the extra cost didn't cause her the panic it once would have, since she now had some money saved up from being able to work the last six months. She signed the paperwork, paid her bill and walked back out the door toward her car.

"I'll pay you back all that money, you know," she called out, moving directly toward him.

He walked toward her. "It's not necessary to pay me back. You can—"

Rosalyn heard the roar of an engine and turned. A car, headlights off, was screeching toward her, swerving back and forth.

"Hey, look out!" someone yelled from a second-floor walkway.

Rosalyn couldn't figure out which way to move to get out of the car's oncoming path. All she knew was that it was going to hit her.

She was still frozen in place, certain of her own demise, when a huge force hit her from the side.

Steve.

He pulled her to his chest and continued their momentum out of the car's direct path, somehow managing to spin them so he took the weight of the fall.

Both of them covered her belly with their arms.

They were on the ground for only a split second before Steve jumped back up to his feet. He pulled his gun from the holster and pointed it at the car.

But the driver put the car in Reverse and began speeding at Steve. The vehicle hit him and knocked him backward.

"Steve!" Rosalyn screamed from where she lay on the ground.

He sat up and got one shot off, but when the car sped toward him again, he had to stop and roll to the side out of the way. He began firing again.

Rosalyn scooted herself back, unsure what the car would do. But thankfully, it sped off.

Steve ran over to her and placed his hands over hers on her stomach. "Are you okay? I'm sorry I hit you so hard."

Her heart was still racing but she didn't think she was injured. "Better you than the car. I'm fine. And I'm pretty sure the baby is okay. You took the brunt of the fall."

The manager ran out of the office. "Oh my gosh, are you guys all right? I just called 911. That guy had to have been drunk."

Two other people ran out from the building. "We saw the whole thing. Did anybody get the license plate?"

They all began to talk over each other.

Rosalyn tuned them out and started to stand up, but Steve's hands kept her gently on the ground. "Just stay there, okay? There's an ambulance coming. Let's just be safe and wait."

She nodded. Her heart still beat erratically but otherwise she didn't feel too bad. But Steve was right—better to let them check her out, just in case.

"Damn drunk driver. You guys are lucky to be alive," the manager said. "I mean, the way he reversed like that? Couldn't figure out which way was forward."

Rosalyn looked over at Steve. His eyes said the same thing as hers. That had been no drunk driver.

"Are you okay?" she asked him. "You're the one who got hit by the car."

He let out a small groan as he sat down on the asphalt beside her. "Yeah, nothing broken, I'm pretty sure."

Activity buzzed around them, but Rosalyn and Steve just sat in silence. His hand was never far from her stomach. Soon the ambulance and police showed up. Rosalyn was assisted onto the stretcher and put inside the ambulance while Steve talked to the cops.

She didn't know exactly what he said to them, but within minutes the ambulance was on its way and Steve was riding beside her. He left her side only when they arrived at the hospital, to talk to some member of the staff.

Again, Rosalyn couldn't hear but twenty minutes later she was being seen by the hospital's chief OB-GYN physician even though it was nearly ten o'clock at night. Dr. Puglisi had her hooked up to an ultrasound machine as soon as she heard what happened.

"There," Dr. Puglisi said, pointing to the monitor. "Good, strong heartbeat. Baby is absolutely fine."

Tears poured down Rosalyn's cheeks as she grabbed Steve's hand beside her. "Thank God."

"A woman's body is pretty amazing at protecting the fetus growing inside it. It generally takes more than a fall to cause real problems." Dr. Puglisi moved the ultrasound wand. "Do you know the gender of the baby?"

Rosalyn shook her head. "Not yet. It was scheduled for my next appointment."

"Would you like to know?"

Rosalyn looked over at Steve but he just shrugged. "That's completely up to you."

She tried not to show the hurt she felt by his nonchalance but knew she couldn't blame Steve. It was too soon.

Rosalyn turned back to the doctor. "Yes, I'd like to know, if you can tell."

The doctor smiled. "Congratulations—your strong resilient baby is a boy."

Chapter Eight

He was going to have a son.

Dr. Puglisi had run a number of tests on Rosalyn, just to double-check that everything was okay. That she was healthy, the baby was healthy and nothing was going to creep up on them unawares.

Some of the tests she did were to establish the gestational age of the child.

Every indication was that the fetus was twenty-five weeks developed. That would mean he was conceived six months ago.

Steve knew that didn't mean the baby was his. But it was definitely a step closer.

The most important thing right now was that both Rosalyn and the baby were healthy. His flying tackle hadn't hurt either of them in any way.

When he'd seen that car speeding toward Rosalyn his heart had stopped. Only years of training, his body responding almost before his mind did, had him moving forward to get her out of the way.

Drunk driver, his ass.

Steve might possibly have believed it if the guy hadn't backed up to run over him.

Someone had been trying to kill Rosalyn or Steve or both of them. He'd made it look like he was a drunk driver, but after everything Rosalyn had told him, that was one coincidence too many.

Funny thing was, until the attack happened, he hadn't really believed Rosalyn about her Watcher theory. To Steve, her description of the situation broke too many of the typical patterns that would be found in a stalker committed enough to kill people.

He'd spent the last hour in a room the hospital had lent him for privacy, on the phone with Sheriff Harvey Palmer. He explained about Rosalyn and her twin, Lindsey. Explained how Lindsey's prints weren't in the system but Rosalyn's were, although he still didn't know why.

Steve also told Palmer what had happened with the car. A dark two-door Toyota with no plates wasn't going to be particularly helpful, but the sheriff agreed to run the description against other incidents in the area. Maybe they'd get lucky.

Steve finished the call by telling Palmer he'd be taking Rosalyn with him out of Florida.

He was going to take her to Colorado Springs. Back to Omega Critical Response headquarters. If they were fighting some villain intent on hurting Rosalyn and her baby, Steve planned to fight on his own turf.

Once he finished with Sheriff Palmer, he called his office.

"Steve Drackett's office."

"Angela, it's me." Someone was in Steve's office twenty-four hours a day, seven days a week to be able to field calls that might come from as far up as the White House. Angela tended to work the evening shifts.

"Hey, boss. I thought you were taking a couple of personal days."

"I was, but my situation has changed. I'm going to need you to book me two tickets on a flight from Pensacola to

Colorado Springs for as early as possible tomorrow. Me and a Rosalyn Mellinger."

"Okay, no problem. I'll text you with the details."

"Anything exciting happening around the office?"

"All in all, a pretty quiet day. If you can believe it."

A *quiet day* might have only meant there were no events threatening national security.

"I'm glad to hear it. I'll be back tomorrow."

"See you then, sir."

A doctor had already looked over Steve's wounds—some road rash and bruises—and declared him free to go. What had happened tonight could've been much worse.

He walked down the hallway and saw Rosalyn joking with one of the nurses. He was struck again by her natural beauty and animation.

It could've been much, much worse.

He'd spent six months angry with her, followed by a day of terrible sadness when he thought she was dead. He'd then been given the precious gift of a second chance when he'd found out she was alive.

Her smile still took his breath away just like it had six months ago.

"You ready to go?" he asked her.

She jumped down from the table. "Yep. Dr. Puglisi said I was done as soon as you were."

"Good. It's getting pretty late. I think we both could use some sleep. We'll go back to my hotel like we'd originally planned."

A uniformed officer had driven Rosalyn's car over from the scene of the accident at Steve's request. He opened the door for her to get in and made his way over to the driver's side.

He eased slowly out of the parking lot and began to drive. He didn't go directly to the hotel, instead took leisurely routes going nowhere near where they would be staying.

After an hour Steve was absolutely positive no one was following them. He'd actually been sure of it for twenty minutes before that, but Rosalyn had fallen asleep and waking her up seemed heartless. She'd had a hell of a day. First Steve pulling a gun on her, then someone trying to kill her. Not to mention dealing with her sister's recent death.

She deserved a nap.

They had so much they needed to talk about. He needed to find out all the details she had about the Watcher. Needed to know where she'd been for the last six months.

Needed to tell her that he was the director of an elite law enforcement agency and was probably more uniquely situated to protect her than anyone else. Even though he'd almost been killed today.

Yes, it was possible it was a drunk driver who had nearly run them over, but Steve would still be on high guard until he knew exactly what it was they were up against.

He drove around a few more minutes before pulling the car up to his hotel on the beach. He got out and looked around for a few minutes, making sure no one had picked them up in the last few minutes. Unlikely but possible.

Nothing. It was completely quiet in the parking lot. The beach was deserted also. All to be expected at nearly midnight on a Wednesday.

Steve walked over and got Rosalyn's duffel bag out of the trunk. She was still clutching her tote bag in her arms, just like she had been when he'd known her six months ago.

He opened her door and nudged her gently on the shoulder. "Hey, Sleeping Beauty, let's get you inside so you can sleep properly."

Her eyes barely opened but she got out of the car. He put an arm around her and led her through the lobby and up the elevator to their room on the seventh floor. He used his key card to get in.

This room was definitely less romantic than the setup six months ago. But from the look in Rosalyn's tired eyes, she didn't care about romance tonight.

"I'm just going to go straight to bed. Is that okay?" She lay down on the bed, on top of the covers, shoes still on. Evidently, having only one bed didn't bother her. She was sound asleep again.

Steve set her duffel bag on the chair and walked over to her. He untied and slipped off her athletic shoes. He then lifted her body with one arm—it shouldn't be that easy; if they hadn't just been reassured by one of the best doctors in the area that Rosalyn was perfectly healthy, Steve would've worried much more about how little she weighed—so he could tuck her under the blankets.

She never even stirred.

Steve shook his head, smiling. She was like a child. He didn't know if that was how she normally slept or if it was a product of exhaustion, pregnancy and stress.

It had been a long day. Steve took a shower, wincing at the sting of the water against his scrapes, and changed into fresh clothes.

Tomorrow he would have Rosalyn in Colorado. He realized she hadn't actually agreed to that yet. He wasn't trying to keep the information a secret, but neither was it up for negotiation. Steve needed to figure out what was going on. The Critical Response Division headquarters was the best place for him to do that.

The body of Rosalyn's sister still needed to be taken care of, but Rosalyn's mother would have to do that. He hoped Rosalyn wouldn't fight him about going to Colorado.

Not because he wouldn't take her if she did. He would still take her. It would just make it much more difficult.

But he'd fight that battle if he came to it. Right now she was sleeping peacefully and he should do the same.

He slid next to her into the king-size bed. His body wanted to grab her and pull her into his arms, but he knew that wasn't wise. Too many unresolved issues between them. Until he knew exactly what was happening, how much he could trust her, he knew he needed to keep his distance.

He looked over at Rosalyn, who had turned onto her side in an attempt to get more comfortable. She looked innocent, lovely, fragile.

But in his line of work he'd learned how very easy it was for looks to deceive.

He would keep on his side of the bed. It was better for everyone that way.

STEVE WOKE UP and immediately sensed something was wrong.

Rosalyn lay completely snuggled in his arms, draped over him like a blanket. So much for keeping his distance from her.

But that wasn't what was wrong.

He looked over at the window. No light was peeking through, so it was obviously still night. He estimated about four o'clock in the morning.

What had awakened him?

He listened for any sounds that would be foreign. Someone trying to break into the room or yells from farther away.

Nothing.

Then he smelled it. Smoke. Too heavy to be just some cigarette somebody was toking on illegally on a balcony.

He shook Rosalyn. "Wake up, sweetheart."

She just mumbled and tried to move away from the hands disturbing her sleep. Steve shook her again. "Rosalyn, come on, you need to wake up." He pulled her until she was in a sitting position.

"What's going on?" she asked, blinking multiple times. "Is it morning?"

"There's trouble, I'm pretty sure."

He ran over to the door. He could see smoke seeping under the crack. He ran back and grabbed the hotel phone. As soon as someone answered, he barked out, "I'm in room 742. There's a fire in the hallway but the alarm isn't sounding. You need to call the fire department and get some sort of alarm working."

He didn't wait for the person to answer. He grabbed one of Rosalyn's shoes. "Can you put these on or do you need help?"

"I can do it. I'm slow, but I can get them."

He handed her one shoe and put the other on her foot himself. "We're going to have to get out of here. I'm not sure how bad the smoke and fire will be."

She grabbed her tote bag and pulled it over her shoulder. Fine, she could take that, but the rest of the stuff would have to stay.

He stood and led her to the bathroom. "Soak these towels. We'll keep them over our faces to protect us from the fire and smoke as best we can."

She began running water over them as he went to check the door again. The smoke was even heavier under the crack.

He opened the door slightly to see exactly what they were up against. He couldn't see three feet down the hall, the smoke was so thick. There was no way they'd be able to wait for the fire department to get up to their floor.

He shut the door, taking the wet towels from her. "It's bad out there. We're not going to be able to see much of anything. But we need to make it to the stairs."

"I don't know where they are." Panic pinched her face. "Are they near the elevator?"

"No." As a force of habit Steve had memorized the general layout of the hotel when he'd checked in. "They're a little bit farther. Just keep hold of my hand, no matter what."

She nodded, eyes big. He wrapped one of the wet towels around the lower part of her face. "I'm not sure the extent of the fire, but the smoke is thick out there. It's going to be rough. Stay low and breathe through the towel as much as possible."

When he opened the door again, he immediately felt heat to the right. The fire was closer than it had been moments ago.

And blocking their way to the stairs.

"We're going to have to go to the far staircase," he told Rosalyn. "Stay with me no matter what."

She nodded and he pulled the door open farther. Smoke immediately filled their room. Steve bent at the waist to get lower than the worst of the smoke in the hall. He knew bending that way would be difficult for Rosalyn. He was glad she was significantly shorter than he was to start with.

He lost all visibility only a few feet from their hotel room. He had to rely on his instincts and his mind's ability to process spatial data to get them to where they needed to be.

He could feel Rosalyn's small hand in his and knew that if he made a mistake, missed the door to the stairs or turned down the wrong hall, it could mean their deaths.

About halfway to where he estimated the stairs were, the smoke got so thick they had to crawl. Steve's eyes burned, although the wet towel at least protected his throat from the worst of the smoke.

He turned back to Rosalyn. Tears were streaming from her eyes. He knew his looked the same.

"Pull the towel all the way over your face," he yelled back at her. "I'll guide you out."

She didn't argue, just pulled the towel past her nose, over her eyes. It wouldn't help her for long, but it had to be better than nothing.

She was putting her trust in him completely to guide her out. He wouldn't let her down.

He crawled as rapidly as he could—feeling her hand on his ankle as she crawled behind him—until he found what he hoped was the right door. If not, they would be in dire straits. He could feel heat licking behind them.

The sound of glass breaking came from the other end of the hall, probably firefighters, but they wouldn't get the blaze and smoke under control quickly enough to help Rosalyn and Steve.

Steve reached up from his crawl to the door handle and sighed in relief when it opened.

They were at the stairs. Steve dragged Rosalyn inside the much cooler stairwell. People were running down the stairs, some crying, some screaming.

Steve stood and scooped Rosalyn up in his arms. He pulled the towel down from her face to find her looking out at him with those blue eyes.

"I'm okay," she whispered, voice a little husky. "I can walk."

He shook his head. He wasn't going to take a chance on her getting trampled or knocked down the stairs by someone in a panic.

He'd almost lost her twice today. And that was *after* he'd already ID'd her dead body.

He carried her to safety himself.

Chapter Nine

Rosalyn found herself being checked out by Dr. Puglisi for the second time in eight hours. Another ultrasound.

And thank God again both she and the baby were all right.

"I can admit you if you want, especially since it seems like fate wants you here in the hospital." Dr. Puglisi peered over her medical chart at Rosalyn. "But honestly, there's no reason for you to stay."

Rosalyn's eyes and throat hurt, like Steve had told her his did. Neither of them had inhaled enough smoke to do any real damage, thanks to Steve's quick thinking and ability to get them to the stairwell and out of the smoke rapidly.

"You're fortunate, of course," the doctor continued. "Both times tonight. Especially for someone who seems to be a magnet for trouble."

"I don't want to stay at the hospital if I don't have to, and if the baby is safe." Rosalyn put a hand protectively over her stomach.

"That little guy is perfectly fine. As a matter of fact, any day now you're going to be feeling him move more pronouncedly."

"All I've felt is like I have bubbles in my stomach all the time."

Dr. Puglisi smiled at her. "Those bubbles, the fluttery feeling, is your son."

"It is?" Rosalyn looked over at Steve. He was looking as shocked as she felt.

"Trust me." The doctor smiled again, then turned toward the door. "It won't be long until it's less like bubbles and more like karate kicks. Now, please, don't let me see you back here again tonight."

The doctor left and Rosalyn turned to Steve. He'd been by her side on the ride to the hospital—he'd driven them himself this time instead of taking an ambulance—and the entire time she'd waited to see Dr. Puglisi. He'd been pretty quiet that whole time too, pensive. The only time he really talked had been when he'd stepped out into the hallway to discuss something with someone from the sheriff's office. He'd also been back and forth on his phone all night.

"I'm going to take a shower." She slid her legs over the side of the hospital bed. They'd been given a private room with a bathroom; she might as well make use of it. She had a change of clothes in her tote bag.

"Good idea. I'll take one as soon as you're done." He walked beside her to the door, as if he was afraid she might need help.

"I'm okay," she told him. "I didn't get hurt."

He flattened his lips, narrowed his eyes, obviously upset. They'd both almost been killed twice tonight, so his anger was justified.

She wanted to talk to him about the fire. That had to have been just a terrible coincidence, right?

Or had the Watcher been so close he'd followed them or heard them talking about where they would be staying.

Rosalyn couldn't stop the shudder that ripped through her at the thought.

Steve was close enough to see it. "Sure you're okay?"

No, she wasn't sure she was okay. The opposite. And now she had dragged Steve down the rabbit hole with her. A dark, dangerous rabbit hole where someone was determined to kill everyone who got close to her. And now it looked like maybe the Watcher was trying to kill her too.

She opened her mouth to ask Steve what he thought, what they should do. But he put a finger over her lips before she could get the words out.

"Shower. You'll feel better. You're safe here—we both are. Let's take advantage of that."

Rosalyn nodded. He was right.

"Do you mind if I borrow your cell phone while you're in there?"

"I don't have one. It was one of the first things I got rid of."

"You haven't had one since you've come back to Pensacola?"

She shook her head. "I haven't had one since the Watcher followed me to Dallas and sent me a series of texts. I destroyed it. Thought it might be the way he was following me."

"Smart girl. I was thinking the same thing."

She shrugged. "I didn't want to give him any extra means of being able to communicate with me."

"Okay."

Steve was right—the shower did help her feel better. Or at least washed away the smell of the smoke that had almost taken their lives.

Steve took one after her but didn't have a set of his own clothes to change into. A nurse brought a set of scrubs for him to wear, as well as a T-shirt.

Steve made a hot doctor as well as law enforcement officer.

Which was another thing they needed to talk about. Exactly what he did in law enforcement. Just add that to the list of all the stuff they still needed to talk about.

Less than an hour after changing they walked out of the

hospital. Steve hadn't said much to her during that time, but he definitely had a plan.

"Do you want to tell me what exactly the plan is?" she asked as they got back into her car.

"I'm a cop who works in Miami. I've booked us a flight there that leaves in a couple of hours."

Of all the things he might have said, that wasn't what she'd expected. "You told me you were from Colorado."

He looked over at her, eyes narrowed. "I guess neither of us was telling the truth that night."

Rosalyn knew she had stolen from him. She was the one who had left him without a word. But somehow finding out that he had been lying about things he'd told her during their time together hurt her. He'd obviously wanted to make sure she could never track him down.

He winced. "Rosalyn—"

She sat up straighter in the seat. "No, you're right. We were both dishonest. And you don't have to take me with you now. As a matter of fact, that's probably better."

"No, you'll stay with me."

Why did he need her to stay with him now when he had gone out of his way to make sure she wouldn't be able to find him six months ago? She wanted to argue further but he had pulled into the parking lot of a superstore.

"Let's go. I need some clothes and you'll need some other stuff."

"Can't this wait until we get to Miami?" Why would he want to buy clothes here when he'd be back to his own home and stuff in just a couple of hours? His scrubs were unusual, but not overly so.

"No. Let's go." He got out of the car and went around to her side. "Bring your bag, everything."

She left the sweater in the seat and got out.

"No, bring that too."

"But I'm not cold."

He grabbed it out of the seat. "Bring it all anyway. Let's go."

She barely resisted rolling her eyes at his gruff tone. What had happened to the man who had been talking to her so kindly—trying to understand everything about what had been happening to her over the past year—a few hours ago at her run-down hotel room?

This gruff stranger had replaced him. He didn't seem to want to talk to her at all.

Maybe it was the two near-death experiences in one night since hanging around her. She couldn't blame him for that. Whether he was in law enforcement or not, it looked like Rosalyn might be back on her own again soon.

His actions inside the store didn't reassure her. He grabbed a cart, then kept her right next to him as they went through both the women's section, where he told her to grab jeans and a shirt, and men's, where they did the same for him.

He even grabbed underwear for both of them. When she tried to protest that she'd had a spare set in the tote bag, he ignored her and grabbed a set anyway. He pulled her to the dressing room, which was thankfully empty of everyone, including an attendant, since it was nearly six o'clock in the morning.

"Change all your clothes." He turned and walked toward the men's changing room.

Rosalyn had had just about enough of the manhandling.

"Look, I don't know exactly what your problem is, although honestly, I can understand if you're upset because of both the drunk-driver guy and the fire. But let's just talk about it, okay?"

Steve looked at her for a long time, then finally just turned away again. "No, not right now."

She could actually feel her eyes bugging out of her head. "Not right now? What is the matter with you?"

"Just go put on the other clothes."

"Maybe I'm just fine in the clothes I'm in. Have you thought of—"

The air rushed out of her body as he grabbed her by the arms and walked forward—forcing her backward into the dressing room. He went in right along with her and didn't stop until her back was up against the wall and he was pressed all the way up against her.

She would've thought he'd lost his mind if she hadn't been so turned on by the feel of him pressed against her. His mouth was just inches from hers and she couldn't stop staring at it.

But his lips didn't kiss her. Instead he dipped his head right next to her ear.

"You're bugged."

At first all she felt was the delicious heat from his breath on her earlobe. Then his whispered words made their way through her desire-addled brain.

"What—?"

She barely got the words out before his lips were on hers. She realized it was a kiss to stop her from saying anything that would give away the information about the bug, but she still couldn't stop her arms from circling up around his shoulders.

His lips moved back down her jaw until he was at her ear again.

"It's important that we not say anything that gives away that we know. I'll explain more later, but right now, we need to ditch everything."

Rosalyn nodded.

"Ahem, excuse me, mister. Men aren't allowed in the ladies' dressing room." A young store associate peeked his head into the room. "I'm afraid you'll have to change in the men's section."

Steve nodded and looked at Rosalyn on the way out. "Everything. Okay?"

As soon as Steve and the clerk left, Rosalyn closed the door and stripped off all her clothes.

A bug? Like a transmitting device?

She'd thought maybe her car was being tracked but hadn't considered some sort of tracking device on her clothing. But as she thought of it more, she cursed herself for being so obtuse. All those times she had thought the Watcher was in her head, he'd really just been on her clothes.

That even explained why sometimes he waited many days between contacting her but sometimes he communicated with her more than once within a few hours.

Because some clothes were bugged and some weren't.

Most of her clothes had been destroyed last night in the fire, along with her duffel bag. She tore off the rest and put on the new clothes Steve had left her. Everything changed, down to a new pair of socks and athletic shoes, bile caught in her throat the whole time.

She was just coming out of the changing room as an alarm started blaring overhead. Steve was standing, waiting for her. He turned to the clerk.

"What does that alarm mean? Fire?"

The kid shook his head. "No. I don't think so. I haven't worked here very long but I don't remember that one from my training. Tornado, maybe?"

Steve grabbed her hand. "We've got to go."

"I'm ready. All new clothes."

"Your bag has to go too. It could also easily be tracked."

She hated to give up the bag—it had been a part of every single move she'd made for nearly a year—but didn't argue. Steve had another similar one he'd grabbed.

"I want to keep my notebook—is that okay? It has all entries about the Watcher."

Steve took it and flipped through it. "It looks clean."

She also took out her money and driver's license. Everything else—makeup, pens, knickknacks—got thrown in the trash with the pen.

The siren suddenly cut off. "It must have been a drill," the clerk muttered.

Steve looked at the guy's name tag. "Hey, Paul, you want to make a hundred dollars?"

Paul stood up. "Am I going to get fired for it?"

"No. I just need you to take the tags off all these clothes and pay for them up at a register. Any change left over is yours to keep."

Nobody had to ask Paul twice. He took the money and the tags from their clothes and left.

Steve took Rosalyn's hand and they walked toward the front.

"Should we do something with our old clothes?"

Steve shook his head. "I found two transmitting devices in your clothes. There's no telling how many more there might be. Hopefully, leaving them in the dressing room will throw your stalker off."

"And we're just going to waltz out the front door?"

"Yep."

"Isn't that dangerous?"

"I think the siren was an attempt to get us to do something stupid like run out the back door. Instead we'll just walk out the front like everyone else."

"And get on a flight to Miami."

"Nope. We were never going to Miami. I was just hoping to mislead whoever might be listening to our conversation."

"Oh. So you really are from Colorado?"

"Yep. And that's where we're headed. That's the best place for me to keep you safe."

Chapter Ten

"We're driving to Colorado Springs? Won't that take like three days?"

They were on their way, via rental car, and were already out of Florida.

"A day and a half at most. Barely more than it would have taken to fly, given the stopovers."

When Steve's assistant had sent him the flight list, they'd all looked pretty miserable: late starts, long layovers. When he'd found the transmitting device on Rosalyn's sweater, he'd known he had to get her out of there right away. Waiting ten hours for a flight wasn't an option.

He glanced over at her. "It's the best way, I promise. It got us out of Florida the quickest. Hopefully your stalker thinks we're on our way to Miami."

"That's how he's known where I was." Rosalyn shook her head. "I thought he might have some sort of tracker in my car, so I ditched it a couple of times. But he always found me."

"I don't know how you've kept away from him for the past few months." The thought of Rosalyn—alone and pregnant—trying to stay ahead of a killer sent ice through Steve's veins. It was all he could do to stop from grabbing her hand, which sat in her lap.

Hell, it was all he could do not to pull over the car at the first hotel and make love to her for a few days. Away from all the crazy surrounding her life and the fanatic trying to hurt her.

"Actually, I haven't heard from him since I last saw you in Pensacola. He left a note under your hotel room door and that's why I left."

He looked at her. *"What?"*

She shrugged. "For six months I haven't heard anything from the Watcher."

Steve brought his eyes back to the road. "No, go back. The Watcher left you a note at my hotel six months ago?"

"He slid it under the door that second night."

"Do you remember what it said?" Now Steve could appreciate why she wanted to keep the notes so badly.

"No, I try not to remember, because it would drive me a little crazy. That's why I write them down in my notebook." Rosalyn reached down in her bag and pulled out the notebook she'd begged him to let her keep. She turned to an entry. "It said 'If you like Steve so much, I guess I'll need to meet him soon.'" She closed the notebook and laid it in her lap.

Steve's hands gripped the steering wheel tighter. "When did this note arrive? What time?"

"At around three o'clock in the morning. You were asleep. I heard it slide under the door."

The Watcher had been at his door. For him to have been so close and Steve to have known nothing about it infuriated him. "So you opened it, right? When you saw what it was, why didn't you wake me up?"

He understood why Rosalyn wouldn't run after a stalker, but Steve wouldn't have any qualms whatsoever about doing so.

She stared at him for a long minute. "I thought you were some businessman. I had no idea you were in law enforcement."

"I didn't have to be in law enforcement to help you.

Any decent human being would've wanted to help you deal with a maniac who was tracking your every move."

"I had already lost two decent human beings for that very reason! I couldn't go through that again. Couldn't drag you into my own personal hell."

Steve gritted his teeth. Logically he could understand why she hadn't wanted to tell him about the Watcher, but he still wished she had. This could've already been settled by now.

"Two? Someone else tried to help you? What happened?"

"A mechanic in Memphis named Shawn. It was before I knew better. And certainly before I knew he had some sort of bug transmitting everything I said."

"He died?"

Rosalyn nodded. "The night I told him about the Watcher."

"Another heart attack, like the detective?"

"No. The news called it a random act of violence. Some sort of gang retaliation, even though the guy had never been involved with gangs and wasn't even near that part of town." Rosalyn turned toward the window. "So no, I wasn't about to tell you about the Watcher and see you die also."

She'd carried a lot of weight by herself for many months, having to worry about not only herself but other people too. And now a baby. Most people would've buckled under the pressure.

He redirected the conversation. "But you haven't heard anything from the Watcher since that night at the hotel when we were together?"

"Well, once I got back to Pensacola three days ago to meet my sister, I heard from him. Another note under my hotel room door." She shuddered.

"This one was worse than the others?"

"No, it had just been so long since I'd received anything."

"So you mean after the morning you left me six months ago, you hadn't heard from the Watcher until you came back to Pensacola this week?"

That meant something. Steve didn't know exactly what yet, but he knew that the Watcher's absence from Rosalyn's life for six months would be a big clue in solving the case.

"Where did you go when you left me?"

She looked over at him and flushed. "I'm sorry I stole your money. I didn't have any left."

"I would've given it to you if you'd asked."

"That would've involved giving you more information than was good for your health."

"I would've preferred that to waking up with you gone and thinking the worst of you for six months."

Actually, he'd thought worse of himself than her. That he'd been a gullible fool. But he'd thought pretty badly of her too.

That wasn't what was important now. "So you took nearly $200…"

"You have to understand, I was at a pretty low place. Everywhere I'd gone, the Watcher had found me. Admittedly, he hadn't tried to hurt me like he has this week, but it was still wearing me down. A note slipped under my door every night or so, knowing he was that close…"

"I'm sure it was nerve-racking."

"It was nerve-racking the first couple of months. By the time I met you, I was considering just killing myself and saving the Watcher the trouble."

He glanced over at her. "Seriously?"

She nodded. "That night at the bar when we met, I ran in because of the rain. I'd been out watching the sunset, considering if taking my own life would be better than letting the Watcher continue to kill innocent people."

Steve couldn't even bear to think about it. "Rosalyn—"

"Then I met you," she continued. "It didn't change anything really, but—"

She stopped and looked away.

"But what?"

"I connected with someone. With you. It was the first time I hadn't felt alone in so long." She tucked a strand of hair behind her ear. "I wasn't using you for money, Steve. I panicked when I saw the Watcher's note. All I could think of was getting away."

He believed her. She hadn't taken his credit cards or stolen his rental car. If she'd been trying to take him for all she could, she wouldn't have left those behind.

"Okay, so what did you do when you left that morning?"

"I took a bus as far as the money I stole from you would take me. I didn't want to go back to my car—I just wanted to get out of town. That ended up being Ellijay, Georgia."

"Never heard of it."

"I'd be shocked if you had. It's a tiny town north of Atlanta, in the Blue Ridge Mountains. Population just over fifteen hundred."

"What was in Ellijay?"

"Nothing whatsoever. That's just where my money ran out."

She stared out the window for a long time.

"Did Ellijay end up being good or bad?"

"Good. Definitely good. I needed to get some money right away, so I asked the couple who owned the small café in town if I could wash dishes or do any odd jobs just for the day, for cash.

"Mr. and Mrs. Ammons—Jim and Cheryl—said yes. I washed dishes a couple of days and didn't really have anywhere to go."

Steve's teeth gritted but he didn't say anything.

"Cheryl invited me to stay at their house, which was

above the café. I slept in their son's room. He had died in the army a long time ago."

"And you had no notes or communication with the Watcher the whole time?"

"Nothing. I thought maybe he'd moved on or I was out of the territory he considered 'his.'" She shrugged. "Or maybe he had followed me but once he saw I was pregnant, I no longer interested him."

Any of those scenarios were possible.

"I definitely didn't tell the Ammonses about him," Rosalyn continued, shifting on the seat to get comfortable. "I didn't want to take a chance with their lives. Plus, Jim was already pretty paranoid since their son died due to a military communication breach or something. Jim and Cheryl live completely off the grid. No cell phone, no television, no computers or internet."

"I'm glad you had someone to help you."

"They're amazing. Gruff and not very talkative, and pretty old-fashioned. When I found out I was pregnant, I was afraid they might turn me out, but they didn't even think about it."

"Why did you leave? If the Watcher had lost track of you, why didn't you just stay in Ellijay?"

From the corner of his eye he could see Rosalyn's hands begin twisting in her lap. "As I was getting further and further along in my pregnancy, I began to think about the future. To worry that the Watcher was playing some sort of game. That maybe he was waiting until the baby was born and then would take me or both of us.

"I like the Ammonses a lot, but they're older, in their seventies. They couldn't take care of a baby. So I decided to call Lindsey. To just meet with her and see what shape her life was in."

She glanced at him, then out the window quickly. Obviously there was more to the story.

"And?"

"And what?"

"And what are you trying to get away with not telling me?"

"Nothing. It's not important."

"Rosalyn, anything having to do with you and the baby is important."

She shrugged. "I had Lindsey meet me in Pensacola because I was going to try to talk the hotel into giving me your info so I could contact you."

"For what, money?" As soon as the words were out of his mouth, Steve wished he could cut off his own tongue.

Rosalyn didn't look at him, just shifted her weight so her back was to him and she was looking completely out the window.

"I'm sorry. I didn't mean that." He wished he could see her face.

"Yes, you did. At least part of you did. The part of you who knows me as someone who lied, stole from you, then showed up pregnant with what may or may not be your baby. The part of you who doesn't want to be taken in again."

"Rosalyn—"

"You know what? I don't even blame you. You're right to be wary. Hopefully that will keep you alive longer."

Steve tried to figure out how to undo the damage his words had done.

She laid her seat back, still facing away from him. "We've got a long drive ahead. If you don't mind, I'm going to rest now so I can take a driving shift later. It'll make it easier on everyone."

He wasn't sure if she meant sleeping now would make it easier or driving later would do so. Clarifying would just make it worse, so he decided to let it go.

He knew she hadn't been coming to find him for money. For physical security, yes, but not money.

He shouldn't have said what he had. Even if he did still mistrust her. She hadn't given him much reason to trust her, truth be told.

Some of that he could alleviate right now. He knew Rosalyn was asleep, so he called his office.

"Cynthia," he said to his assistant by way of greeting. "I need everything you can give me about Rosalyn Mellinger. And anything you can find on Jim and Cheryl Ammons. North Georgia."

"Got it."

"I'll need you to call me back and read it to me. There's been a change of plans. We're driving from Pensacola back to HQ."

"That's quite a trek."

"Couldn't stay in Pensacola any longer. Had two attempts on our lives in under twelve hours." Steve explained about the driver and fire.

"Damn, boss. Do you want me to redirect an Omega plane to you? Or send Liam or one of the guys out to meet you for protection?"

"No, I got rid of how he was tracking us. We should be fine now. We'll stop at a hotel tonight, but I should be in the office by tomorrow afternoon."

"I'll make sure Joe has all the party paraphernalia gone by then."

Steve snickered. Joe Matarazzo was the team's hostage negotiator and was known for his partying. Or had been until his wife, Laura, reined him in a few months ago.

Rosalyn hadn't budged during his entire conversation. Her breathing hadn't changed; there'd been no sudden tension to make him think she was awake. She was exhausted. She'd barely gotten any sleep before the fire had awakened them again.

She was still sound asleep two hours later when Jon Hatton, one of Omega's best profilers and Steve's personal friend, called him back.

"Hey, boss, Cynthia and I have been gathering the info you wanted."

"Anything interesting?"

"Rosalyn Mellinger, twenty-four years old. Daughter of Crystal Mellinger and twin sister to Lindsey Rose. Hey, I see what the mom did there with the names—"

"Yeah, already got that, Jon. Keep going."

"No father listed on the birth certificate. Arrested as a teenager for shoplifting. That's where her prints are from and that sealed juvenile record was a bitch to get opened. But that little run-in with the law must have scared her straight because she's been straight as an arrow as an adult. Went to college, became an accountant. Worked every day until the day she quit. Not even a parking ticket."

Steve glanced over at Rosalyn, still asleep. "Okay."

"Sister has been in and out of juvie rehabs, then adult versions since her mid-teens. No college, barely finished high school. The mom is pretty much a deadbeat also. Alcoholic. Lives on welfare."

Okay, so no family support for Rosalyn. That explained why she'd been on the run by herself for a year.

"In the last few months Rosalyn's name has been mentioned in multiple police reports, all over the Southeast and Texas. She's been talking to them about a stalker, but nothing has come of any of the investigations. Nobody has been taking her seriously."

"Well, I'm taking her seriously now, Jon. Someone nearly killed us twice in the last day."

"I'll see what I can dig up on the reports."

"Thanks, Jon. And if you can find out all you can about a Detective Johnson in Shreveport—he would've died of a heart attack eight or nine months ago—and a mechanic in Memphis who was killed in a random act of gang violence. Shawn something."

"Okay, these two related?"

"Just look for anything suspicious in either."

"All right, and we're still checking on the Ammonses. All I can find so far is a dead son in the military nearly fifteen years ago. They keep a low profile, whoever they are. I can't even find a bank account."

"That fits with what Rosalyn told me. Let me know if there's anything else."

"Got it. You watch your six, boss. I've already got a hinky feeling about this whole thing."

Steve took Jon's "hinky" feelings very seriously. Not to mention, Steve felt like they were dealing with something pretty major too. He said his goodbyes and disconnected the call.

Rosalyn turned in her sleep toward him, obviously finding it difficult to get comfortable. He had thought about driving all the way through the night and getting to Colorado Springs in one push.

But that wouldn't work. Rosalyn needed a bed where she could get a proper night's rest. Somewhere where no one was trying to run her over or set the building on fire or slipping notes under her door.

Rosalyn had been on her own for way too long. Steve planned to show her she wasn't alone anymore.

Chapter Eleven

She awoke to Steve's voice again, but at least this time he wasn't trying to tell her the building was on fire.

"Let's get you inside. Then you can go back to sleep if you want."

She looked at the handsome man, so strong and able, who had her tucked into his side leading her into the hotel lobby. Oh, she wanted, but sleep wasn't it.

She wanted him. Sometimes he said stupid stuff, but she still wanted him.

He used the key card to enter their room and turned on the light. This was a much nicer room than the ones she'd slept in for the last year when she hadn't been at the Ammonses' house. Generic, sure, but clean, tasteful, new. With a king-size bed in the middle of it.

She walked all the way in, then turned to him. "No hot tub this time."

She almost smiled at the speed with which his eyes flew to hers. Good. She wasn't the only one affected by the heat between them.

"Yeah, a shame." He pulled himself together and turned to close the door behind them. "Sorry we don't have any change of clothes. Once we get to Colorado Springs, I'll make sure you get something right away."

"It's no problem. I'm sure I'll be okay for one more day in these."

Maybe it was the fact that she'd slept most of the day or maybe it was because Steve had found the electronic transmitters and that just explained so damn much, but Rosalyn felt different.

For the first time since this nightmare began nearly a year ago, she was positive there would not be a note under the door tonight.

All those times she thought she was crazy, that the Watcher could hear her thoughts, that he lived inside her head? He'd simply lived inside the fiber of her clothing, able to hear who she'd talked to, where she'd checked in. That's how he'd found her.

All the times Rosalyn had talked to herself, he'd been privy to those conversations. Embarrassing, but at least it all made sense now.

The fact that he had gotten close enough to put transmitters on her clothing was terrifying. Steve had found two. Who knew how many more there might have been in the clothing that had been destroyed by the fire.

But there weren't any transmitters anymore. Rosalyn didn't even mind the ill-fitting supermarket clothes she was wearing now, because it meant nobody could hear her. Nobody but she and Steve knew where they were.

She hadn't realized how much weight she had shouldered for so long until a great deal of it was lifted. It allowed her to focus on other things.

Like how she was in a hotel with a gorgeous man. Six feet of muscle and awareness. Dark hair and green eyes staring at her like he was slightly nervous about what she would do next.

She hadn't had anyone but him hold her in the last year. No one had kissed her or pulled her into any embrace at all except for Steve. No one had touched her.

Sure, Jim and Cheryl Ammons had given her a brush on the shoulder or pat on the back here and there. Physical demonstration of affection wasn't the older couple's way. They weren't heartless, and cared about her for sure, but they just weren't very demonstrative in showing it.

It wasn't like she missed it. Rosalyn had been raised in a house where affectionate touches were few and far between. It was one of the things she'd promised herself her child would never go without. Her son would be hugged and kissed until he squirmed to get away. He would know every day he was loved, not just by words but by gestures.

But watching Steve cross the room, secure the door to make sure they were safe and turn those intense green eyes back on her, Rosalyn was quite sure of the type of touch *she* wanted right now.

And a hug wasn't it.

She wasn't looking for comfort, like she had been six months ago. She wanted the heat she and Steve had felt together.

He slowly took a step toward her. She smiled at his hesitancy. The cop in him must be aware of the predator in the room.

Her.

And he was the prey. Big, strong sexy man probably wasn't used to that.

"Do you want to take a shower first or do you want me to?" he asked.

"What about taking one together?"

"Rosalyn…" His words were a protest, but she saw the tightening of his body. The slight flare in his eyes.

She took a step toward him. "We'll at least save water that way."

"I have a feeling we'd be in there too long to save any water." He tried to step around her so he could get to the other side of the room, but she moved so she was right in front of him.

"So take a shower with me and don't save water."

She could almost see his conscience pour over him. "Rosalyn, it's been a really long couple of days. Traumatic couple of days."

The words were for her benefit, not his. She raised one eyebrow and gave him a little snicker. "And you're tired? Need a little you time? Drink a chai latte or something?"

She saw the smile he fought against. He wanted her— she knew he did. She wasn't going to give up at his first token protest.

"No, I'm talking about you. You've had a rough couple of days, hell, a rough few months. There's no need to jump into anything just because you're relieved or grateful or whatever."

"Generally I don't pay my debts with sex, if that's what you're thinking."

He winced. "No, I didn't mean you were trying to pay me. I just meant—"

She stepped closer to stop him from saying anything further. He was digging himself a hole and she was afraid he was going to piss her off with whatever asinine thing came out of his mouth next.

"Steve, don't overthink it."

"Somebody needs to overthink it. Or at least think at all."

He was protective of her and she appreciated that. But right now she didn't want him to use his strength to protect her. She wanted him to use his strength to help her celebrate how good it felt to be unfettered for the first time in as long as she could remember.

She ran both her hands up his arms. She felt him tense but he didn't pull away. She leaned in closer.

"I'm happy to be alive. I'm happy no one is going to find me and slip a note under the door tonight. I'm happy we're both safe here together."

She slid her arms to his shoulders, then around his neck, pulling his lips down to hers.

The heat was still there. Thank goodness it wasn't just something she'd remembered, something she'd dreamed about. His lips were still as firm and hot and inviting as she'd known they would be.

But he wasn't pulling her to him. His hands were on her waist, but they seemed neutral—neither encouraging nor discouraging.

"Rosalyn…" he groaned against her mouth.

He was going to let her go, she could tell.

"Steve, you got me away from a lunatic. I want to celebrate that."

Those were the wrong words. He stepped back from her. "You don't owe me anything."

Were they really back to that again? "I know. And I appreciate very much that you're not the type of guy who would try to lord that over my head. But that's not the point."

He grabbed her arms and set her back from him. "Look, I've worked around people who have been traumatized by violence. Sometimes it's hard to recognize the symptoms in yourself. I just don't want you to do something you might regret."

Rosalyn smiled. She appreciated his concern, she really did. But this wasn't something she was going to regret—she was positive about that. "Believe me, I'm not going to regret this."

She tried to step forward but he stopped her.

"Well, have you considered that maybe I don't want to do this? That it's something I'll regret?" Frustration flavored his tone.

He didn't want her. The reality hit her like a bucket of ice. She immediately stepped back from him.

What did she expect, really? She'd lied to him, stolen

from him, dragged him into a situation that had almost gotten him killed twice. Not to mention shown up pregnant with his baby.

Of course getting involved with her physically wasn't a good idea for him. Yeah, there was heat between them, but he was smart enough to know that wasn't enough to justify getting close to her.

All the perk, all the joy seemed to drain out of her. "You're right—I hadn't thought of that. Smart move on your part."

"Rosalyn…" He took a step toward her.

She immediately jerked back. He couldn't touch her. Not now. If he did, she might shatter into a million pieces. "I'm going to take a shower."

She turned and all but ran.

STEVE WATCHED ROSALYN nearly run across the room to the bathroom.

Damn it. What the hell was the matter with him? Why would he say that to her?

He was the director of one of the most prestigious law enforcement agencies in the country. He regularly spoke to the congressmen, senators, the president's advisers. Hell, he'd even spoken to two different presidents in his tenure as the director of the Critical Response Division.

He was known for being well-spoken. Known for reading a situation and doing and/or saying whatever was needed. He had a team of dozens of people who looked to him to provide guidance and leadership. To know the words that needed to be said when everything around them was falling apart.

Yet somehow he'd just managed to say the worst possible thing to one small, fragile woman who'd just been reaching out to him for human contact.

And the worst thing about his ridiculous words? None of them were true.

Not want her? That was so far from the truth he could barely wrap his mind around it.

But he was convinced she felt beholden to him. That she wouldn't really want him under normal circumstances that didn't involve life-threatening situations.

Of course, he wanted her pretty desperately, and life-threatening situations were commonplace for him.

His fingers itched to touch her. To run through her hair and along her body. To see the changes pregnancy had made, beyond what he could make out from beneath her clothes.

He wanted her with a passion that went against everything in his calm, collected nature. He couldn't ever remember wanting anyone this much. Not even his wife, Melanie. They'd loved each other, absolutely, but with the low simmer of the knowledge that they would have the rest of their lives together to work through their love.

The rest of their lives together had ended up being only six short years.

The fire that consumed him every time he was around Rosalyn was so different from that it almost couldn't be compared. Being around her caused him to lose his cool. Lose his focus.

Melanie would approve. Deep in the back of his mind, Steve knew his wife would approve of the young woman in the bathroom who had stayed alive under some pretty desperate circumstances. Would approve of the fact that Rosalyn shook him up enough to make him say stupid things.

He heard the shower turn on in the bathroom.

And maybe Rosalyn just wanted him because she wanted him. Not because of anything else but this damn heat between them. An itch that had just barely gotten scratched six months ago and had been driving them both crazy ever since.

Maybe he'd just sent her running despondent into the bathroom not because he didn't want her—he almost laughed outright at the thought—but because of some ridiculous, completely wrong feeling of overprotection.

He was an idiot.

The bathroom door opened but her head didn't pop out. "You know what, Drackett? You're an idiot."

His legs were moving before his brain had even processed what was going on. He caught the bathroom door just before it shut and pushed it all the way open.

Rosalyn's mouth made a little o.

But the heat burned in her eyes the way he knew it burned in his.

"You know what? I *am* an idiot."

He kissed her.

There was no gentleness in the kiss. No finesse.

But there was plenty of heat and need and passion.

He lifted her up and set her on the bathroom vanity, then grabbed her hips and slid her all the way to the edge until she was flush up against him. They both groaned as her calves hooked around the backs of his thighs. Her fingers linked behind his neck, keeping him against her.

"Rosalyn, I'm sorry—" He began his murmured apology against her mouth, but she stopped him.

"No apologies. No talking. No thinking."

He couldn't hide the effect she had on him, didn't even try to pretend he could control his response. He just let the heat take over.

As he stripped them both out of their clothes and slipped his arms around her hips to carry her with him to the shower—unwilling to separate their bodies for even the few steps it would take for them to walk—he hoped the heat consuming them both wouldn't burn them away.

Leaving nothing but ash in its place.

Chapter Twelve

They got on the road again early, after catching a quick breakfast. By lunch they were only a few hours from Colorado Springs. They stopped at a truck-stop diner just outside Dalhart, Texas, off Highway 87.

Rosalyn felt rested. She shouldn't, since she'd been awake for a big chunk of the night for the best of reasons, but she did.

Steve had seemed fascinated by the changes in her body that had come about from the pregnancy. She was right at the perfect stage: not sick and tired all the time like she'd been in the early days, but not so big that she was waddling around. She knew that would be coming soon.

There were a lot of things unsettled about her future. What was she going to do when she got to Colorado Springs? Get a job and stay there? She had some money she'd saved from working at the diner, but not enough. Especially not when the baby came.

Another thing she and Steve needed to talk about. The list was getting pretty long.

She was concerned about the future but for the first time the thought didn't send her into a near panic.

Maybe it was the knowledge that the Watcher could no longer find her now that the transmitting devices in her clothes were gone. Maybe it was because Steve was here and believed she was in danger.

But she had slept like she hadn't been able to sleep in months. Even when she'd been at the Ammonses' house and it seemed liked the Watcher couldn't find her, she hadn't slept this good.

She was sure having Steve's arms around her helped.

But even if they hadn't made love, if he hadn't held her, she knew just his presence made a huge difference to her psyche. She wasn't alone. And although there was a lot she and Steve still needed to work out, she knew it would happen eventually.

He was looking through her notebook now, the one with all the dates and recordings of the notes or messages the Watcher had given her.

"I wish we hadn't lost all the notes in the fire." She sipped on her iced tea, knowing she shouldn't be drinking caffeine, but surely one cup wouldn't hurt. She savored it as well as her large lunch.

Steve shrugged. "They would've helped for sure, especially with prosecution for stalking. But this notebook gives us a lot of information. My people will be able to see what patterns can be established from this."

"Detective Johnson steered me right by telling me to write everything down. Actually, at the time, I think he just told me that to give me something proactive to do. Make me feel less like a victim, more like an active part in an investigation."

And it had worked. For the first time Rosalyn had felt hopeful. Right up until Johnson had died two days later.

Steve took her hand. "I already have people looking into his death and the mechanic's. They'll dig through what it looks like on the surface to what's actually underneath, okay?"

Rosalyn nodded. "Thank you."

He handed the notebook back to her. "I'm going to pay

and use the restroom. Then we'll hit the road again. We should make it to Colorado Springs by this afternoon."

She smiled. "I'll try not to sleep the entire day away this time."

He stood up. "You can do whatever you need to—don't worry about that. It's been a stressful couple of days. Your body needs rest."

It had been a stressful year. But she just nodded.

She was thankful Steve was looking into Detective Johnson's and Shawn the mechanic's deaths. She still didn't know exactly what Steve did in law enforcement, but evidently he was pretty high up. He hadn't offered any information and she hadn't wanted to ask.

She needed to call the Ammonses before they got back on the road. She needed to let them know she was okay. They didn't have a phone upstairs at their house, due mostly to Jim's paranoia that the government was listening or watching them, but had one at the café.

Rosalyn got change from the waitress and went into the hallway lined with phones, a throwback from before everyone had cell phones and truckers used to have to make calls to their loved ones from pay phones. She dialed the number for the Ammonses' café, then put in the change required to connect the call.

"Main Street Cafe."

"Hi, Cheryl, it's—"

"Oh, Rosalyn, honey! Thank goodness you're okay."

It was the most emotion she'd ever heard out of the stoic Cheryl.

"I'm sorry if you've been worried about me. I should've called earlier."

But a deranged stalker found me again, killed my sister, then tried to kill me twice.

Rosalyn had never told the Ammonses about the Watcher. She suspected they knew she was on the run from someone but had never pressed for details and she'd never given any.

"That's all right. I'm just glad to hear you're safe now. Jim was worried too."

Rosalyn laughed. "I don't think Jim worries about anything but the government encroaching on his boundaries."

"Well, he talked yesterday about putting a phone line in the house so you could call there if you needed anything."

Rosalyn felt tears come to her eyes. For Jim to have considered that, he really did care about her. "Cheryl, I'll just call the café, okay? Tell Jim he doesn't need to do anything so drastic like get a phone in the house."

The words were in jest, but Rosalyn meant it. She knew what it meant for Jim to have even considered it.

"Are you coming back? You know you're welcome anytime. You and the baby."

"Thanks, Cheryl." Emotion choked Rosalyn's voice. "I've got some things to take care of. But I might be back. I don't know yet."

"Well, we both mean it when we say we want you here. Don't forget that, okay?"

"Yes, ma'am. I'm with the baby's father now and we're trying to get some stuff figured out." Probably not the stuff Cheryl was thinking of, but that didn't matter. "I'll call in a couple of days with an update, okay?"

"You be careful, hon. And remember you've always got a home here if you want it."

"Thanks, Cheryl. Give Jim my love."

"I will. Bye."

Rosalyn put the phone receiver back in its cradle and leaned her head against it. It was nice to know she had someone who cared about her. That she had options. But she wondered if she was opening up the Ammonses to the Watcher's clutches. What if he found her again? If she went back there, would she be leading him to them? She couldn't stand the thought of the older couple falling victim to him.

Maybe she'd done the wrong thing by calling them at all. But surely with the transmitters gone, no harm would come to them.

She looked up to find Steve staring at her, eyes narrowed. She gave him a little wave as he walked over, but all the easy camaraderie they'd had at lunch, the closeness they'd shared last night seemed to be gone.

"I would've let you use my phone if you needed to make a call. You didn't have to pay for it."

"That's okay. I didn't want to bother you. And I didn't want to waste time. I know we're trying to make it to Colorado Springs as quickly as we can."

Rosalyn was still a little overcome with emotion after talking to Cheryl. It must be pregnancy hormones or something. But the thought of Jim agreeing to put a phone in his house just because of her had tears rushing to her eyes again. She turned away so Steve wouldn't see.

"Ready to go?" she asked.

Steve grabbed her arm. "Who were you talking to, Rosalyn?"

The anger behind the words took her aback. "Who do you think I was talking to?"

"I don't know. All I know is I leave you alone for the first time in twenty-four hours and you're making mysterious phone calls."

"I was calling Cheryl and Jim Ammons. The people in Ellijay with whom I had been staying. I wanted to let them know I was all right."

"And you couldn't wait to do that in the car on my phone?"

He was still holding her arm. Rosalyn snatched it away. "I didn't think of that, okay? I've been on my own for a while now and I'm not used to having other people around or their resources."

Steve's eyes narrowed more, so she turned and walked out toward the car. Let him believe whatever he wanted to.

It was going to be a long ride to Colorado Springs.

THE HOURS ON the way to Colorado Springs were tense at best. Rosalyn never told him exactly who she had been contacting, but he didn't believe her when she said it was the Ammonses, the couple in Ellijay who had taken her in. After all, hadn't she already told him the husband didn't trust the government and they lived off the grid?

No computer, no phone. So how exactly had she called them?

Steve didn't want to let it, especially after last night, but true doubt about Rosalyn crept in. He was trained to see evil in innocent actions, to question all possibilities.

He had to face the fact that Rosalyn could be using him right now. That she had initiated contact with him in Pensacola for a particular purpose that had nothing to do with the baby or the Watcher.

To what end, he didn't exactly know. But he had to admit she could be working with some sort of partner to get something from him or maneuver him in some way. Maybe she knew who he really was in Omega. He had access to top secret information on a regular basis. Maybe she was hoping to obtain something through him.

He just couldn't get out of his mind how sad she'd looked when getting off the phone. How guilty.

Like she'd done something distasteful and wished she could take it back.

Why would she feel that way after talking to a couple she'd been close to for half a year? And for that matter, why wouldn't she just have used his phone to contact them? It would've made a lot more sense.

Or was it just like Rosalyn had said? She wasn't used to depending on other people. She hadn't had a cell phone in a while. Maybe she hadn't even considered it. She'd just seen the pay phone—a rarity these days—and decided to make the call while Steve was doing other things.

Certainly not nefarious when thought of that way.

Steve's hands gripped the steering wheel tighter. It wasn't often that he called his own judgments and gut feelings into question.

But when it came to Rosalyn, he had to admit that he was not neutral.

He decided to try to talk to her. They couldn't spend the rest of the five hours in silence.

"I'm going to take you into my office. I have people looking into your situation."

She nodded. "Okay. You still haven't told me exactly what you do or who you work for."

He didn't answer. Was it interesting that she would be pressing for info on that topic now or was he just reading into things that weren't there? He looked over at Rosalyn, her crystal-blue eyes staring at him.

He'd swear she was guileless. But he couldn't take the risk. The Critical Response Division wasn't one of the covert divisions of Omega, but Steve still couldn't take a chance on giving Rosalyn any information if he suspected she was working with someone.

God, what a mess that was going to be if she was. Because what if a paternity test proved the baby was his but Rosalyn was really in cahoots with a criminal?

Complicated was an understatement.

Chapter Thirteen

Great. She was trapped in the car with Broody McScary.

What had happened to the passionate man she'd made love with last night? He been here with her until they'd eaten lunch.

Maybe he had indigestion.

No, it wasn't lunch. It was her phone call. He didn't like that she'd had a conversation he couldn't hear. It didn't take a genius to figure out why.

He didn't trust her.

She didn't know exactly what bad thing he kept expecting her to do. Hell, she didn't think *he* knew what bad thing he expected her to do. But obviously he expected something.

She didn't even really want to talk to him, and avoided doing so by pretending to sleep part of the way. But about an hour outside Colorado Springs, she had to go to the bathroom.

"Can we make one short pit stop?"

"We've got less than an hour. We're almost to Pueblo. Can't you hold it?"

If he'd been annoyed, she would've argued with him. But he didn't look annoyed. He looked distrustful.

"Fine." She would hold it, even if it killed her.

Thirty minutes later she was afraid it really would.

"Look, we're going to have to stop, okay? I know you

think I'm planning some sort of nuclear attack or whatever, but my pregnant body is not going to wait to go to the bathroom."

He almost cracked a smile at that. "Fine. I'll get gas while we stop."

He pulled up at the gas pump and Rosalyn ran inside to use the restroom. She felt much better when she came back out. She wondered what she could do to help ease the tension between her and Steve. She had to accept it was his job to be distrustful—he was a cop, after all. She shouldn't be offended if he was butting into her business with questions all the time. Especially if it was because he was trying to keep her safe.

She would be the better person. Maybe buy him a candy bar as a peace offering. Who could resist chocolate? Plus, she was hungry.

Then again, she was always hungry.

She looked out the gas-station convenience-store window at Steve, wondering what he would like. A guy on a motorcycle was moving slowly toward Steve as he pumped the gas. Steve was looking at her. Probably to make sure she wasn't robbing the cash register.

At first she didn't pay any mind to the motorcycle except to wonder why he was coming up directly behind their car rather than to one of the empty pumps. But then she saw the rider pull something out of his jacket. It looked like a small stick.

Then he flicked his wrist and it grew into a much longer club.

He was going to hit Steve with it.

Rosalyn dropped the candy and ran toward the door knowing there was no way she'd make it outside in time to warn Steve or stop the motorcycle guy.

Something in her face alerted him, or maybe just his

cop instincts, and he spun and threw up his arm just as the club came at his head.

A soft scream came out of her mouth as she saw the impact. It had to have hurt—had maybe even broken his arm—but at least Steve was still on his feet. A blow that severe to his head would've killed him.

In the corner of her mind the agony of what this meant—the Watcher had found her again—tried to take control, but she wouldn't let it. She couldn't have a breakdown right now. She had to help Steve.

"Call the police!" she yelled at the cashier. "My friend is being attacked."

She didn't wait to see if the cashier did it; she just ran through the doors.

The guy pulled the club back for another swing, but Steve was more prepared this time. The attacker swung from the side rather than in a downward motion and Steve ducked. He brought his uninjured arm up like he planned to use it to punch the guy, but the man was too far away for Steve to be able to reach him. The stick gave him all the advantage.

He brought it down at Steve again, with not as much force, but it still knocked Steve to the ground as it hit his shoulder. He got back up, but the attacker was already bringing his arm around again.

"Hey, leave him alone!" Rosalyn didn't think through the wisdom of being unarmed, smaller and pregnant when facing the attacker, just knew she had to get him away from Steve. The best way to do that would be to bring as much attention to the situation as possible.

The motorcycle man looked at her, but she couldn't see his face through the darkened visor.

"Yeah, you, get away from him. Somebody help us!"

Rosalyn might not be able to do much but she could scream her head off. She also reached for bottles of oil that were stacked by the front door as she ran past them, throwing them as she went. None of them got far enough to hit the attacker, but at least she was making enough of a spectacle of herself to draw even more attention.

Other people were coming out of the store and a car on the road had pulled in to see what was going on. The motorcycle man realized the situation and threw his stick down and sped off. Nobody could do anything to stop him.

Rosalyn ran over to Steve.

"Are you okay?"

He was still cradling the arm he'd used to block the first—and hardest—hit. "Yeah. I'm okay. I don't have much feeling in my arm, but better than if he had hit me in the head."

Rosalyn clenched her teeth to keep them from chattering at the thought. "It would've killed you."

"Probably not. But it definitely would've knocked me unconscious long enough for him to finish the job."

They heard sirens heading toward them.

"I told the clerk to call the cops. I didn't know what else to do."

Steve tilted his head sideways and looked at her. "You had the clerk call the police?"

"Yeah, well, I wasn't sure my oilcan throwing was going to stop the motorcycle guy, so I thought we better get reinforcements here as soon as possible. Is your arm okay? Let me look at it."

She took a step toward him but stopped when he backed up. She tried not to let his actions hurt her feelings. It probably wasn't personal. He was in pain. Trying to figure out what had happened. Cop mode.

It wasn't long before two police cars and an ambulance were pulling up.

"Do you mind waiting by the car?" Steve asked. "It'll be less complicated if I talk to the locals alone at first."

"Yeah, okay." She shrugged. "I'll be over at the car."

A paramedic walked up to them before she went, so Rosalyn waited. She wanted to make sure Steve was okay.

"Ma'am, were you hurt in any way?" the paramedic asked her.

"No. I was in the store, nowhere near the guy with his club."

"Guy on a motorcycle came up, had an expandable baton." Steve began rolling up his sleeve so he could show his injuries to the paramedic.

Rosalyn gasped when she saw his forearm. It was swollen and already turning purple.

The medic took Steve's arm in his hand. "Can you move all your fingers without pain?"

Steve wiggled them. "Nothing sharp. Just an allover ache."

The medic probed gently around the bruise. "It doesn't seem to be broken, but you should probably get it x-rayed to be sure. You're fortunate. Whoever did this was trying to do you serious harm. It could've shattered your arm."

Steve nodded. "It could've done much worse if he had gotten me on the skull like he was aiming for."

The medic whistled through his teeth. "Yes, for sure. Do you have any other injuries?"

"He got me across the shoulders also, but not with nearly as much force." Steve turned so the medic could see.

"You'll want to get these photographed so it can be used against whoever did this when they catch him," the medic said. "But beyond that, there's no reason for you to come with me. You'll probably be hurting pretty bad for a few days."

"Thanks. I'll take care of it." Steve turned to her. "I'm going to talk to the officer. You stay right at the car, okay?"

Rosalyn nodded and walked over to lean against the trunk. Steve went to talk to the two officers who had shown up, turning so he was facing her. She saw him pull out some sort of badge or ID and show it to the officers.

Now that she was alone and not worried for Steve's immediate well-being, the weight of what had just happened hit her.

The Watcher had found her again.

There was no way this incident could be a coincidence.

But how? They had left all the clothes, with the electronic transmitters, in that superstore dressing room. The only thing she'd kept had been her notebook.

And she'd searched every single sheet of paper in it during the car ride. There had been absolutely nothing unusual.

She didn't know how he had found her, only that he had. And Steve had almost paid the price for it right before her eyes.

Maybe she should run. Right now. Maybe if she left and got away from Steve, the Watcher would leave him alone.

She turned and put her elbows against the passenger-side window, cradling her head in her hands. What was she going to do? She was going to have the baby soon. She couldn't keep running forever.

Especially since running didn't seem to matter. The Watcher found her no matter where she went. The only place he hadn't found her was at the Ammonses' house. Or if he had, he'd never made his presence known.

Rosalyn turned and glanced at Steve. He was still talking to the officers, but he was looking at her. One of the men nodded at whatever Steve was saying and looked at Rosalyn too. The other gave something to Steve that he put in his pocket. Steve shook hands with both men again and began walking toward the car.

"You seem pretty upset. Are you okay?" he asked her.

Rosalyn laughed, but there was no humor in the sound.

Was she okay? No. She wasn't certain she was ever going to be okay. "No, I'm definitely not okay."

"Why? Because he didn't succeed or because you changed your mind?"

She studied his face more carefully. His green eyes were cold. The angles of his jaw set in anger.

"What?"

"I saw you looking at the guy on the motorcycle. You were looking at both of us right before he hit me."

She shook her head, trying to process exactly what Steve was implying. "Yeah, I noticed him, but I didn't think anything of it."

He took a step closer to her, his height intimidating rather than comforting. "Why were you studying me so intensely from inside the convenience store, then?"

"I was trying to figure out which candy bar to get you." Her words were small. They sounded ridiculous even to her own ears.

"You called someone earlier, someone you didn't want me to know about. Was that him? The Watcher? Are you working together?"

Rosalyn could feel the blood leaving her face. "Wh-what?"

He grabbed her arm with his good hand. "Did you decide you didn't want me dead at the last minute? Did you change your mind? Is that why you made that horrified face in the store and tipped me off?"

"I made the face because I saw he was going to hit you—"

"Which was the plan all along, right? Except you had some sort of change of heart and decided to tip me off. If you hadn't made that face, I have to admit, I'd be dead now."

She couldn't believe what she was hearing. "No. No, I

didn't know what he was going to do until he flicked out that stick thing—"

"Really? You expect me to believe he just happened to find us right after you just happened to make a secret call at lunch today? Is that why you had me stop here when we were so close to Colorado Springs?"

"No. Steve, I—"

He took a step back. "You know what? Save it. We'll do official questioning when I get you into the Critical Response office."

"The what?"

He didn't answer. Instead he pulled a set of handcuffs out of his pocket. That's what the officer had handed him. Rosalyn looked over at them. They were watching her and Steve. Evidently he had already told them why he would need the handcuffs.

Almost as if from a distance, she felt a cuff slip around one wrist, then the other.

"Rosalyn Mellinger, you're under arrest."

Chapter Fourteen

She was playing him. Had to have been this entire time. There was no other explanation for it.

Steve could feel the anger coursing through his body. Not just at Rosalyn, although he was plenty pissed at her, but at himself also.

She'd taken him as an easy mark once, six months ago, and obviously had found he was still just as dense even after being fooled by her before.

Even worse? He still wanted to believe her now. That the crushed look on her face was real, that he'd made a mistake in slipping her into handcuffs.

But damned if he'd let himself fall prey to her for a third time.

And the baby… He couldn't even think about that right now.

She had to be playing him. Had to be conspiring with the Watcher. There were no tracking devices anywhere on either of them. He had meticulously searched her clothes, his, her notebook and wallet and found nothing.

He'd watched mile after mile in the rearview mirror to make sure they weren't being followed. There was no way any one vehicle—hell, even two or three taking turns—could've followed without his knowing. Steve had been watching. No one had tailed them.

The only suspicious happening since they'd left Pensacola had been Rosalyn's call to the Ammonses. To a couple she'd previously stated had no phone in their house.

How exactly did you call someone who didn't have a phone?

You didn't.

But you could be calling a partner you were working with. Tip him off about where you were going. She might not have been able to give her partner specifics, but she could get him close enough that he could start tailing without Steve's awareness.

He remembered her head against the telephone cradle at lunch today. The same guilty expression she'd had while standing over at the car while he'd been talking to the local cops.

Like she felt bad for tipping her partner off, then felt bad again that Steve had been hurt.

He should be thankful for her guilty conscience. Without it, he would be dead.

Or maybe—if he was willing to give Rosalyn a slight benefit of the doubt—*maybe* she hadn't known exactly what her partner's plan was. Maybe she hadn't known the plan was to kill Steve outright.

Maybe she was a thief and a con but not a murderer.

The thought made him feel slightly better, which made him even angrier, which made his arm hurt like a bitch. Steve gritted his teeth. He'd have to take some aspirin when he got to Omega HQ, because he wasn't going anywhere else but there.

Not giving Rosalyn any chance to escape. He could've sworn she was about to run while he was talking to the cops. Maybe she'd known he was onto her.

He was surprised she didn't try to plead her case while it was just the two of them in the car. She had to know that once other people were involved—people not so blinded by their obvious gullibility for her like Steve—it would be harder for her to fool them. To fool him.

But she hadn't said anything. Not a single word since he'd put the cuffs on her. Hadn't gotten angry. Hadn't cried. Hadn't reasoned with him.

If he hadn't known better, he would've said she'd just shut down. Even now, she had her arms wrapped protectively around herself, around the baby. She was looking straight ahead, but it didn't seem like she saw anything.

Obviously she hadn't thought he would figure it out. At least not this soon.

There was only one thing Steve knew for absolute certain. He was going to get some answers. Maybe he couldn't trust his own judgment around Rosalyn. Was too close to her.

But he was taking her to Omega's Critical Response Division. He had some of the best profilers and behavioral analysts in the entire world working on his team. He might not be able to get to the truth with Rosalyn.

But they would.

STEVE SAW ROSALYN perk up a little when he pulled into the Omega complex. Obviously she hadn't been expecting him to take her somewhere as sophisticated as his unit.

That's right, sweetheart—you didn't just pick some local yokel to mess with. You're in the big leagues now.

"Not what you were expecting?"

She looked over at him. "I don't know what you think I was expecting, but no, this wasn't it." She turned back to look out the window. Her hands were rubbing at the handcuffs on her wrist.

He wondered if she wished she'd chosen her mark better. Or maybe getting some sort of information about Omega had been her plan all along.

He steeled himself against any softness toward her. He

couldn't allow her to get the upper hand again. The cuffs were probably overkill, but it was a necessary reminder— for both of them—that she was a criminal.

When Steve walked in through the front door with Rosalyn, the guards did a double take. They were probably equally as disconcerted to see Steve in a casual shirt and jeans as they were to see him bringing in a prisoner. Neither were commonplace for Steve.

He went through standard procedures to enter the building, ID scan, weapon check-in. He signed in Rosalyn as being in his custody and walked her through the metal detector. She set it off, of course, because of the handcuffs.

The guard looked uncomfortable. "Um, protocol says we scan all prisoners entering the building, Mr. Drackett."

"That's fine." Steve didn't really like it, but damned if he'd give her preferential treatment.

Rosalyn raised her cuffed hands in front of her face so the guard could use the wand to run up the front of her body, then down the back. Nothing else set off the detector.

Steve had to admit he was a little relieved. If she'd had a hidden cell phone or weapon on her, he would've never been able to trust his own judgment again.

The guard allowed them through and he took Rosalyn's arm to the elevator and into the division offices.

As soon as he walked into the large open area that housed most of the desks of the Critical Response Division, Steve knew he had made a mistake. He should not have paraded Rosalyn in like this. He should've let the locals handle her arrest. There were going to be too many people with too many questions about who Rosalyn was and what was going on.

Personal questions.

Steve wanted answers from Rosalyn. But at the same time he did not want his private life being broadcast all over the office.

He looked over at her. Her head was bowed and her hair was framing her face on either side. Between her hunched shoulders, pregnant belly and handcuffs, she made quite the pitiful picture.

Steve wasn't surprised when Andrea Gordon, one of the most naturally gifted behavioral analysts Steve had ever known, approached them, her concerned look focused on Rosalyn.

Hell, even Steve felt sorry for her and she'd almost gotten him killed an hour ago.

"Steve, is there anything I can help with?" Andrea asked him.

"In a minute, Andrea." Steve glanced around until he found the person he wanted. He wasn't surprised to see him leaning against the wall on the other side of the room watching what was going on.

"Waterman!" Steve jerked his head to the side, indicating Derek should come over.

Derek Waterman, head of the Omega SWAT team, was always aware of what was going on around him. He was focused and deadly and an asset to the team for multiple reasons.

But right now Steve wanted Derek because of what he wasn't: friendly. Steve needed Rosalyn escorted down to an interrogation room. Most of the other men on the team would be friendly, try to set Rosalyn at ease. That's not what Steve wanted. He wanted Rosalyn nervous, uncomfortable, unhappy.

That's how he would get answers.

And if a little voice said he was making a huge mistake, well, he'd just squash that. He was done giving her the benefit of the doubt.

"Derek, will you please escort Ms. Mellinger to interview room 2?" It was the starkest of the interrogation rooms, the least comfortable.

Out of the corner of his eye he saw Andrea stiffen. She didn't like how he was treating Rosalyn. But then again, Andrea tended to be tenderhearted toward everyone.

Derek didn't even bat an eye. "No problem, boss." He turned to Rosalyn. "If you could come with me, ma'am." Respectful yet distant. He took her arm and escorted her down the hall.

Steve turned back from them and found at least a dozen of his team watching him.

"All right, people, let's get back to work. I know you have other things to do besides gape at me."

Many of them sat back down at their desks or went back to their normal tasks. Liam Goetz, hostage rescue team captain and resident smart-ass, just walked closer.

"But, boss, how are we supposed to go back to work when we know there's such a big, bad criminal nearby?"

That got a couple of snickers. Steve turned to Liam. "I can fire you, you know."

"If I had a dollar for every time you said that," Liam muttered, but eased back down to his desk.

The good thing about his team was that the members knew each other well enough to know when to leave something alone. He also knew he could trust them to provide him with the information he didn't seem capable of getting himself. Or have the neutrality required to do it.

"Brandon, Andrea, Jon, I need to see you in my office."

He turned and walked out of the main room. He didn't check to see if the people he'd asked for were following. He knew they were. If for curiosity's sake as much as anything else.

He walked through his outer office door. Cynthia and his other assistants stood when they saw him, all with pressing matters that needed his attention, he was sure. He held out a hand.

"For the next few hours, unless there is a national or international crisis, consider me still unavailable. I don't want to know about it." He saw Brandon and Andrea make eye contact with each other at his words but didn't care. For his own sanity, unless there was some sort of real emergency, he had to get this issue with Rosalyn settled.

"Do you need something for your arm?" Andrea asked. All eyes flew to it. Damn it, he'd been trying not to let anyone know about the throb and what he was sure was going to be stiff and painful tomorrow. He glared at Andrea for bringing it up. He should've known she'd be able to read his nonverbal communication too accurately for him to hide or fake.

"Sorry." She shrugged. "It wasn't that noticeable, but I could tell."

"What happened?" Brandon asked.

"I was on the wrong side of a steel telescopic baton." Steve grimaced. "I'm fine."

"I'll get ice and ibuprofen. It will help with swelling and pain. We'll handle everything, Steve." Cynthia, the assistant who'd been with the team the longest, the one he trusted the most, nodded at him. "You handle your crisis. We'll handle anything else."

Steve opened the door for his inner office and held it for the others. Jon Hatton and Brandon Han were two of the finest profilers—honestly two of the most brilliant, trustworthy men—Steve had ever known. Andrea was much quieter and kept to herself more due to her past, but as a behavioral analyst she couldn't be beat.

"What's going on, Steve?" Jon asked. "I'm assuming that woman you walked in with was the Rosalyn Mellinger you had me looking into."

Steve went over to the window looking out at the Rockies. Normally the view gave him a measure of peace, but not right now. "She is."

"You didn't mention she was having a baby."

"No." Steve shook his head. He really didn't want to get into that yet if he didn't have to. "I didn't."

"You also didn't mention that she was a suspect." He could hear the frustration in Jon's voice. "That would've changed how I was reading the information."

Steve turned and looked at them. "She wasn't a suspect until lunchtime and then about an hour ago."

He explained what had happened with the phone call and the attack at the gas station. He was just finishing as Margaret, another one of his assistants, brought in the pain medication and some ice. Someone had also dug up a sling. That would at least take the pressure off his shoulder and hopefully ease some of the throbbing. He thanked her.

"What did Rosalyn say to your accusations?" Brandon asked as Steve took the medication.

"She denied them, of course."

Andrea walked over and helped him ease his arm into the sling. Immediately the pain eased somewhat.

"And you're not completely sure about your accusations either," she said softly. "You're angry with her, but also protective. And confused most of all."

Steve nodded. "Yes. All of those things." He looked over at the other two men. "I've lost my perspective when it comes to Rosalyn Mellinger."

"Because the baby is yours," Brandon said. Jon nodded, not looking surprised.

Steve shrugged. "She says so."

Andrea touched his arm. "It's okay to believe her. Until you know for sure otherwise, it's okay to believe that what she says about that is true."

"Well, if it is, then it seems an awful lot like she was

just part of a plan to kill or at least seriously injure the father of her baby."

He walked around his desk and looked out at the three of them. "I can't be neutral around her. So I need you three to figure out the truth for me. To be my eyes and ears."

Chapter Fifteen

Rosalyn sat in a room that was like something out of a crime-investigation show on television. A table with four chairs around it, none of them comfortable, cement walls all the way around painted a gray color that wasn't very different from their original hue. Fluorescent lights blared down from overhead, unflattering at best, downright painful after a few hours.

And on one wall was a large mirror covering half the surface. Of course, it would be a two-way mirror.

She'd known Steve was in law enforcement, but she'd had no idea he worked at a place like this. That he was evidently the *boss* in a place like this.

She'd told him everything she knew about the Watcher and he'd just made it seem like he was a beat cop or something. He was obviously so much more than that. He hadn't tried to give her any insight or any knowledge about what he thought would be the next steps.

Because he hadn't trusted her. She could almost understand the misunderstanding with the phone and the guy on the motorcycle. But Steve hadn't trusted her from the beginning. Not today, not last night when they were making love, not ever.

She'd started feeling like she was finally not alone, not knowing she was actually more alone than ever.

The guy who had brought her down to this stark room

hadn't been mean or rough. He hadn't said much to her at all, beyond reading her the Miranda rights. Rosalyn wondered if she should call a lawyer but didn't know one to call here. Plus, she hadn't done anything wrong.

Besides trust that Steve Drackett was looking out for her best interests.

The big guy—what had Steve called him? Derek?—had escorted her to her seat.

"Stay here," had been all she'd gotten out of him before he'd left, closing the door behind him with a resounding click.

How long ago had that been? Probably twenty minutes. It felt like hours. Rosalyn could feel panic scratching at her subconscious, trying to work its way in. She refused to let it. She hadn't done anything wrong. Surely someone would believe her.

Although she was quite sure it wouldn't be Steve.

And once someone did believe her and she got out of here, where was she going to go? The Watcher had found her again. She wrapped her still-handcuffed arms around her belly, rocking back and forth, fighting panic once again.

What was she going to do?

Rosalyn nearly jumped out of her seat as the door opened. Two men, both of whom had been out in the office when Steve had brought her in, entered.

"Are you okay, Ms. Mellinger?" One, a stunningly handsome Asian man, asked her. He looked genuinely concerned.

"I just…I just…" The words wouldn't come out.

I just realized the enormity of the fact that a killer has found me again and the one person I thought I could trust wants to throw me in jail.

"I was just startled. That's all," she finally finished.

They both came and sat in the chairs on the other side

of the table. The other man, very tall and also handsome, had a key in his hands. "Can I take those handcuffs off? I'm sure you'll be more comfortable without them."

Rosalyn brought her wrists up to the table so he could release her. She had to get some measure of control over herself. She could do this.

"Are you sure you fellas will feel safe with me unfettered?" She raised an eyebrow at them. They both had her by nearly a foot and at least fifty pounds apiece. Not to mention her range of motion with her extended belly would make her escape skills almost nonexistent.

Both men glanced at each other and cracked a smile. "We'll be sure to keep our guard up," the tall one said. "I'm Jon Hatton and this is Brandon Han. We're both profilers and behavioral analysts here at the Critical Response Division of Omega Sector."

"I'm not sure I know exactly what Omega Sector is."

Agent Han leaned back in his chair. "We're an interagency task force. People working together with backgrounds in the FBI, DEA, ATF and other relevant agencies. We even have some Interpol and other international agencies as part of our ranks. Helps us cut through red tape."

"We'd like to ask you some questions about what happened at the gas station a couple of hours ago," Hatton said. "Did you know the man on the motorcycle was going to attack Steve?"

"No." She looked at one man and then the other. "I was inside the store when I saw the guy pull up. I thought it was pretty stupid that he was coming right behind our car when there were other pumps open, but I didn't know who he was or that he was going to hurt Steve until I saw him flick out his stick thing."

Agent Han had pulled out a notebook and began writing. "It's called a telescopic baton. A weapon that can be easily transported and then, like you said, be fully expanded with just a flick of the wrist."

She nodded. "Steve was looking at me, so I knew he wasn't paying attention to the guy and was going to get hurt." She remembered knowing she wouldn't get outside in time to warn him. "Fortunately, Steve turned at the last second and blocked the hit with his arm."

"And you had no idea who the man was or that he was going to be there at that time?" Han asked.

"No." Rosalyn could feel the panic pulling at her again.

Hatton tilted his head to the side. "You didn't notify him in any way that you were traveling to Colorado Springs with Steve?"

It was almost like it was a friendly question. That this was all some dinner-party conversation. Rosalyn could feel hysteria building up inside her and fought to keep it tamped down.

"No. I did not contact the man who has been stalking me almost daily for the last year, who has caused me to leave my job, all my friends, and for six months live on the run in sleazy hotels. I did not contact the man who has driven me to the precipice of insanity and thoughts of suicide more than once."

She leaned forward in her chair. "I did not contact the man from whom I, for the first time in a year, had found a measure of peace because I had finally felt like I had gotten away from him for good. I did not bring that man back into my life."

Agent Han leaned forward too. "Then how did he find you and Steve?"

Rosalyn couldn't stop the tears now. "I don't know," she whispered before huddling back into her chair. "He always finds me."

The two men looked at her for a long time. Rosalyn finally just covered her face with her hands.

After a long pause she heard Agent Hatton say, "I think we need to start at the beginning."

STEVE WATCHED IT all from the adjacent room, able to see everything through the two-way mirror and hear everything through the audio that was pumped in. Andrea had wanted to go in with Brandon to help question Rosalyn, but Steve had asked her to stay.

He needed Andrea's opinion. Not only could she read other people's nonverbal communication with remarkable accuracy, she also had a sixth sense about their emotions. She could feel what they were emoting even if it didn't match what the person was saying.

He'd trusted Andrea's abilities when he'd pulled her out of a pretty horrible situation nearly five years ago; he trusted them even more now.

"Steve, I've got to say, there is nothing Rosalyn has done nonverbally that has given me any indication that she's not telling the truth."

Rosalyn had started back at the beginning like Jon had asked her to do. She'd spent the last hour telling Jon and Brandon about the Watcher and everything that had happened. She was giving much more detail than she had to him.

It made him physically ill to think about what she'd gone through.

Steve rubbed his good hand over his face, his hurt arm still in the sling. He didn't have to have Andrea's talent at reading people to see that Rosalyn was telling the truth.

"I've made a pretty bad mistake."

Andrea looked at him, eyebrow raised.

"When the attacker showed up at the gas station, just a couple of hours after she'd made what I deemed to be a suspicious phone call, I was positive she'd played me again."

"Again?"

Steve realized this all came back to when Rosalyn had left him at the hotel six months ago without a word.

"She fooled me. Snuck out in the middle of the night. Took all my cash."

Andrea studied him. Steve knew he wouldn't like whatever it was she was going to say.

"She hurt you."

"My pride, sure. Personally and professionally. I'm the head of one of the most prestigious law enforcement agencies in the world. If I can't tell when I'm being set up as a mark, maybe I don't deserve to run this place."

Andrea shook her head, the tiniest of smiles on her face. "No, it's a lot more than that. You opened yourself to her and she hurt you."

Steve thought of that time in Pensacola before Rosalyn had fled. He had known she was scared of something, that something was happening in her life. He'd planned to ask her to stay with him the rest of the week. Hell, if being outside made her nervous for whatever reason, they could stay in the bungalow.

He'd planned to keep her there, to make love to her, to talk to her and listen to her until she realized she could trust him. Then they could solve whatever scared her together. Maybe he'd even see if she needed a fresh start in Colorado. She'd mentioned the beautiful mountains.

Steve ran his hand through his hair. He couldn't deny it to himself any longer. He, jaded law enforcement officer who saw the worst of humanity on a daily basis, who hadn't been on more than a handful of dates since his wife died, had fallen in love at first sight. Or at the very least had been willing to try a relationship with Rosalyn, invite her into his life.

But she'd bailed before he had the chance.

So yeah, she had hurt him.

And evidently he still hadn't forgiven her for any of it.

Because he'd put cuffs on her, for God's sake, and had her dragged into their least comfortable interrogation room like she was a terrorist or murderer or something.

"Damn it." He ran his hand over his face again. "I'm an idiot. I've got to get her out of there."

Andrea touched him on his arm. "Let Jon and Brandon finish talking to her. It's helping her, Steve. To go through the details. To talk about it with someone else."

Steve watched through the mirror again and saw Andrea was right, as she most always was. Rosalyn was sitting up straight, had unwrapped her arms from the protective stance around herself. Her shoulders weren't hunched. She had more color in her cheeks.

Brandon had asked for Rosalyn's notebook when she'd mentioned it, and it had been brought to them. The three of them were now poring over it.

Obviously Jon and Brandon believed Rosalyn, and were trying to help her make sense of it all. To discover the pattern in the Watcher's actions concerning her.

Exactly what Steve should've been doing rather than worrying about whether she was in on her own terrorizing.

Derek Waterman entered the room. "Some more info for you, boss, about the Ammonses in Georgia. Seems like they don't have a phone in their house, but they do have one at their café, for orders and such."

Of course they did.

"We checked, and there was a record of a call from Dalhart, Texas, made to them this morning at ten o'clock Eastern time. I think that would line up with the call Rosalyn was making."

"Yep, it definitely would. Thanks, Derek."

And just like that, Rosalyn was cleared. Although he'd already cleared her in his mind anyway.

Derek turned toward the mirror. "She looks a lot better than she did when I brought her in there."

"That's because the idiot quota surrounding her has dropped significantly." Steve grimaced.

Derek chuckled. "Hey, only my wife is allowed to call me an idiot."

"Your wife is a certified genius. She's at liberty to call everyone an idiot." Derek's wife, Molly, was the head of the Omega forensic lab. "But in this case, I was referring to myself."

Derek slapped him on the shoulder and Steve winced from the blow he'd taken there but didn't say anything. "We all can be idiots when it comes to the women we care about."

Steve heard a muttered "Amen" out of Andrea.

"Andrea, will you take some food and water in to them? Make sure Rosalyn is okay? I don't want to disrupt their progress by going in there myself."

"Sure. That's a good idea. I'm sure she'll appreciate your thoughtfulness, Steve."

He shook his head. "No, don't say it's from me. Just make sure she has what she needs."

Steve wasn't sure Rosalyn was ever going to want to talk to him again after how he'd treated her. All he could do now was catch the psycho trying to harm them both.

Steve would do whatever it took to keep Rosalyn and their baby safe. And would pray she would give him another chance.

Chapter Sixteen

They believed her. She wasn't exactly sure when it happened, but Rosalyn knew Agents Hatton and Han believed her.

The gorgeous blonde who'd first approached her in the offices before Steve stopped her came into the room. She had a tray of food—some soup and crackers—and water and coffee.

"We thought you might want something to eat. And Steve mentioned you like coffee."

"Steve sent you in here with food and drink? I thought he wanted me thrown under the jail."

The woman set the tray down in front of Rosalyn, then went to stand beside Brandon's chair. He hooked a casual arm around her hips. What a striking couple those two made.

She smiled gently at Rosalyn. "Sometimes it's difficult to see things that are right in front of you when there are feelings involved. I'm sure that's true for Steve."

"I think Steve made it quite obvious he has no feelings for me when he arrested me a few hours ago."

The woman smiled. "Sometimes men are a little bit slower in recognizing their own feelings." The woman looked over at Brandon and a moment of tenderness passed between them. Obviously at some point Brandon had been a little slow in recognizing his feelings for the woman. Although obviously not anymore.

"I'm Andrea Gordon, by the way." Andrea looked back up at Rosalyn. "And just for the record, you are not under arrest. You're free to leave at any time, although we would very much like you to stay so we can continue working on the case with you."

"Does Steve Drackett know I'm free to go?"

Andrea nodded. "He's the one who gave the word."

Rosalyn didn't know what to make of that, so she just started eating her food.

The other three agents began looking at the papers on the table.

"Steve found two transmitters on Rosalyn's personal effects. One was on a sweater, one on her bag," Jon said and turned his attention to her. "He found those after the fire at the hotel, right?"

Rosalyn nodded. "While we were at the hospital, I think."

"And you went immediately to the superstore and changed out of everything?"

"Yes, the only thing I took with me out of that store that I had brought in was this notebook." She pointed at the one on the table.

Jon looked through it. "It's highly unlikely that there's any sort of transmitter in here, but let's get it scanned just in case." He walked out of the room with it.

Brandon sat back in his chair, taking a cracker Rosalyn offered him from her tray. "Let's say he got the transmitters on you at the very beginning. That he broke into your house and put one on every piece of clothing you had. That would be excessive and expensive, but this is obviously no garden-variety stalker we're dealing with here."

"That's how he followed you for the first six months.

He knew where you were and could show up there," Andrea continued.

Jon walked back into the room. "Derek's going to take the notebook over to Molly in the lab."

"We're trying to figure out the transmitter pattern," Brandon told him. "I'm running with the possibility that he put trackers on everything she owned at the beginning."

"Okay," Jon said. "Possible. And scary."

Rosalyn had to agree.

Brandon continued. "When we get your notebook back, we'll double-check for patterns to see if there's any consistency, but maybe he was working around his own schedule. He has a job that requires him to be in an office at least part of the time. That's why some weeks you had notes multiple days in a row, and sometimes you didn't hear from him for a while."

Jon nodded. "That would suggest someone with a career. We can see if weekends were more active with the notes—that might help confirm."

Rosalyn looked at them. "I don't understand. You're saying the Watcher is just a normal guy? Like a businessman or a lawyer or something?" The thought made her feel a little ill.

Andrea reached over and touched her hand. "A lot of times minds of pure evil can be dressed in very professional packages."

Brandon shrugged. "Times you thought he was toying with you by leaving you alone, making you think you'd gotten away? Maybe he just had something in his schedule that required his attention and he couldn't get to you that day."

"And it is highly likely that the Watcher is from your hometown of Mobile, since that's where it all started. Not only that, but that you know him or met him briefly." Jon grimaced.

Rosalyn shuddered, glad she was almost done with her food. She wouldn't have been able to eat another bite after thinking about this. "I was an accountant. I met with clients all the time."

"We'll check into that right away," Jon said. "Clients you've met with, coworkers."

"But really, it could be anyone. Someone I met at the grocery store or while waiting for the elevator."

Rosalyn saw the compassion in Andrea's eyes. "Yes, unfortunately."

The thought that she might recognize the Watcher's face when they caught him made her want to be physically ill. Every person she'd known was suspect.

But for the first time, Rosalyn actually had hope that they—this Omega Sector team—might really catch him. Before today her only hope had been she might be able to outrun him at some point. Get somewhere he couldn't find her. But there hadn't been much chance of that with the baby coming.

Jon, Brandon and Andrea were discussing particular aspects of the Watcher when the door to the room opened and Steve walked in.

They just stared at each other for a long time. Apology was clear all over his face.

But even with his arm in the sling and the stiffness in his frame—pain from being hit with that telescopic baton thing—Rosalyn found she wasn't quite ready to let this go just yet.

Steve eventually stepped away from the door.

"All right, I've cleared conference room 1 for us to use. I think we'll all be more comfortable there."

Everybody stood and began packing up their notes, still talking about the Watcher they were trying to profile.

"Rosalyn and I will meet you up there in a few minutes."

They all shuffled out quickly after that. Rosalyn remained in her chair. Steve came and sat across from her.

"I overreacted. Made a mistake."

She cocked her head to the side. "You thought I tried to have you killed."

"You made a suspicious phone call and a few hours later someone took a swing at my head with a metal rod. That seemed pretty dubious at the time."

"I told you I called the Ammonses." Her volume began to rise.

His did too. "You also told me the day before that the Ammonses didn't have a phone. It seemed like an inconsistency in your story. You know who tends to have inconsistencies in their stories? Liars and criminals."

Rosalyn rolled her eyes. "I called their café. They have a phone there."

His eyes narrowed. "I know that *now*. But you didn't tell me that."

Rosalyn stood, bracing her hands on the table and leaning toward him. "Because you didn't ask. Because you were convinced I was up to no good. That I was playing you."

"Damn it, Rosalyn, I'm trained to look for suspicious patterns. To see bad things before they happen."

"And that's what I was, right? A bad thing."

"No, it's just—"

She slammed her hand down on the table. "You put handcuffs on me like I was some common criminal that might try to run at any second. You didn't ask. You didn't give me a chance to explain."

"Rosalyn—"

"We made love last night. And today you were convinced I was trying to have you killed. I guess that tells me how you really feel about me."

He stood then. "No, it wasn't like that. I had to force myself to try to look at you objectively."

He reached out toward her, but she snatched herself back. When Steve touched her, she couldn't think straight. Her attraction to him overpowered everything else. She didn't want that now. Maybe never wanted it again.

She rubbed her eyes. She was tired, not just from today but from everything. The only thing good going for her now was the fact that everyone here believed her. The agents seemed ready and willing to put their resources and brainpower into figuring out who the Watcher was and what Rosalyn could do about it. It was more than she'd had in a long time.

"You know what? Just take me to the conference room. The faster we can get this situation resolved, the sooner I can get myself out of your life."

Because Steve obviously didn't want her there.

STEVE DIDN'T MAKE a lot of tactical errors. Nor did he make many errors in judgment. His job and the lives of the people on his team, not to mention those of the American public in general, depended on it.

But he'd done both with Rosalyn.

They walked to the conference room together in silence. Not the comfortable kind.

She was mad. He didn't blame her.

But she was right. They needed to concentrate on figuring out all they could about the Watcher. Not because Steve wanted Rosalyn out of his life—he'd be damned if he was going to let that happen—but because obviously the Watcher had escalated in violence over the past few days.

Steve would do whatever was necessary to keep Rosalyn and the baby safe. Even if she didn't want anything to do with him right now.

He held the door open for her as they entered the conference room. Jon, Brandon and Andrea were already there. Roman Weber, a member of Omega's SWAT team, had joined them.

One entire wall of the conference room was made up of an electronic whiteboard. Brandon and Jon had already started making a timeline on it. Everything they wrote could be saved onto a computer file to be used later.

"Molly brought Rosalyn's notebook back over from the lab," Andrea said as they walked in. "Nothing suspicious about it."

Steve nodded, not surprised.

Brandon turned to them from the whiteboard. "Basically, we have two inconsistencies that need to be addressed before we can go much further. First, why didn't the Watcher have any contact with you for the six months you were at the Ammonses' in Ellijay? What was different? Something in your life or something in his?"

"I don't know." Rosalyn shrugged as she sat down at the table.

"How did you meet them?" Andrea asked.

"I took a bus from Pensacola as far as the amount of money I had would take me." She glanced over at Steve, then looked away quickly. "That ended up being Ellijay.

"The Ammonses own a small café in town. They've lived there all their lives. They live right on top of the café, although I know Mr. Ammons also has a fishing cabin somewhere." Rosalyn smiled. "I got off the bus, went in to eat and felt like I never really left there again until I went to meet my sister in Pensacola."

Her smile faded into a flinch at the mention of her sister.

"Anyway, I asked Mrs. Ammons if I could make some cash washing dishes or whatever. They're not big fans of the government, so they didn't mind paying me cash under the table."

Jon smiled. "I like them already."

She shrugged, shaking her head with a smile. "The Ammonses are odd. Definitely keep to themselves and don't want people, especially the government, in their business. But they took me in. Let me wash dishes, then started letting me wait tables. When they found out I was sleeping out back under the café's overhang—"

"What?" The word was out of Steve's mouth before he could catch it. But the thought of her homeless, pregnant, sleeping outside.

"Honestly, it wasn't so bad. And it was just for a few days."

Steve's fist clenched but he didn't say anything further.

"Anyway, they invited me to live with them, and that was that. I pretty much never left their property. I worked, then went upstairs. For the first couple of weeks I would run downstairs every morning to see if there was a note from the Watcher."

"And nothing? Ever?" Brandon asked.

"No. Never. I just began thinking of the house as my force field." She scoffed at herself. "Stupid, I know."

Andrea walked over and touched Rosalyn on the shoulder. "No, not stupid at all. No one would blame you for staying somewhere where you felt safe. Where, for all intents and purposes, you *were* safe."

"Why did you leave?" Jon asked.

"The baby." Rosalyn put a hand on her stomach. "Soon it wasn't just going to be me anymore. The Ammonses are in their seventies. I knew I needed to have a backup plan in case…" She trailed off, then finally picked back up. "In case something happened to me."

In case the Watcher killed her. She didn't say it but everyone in the room knew what she meant.

"So you contacted your sister," Andrea prompted when Rosalyn didn't go on.

She nodded. "I asked Lindsey to meet me in Pensacola.

I was going to go back to the hotel and see if they would give me Steve's name. Or, if there was some sort of privacy law, see if they would at least contact him on my behalf."

Until that moment Steve hadn't realized he'd held a hardness inside himself against her about that. He'd silently, subconsciously, assumed she'd never planned to tell him about the baby. But she had. He took a step toward her, catching her eyes with his.

"I didn't know who you were," she continued, looking at him. "And I definitely didn't know about all this—" she gestured around the room with her arm "—but I knew the baby had a better chance with you than with me."

He wanted to move closer. To pick her up and plop her down on his lap. To promise her it was all going to be all right. To apologize for being an idiot earlier today.

Andrea looked over at him, sympathy in her eyes. She could clearly read his pain, his concern. Steve didn't care if it was noticeable to everyone.

"And Steve was there identifying what he thought was your body," Jon said.

"With all your sister's drug troubles, I'm surprised her prints weren't on file. But yours were," Steve said. "At least from juvie."

Rosalyn rolled her eyes. "That's when we were sixteen and Lindsey shoplifted. Left me to take the blame."

It explained a lot.

"Okay." Brandon got them back on track. "And once you were in Pensacola, you were immediately contacted by the Watcher again."

Rosalyn's lips pursed as she nodded.

"We know your clothes had the transmitters. Maybe they were short-range and the Watcher couldn't pick them up from that far away," Jon mused.

"Possible, but Rosalyn also traveled nearly as far when

she was in Dallas and Memphis and he found her there."
Brandon turned back toward the whiteboard.

It was time to take action. Steve turned to Roman. "I
need you to get to Ellijay. Talk to the Ammonses, scope
out the situation. See why the Watcher might have left
Rosalyn alone while she was there."

Roman headed for the door. "You got it, boss. One-
horse towns are my favorite." He winked at everyone as
he walked by. "I'll call as soon as I have info."

Brandon nodded. "Good. Having solid intel on the Ammonses will help. The other big inconsistency is how the
Watcher found you here in Colorado, after you'd removed
all the bugs."

Steve ran a hand over his face. "I could've sworn we
weren't followed. I was actively watching the entire time."
He looked over at Rosalyn and shrugged. "But today hasn't
been my finest day when it comes to judgment calls."

Jon had been looking at Rosalyn's notebook but now
looked up to address everyone. "I think we all have to
agree. We're either missing something big, or the Watcher
isn't just one person."

Chapter Seventeen

The thought that she had one psychopathic stalker had been bad enough. Jon Hatton's idea that it might actually be more than one person had been enough to put Rosalyn into a panic.

She hadn't said anything, had just tried to keep it all together while all the discussion continued on around her. They'd sent someone out for pizza, and Rosalyn had done her best to eat, but it had been difficult.

Eventually she'd put a hand on Steve's arm. Once he'd gotten a good look at her, he'd immediately announced he was taking her home.

His home.

He called Derek Waterman and another SWAT member she hadn't met yet named Liam Goetz. They were tasked with making sure no one followed them to Steve's house. Liam joked and flirted with her, when he wasn't showing her pictures of his newborn twins, while Steve personally inspected the Omega vehicle they'd be using. Evidently it had already been swept thoroughly for bugs, but he wanted to double-check.

They drove around for more than an hour. Derek went to Steve's house and checked it out for them. They even switched vehicles halfway through their journey. There was no way anyone could've followed them. Hell, Rosalyn was in the car and she hardly knew where they were.

"I couldn't find my way back to your building now if my life depended on it." She had long since closed her eyes, but having them open wouldn't have helped anyway.

"Believe it or not, my house is only a few miles away from the office. We're just taking the scenic route."

"I don't think anyone could've followed us."

Steve grimaced. "I thought the same was true earlier today, but I was wrong. But both Derek and Liam have given us the all clear. So I'm certain no one has followed us now. Plus, we'll have a guard in a car outside the house watching for anyone."

"Derek?"

"No, someone else. Derek will want to get home to his wife and their daughter."

"Yeah, Liam was showing me pictures of his twins and his daughter, Tallinn."

Steve smiled. "Yes, he and his wife, Vanessa, adopted her after a human-trafficking case last year. And the twins…they're just exhausting. Keeps Vanessa and Liam busy."

Rosalyn realized how little she knew about the man she was about to have a baby with. She opened her eyes. "How about you? Do you have any kids? You were married once right?"

"Yes. Melanie. She died in a car accident twelve years ago. But no, we didn't have any kids."

"I'm sorry about your wife." Rosalyn wondered if Steve still loved her.

"Don't take this the wrong way, but you two would've liked each other. Both of you are smart and strong." His smile was pensive, but not sad.

"Do you still love her?" The words were out before she could bite off her tongue. Damn it. "Never mind. You don't have to answer that."

"No, it's okay. I'll always love Melanie—she was a huge

part of my life." He looked over at her before returning his gaze to the road. "But no, I'm not in love with her anymore. Not pining after her. As a matter of fact, she'd probably lay into me for taking this long to get serious about someone."

Was that what they were? Serious?

"Do you mean us?"

"You're the only person I'm having a baby with."

"You arrested me earlier today, for heaven's sake."

He grimaced. "I was trying to do the right thing. To keep some perspective. My perspective has been blown to hell since the day you ran into that bar in Pensacola trying to get out of the rain."

"Because I stole from you?"

"No. I couldn't care less about the money. Because you got under my skin the way no one else has."

He pulled the car into a driveway of a small house, then used his phone to activate a code that opened the garage door.

She turned to look at him more fully.

"I did?" She had figured he'd be a little irritated at her running off with his cash, then would never think about her again.

He pressed the button to shut the garage door and turned off the car but still stared straight ahead with his hand on the wheel. "Why do you think I happened to be in Pensacola to identify your body? I had the Pensacola police report sent to my desk every day."

"To look for me? Because you thought I would be arrested?"

"I figured if you were looking for businessmen as marks to steal from, you would eventually get caught."

After her behavior in Florida, she really couldn't blame him for that conclusion, although it still sat heavy in her heart. "And you wanted to press charges too."

"That's what I told myself." He finally looked at her.

"But really it was so I could find you again, rescue you from the terrible path I thought you were walking down and bring you back here. Set you straight."

"You sound like a parole officer."

He continued as if she hadn't spoken, his eyes softening. "And then once you were more settled, with a good job and happy with your life, I planned to court you properly. To go out on dates and get to know you."

"Oh."

"Because there has not been one single day that I haven't thought of you. I'll admit, I wasn't always happy with you. But I also have to admit that my plan, once I found you again, was to make sure we were together. Even when I thought you were a petty criminal."

"But you don't think I'm one anymore?"

He reached over and tucked a strand of hair behind her ear. "No."

She asked the question she'd been afraid to ask. "And you believe me when I say the baby is yours?"

"Yes." His hand slid into her hair and pulled her closer. "And I'm going to do whatever it takes to keep you and the baby safe."

He closed the distance between their lips. Soft, this time, full of promise but not demand. His thumb brushed along her jaw, sending a rush of sensation racing across her skin. She leaned in closer but stopped when she felt the oddest sensation in her belly.

She jumped back from Steve. "Whoa." She put both hands on her stomach.

"What? Are you okay? Is something wrong?"

She smiled. "I'm fine. He just kicked. Like, kicked *really* hard."

She grabbed his hand not in the sling and put it on her stomach under her hand. They waited a moment, and then she felt it again.

Steve's eyes grew wide. "I felt that."

Rosalyn's smile felt so big that it might split her face. "I know! He must be a soccer player or something."

"Have you felt him move before?"

"I think so, but I thought it was indigestion or something. Never anything this strong."

They waited a few minutes more, but evidently their little soccer player had gotten tired. Both Rosalyn and Steve were still grinning as he helped her out of the car and led her into the house.

In the midst of all the heartbreak and chaos of the last two days, feeling their baby move so lively inside her made everything seem like it was going to be okay.

But that didn't stop her from being tired. Steve showed her around as they talked. He stopped and turned to her when they got to the kitchen.

"I don't have much food." He grimaced. "Honestly, I don't usually come here very often during the week. There's a small apartment within the Omega complex I use. Or just crash on the couch in my office. But I could have an agent deliver us something."

"No, I'm fine tonight. Although I know I'll be hungry in the morning." She was always hungry first thing in the morning, but at least she didn't wake up sick anymore like she had in the first few months.

"I've got waffles and toaster pastries."

"Do the important people you work with know you eat Pop-Tarts for breakfast?"

He winked at her. "Please don't tell."

"Would it ruin your big, bad reputation?"

"No." He rolled his eyes. "They would all just want me to bring them some every day."

Rosalyn's laugh turned into a huge yawn.

Steve walked over and slid his good arm around her

shoulder. "I guess that answers my question about whether you're ready for sleep or not."

He led her up the stairs to a bedroom. "This is my room. You can sleep here and I'll sleep in the guest room."

She grabbed his arm as he turned to go. "No, stay here with me."

"Rosalyn, are you sure? What I did today…" His head dropped.

"A little overdramatic to be sure, Director." She put a finger under his chin and lifted until they were looking at each other. "But the situation is complicated. If nothing else, I can definitely agree with that. So don't worry about it. We have a big enough enemy to fight without fighting each other."

"Then I would very much love to sleep in that bed with you, where I can hold you and know you and the baby are safe."

She pressed herself up against him and smiled. "Well, I hope not *just* hold…"

TRUE TO HIS WORD, Steve was still wrapped around Rosalyn when she woke up the next morning. Despite all her naughty intentions, she had fallen asleep not a minute after her head hit the pillow.

She eased herself away from Steve and out of the bed so she could use the bathroom and go make some breakfast. Actually, the infamous toaster pastries sounded just about perfect right now, although she still had to snicker a little bit.

She was dressed in one of Steve's T-shirts, a soft gray one that fell to her knees even over her extended belly. She never wanted to get out of it. But it would probably look a little weird if she wore it back to the Omega offices.

Rosalyn made her way down the stairs and into the kitchen, trying to rub sleep out of her eyes. She easily found the breakfast food in Steve's pantry—he hadn't been kidding when he said he didn't have much food here—and started decaf coffee. She ate the first Pop-Tart right out of the toaster to ease her growling stomach, then poured herself some coffee.

Hopefully they would make progress today. Real progress. If anybody could, it was Steve's team. They were trained and obviously good at what they did.

She grabbed a plate of the breakfast food whose name was not to be spoken and another cup of coffee to take up to Steve. They'd have to leave soon, but maybe she could talk him into a little naughtiness before then.

She stepped out of the kitchen into the front hall and froze.

An envelope sat there on the ground, a garish white on Steve's dark hardwood floors. It had been slid under the front door at some point—she had no idea when. She could see her name on the front in bold letters.

Just like all the others she'd received over the past year.

The coffee cups slipped through her numb fingers and crashed to the floor, shattering. Rosalyn felt the drops of hot coffee burn her bare legs and feet almost from a distance.

She couldn't take her eyes off the envelope.

The Watcher had found her again.

Chapter Eighteen

Steve heard the shattering cups and jumped out of bed. He instantly realized Rosalyn wasn't in the room with him. Habit had him grabbing his sidearm before running toward the stairs.

"Rosalyn?"

He saw her standing there, perfectly still. Two cups lay broken at her feet.

"Are you okay? Don't move. You might cut yourself. What happened?"

Now that he knew she was safe, his adrenaline slowed just a little bit. He set his gun on the hallway table and walked toward her.

She'd dropped the coffee cups, but it didn't look like she was cut or burned.

"Are you all right?" he asked again. "I don't see any cuts."

When he looked up and saw her face, his concern came rushing back. She stood devoid of all color, fists pressed to the sides of her head. She was looking at him, trying to say something.

Glass be damned, he walked all the way to her.

"What, sweetheart? What's wrong? Is it the baby?" He put his hand on her belly. She lowered her hands and he looked down to see her pointing to something on the floor.

"It's him," she whispered. "I know it's him. He found me."

It was a letter. Steve muttered the foulest expletive he knew. How the hell had the Watcher found them here? Ignoring the ache in his arm, Steve reached down and scooped Rosalyn up and carried her over to the stairs.

"Stay right here, okay?"

She nodded, but he wasn't sure she was processing anything he said. She just stared at the envelope on the ground, face ashen.

Steve got his weapon and did a sweep of the house to make sure no one had entered unawares, then called Derek.

"My house has been compromised," Steve said before Derek could even get a greeting in.

Derek's expletive matched Steve's.

"There's a letter here on my floor. Has been slid under the door. The house is secure now." Steve looked over to where Rosalyn sat huddled on the stairs, arms around her knees, rocking herself back and forth. "Who was on patrol last night?"

"Wilson. I'll call you back in two minutes." Derek disconnected the call.

Steve wanted to go over and open the letter. Read it. But more than that he wanted the forensics team to be able to get off any possible information. He walked over to stand by Rosalyn, rubbing her hair gently. He wished he could pick her up and carry her away but knew they had to deal with this while they could.

True to his word, Derek called back in a little over a minute. His voice was grim. "Wilson hasn't reported in for the last three hours and is not answering his phone now."

"Damn it." That was not a good sign.

"You should have agents at your door in three to four minutes. Liam is on his way, ETA ten minutes. I called Brandon and Andrea too. I figured Andrea might be good for Rosalyn."

"Thanks, Derek."

He could hear Derek's muted talking to someone before he came back on the line. "Molly and I are coming too. She wants to check out the scene herself. She says not to touch anything."

"Okay."

"Just hold tight, boss. We're on our way."

THIRTY MINUTES LATER his house was a circus.

He'd gotten Rosalyn back upstairs before anyone arrived. Helped her wash off the coffee that had spilled on her legs and they both got dressed.

She still hadn't said much. Still had no color in her face. But she was holding it together. That was all he could ask for.

Agent Wilson was dead. Had been shot at close range in his car. Initial estimates put his death at around 3:00 a.m.

Molly Humphries-Waterman and her forensic lab team were doing their job all over his front porch, Agent Wilson's car and around the letter itself.

When Brandon and Andrea got there, Steve sent her straight up to his room to where Rosalyn still sat on the bed.

The rest of his inner team—Derek, Jon, Liam and Brandon—were with Steve in the kitchen. Those were the men he trusted most in the world.

"We need to get Rosalyn moved to Omega," Jon said. "At least we know there that she'll be safe. That he can't get to her."

Brandon nodded. "I agree. There's something we missed, obviously. Some way he's finding Rosalyn's location."

"Because they sure as hell weren't followed." Liam leaned his large frame against the fridge. "I can guarantee that."

Steve agreed. There was no way someone could've followed them last night without their being aware of it.

"I don't want to be the bad guy here," Derek said. "But, Steve, yesterday you were sure Rosalyn had contacted the Watcher. Are you sure something like that didn't happen again?"

Steve wasn't going back down that road. "Yes, I'm sure. However he's finding her, it's not because she's telling him."

Derek held out his hands in surrender. "All right, don't kill me. All I'm saying is sometimes the simplest answer is the most likely one."

"Well, start looking for complex answers because Rosalyn isn't helping the Watcher." If they had seen her face when she'd found that letter, they wouldn't question it either. Steve would give everything he had to never see that look on Rosalyn's face ever again.

Jon jumped in before things got out of hand. "We need to get Rosalyn back to HQ. You too, Steve. We'll work out the hows and whys from there. And I have some other cases I've found that I think might have an interesting tie to what's happening to Rosalyn."

"Steve, I'm going to open the letter now," Molly called out from the hallway. "I've gotten all the forensic evidence I can from the floor around it and the outside of the envelope."

They all moved into the hallway.

Molly looked up, shaking her head. "I had hoped he had licked the envelope. That would've been our best shot at DNA."

"He never licks the envelope." Rosalyn's voice was tight at the top of the stairs. "Not once. He's too smart for that."

"I was going to read the note." Molly looked up at Rosalyn. "Is that okay?"

Rosalyn nodded.

Molly opened the envelope and her eyes flew to Steve. This had to be bad.

"Go ahead," he murmured.

"'I can't wait to meet your baby. Maybe he'll decide to come live with me. But I'll get rid of Dad first.'"

Rosalyn let out a sob and held on to the banister for support. Steve took the stairs two at a time to get to her, then pulled her hard to his chest. He could feel shudders racking her small frame.

"He'll kill you. He'll take the baby."

"No," he whispered in her ear. "Do you hear me? That maniac will never touch our child. I promise you that. And I can take care of myself."

"Not all the time, you can't. He'll wear you down. That's what he does." Her quiet sobs broke his heart.

He held her close, fury streaming through his blood. He looked down the stairs at Liam and Derek.

"I want to get her back to HQ, now."

Within minutes they were on their way. They left the forensic team and coroner's office representatives, as well as members of the SWAT team. Derek stayed to oversee everything but really to keep an eye on his wife if the Watcher decided to come back for any reason.

Everyone else made a caravan to get Rosalyn back to Omega. Liam was in the car in front of Steve, Jon in the car behind. Weapons hot in case there was any problem. Rosalyn sat in the backseat in Steve's car. Andrea was beside her, arm around her shoulder. Brandon was on the other side.

Every time he caught a glance at Rosalyn's face in the rearview mirror, his heart sank a little more. She was pale to the point of gray, her lips pinched until they were colorless. Her blue eyes, usually so full of life, were dull, lifeless.

Like she had given up.

Steve felt marginally better as they pulled into Omega and he got her into the building. The Watcher's violence seemed to be escalating, and now he was using guns. Rosalyn would be staying inside the Omega compound until they caught the Watcher.

They moved quickly past the security guard, Steve biting his tongue when Rosalyn once again set off the metal detector. The guard ran the wand up the front and back of her body but found nothing.

This was ridiculous. "Get those things looked at," he barked to the guard. The man nodded quickly.

He slipped his arm around Rosalyn, keeping her close to his side as they walked down the hall.

"I need to write this note in my notebook. It's important for me to keep an accurate record. Detective Johnson said so."

Rosalyn's voice sounded unnatural. Distant. Steve shot a concerned look over at Andrea.

"Sure, honey." Andrea rubbed Rosalyn's arm. "Your notebook is in the conference room. I'll help you write it down."

When they got to the room, Jon grabbed Steve's arm. "Brandon and I found something interesting last night after you left."

"Okay."

Brandon and Jon both turned to look at the two women, who were settling in at the conference room table. Jon shook his head. "I'm not sure if it's something we should say in front of Rosalyn. Especially given her fragile state right now."

"Okay, let's go into my office. You can run it by me and then we can decide whether to tell Rosalyn. Although I don't want to keep secrets from her if it's going to affect her safety. More information is better in this case."

Brandon nodded. "I think we both agree. It's some other cases we found that are interesting."

As soon as they were in Steve's office, Brandon pulled out four files. He opened one and laid down a picture of a young woman.

"This is the one I remembered. It's from two years ago." Brandon's genius mind didn't forget much of anything. It had helped them on cases more than once. "Her name was Tracy Solheim. From Jackson, Mississippi."

Steve picked up the file and looked over it. "Says she committed suicide."

Brandon nodded. "She did. She was twenty-one. But for six months before she killed herself she told multiple people, her family, friends, even the police, that she had a stalker. Said she was receiving notes."

"Nobody believed her," Jon continued. "Tracy had a history of emotional trauma. Did a lot of weird stuff to get attention over the years. Police reports did say she had notes but that none of them were threatening in any way."

Steve shrugged. "Okay, there are some similarities there. But not enough to convince me it's the same guy."

Brandon nodded. "I agree. But look at these three others. One's from Tampa, one's from Birmingham, Alabama, and one's from New Orleans."

"I'm assuming the point is the radius to Mobile, Alabama, Rosalyn's hometown."

"It's almost a semicircle," Jon said. "And within the last six years there's been a woman who has committed suicide in all those cities. All white females within twenty to twenty-five years of age. All who complained to family and at least once to the police about receiving 'strange' notes. In all the cases nothing was done to help them, because they were deemed nonthreatening."

Brandon pulled out a piece of paper. "This is what clinched it for me. One of the officers from the New Orleans case at least wrote down in his official report what some of the notes said."

Brandon had blown them up so they were each on a separate sheet of paper.

The park was nice today, wasn't it?

I would've chosen the red sweater, but the blue one looks nice too.

Did you enjoy dinner with your friends? I was hoping you'd get the shrimp rather than the chicken.

"Those are all similar in tone to some of the notes Rosalyn has quoted in her notebook."

Brandon nodded. "Exactly. And also, innocent enough to not be taken seriously by the police."

Steve sat down in the seat next to the table and leaned back. "Okay, let's assume this is the same guy. So what happened? The Watcher killed them? I thought you said they were suicide."

"Yes, all confirmed suicide." Brandon sat in the other chair. "We think that's his MO, Steve. He drives these women away from their families, away from their loved ones. He isolates them. He's smart enough not to threaten them in the notes, so nothing can be done with the police."

"To what end? He's obviously not living out any fantasies with these women." That was almost always part of a violent stalker's MO—having the women with him. "He's not killing them, right?"

"He's a serial killer, Steve." Jon braced himself on the table with both arms. "Every bit as much as ones that we profile. But instead of using a certain weapon or certain ritual, he pushes and pushes until they do it themselves. That *is* his ritual."

It was so sick and yet made so much sense at the same time.

A serial killer who didn't actually kill his victims. Drove them to killing themselves by isolating them from everyone they loved, by terrorizing them until they felt they had no other choice.

It took a special sort of evil to inflict emotional trauma of that magnitude.

Steve realized the Watcher could've killed Rosalyn at any time. She'd been alone, undefended, for months before she met him and months afterward. The Watcher hadn't tried to harm her. It was only within the last few days that he'd turned violent toward her.

And actually, he really hadn't turned violent toward *her*. True, he'd killed Rosalyn's sister, but probably because he found out it was Lindsey and not Rosalyn. He'd also been trying to kill Steve, not Rosalyn; she'd just been near collateral damage.

Brandon cleared his throat, dragging Steve's attention back into the room. "If you think about it, the fact that Rosalyn is still alive is a testament to her strength. We're still gathering information about these other women, but so far it seems that none of them lasted as long as Rosalyn has."

Steve stood. "Because she was alone a long time before the Watcher found her."

"She doesn't have family?" Brandon's brow wrinkled. "That would go against our profile."

"No, she has family. Just none of them have ever been there for her. She has, in essence, been alone her whole life." Steve began restacking the files. "Let's go tell Rosalyn what we've found. I think it will definitely help, not hurt. At least give her an understanding of what's going on."

Yeah, she'd been alone. But she damn sure wasn't anymore.

Chapter Nineteen

Steve had been correct—telling Rosalyn about Jon and Brandon's theory had been the right thing to do. She felt sad for the other women and angry that the Watcher seemed to be getting away with a horrible crime without anyone even knowing. But mostly she was relieved to finally understand what was happening.

"So he was trying to get me to kill myself." She was sitting across the table from him, next to Andrea. Her voice was still soft but at least she didn't look as fragile as she had before. "I almost did, you know. That night I met you."

"He wanted you to feel that way," Steve said.

"Yes," Brandon agreed. "That's his pattern. From what we can tell, he's very methodical about what he does. Almost like this is some sort of experiment to him. He wants to see how far he can push each woman before she breaks."

Jon nodded. "He's smart. Knows about law enforcement. His notes are never threatening and don't mention anything that would raise a red flag with police."

"Like what?" Rosalyn asked.

"Anything that would show obsession. 'We'll be together forever' sort of stuff. Instead the Watcher mentions normal everyday occurrences. Meals. Activities. Something a friend would mention casually, not someone obsessed."

Steve sat down in a chair across from Rosalyn. "Because he's not obsessed."

Brandon nodded. "Exactly. He's scientific. Experimental. He's not obsessed with the women themselves, just what sort of reactions he can get from them."

"And he doesn't actually harm them himself," Brandon continued. "But he uses tools of psychological terror instead—isolation, fear, imbalance. Then it's just a matter of time before they crack."

"You didn't," Steve told her.

A single tear escaped and rolled slowly down the side of her cheek. "I almost did. If I hadn't met you that night…"

He leaned forward, closer to her. "But you did meet me, not that I was of much help at the time. And if you hadn't, you still would've made it through. You're one of the strongest people I've ever met."

Her smile was breathtaking.

She now knew the Watcher's endgame—her taking her own life—and she was bound and determined not to give it to him. It was all Steve could do not to pull her up into his arms right there in the conference room in front of everyone. She was amazing.

And she was his. She might not realize it, but he had no intention of letting her out of his sight even after this was over. The baby was part of that, true, but he wasn't the only part. Steve wanted Rosalyn—with all her strength, beauty, radiance—in his life. If she would have him.

"The Watcher doesn't hurt the women," Steve finally said, "but he's obviously not above violence. We've got a dead agent and Rosalyn has a dead sister that proves that. He's a killer."

"Yes, absolutely." Brandon nodded. "But killing the others are him manipulating variables in his equation. A means to an end. I don't think he's killing because he likes it. He's killing to further the reaction in his victims. To isolate them further."

"Everything's different now," Rosalyn looked around the room. "He hasn't got me isolated anymore. But he threatened the baby, Steve."

"That's his way of trying to continue his manipulation of you." Steve squeezed her hand. "There's no way he can get to you here. We'll put protective custody around your mom."

"The Ammonses too. In Georgia," Rosalyn whispered.

Steve nodded. "Roman should be checking in soon. He was meeting with them this morning."

"We've still got a lot of holes," Jon said. "The same ones Brandon was mentioning last night. Mainly, why didn't you hear from the Watcher for the six months you were in Georgia, and how he keeps knowing where you are, even though there aren't any more tracking devices on your clothing. There's no way he should've been able to find you at Steve's house last night."

"I swear I didn't tell him where I was," Rosalyn was quick to interject.

"No one thinks you did," Andrea murmured, leaning closer to Rosalyn.

Steve nodded quickly. "No one is idiot enough to think you're involved."

She raised an eyebrow at him.

He shrugged, grinning sheepishly. "At least not today."

She rolled her eyes. Steve was so happy to see her more lively that he couldn't be the least bit irritated.

When he'd seen the note that threatened their baby... Renewed rage caused Steve's fists to clench. He would make this right no matter what it took.

"We're still looking for other cases," Jon said. "Because of the intensity of his crimes, we're pretty sure he can only stalk one woman at a time, maybe two at the most.

None of the cases overlap. There are probably others but we haven't found them yet. And we're still gathering info on the cases we have found."

A call beeped through to the conference room's phone. Steve pressed the speaker button.

"Roman Weber is holding for you, Steve," Cynthia told him. "He's in Ellijay, Georgia."

"Good. Maybe he can provide some answers. Put him through."

"Hey." Roman's voice came through clearly. "Remind me next time you want me to go to some tiny town in Georgia to make you send someone else."

Steve caught the slightest hint of a smile on Rosalyn's face.

"Roman, I have you on speaker in the conference room. Everyone's here."

"I talked to the Ammonses this morning. Like Rosalyn said, they're good people. Just don't trust the government much. Their son died in the military, years ago, but I think they were probably pretty skeptical before that."

"Okay. Did you find anything of interest?"

"I tell you what, these people are more than ready for a TEOTWAWKI event. They've got a cellar full of food, water purifiers, ammunition. You name it."

Rosalyn looked confused. "What does *TEOTWAWKI* mean?"

"The end of the world as we know it," Jon explained. "A lot of survivalists use the term."

"They're definitely off the grid. No computers, only one phone. The whole town is prepared for a zombie apocalypse or whatever, but the Ammonses are definitely the most paranoid."

"Did you talk to them yourself?" Steve asked.

"Yes, they said to give you their best, Rosalyn. And to let you know you are welcome back at any time."

Rosalyn smiled. "If you see them again, send my best too. I know they're not very talkative."

"That's for sure. Steve, in all their survivor gear—and believe me, it's extensive—they have some jamming devices. They didn't want the government listening in on them in any way. This wouldn't stop a lot of the higher-end devices we have now, but it would've protected them from the basics."

And there they had it. One mystery solved. Steve looked at Rosalyn across the table. "And their equipment would have interfered with transmissions of all kinds."

"No doubt. I thought you would find that interesting, given the transmission devices you found on Rosalyn's clothes."

"Great, Roman," Steve said. "I need you to stay there and keep an eye on the Ammonses. If you're right about everything, there shouldn't be a problem. We think we have a profile on the killer. Doesn't look like he'll be coming your way, but just in case."

"Got it, boss."

Roman gave a little more information before hanging up, promising to keep a watchful eye for anything unusual.

"Well, that solves question one of the two. The Watcher couldn't find you while you were at the Ammonses' because the equipment they were using to block the government from hearing them—not that the government is listening to a couple in their seventies who have never broken the law—also kept the Watcher from being able to hear or find you."

He could see Rosalyn's relief at one more piece of the puzzle falling into place.

"Thank God." She leaned back in her chair. "I was afraid he'd just been toying with me. That he was going to hurt the Ammonses in some way, even though I never mentioned him to them."

"Looks like the Watcher may not know about them at all. Their government paranoia saved them from a serial killer." Steve reached over and grabbed her hand again. He didn't care if anyone else knew about his feelings for Rosalyn. It's not like he'd done such a good job hiding them up to now.

They all took a break to eat lunch. Steve walked with Rosalyn to the small cafeteria in the building. He wanted to make sure she wasn't missing any meals she couldn't afford to miss. He saw her hands suddenly fly to her belly and a little smile cross her face. He knew the baby had kicked again.

It just made him all the more determined to keep them safe.

But to do that they had to figure out how the Watcher was finding them now.

Back in the conference after lunch, they pored over the case files, comparing what little dates and specific information they had to Rosalyn's much more in-depth notebook. Jon and Brandon had already left, Jon to Tampa, Brandon to New Orleans, to see if they could gather more intel from talking to the victims' families and the local police.

They wouldn't give the families all the details in the cases, especially since right now it was only a theory, but they would let them know that there had been others who had suffered similar fates. Maybe there would be something—or someone—else the family members could remember.

Andrea worked with Joe Matarazzo to see if they could find any ties between the other four victims and Rosalyn. They'd shown Rosalyn all the women's pictures, but she hadn't recognized any of them.

Steve couldn't stay with Rosalyn the entire day like he wanted to. He had to deal with Doug Wilson's death; the tragic job of notifying the family belonged to him. He also had to catch up the local PD with what had happened at his house this morning.

He wanted Rosalyn's case to be the only thing he had to work on, but it couldn't be.

When he got back to the conference room at nearly nine o'clock that evening, she was still poring over her notes with Andrea and Joe.

"Time for everyone to go home," he announced. "We'll pick up fresh tomorrow."

Joe nodded before hugging both women. Steve wasn't offended or threatened. Joe was a people person to his very core.

"Tomorrow, boss," he said on his way out.

"Tell Laura I said hello." Steve and Laura, Joe's bride, had become close since they both were almost burned alive by a psychopath a few months ago.

"I'm sure she's going to want you to come to dinner with your new girlfriend." Joe said it in an exaggerated stage whisper, winking at Steve.

Steve's eyes met Rosalyn's. She was shaking her head at Joe's antics, as they all tended to do.

"I'll see you guys tomorrow too," Andrea said as she put her blazer back on. She hugged Rosalyn. "We'll start again first thing. Welcome to real-life police work. It takes time."

Rosalyn's frustration colored all her features as she looked down at the case files and papers spread out all over the table. It wasn't messy but it was chaotic.

He slipped an arm around her shoulders and pulled her to his side. "Andrea's right, you know. It takes time."

She eased against him but rubbed her face with her hands. "We've gone over so much my brain hurts. And I don't know that we're any closer to catching the Watcher."

"We are. Every day we put together more of the puzzle pieces. Soon we'll have a good view overall."

"I can't stay here forever. He has me just as much trapped here as he did when he had me on the run before."

He grabbed her by both shoulders so they could look eye to eye.

"No. You're not alone here. You have people who will do whatever it takes to keep you safe. We will catch him, Rosalyn."

She shrugged. "I hope so. Everyone has lives they need to get on with. They can't spend all their time just on this one case."

He pulled her to his chest and felt her arms wrap around his waist.

"You let me worry about that. Working cases, hunting down people who hurt others? That's what we do here. We find the patterns nobody else sees. And we're damn good at our job."

"Okay." She nodded her head against his chest.

"We'll catch him." He brought his lips down to her forehead. "I will do whatever it takes to make sure you and our baby are safe. I promise you that."

It was a promise he had every intention of keeping.

Chapter Twenty

Rosalyn awoke to sounds of voices in the small living room area of the Omega Sector apartment. Evidently the apartment was used by experts who came to help with cases or by agents who needed a night's rest and didn't want to go to their homes.

Or for people who were being hunted by psychopaths.

The apartment was within the compound but outside the main section of offices. Members of the SWAT team, angry over the death of an Omega agent, were taking turns guarding the door. Ashton Fitzgerald had been there when she and Steve had arrived.

Rosalyn had fallen to sleep knowing the Watcher couldn't find her here. Or at least couldn't get to her.

But she had dreamed that he sat right outside the gate. In a lawn chair. Drinking coffee and reading a newspaper. His face was hidden from her in some sort of unnatural darkness, but she could clearly see a giant knife sitting on a small table by his side.

Just waiting for her to exit Omega so he could kill her.

Worse than that, the bodies of everyone she'd come to know and care about at Omega Sector—Jon, Brandon, Andrea, Derek, Joe—lay around him. Murdered.

Steve's body sat propped up closer to the Watcher, blood staining his T-shirt. Steve's green eyes were open, lifeless, staring out blankly.

Rosalyn took a step outside the gate. The Watcher folded his paper and stood.

"I was beginning to think you'd never come out of there," he said, his voice sounding like it was coming through one of those modulator things. "But I had fun with your friends since you were so busy protecting yourself."

She watched in horror as he kicked Steve's body over and rushed toward her.

"I'm so excited to meet the baby!"

She'd awakened sobbing right before he reached her.

Steve had held her in the bed as she fought him at first—caught in the terror of her dream—then as she sobbed.

"You're all going to die because of me. Because I'm hiding and the Watcher wants to keep his sick game moving forward."

"Nobody else is going to die. We are all on high alert and everyone can handle themselves."

He'd stroked her hair and held her close to his chest, murmuring soft words of comfort and encouragement. But she still couldn't fall back asleep until the light of dawn crept up through the small window.

She heard the deep timbre of Steve's voice right away and soon recognized the other voices to be Derek and Molly Waterman. Maybe Molly had found something when analyzing the crime scene at Steve's house yesterday. Rosalyn got dressed and went out into the small living room. She didn't have any makeup to put on even if she could have been bothered to do so.

Steve immediately crossed to her and kissed her on her forehead.

"You okay?" He led her over to the small kitchen island so she could have something to eat and some coffee. "I'll make you eggs and toast."

"Thank you. Rough dreams, but yeah, I'm okay now."

She turned to Molly and Derek. "Good morning. Anything new?"

Molly surprised her by coming over to give her a hug. It had been a long time since she'd had friends, really anyone besides Steve, who cared about her. She returned Molly's hug, trying not to be as awkward as she felt.

"We didn't find anything useful at Steve's house. Like you said about the other notes, there was no usable DNA available."

Rosalyn swallowed and nodded. She hadn't really expected them to find anything. "I'm not surprised. I had hoped maybe a professional would find something I had overlooked all these times."

Molly shook her head. "There was nothing to be found, not by you, not by anyone. I'm sure that was true for the other notes, as well."

Rosalyn felt a little bit better.

"But Jon found a transmitter on an article of clothing of one of the other deceased victims. He's bringing it back here so I can analyze it."

Steve looked over from where he was cooking at the stove. "Our primary focus with your case as of now is figuring out how the Watcher has found you after we removed the trackers in Pensacola."

"Being able to look at a functional transmitter will help me," Molly said. "I might be able to pinpoint where it was made."

Steve fed not only Rosalyn but Derek and Molly breakfast. Molly and Derek told humorous stories of Molly's own pregnancy—their daughter had been born five months ago—and some of Derek's outrageous behavior in the delivery room.

Evidently the big, bad SWAT agent who towered over his petite wife had been reduced to "less than useless"—

Molly's words—while their child made her entry into the world.

"It was time to go to the hospital, and he got lost." Molly rolled her eyes. "The man navigated his way through a Colombian jungle once to rescue me and he couldn't figure out how to get to a hospital eight miles away."

Derek nearly choked on his piece of toast. "I made one wrong turn. That is not the same as getting lost."

She slapped him on the back to help with his coughing. "Of course, honey." She turned to Rosalyn. "He was lost," Molly said in an exaggerated sigh.

Steve laughed.

"Just you wait." Derek stabbed some of his eggs, glaring at Steve. "Your time is coming. I'm going to follow you around with a camera."

The normal conversation, the joking, even the glares, made Rosalyn feel better. Made life seem a little more normal.

But then the vision of the Watcher in her dream came back.

If the Watcher killed Molly and Derek, their daughter would be an orphan. Rosalyn fought to keep down the food she'd just eaten.

Steve moved closer to her. "Whatever you're thinking right now, stop," he whispered in her ear as Derek and Molly gathered her papers so they could all leave.

"But…"

Steve tilted her chin up. "I know it feels this way to you, but the Watcher is not the baddest bad guy we've ever faced. Isn't that right, Derek?"

"Not even in the top ten," Derek confirmed.

"That man is not going to let anything happen to Molly, so don't even let that enter your mind."

"Nope." Derek confirmed again, reaching down to wrap

both arms around his wife's hips and lift her so he could kiss her. "Never again."

"And I'm not going to let anything happen to you."

They got the rest of what they would need for the day and the four of them walked out the door and down the hall. Rosalyn tried to hold on to the good feeling she'd had for a few minutes, but it was lost in the weight of what was happening.

They had to go through the security section again as they entered the main offices. Everyone made it through the metal detector without it going off but Rosalyn. Again. Always her luck.

The poor guy looked as though he feared for his job when he used the wand on Rosalyn and she set it off once more.

"Eastburn, I thought I told you to get that wand checked." Steve spoke through his teeth with forced restraint.

"Yes, sir, this is a new wand. There shouldn't be any problem with it."

"So, you're suggesting that Ms. Mellinger has a weapon in her mouth?" That was where the wand kept beeping.

"No, sir. I'm not sure what is wrong."

"You ever have problems in airports or anything?" Steve asked her.

Rosalyn shook her head. "I haven't been in one for a few years, but no, not that I recall."

Molly put the files she'd been carrying down and walked over to Steve and Rosalyn. "You've set off the metal detector every time you've come through?"

"Yes." Rosalyn shrugged. "Well, the first time I was in handcuffs, so I'm pretty sure that did it. Yesterday we were assuming it was just a defective wand."

Molly, Derek and Steve were all giving each other looks.

"What?" Rosalyn asked.

Steve tossed some keys to Derek, who put them in his pocket. Steve took the wand from the guard and scanned Derek. It beeped when it got to his pocket, signifying the presence of the keys.

Without Steve asking, Derek took the keys out of his pocket and handed them to Molly. Steve scanned Derek again, with no beeps this time.

"Scanner seems to work correctly," Derek said. They all turned and looked at Rosalyn.

"What?" she asked again.

"I need you to come with me over to the lab," Molly said.

"Why?" Rosalyn had no idea what was going on.

"We need to take an X-ray of your mouth. Your teeth in particular. I think we've just discovered how the Watcher keeps finding you."

ONCE MOLLY MADE her announcement, everyone flurried into action. Rosalyn wasn't quite sure what to do except go along with it.

"The X-ray equipment in the lab is not really for use on a human," Molly stated as she walked with Steve and Rosalyn toward the lab. Derek had gone to research transmitters.

"Is it safe for the baby?" Steve asked. "I won't risk any harm to Rosalyn or the baby just for quicker results. If we need to get her to a hospital, we can make that work safely."

"No X-ray machine is great for any human. It's radiation. But it's a small amount for a very short time. And we'll use a lead covering." Molly turned to Rosalyn and took her hand. "Under the same circumstances, I would've allowed the X-ray when I was pregnant. That's the best assurance I can give you."

Rosalyn nodded. It was enough.

Molly's comfort inside her lab was evident. She slipped

on a white coat and began giving orders and answering questions the moment she arrived. Obviously how things occurred here every day.

Molly led them into a smaller room with an X-ray machine. "We're fortunate. We got the X-ray as part of the new lab."

Rosalyn looked over at Steve as Molly set up the machine so it could be used on her rather than objects.

"New lab?"

Steve nodded. "About eighteen months ago a terrorist group bombed the lab to try to hide some evidence concerning a bigger crime. We rebuilt a newer, better one."

"I'm glad you weren't in here when it blew, Molly."

"Me too. We did lose one tech, though." Rosalyn saw the glance between Molly and Steve. There was more to this story than they were saying. She was about to ask when Molly brought her over to sit on a step stool.

She arranged the X-ray machine while Rosalyn held her head in an awkward position. Like Molly had said, the machine wasn't meant for humans. But in the end, they got what they wanted. Ten minutes later they were sitting around Molly's computer as the X-ray image came up.

"There." Molly pointed to one of Rosalyn's teeth from the X-ray.

"My tooth?"

"No. It's a crown. And beyond that, it's a transmitting and locating device. It's how the Watcher has been finding you."

Chapter Twenty-One

They were out in the hall talking about her. As soon as Molly announced about the transmitter, Steve and Molly had immediately stopped talking. It took Rosalyn a minute to understand why.

They were afraid the Watcher could hear everything they were saying.

Steve wrote her a note explaining that, but Rosalyn had already figured out that he and Molly weren't just being rude.

Meanwhile, Rosalyn was fighting the urge to find some sort of pliers and yank the crown out of her jaw.

The Watcher had a transmitter *inside* her body. Rosalyn laughed out loud, although she could recognize the hysteria that tinged it.

All these weeks when she thought the Watcher was inside her head she'd been literally right.

She glanced around for pliers again. Yeah, it would hurt, but the pain might be worth knowing he was out of her thoughts once and for all. But she couldn't find anything in the lab.

Steve and Molly came back in about ten minutes later.

"It's okay—we can talk." Steve came to stand in front of her, putting his hands on her shoulders and rubbing them gently.

"But can't he hear us? The transmitter?" Rosalyn fought to keep her voice even.

"No. Not here at Omega. We use a similar jamming device as the Ammonses use in Georgia. We want to make sure criminals are not privy to our private conversations."

Molly looked up from where she had sat down at her computer. "And ours are on a much greater scale and more sophisticated than the jammers in Georgia. Anything you say here is safe."

Steve wrapped an arm around her shoulder. "Let's go up to the conference room. We need to get Jon and Brandon on a conference call and figure out our next step."

"I want to get it out as soon as possible," she told both of them. "Fortunately, I couldn't find a pair of pliers while you were in the hallway talking or I might have already taken care of it myself."

"Absolutely," Steve agreed. "I want that thing out of you just as much, believe me."

"It's still a crown. It's cemented in," Molly reminded them. "A dentist will be much less painful and ready for any emergency."

She and Steve were both deep in their own thoughts as they made it back to the conference room. He had Brandon and Jon on the line within minutes, explaining what they'd found.

"That makes so much sense," Brandon said. "The reason why he could find Rosalyn at Steve's house but can't find her at Omega."

"Yes," Steve agreed. "Molly and I already double-checked. Omega's frequency jammer is keeping the signal from being broadcast any farther than the building."

"So he probably has no idea where you are, Rosalyn," Jon said.

"That's right," Steve agreed. "And even if he somehow followed her, there's no way he can get in."

She felt safe, but she still wanted the thing out of her mouth.

"More important," Brandon said, "this gives us a big clue as to who the Watcher is."

Steve turned to her. "Your dentist, Rosalyn. There's no way that transmitter could've been put in the crown by accident. Whoever did your dental work is most likely the Watcher."

"Fits the profile," Jon agreed. "Intelligent. Professional. My personal bet had been on some sort of doctor, but I guess a dentist is close enough. Plus, he would've had days he could devote to following you and days he couldn't, thus the gap in notes sometimes."

Of course. Rosalyn felt a little stupid that she hadn't thought of that immediately.

"I'm going to bet you had that done about a year ago?" Brandon asked.

"Yes." Rosalyn sat down in one of the conference room chairs. "I don't like going to the dentist. So I found one who would put me under general anesthesia to do the root canal."

She looked at Steve. "Actually, my sister was the one who told me about him. I think he practices all over the Southeast. Gunson was his last name. I don't remember his first."

Steve reached down and kissed her on the forehead. "That's enough. We'll get him now."

CHRISTOPHER GUNSON DIDN'T know it, but his days as a free man were numbered.

Even without the first name it hadn't taken long for them to find him. His primary practice was based out of Mobile, but he also did work in New Orleans.

It said so right there on his website. The website also explained that he understood the fear people had of dentists, that the fear wasn't unreasonable. That he would rather work with patients by whatever means necessary—including general anesthesia for procedures—than for them not to have dental care at all.

It was easy to see how he drew patients in. And then, when they were out cold for their procedures, he could easily place a transmitter and tracking device like he had in Rosalyn's mouth.

Brandon was on his way to Gunson's New Orleans office right now. Jon was flying from Tampa to Mobile to investigate the practice there.

Steve didn't expect them to find the man at either site, because he was sure Gunson was still here in Colorado. He might not know where Rosalyn was exactly, since he couldn't track her or listen to her while she was in the Omega building, but Steve had no doubt he would be waiting to make a move as soon as she wasn't in their protection.

They hadn't found a good picture of Gunson on his website. The most recent picture they had was taken of him ten years ago at a dental convention in Las Vegas.

In the picture he was in his late thirties, already balding and pretty thick around the middle. Steve imagined the ten years since hadn't been kind. He wondered if that was the reason Gunson stalked women. If it gave him a sense of power he didn't otherwise have in real life.

Maybe he wasn't so different from the average stalker, after all.

Rosalyn was holding it together, but barely. Every time he looked over at her, she was rubbing her jaw where the transmitter was. She wanted it out and he didn't blame her. But they couldn't do it here. And right now it was more important that they make their move on Gunson, before he realized they were onto him.

Once the transmitter was gone from her mouth, Gunson would know his identity was blown.

So as long as Rosalyn wasn't in a panic, they needed to leave it in. At least for a few more hours.

Steve wished he could distract her. Take her back upstairs to the apartment and let her rest. He knew she hadn't slept very well last night.

But he couldn't. He was coordinating with both the New Orleans and Mobile Police Departments to provide back up when Brandon and Jon arrived. They needed to make sure nobody got a call in to Gunson once they raided the offices. They had to collect as much information as they could without clueing in Gunson.

A few hours later Steve received the call. Brandon and the New Orleans police had moved in on Gunson's office. Gunson had surprised everyone by actually being there, in his office, with patients. Definitely not in Colorado. The locals took him into custody and allowed Brandon to use their facilities to interrogate him and were providing Omega with the live feed of the questioning.

As soon as Steve saw the man through the monitor—and Steve had been right; the ten years hadn't been kind to him—crying, before Brandon even asked a question, Steve knew this wasn't the Watcher.

But still he hoped.

Rosalyn sat next to him watching the screen too.

"Yes," she whispered. "That's Dr. Gunson. He's really the Watcher?"

"Let's see what Brandon can find out."

Gunson had already been read his rights but hadn't insisted on an attorney. Probably not a smart move on his part.

Also another clue that he probably wasn't the killer. Steve grimaced.

But if anybody had to be in there questioning him,

Brandon Han was the perfect person. His ability to get inside the minds of criminals was unparalleled. Brandon might not be able to get a confession, but he would definitely walk out of there with a pretty damn educated guess about Gunson's involvement.

Andrea came running into the room. "Brandon's about to interview Gunson?"

"Yeah." Steve gestured to the seat beside Rosalyn. "Join us, please. Give us your opinion."

They all tuned in to the screen.

"Can you tell me why you're crying, Dr. Gunson?" Brandon's voice was even, nonthreatening.

"I didn't want to do it."

Rosalyn strained closer to the screen.

"Didn't want to do what, Christopher? Is it okay if I call you that? But I don't mind calling you Dr. Gunson, if that's what you prefer. A title of respect."

"That's my man," Andrea murmured. "He always knows the best route to take."

And in this case showing regard to a person feeling dejected was that route.

"Christopher is fine. Or Chris."

"Okay, Chris. Tell me what you didn't want to do."

"I had gotten into financial trouble. Done too much online betting. Lost too much. I was about to lose my house. My practice. Everything."

The crimes against Rosalyn hadn't been of any financial gain, the opposite, in fact. He would probably lose money being away from his practice to follow the women.

Brandon had to know that, but he didn't let it show. Instead he nodded. "So you did something you shouldn't."

"The transmitters. I knew they were wrong."

Steve heard Rosalyn's soft gasp at Gunson's admission.

Gunson sat back in his seat, defeated. At least he wasn't crying anymore. "I really don't know much. I didn't want to know what he was studying. I didn't want to know how it worked or anything about the transmitters themselves."

"Someone paid you to put transmitters in dental work."

"He's not the Watcher," Rosalyn murmured.

Steve squeezed her shoulder, keeping his frustration at bay. He'd wanted this to be over. Wanted Rosalyn to be able to walk out of here completely free of the Watcher.

That wasn't going to happen today unless Gunson had a lot more info than he was letting on.

"Who paid you, Chris?" Brandon leaned in toward the other man.

"I don't know. I never met him face-to-face. About six years ago I was really in deep with some loan sharks. They were going to break my fingers."

Gunson looked at Brandon as if that explained everything. Brandon gestured for him to continue.

"So when a man approached me and said he was doing some unorthodox experimentation and needed me to put some transmitters into crowns, I finally broke down and did it."

"How many transmitters have you put in in those six years, Chris?"

"I don't know."

"He's lying about that," Andrea said. "Everything else he's been telling the truth about. But about this he's lying."

"How do you know he's lying?" Rosalyn asked.

"The way he looked down and to the left."

"I didn't even see him look anywhere." Rosalyn leaned closer to the screen.

"Andrea is very good at what she does, sweetheart. Don't feel bad—I didn't see it either."

"Brandon did," Andrea murmured. "I can tell."

Brandon leaned in toward Gunson. "Chris, this is only going to work if we're honest with each other. I think you know how many transmitters you put in patients' mouths. That's not something you would forget."

"Twenty-nine," Gunson finally responded. "All women. Over six years. He paid me $10,000 for each one."

Rosalyn sat ramrod straight and Steve sucked a breath through his teeth. Twenty-nine women had transmitters in their teeth. So far, including Rosalyn, they knew of five. And four of them were dead.

They watched as Brandon showed the pictures of the dead women. Gunson remembered each. Brandon didn't tell him the women were dead, a good call since the dentist seemed to be holding on by a thin thread anyway.

Brandon confirmed that Gunson had been in town the last forty-eight hours. The man gave a detailed report of what he'd done and with whom. Brandon would follow up, of course, but there was no doubt in Steve's mind.

Christopher Gunson wasn't the Watcher. He was pathetic and would be going to jail, but he wasn't the Watcher.

He could tell Rosalyn knew it too. When she looked back at him, devastation was clearly written across her face.

The worst news hit them at the very end. Brandon asked for information about the other patients. These women, even if they had never been contacted by the Watcher, even if their transmitters weren't live, needed to know what had happened to them.

Gunson looked ashamed as he explained that once the procedure had been done, he had given the patient records over to the man in order to receive payments. Although Gunson recognized the pictures of the women Brandon had shown him, he could not provide the names or any information about the other women he'd performed the procedure on.

They still had no idea who the Watcher was. All they

knew was that he had two dozen other victims to whom he could turn his attention at any time.

If he hadn't already.

Chapter Twenty-Two

Rosalyn dreamed of the Watcher again that night.

He was still waiting outside the fence of Omega, toss-ing something small up in the air and then catching it as it came back down. Rosalyn didn't have to be able to see it to know it was a transmitter.

All the Omega agents lay dead around him again. Rosalyn tried not to look at them, knowing she'd never make it if she did.

Make it where? Away from the Watcher? She could go now. He wouldn't be able to follow her.

But now not only did the Watcher have all the Omega agents, he had twenty-eight women tied up in chairs. Blindfolded. Helpless.

Four were obviously dead.

He walked up and down the line of the other women as if he was trying to decide who to choose next.

Rosalyn woke up sobbing again.

"Hey, it's okay."

Steve. He was here, holding her again like he had last night.

"He's going to kill those women. There are twenty-four other women and he's going to kill them. Or get them to kill themselves."

Steve pulled her closer. "We'll stop him."

"How? Dr. Gunson doesn't have any idea who he is."

"We know his pattern now. His MO. We'll catch him, Rosalyn. This is what we do."

"But more women will die first."

Steve was silent for a moment. "Not necessarily. We'll do whatever it takes to keep that from happening."

Rosalyn twisted around, forcing Steve onto his back so she could see his face in the dim light of the moon through the small window. "I'm your best shot at keeping that from happening."

"Why do you say that?"

"If we leave the transmitter in my mouth, we can use it to catch him."

"No. I know how much that thing bothers you. It bothers me too. I don't want him having the means of finding you." He pulled her closer to his side and put his lips against her forehead. "The dentist is coming in the morning. The transmitter comes out. We'll see if it can be salvaged and still used, but your part ends there."

She snuggled into his side. It felt good to have someone care about her. To have someone she could lean on literally and figuratively.

"Go back to sleep," he whispered.

Rosalyn's eyes drifted closed but she knew she would still see the Watcher's other victims when sleep claimed her.

THEY HAD DEEMED it safer to bring a dentist in rather than have Rosalyn go out where she could be tracked. Once they had the transmitter out of her mouth, Steve hoped to be able to use it to trick the Watcher in some way. To trap him.

Molly had offered one of the rooms in her lab for the dentist to do his work. Rosalyn was less than thrilled with dentists in general—thus how she'd gotten into this mess in the first place—and the thought of one working on her while she sat in a reclinable office chair did not reassure her.

But she wanted the transmitter out. Wanted to know for sure her baby was safe.

She took one look in the room where the dentist was setting up and knew she couldn't do it. But not because of her fear of the dentist.

Because she knew if she had this transmitter taken out of her tooth now, she wouldn't be able to help stop the Watcher.

"Everything okay?" Molly stepped up to her as Rosalyn stood paralyzed in the door. "I know this looks a little rough. But you won't be able to feel anything once he gets you numb."

"I can't do it."

She felt Molly's hand rubbing her back. "Dr. Mitchell is an excellent dentist, I promise you. It won't hurt."

"No, it's not because of the dentist. Believe me, I want this thing out of me enough to probably let him go at me with no numbing at all. It's the Watcher. This is our best link to him. To stopping him."

Molly nodded. "That's another reason we chose Dr. Mitchell. He's one of the most likely people to be able to get the transmitter out intact."

"The Watcher listens to me with the transmitter, right? I mean, it tells him where I am, but he also physically hears my voice."

"Yes, from what I can tell from the X-ray."

"So if we take it out of my mouth, he's going to know something's different, right? He's going to be able to tell."

"Rosalyn…"

"If I get this removed, I'm making myself safe, but we'll lose our best chance of catching him."

Molly shook her head. "We'll find another way of catching him. You don't need to risk your life. Risk your mental health."

But Rosalyn had already made up her mind. "I'm not going to let another woman go through what I've gone through. Not if it's in my power to stop him."

Molly spent a few more minutes making sure that was what Rosalyn really wanted, but Rosalyn knew it was. She couldn't live with herself if more women got hurt.

She wanted to take this bastard down.

Molly escorted Rosalyn back to the conference room. Steve was there. Jon and Brandon had made their way back from the interviews in Mobile and New Orleans. Derek and Ashton Fitzgerald from SWAT were there also.

They were coming up with a plan. Everyone stopped talking when she and Molly entered.

Steve rushed to her. "Hey, are you done already? That took a lot less time than I th—"

"I decided not to do it," she told him.

Steve grabbed her arm gently and backed her up so they could have a more private conversation in the hall. "Last night we agreed for you to get the transmitter out."

Rosalyn looked down at his arm where it gripped her shoulder. He'd rolled up his sleeves as he was working and she could see the bruises from when the Watcher had hit him at the gas station.

"I can't let him hurt someone else."

"We will stop him. That's our job, Rosalyn. Not yours."

"No." She gently kissed his wrist, then ducked under his arm and into the conference room.

She crossed to the head of the table. "The best shot we have of catching him is if the transmitter is still in my mouth and we use me to set him up."

Steve wasn't willing to let it go. He came and stood beside her. "We already have a plan. We'll use an agent of your general build and coloring—probably Lillian here—"

he pointed to a woman at the table "—to impersonate you. We'll give the transmitter to her and put her somewhere, he'll follow it and we'll catch him."

Derek nodded, supporting Steve. "Using a trained agent rather than you is a better tactical position for us."

Rosalyn shook her head. "That's assuming the dentist can get the transmitter out unharmed, which is no guarantee."

"Dr. Mitchell is one of the best oral surgeons in the state," Steve said.

Rosalyn rolled her eyes. "And I'm sure he's had lots of practice taking transmitters out of crowns, because that happens so often. No matter how good he is at normal dental stuff, he's never done anything like this before. You can't deny it's a huge risk."

Steve crossed his arms over his chest. "It's an acceptable one."

Everyone was looking at her now. "Even if we get the transmitter out safely, the Watcher is still going to know something is different. He can hear my voice. Has months of practice listening. He'll know if my voice is different."

Derek looked at Molly, "Can anything be done after the removal of the transmitter to make it sound like it's still in?"

"I can manipulate it somewhat, but it would just be a guess. I agree with Rosalyn about the sound. After all the time he's spent listening to her, he would notice a difference."

"I agree," Jon said. "Part of the thrill for the Watcher is probably listening in to the women. He wants to think of it all as just a science experiment that he's controlling, but listening probably gives him some measure of sexual thrill."

"And he would definitely be aware of changes," Brandon agreed. "He knows not only the sound of Rosalyn's voice but the pitch and the patterns."

Rosalyn couldn't help the shudder that ran through her.

"It's probably part of how he's known what buttons to press to get the biggest reactions out of his victims," Brandon continued. "He studied their voice patterns to see what caused the stress and then preyed on that."

Rosalyn nodded, trying not to lose her nerve. "So we all agree that taking it out is not the best thing to do."

Everyone around the table began talking at once. There was no clear consensus about the best plan.

Steve held up a hand to quiet everyone. He turned to Derek. "Derek, you and Ashton and the rest of SWAT will be heading up most of the sting. What's your opinion?"

Derek leaned back in his chair. "It's never my first choice to put a civilian in the line of fire. A pregnant one makes the situation even more complicated."

Rosalyn refused to be cast aside because of what *might* happen. "But…"

Derek held up his hand in a gesture that encouraged her to let him finish. "But I agree with what you're saying about the transmitter. The Watcher knows your voice. Changes now might spook him."

"We can use you to give all the verbal cues," Ashton said from his place beside Derek. "Then use a replacement agent in the actual location where we plan to arrest him."

Steve looked over at Derek. "You agree?"

Derek shrugged and nodded. "I understand you wanting to keep Rosalyn completely out of this, boss, truly I do. But she's right. Using her is our best bet at catching this guy before he hurts someone else. And if we use Ashton's plan, the risk to Rosalyn is minimal."

Rosalyn reached over and touched Steve's arm, bringing his attention to her. "I want to do this. I *need* to do this."

"And I need to keep you safe. Keep the baby safe."

"We will be safe. You'll be there to protect us every step of the way."

She knew Steve understood. Knew he knew this was the best plan. But she could also understand his hesitancy.

"Fine." He turned back to everyone. "But we don't leave here until we have a plan with no holes. And time is of the essence. Rosalyn has been out of the Watcher's ear for over two and a half days. If we wait too much longer, we'll lose him for good."

Rosalyn knew if that happened, they might never find him again.

Chapter Twenty-Three

"I'll keep hunting him, Rosalyn. We know he's here in the Colorado Springs area because of the note at my house. But I don't think you should leave."

"I don't want to leave you, Steve. We just found each other again. But I have to. We can't be together."

Even knowing the words were fake—an act of theater put on for the Watcher's benefit—Steve didn't like them.

They were about a mile away from the Omega offices. Nothing blocked the transmitter now. The Watcher should be able to hear everything they were saying.

Rosalyn sat inside a café. In the very back corner in a booth. She was huddled down near the table as if she was cold, but really she'd been told to keep her head down in case the Watcher decided to change his MO and take a shot at her.

There were three exits in this café—a front door, a window in the bathroom and the back delivery door. Every person in the building, from the waitstaff to the cooks to the customers, were Omega Sector employees. Not all were active agents, but all were trusted.

Steve wasn't sure exactly how they'd gotten the café completely emptied in the three hours since they'd finished their planning in the conference room. Steve had asked Joe for a favor, something he'd never asked Joe in the six years he'd known him. He'd asked Joe to use his money and connections to find them a building to pull this off in a ridiculously short amount of time.

Joe hadn't even blinked an eye. He'd called Deacon Crandall, Joe's sort of jack-of-all-trades, and next thing Steve knew, they had a café that could be used for the next week for anything Omega needed. Maybe Joe had used some of his millions of dollars and bought or rented the place; maybe he had just smiled prettily for the owner; who knew? Joe had a way with people. And Deacon was just a man who got stuff done.

Steve wanted to control as many circumstances as he possibly could. He already had a bad feeling in his gut about this situation. But maybe he would have that in any situation that might jeopardize a pregnant civilian.

The building was surrounded by four snipers. Ashton Fitzgerald, by far the best long-range shooter Steve had ever known, had the restaurant in his sights. He wouldn't let anything happen to Rosalyn there.

Steve couldn't be in the café with her. This had to be a telephone call between them for it to work. They didn't plan on it being long enough for the Watcher to get a bead on her location right now. Just enough to get him here tomorrow, when they'd be ready for him. Steve was watching the entire scene from multiple camera angles at the home base inside Omega. But still he itched to be there with Rosalyn. Didn't like having her so far out of his reach.

But he trusted his team.

"You don't need to leave." Steve continued their scripted conversation. "I'll track him down. Just give me more time."

"I can't risk you, Steve. He almost killed you on the motorcycle. If you hadn't turned in time—"

The emotion in Rosalyn's voice was real. And he could see it on her face in the monitor.

"But I did. And I'm okay."

"But how long before the Watcher tries again? I can't take the chance. I have to go."

"No, Rosalyn, just tell me where you are. Where you've been for the past two days."

This was part of the plan. To assure the Watcher they didn't know about the transmitter in her tooth. To make sure Omega wasn't part of his thought process.

"Just at a hotel."

"You're not safe at a hotel. He might find you."

"I'm not safe at your house either, Steve. He found me there."

Steve pulled from his own frustration at not being there next to Rosalyn and put it in his tone. "I can protect you. The Colorado Springs Police Department can protect you."

Steve and Rosalyn realized that they had never talked about Omega outside the Omega building itself. Therefore, the Watcher would not know Steve worked for the multifaceted law enforcement agency. They would convince him Steve was just a member of Colorado Springs PD.

A lone member with no real backup.

"Did you tell your bosses there about the Watcher?"

Steve waited a beat. "Yes."

He could see Rosalyn stir her coffee on the screen. "They didn't believe you, did they?"

"Look, just tell me where you are."

"I can't right now, Steve."

Jon pointed at his watch. They needed to wrap this up. Not give the Watcher enough time to find her today. It had to be tomorrow, when they were ready.

"When are you leaving?"

"Tomorrow. I'm taking a bus. That worked before and the Watcher didn't find me for a long time. I'm hoping that will work again."

"Okay, well, just meet me for breakfast or coffee or something before you go, okay? I just want to see you. To feel the baby kick one more time. You might have him before I can catch the Watcher."

"Okay, fine. My bus leaves at 9:45 a.m. tomorrow."

"Good. Let's meet at eight."

"Fine. There's a little café I'll meet you at." Rosalyn gave him the name and directions to the place she was at now.

"I'll see you tomorrow, sweetheart."

"Be careful, Steve. I don't want anything to happen to you."

Then she clicked the off button.

Steve tapped his communication button to Derek's earpiece. "Okay, get her out of there."

Derek was wearing an apron, posing as a cook in the back. He could see the entire seating area from where he stood.

"Roger that. Everyone in here is still Omega."

Steve watched on the screen as Derek nodded to Lillian, a SWAT team member no less deadly just because she stood barely over five feet tall. She brought Rosalyn a bill. "Here's your check, ma'am."

"Thank you." Rosalyn made a wincing sound as if she was in pain.

"Are you okay?"

"Just my tooth. Something's wrong. But I hate going to the dentist, you know?"

Hopefully the Watcher would buy that there was something wrong with the transmitter. It would force him to move up any timetable he had. To come after Rosalyn tomorrow even if he wasn't planning to. To make a mistake.

"I hope you feel better." Lillian touched the check. "I can take that whenever you're ready."

"Thank you."

That was the agreed-upon code that it was time for Rosalyn to leave. Steve watched as she got up and went out the front door and around to a car in the side parking lot. The camera lost her then, but he knew from there she would drive, as if she was looking for a tail.

Just like she always had done before she'd known how the Watcher was following her. Four different Omega vehicles would be following her, piggybacking off each other so they wouldn't get made. Once they gave her the signal that she was clear, she would drive immediately to Omega, where the transmitter would once again be jammed.

The Watcher would think he'd lost her again for whatever reason. Maybe it was the mountains, or maybe the transmitter itself was faulty—after all, he hadn't had a signal from her the entire time she'd lived with the Ammonses. But hopefully he wouldn't decide to dig too far into it tonight.

But Steve didn't feel like he could draw a complete breath until Rosalyn made it safely back through the gates of Omega. As soon as a member of SWAT brought her up to the offices, Steve pulled her to him, breathing in the scent of her hair.

"How do you think it went? Do you think he bought it?" she asked.

"I hope so."

Jon walked out of the control room. "You did great, Rosalyn. If he doesn't buy it, it's definitely not because of anything you did or didn't do."

She looked up at Steve. "I just want this to be over with."

He kissed her forehead. "Tomorrow it will be."

But Steve knew that even the most well-thought-out plans, the no-holes plans, could sometimes fail.

THE NEXT MORNING all the Omega Sector employees were back at the café. They opened the restaurant at 7:00 a.m. as if they had been doing it for years.

Derek was in the back again as a cook. Jon was in the command room, but it was a van parked around the corner rather than at Omega. He would be calling the shots today, having the bird's-eye view of everything.

Steve had a different role to play: concerned lover.

It didn't require much acting on his part.

Steve would arrive at 7:45 a.m. Rosalyn would come in at 7:55 a.m., say something briefly to him, then excuse herself to go to the restroom.

From there, she would be taken out the back door and directly to Omega HQ. Steve categorically refused to risk her life by having her in the middle of a sting operation.

And the operation was huge. Not only were the dozen employees and customers in the restaurant Omega agents, but there were SWAT agents all around the building, and most of the people outside were theirs too. The lady walking the dog. The jogger a few blocks over whose route happened to go by the café a few times.

Others. All watching the café. Anyone who entered would be tagged: faces captured on camera, fingerprints collected and filed. Anyone who could possibly be the Watcher—so any male under the age of sixty—would be followed and/or tracked.

Steve had decided to use the Watcher's own means against him. Lillian was still playing the waitress. Her petite form belied the fact that she could kill a person in a dozen ways with her tiny bare hands. She would make sure that anyone who could possibly be the Watcher got a transmitter put on him.

It was a complex operation, but complex was what Omega did.

And it was showtime.

He parked his car, trying to make this all as normal as possible, and walked in the front entrance. Lillian greeted him with a perky "Good morning" and told him to sit wherever he wanted to.

He chose the booth near the corner and sat with his back to the wall so he could see the door. Just like he would do in any given restaurant. At least he didn't have to pretend that he wasn't law enforcement.

The place was relatively empty outside the people working for Omega. There was an older couple at one table and a young mother with her toddler at one of the booths. They would all be checked out but none of them were viable suspects.

The building had been thoroughly swept for explosives—at this point Steve didn't put it past the Watcher to just take out the whole place. They'd also been sure to search the closets and attics and crawl spaces. After what happened earlier this year—a psychopath deciding to reside in an agent's attic until the time was right for a kidnapping—they'd all learned their lesson.

Now all Steve could do was wait and watch. And pray that nothing tipped off the Watcher. It wouldn't take much.

Five minutes later a man came in, their first real possible suspect. He was tall, sort of bulky, wearing business attire. Jon's voice came on in Steve's ear.

"We've got him. Got a good shot of his face. Running it now to see if he shows up in any of our facial-recognition software."

"He's got a briefcase," Steve murmured behind his hand.

"Roger that."

A briefcase could carry explosives or a weapon.

"Infrared on the briefcase suggests no explosives," Aidan Killock, SWAT's explosives expert, said through the earpiece. He was in a different van outside.

The man was getting a coffee and muffin to go.

"Tag him anyway, Lillian."

He saw her nod briefly before she came around the counter and stood before the man.

"Here," she said, reaching up and messing with the back of his collar. "That was folded up a little, but now it's perfect."

"Thank you." The man seemed relieved and flattered to have received such attention from someone with Lillian's looks.

And the transmitter in his collar would allow them to track him.

"We've got him," Jon said. "He's not showing up in any of our facial software."

"I don't think that's him. Build isn't right for the guy who came at me on the motorcycle."

But Steve knew they would follow him anyway.

Business began to pick up as a number of people entered, some couples but a few single guys. Steve had to trust his team to do their jobs, because right at 7:55 a.m. Rosalyn walked in the door.

She waved to him and he stood and hugged her as if he hadn't seen her in two days rather than just the hour it had been.

"Are you hungry?" he asked her as they sat down at the booth.

"I'm always hungry."

This, again, was part of the script they had worked out last night. The Watcher had to be listening.

"What do you feel like?"

"Something soft. I have a bad toothache."

Lillian came over and took their order. Steve asked Rosalyn how she was feeling and if the baby had moved again.

He wanted Rosalyn out of there. The more crowded it got in the café, the more tense Steve became.

There were three men in the café right now who could

possibly be the Watcher. One in particular looked nervous. But then again, Steve didn't think the Watcher would look nervous.

Something wasn't right.

Steve brought his hand up to his mouth and turned his head to the side. "I'm sending Rosalyn out now."

"Are you sure it's not too soon?" Jon asked.

"I don't care. There are too many unknown variables."

"Roger that. The car is waiting."

Rosalyn didn't have an earpiece in case the transmitter also picked up on what was being said to her.

Steve nodded at her. She nodded back, knowing it was time to go. She reached over and grabbed his hand, squeezing it. He winked at her.

"I've got to go to the restroom."

"Okay."

She stood and walked to the back. The agent in the car reported a few minutes later that he safely had Rosalyn and they were headed back to HQ.

Whatever happened now, at least Rosalyn was safe. He breathed a sigh of relief.

It was short-lived, as a man—the nervous one he saw earlier—sat down in the booth across from him.

He pulled at a gun and pointed it straight at Steve.

"I don't think we've met. I'm the Watcher."

Chapter Twenty-Four

A cascade of emotions flooded Steve.

Rage that this bastard had terrorized Rosalyn for so long. And other women too, to the point of them killing themselves.

Relief that Rosalyn was gone, safe. Out of his clutches. She'd never be in this man's clutches again.

Surprise. This wasn't what he'd thought the Watcher would look like. He wasn't sure exactly what he'd thought the Watcher would look like, but it wasn't unkempt and sweaty like this man. But how did you put a face to a monster?

Either their plan had worked perfectly and the Watcher had grossly underestimated who Steve was and what sort of weight he carried in law enforcement, or the man had nerves of steel. He'd just pulled a gun on a cop in broad daylight with dozens of witnesses.

Or perhaps his intent had always been to kill Steve and he didn't care who saw.

Over the man's shoulder Steve could already see Lillian and the other Omega agents escorting the patrons out of the restaurant.

"Don't let any of them go," Steve said into his communication device. He didn't care if the man across from him knew he had backup. Let him worry.

"We're getting everyone's info. Why don't you worry about the guy pointing a gun at you."

"I'm assuming Ashton has him in his sights."

"Roger that, boss," Ashton's voice came through his ear. "But you'll be scrubbing brain matter off yourself for a long time."

Steve was tempted to tell him to take the shot. He had a gun, was pointing it at Steve, might turn and start shooting innocent people any moment. It would be considered an unfortunate but necessary kill.

Steve wasn't even sure he'd consider it that unfortunate.

But something wasn't right. Since his one sentence introducing himself, the man hadn't said anything. His hands were shaking. He was sweating.

"Nervous?" Steve asked.

The man nodded. "I'm the Watcher."

"Yeah, you said that." Steve took a sip of the cup of coffee Lillian had given him while Rosalyn was here, more to put the other man at ease than anything else. "Don't you have anything else you want to say to me? You know we have the place surrounded, don't you?"

"I am the Watcher." The man was sweating and the gun in his hand was shaking.

"Jon, you got an opinion of what's going on here?"

"Obviously the guy is highly stressed. I don't know, Steve. If I had to guess, I would say this isn't him. But then why is he pointing a gun at you?"

Tears squeezed out of the man's eyes. "I am the Watcher."

Steve gestured to Lillian to come over and plucked a pen out of her pocket. The Watcher continued to point the gun at Steve, not paying attention to Lillian.

Because he thought she wasn't a threat or for another reason entirely?

Like being given instructions to keep the gun pointed on Steve.

"What's your name?" Steve asked the man.

"I am the Watcher."

"How about I arrest you and we figure out your name once you're in custody."

The gun shook more, but the man didn't pull the trigger. Steve wrote on the napkin. *Are you being forced?*

He spun the napkin and pushed it over where the man could read it. Tears poured out of the man's eyes as he nodded. He reached up and flipped his collar.

It was a transmitter just like he'd found on Rosalyn's clothes.

The Watcher was using this man as a patsy.

"All right, look, let's just talk this out. Okay?"

The man nodded that he understood. Steve wrote on the napkin. *Can he see you?*

The man shook his head no. Steve gestured for him to put down the gun. After a few moments he did so.

"You know I'm police, right?"

"I am the Watcher."

Evidently that was all the man was allowed to say. Steve grabbed another napkin. *Where is the man who did this? At my house. Will kill my wife and kids.*

"Look, just put the gun down. It's me you want. I don't want anyone else to get hurt by accident." *Address?*

The man wrote it. Then, *I have to kill you or he will kill them.*

Jon's voice sounded in his ear. "I've got the address, Steve, and we have agents en route to the guy's house. They'll go in silently."

Steve picked up the gun and handed it to Lillian.

"You have to put the gun down. If you were going to shoot me, you would've done it by—"

Lillian shot the gun over his head into the wall.

"Oh my God, that guy just shot that guy. He's got a gun!" she screamed at the top of her voice.

"Hey, he's running away—" Derek yelled out, helping along the charade.

Steve reached out and grabbed the transmitter from the guy's collar. He dropped it to the ground and stomped on it.

"Any others?" he mouthed.

The man shook his head, confusion plain in his eyes.

"We've got law enforcement en route to your house," Steve told the man. "What's your name?"

"Donny Showalter. He told me I had to come in here and shoot you. He told me all I could say was that we hadn't met and that I was the Watcher." The guy put his face in his hands. "I have to get to my house."

"How far do you live from here?"

"Only a few blocks."

"Steve, our agents are there," Jon told him. "We have eyes inside. The family is tied up but no one is hurt."

He relayed the information to the man, who promptly deflated on the table in relief.

"Is anybody there with them?" Steve waited for the information to be relayed back to him.

A few minutes later Jon was back in his ear. "Steve, the wife says the guy who tied them up left right after Donny did."

He'd been around here. Maybe in the coffeehouse or directly outside. Seeing what happened. Probably hoping they would kill Donny and cause even more chaos.

"Is my family really okay? I need to see them."

"I'll have them call you in just a minute, okay?"

Donny nodded.

"Can you tell me anything about the man who put you up to this? What he looked like?"

"No. He broke into our house this morning while we were having breakfast. He was wearing a mask."

Damn it. The Watcher had been smarter than they thought. He'd been making sure this wasn't a setup, and if he was anywhere in the vicinity, he would know that Steve was much more deeply entrenched in law enforcement than just some sort of beat cop.

Taking him by surprise was no longer an option.

"Steve." Jon's voice was more somber than he'd ever heard it.

"Go, Jon." He pressed the earpiece farther in his ear so he could hear over the chaos going on around him.

"I just got word from HQ. Travis Loveridge and Rosalyn never checked in. They found the car about a half mile from HQ. Loveridge is dead. Rosalyn is missing."

ROSALYN HAD AGENT Loveridge's blood all over her. Her arms, her neck, her hands. She couldn't get it off.

Of course, dried blood was the least of her problems.

She stared at the man driving the car. "I remember you. You're Lindsey's psychologist from when she was a teenager. Dr. Zinger."

"Zenger." He turned and smiled at her. Like they were old friends or something. Like he hadn't walked up to the car while they were stopped at a red light and shot the agent driving. Like he hadn't been stalking and terrorizing her for the better part of a year.

Rosalyn shrank back against the car door. He hadn't touched her at all, except to catch her when he drugged her and tied her hands, but she didn't want to take a chance.

She was barely holding it together. If he touched her, she might start screaming and never stop.

"Lindsey liked you," she whispered. "Thought you were so handsome."

Rosalyn remembered. They'd been eighteen. Lindsey had been in trouble again and sent to group counseling this time. When Rosalyn had come home from college for a semester break, she'd asked her sister how things were going.

Rosalyn hadn't been encouraged when all her sister would talk about was how hot the counselor was rather than showing any interest in truly kicking her drug habit.

He was handsome, if Rosalyn could distance herself enough from the terror. Clean-cut, short brown hair. Good physique. But all Rosalyn saw was the monster.

"You killed her," Rosalyn whispered.

He shrugged, not looking at her. "If it helps, she never knew it was me."

It didn't help at all.

Rosalyn's hands were tied with some sort of zip tie. "Where are you taking me?"

"We have to get out of Colorado, of course. Your boyfriend is already dead—I sent a friend of mine in to shoot him. Since Steve didn't know who I was, I'm sure he won't care that it wasn't me who actually killed him."

Rosalyn stared and could hear her breath sawing in and out of her nose and mouth. Was he telling the truth? Was Steve really dead?

"I wasn't exactly sure how the whole café scenario was going to play out. But when I saw you leave out the back door, I knew it had been some sort of setup. How did you know I would be there?"

Rosalyn tried to get her panic under control. She had to keep the fact that Omega Sector was onto him a secret. "We didn't. I guess Steve was doing stuff just in case. I was hitching a ride from that guy to the bus station. You didn't have to kill him."

Zenger's eyes were narrowed as he turned to look at

her. She wasn't sure if he was buying her story. "Hitch-hiking is dangerous."

She bit back a hysterical laugh. "Ended up being much more dangerous for him."

She looked out the window again. They were on the interstate. There was no way she could jump out of the car now and survive.

She refused to believe him when he said Steve was dead. Zenger hadn't been there; he'd been too busy killing that poor agent who'd been with her. There was no way he could know for sure Steve had actually died. Maybe the shot hadn't killed him.

Steve was alive and would be coming for her. He and Jon and Brandon…they would figure out who Zenger was; they would find him.

Steve would rescue her. He wouldn't leave her and the baby in the hands of this madman.

She had to hold on to that or there was no way she would survive.

They sat in silence for miles.

"Where are we going?" she asked again finally.

"Back to familiar ground. I'm from Mobile too, you know. I have a nice little place where you can stay."

"And do what?" She couldn't keep the revulsion out of her voice, not that she tried.

He laughed, a friendly sound under any other circumstances. "Rosalyn, I'm not like that at all. I don't plan to force myself on you in any way. That's beneath me."

"But killing people isn't?"

He sighed. "I don't kill out of choice or some sort of sport. Honestly. It brings me no pleasure."

"Then why kill at all?"

"For the research. This is all for science, Rosalyn."

Oh God, Jon and Brandon had been right all along with

their profile. That gave Rosalyn hope that they would be able to follow through and find her.

"Science?"

"I am a psychologist. I help people. The data I'm collecting about isolation will be used to help disturbed people for decades to come."

He honestly believed it.

"Isolation?"

"Yes, yes, that's what all of this has been about. I take young women and divide them from everyone in their life. I prey upon their worst fears and then see what they do to cope. How long they can last."

She wondered if he would tell her, if she asked, about the tracking devices. About the dentist and the one in her tooth. But she didn't want to tip her hand.

"What happens to them when they can't last any longer?"

Zenger shook his head sadly. "Unfortunately, they commit suicide. It's a regrettable side effect of this research. But don't you understand? The loss is acceptable for the greater good. I am on the forefront of research that every mental-health-care professional would love to be a part of."

If it hadn't been absolutely sickening, Zenger's zeal for his work would almost have been commendable.

"Was that what you wanted with me? For me to kill myself?"

"You, my dear, you have been the longest-lasting subject in my research." He glanced at her again. "And to think, you weren't supposed to be my original subject."

"Lindsey was."

"Exactly. But I realized that the drug abuse made Lindsey a poor test subject. You were much stronger, more resilient. I just had to wait for the right time."

She assumed that meant wait until she went to the dentist. The dentist that Lindsey had suggested. Had suggested because a doctor mentioned it to her.

Zenger had been that doctor. Had helped orchestrate the entire thing from the beginning.

"I'm sure your pregnancy has played an important role in your resilience. You don't want to die. You want to live for your baby."

Maybe she could get him to understand that. Make him think that she could understand the importance of his research so he would let her go.

"Yes. The baby is an unforeseen variable with me, I'm sure." Rosalyn nodded. "It must mean I can't fit into the conceived categories and corrupt your data analysis."

He nodded, obviously glad she understood. "I forgot you majored in accounting. So you are familiar with data and experimentation."

"Yes. You're obviously the expert, but I do have some knowledge. I know the baby changes things."

"You're absolutely right. He does. I had to really think about what needed to be done when I found out you were pregnant."

"Dr. Zenger, now that you've explained it to me, I see how important your research is. Like you said, the baby changes things for me. I can never be truly isolated from people when I have a little person growing inside me."

"That's exactly right, Rosalyn. I'm so happy you understand."

"So you'll let me go? You know I will never tell anyone about your research. Unless you want me to, of course."

She meant it with every fiber of her being. If she could get out of this with both her and the baby unharmed, she would do whatever Zenger wanted.

Steve would hunt him down to the ends of the earth, but Rosalyn would stay out of it.

"No, I can't let you go, Rosalyn. I'm sorry."

She tried not to let the disappointment crush her. She needed to reason with him. "But what about the baby? Like you said, I don't fit any categories anymore. I'm not useful for your research."

"Rosalyn, you were an outlier even before the baby. I'm not sure you would've ever been statistically useful."

"Then why are you taking me to Mobile?"

"I'll keep you there until you have the baby. Then, unfortunately, I'll have to kill you. Like you said, you're not useful for my research anymore."

"What about the baby?"

"Oh, he will give me a lifetime worth of data. Just think of what I'll be able to do."

Suddenly there wasn't enough air in the car. Rosalyn reached for the handle of the door. She didn't care that they were on the interstate. She couldn't stay in this car a moment longer. She would have to take her chances with jumping.

Zenger swung the car toward the shoulder, slowing rapidly, grabbing her arm tightly to keep her from jumping out.

She fought him. Slowing was what she wanted him to do. It gave her a better chance to survive.

"Stop, Rosalyn."

She kept fighting.

He pulled the car to a stop, both of them slamming forward as he hit the brakes hard. Now he had both hands to hold her with.

She didn't care if she had to stay here and fight him for the rest of her life. She was not going to let him drive her somewhere where he could keep her baby and do experiments on him.

She felt a sharp sting on the side of her neck. It took

only a few moments before all her movements began to feel slushy.

"No…" she whispered. She felt tears leak out of her eyes, but her arms were too heavy to wipe them.

"You fought the good fight. Now go to sleep."

She tried not to, but in just moments the darkness pulled her under.

Chapter Twenty-Five

Steve did what he did best: worked the problem.

He did not focus on the fact a psychopath had Rosalyn in his clutches. Did not focus on the fact that they had no idea where said psychopath was taking her or how they would find her. That they still had no idea what the Watcher looked like or where he was from.

Because if he focused on those things, the fear and agony would overwhelm him.

He'd known helplessness when Melanie had died; it had ripped a hole in his heart.

But he knew he wouldn't survive if Rosalyn didn't make it.

He kept that all pushed aside because it would do nothing to help them find her now.

Travis Loveridge was dead. Evidently the Watcher had walked up to their car while they were stopped at a red light and shot him point-blank in the head. There had been witnesses, but no one had been able to see the Watcher's face. They'd seen him pick up a woman—an unconscious woman with long black hair—and carry her to his car parked at the side of the street.

A gray sedan. There were thousands of them on the roads. They were checking, but so far a dead end.

They'd pulled up the feed from the traffic camera, but it had been pointing in the wrong direction. Another dead end.

Brandon was interviewing Gavin from the café and his wife. Molly's lab crew was checking for forensics at the house. But so far…

Steve was studying computerized maps. Working on the assumption that the Watcher was taking Rosalyn out of Colorado. He assumed back to Mobile.

But it was too far to make it in one day. Steve knew from personal experience a week ago going the opposite way. He had every Omega person who could be spared making calls to hotels along the interstate heading south.

Steve personally had called the state and highway patrols for New Mexico, Kansas and Texas. He wanted them to understand the direness of the situation; he didn't want it to be just be another report that came across their desks.

It was all long shots, but Steve would keep taking long shots until one of them paid off. It was getting late now. Dark. The thought of her alone with the Watcher overnight…

Derek put a hand on Steve's shoulder. "How are you holding up?"

Steve wiped a hand across his face. What could he say?

That panic was crawling up his spine, threatening to take over not only his whole body but the whole world?

How would anyone understand that?

"She's alive, Steve. When the panic starts to overwhelm you, you push it back down with the thought that until we know definitely otherwise, Rosalyn and the baby are both alive."

Maybe someone could understand that.

Derek could. Hadn't Steve seen the very agony in his own eyes in Derek's eighteen months ago when a sadistic bastard had kidnapped Molly?

Derek had moved heaven and earth to get her back. Steve had helped. He prayed he would get his own happily-ever-after with Rosalyn and their child.

"I thought she was dead once, Derek. And that was before I knew what she meant to me. I'll be damned if I'll let her die again not knowing I love her."

Molly walked through the door. "You're not going to have to."

Both men turned to her. "What do you mean?"

"I've found the frequency the Watcher was using to track Rosalyn from a transmitter Jon and Brandon brought back from other victims. The transmitters were still live."

"What?" Derek asked.

"I don't know if the Watcher was trying to keep tabs on the families or what. But I was able to use them to find other transmitters. Actually, I've found *all* the women—since he used the same frequency for all the transmitters."

"How do we know which one is Rosalyn?"

She ran over to the computer and brought up a navigation system on the screen.

"I'm going to assume she's the one halfway between here and Mobile." She pointed to a red dot near Oklahoma City.

Oklahoma City was less than six hundred miles. They could've made it there if the Watcher drove at a rapid pace.

He would've been moving at a rapid pace.

Derek kissed Molly and ran for the door. "The team and I will meet you at the helicopter in ten minutes," he called back to Steve.

Molly touched Steve's arm as he moved toward the door and handed him a small GPS screen. "You're going to need this. Outside Oklahoma City is the best I can do from this far away. As you get closer, this monitor will provide more details."

Steve kissed her forehead. "Thank you, Molly."

She shrugged. "You once broke all the rules and gave Derek a plane to come after me. If you hadn't, I wouldn't be here now." She pushed him. "Go get your girl."

TRUE TO MOLLY'S WORD, the GPS continued to become more detailed the closer they got to Oklahoma.

The transmission wasn't in Oklahoma City at all; it was in Guymon, a much smaller town northwest of the city.

At some point the Watcher had gotten off the main interstates, which had been a smart move on his part.

"Boss, there's no actual helicopter landing site big enough for us in Guymon. But we've been given permission to land on the high school field." Lillian was flying the helicopter. One of her many skills.

"Good." Steve spoke into the headset he and the five members of the SWAT team were wearing.

As they got closer, Steve was able to pinpoint Rosalyn's location. A hotel about two miles south of the high school. Steve provided the info to Lillian, who relayed it to the local police, who would also be providing them transportation to the hotel. They landed a few minutes later.

The local deputies were there with a county van to take the SWAT team and Steve to the location. Steve could tell the team was ready.

There wasn't anybody he would want at his back more than these men—and this woman—right here.

"You guys…" He looked at Derek, then at Lillian. He needed to express how important Rosalyn was to him.

"No need to say it, boss," Derek told him. "We'll get her out, safely."

They were less than a minute out when the news came over the van's CB unit.

"We've got reports of shots fired at the Best Holiday hotel on Thirty-Second Street."

That was the hotel where Rosalyn's tracker had stopped.

Steve's curse was foul. The van squealed into the hotel parking lot and Steve and the team poured out the back door before it even stopped moving.

The place was surrounded by cop cars, officers using their vehicles for cover, weapons drawn.

Steve rushed up to the officer in charge, a kid, probably in his mid-twenties. Doubtful he had any experience with this sort of situation. "I'm Steve Drackett, head of the Critical Response Division of Omega Sector. I need your name and a rundown of the situation."

"Keith Holloway, sir. Evidently a man was bringing in his exhausted pregnant wife, who'd been very sick. He was half carrying her, according to one witness. But then she started screaming that he was kidnapping her and he pulled out a gun. Shot the clerk."

"How long have you been out here?" he asked Holloway.

"Less than two minutes, sir."

Steve looked over at Ashton. "Got any ideas for a distance shot?"

Ashton was already putting his distance scope on his rifle. "It will be hard without knowing where Rosalyn is."

"I'm going in to draw him out. As soon as you can get a good shot, you take it."

"Steve—" Derek put an arm out as Steve stood up.

"He's trapped. He knows it. Getting out with Rosalyn will be nearly impossible. He'll cut his losses and shoot her as a distraction. And he knows the longer he stays, the less chance he'll have to get away."

"He'll shoot you."

The other members of the team were taking out their rifles too. None of them were as good a shot as Ashton, but that didn't matter now.

Steve looked at them. "I'll draw him out. You take him down."

Mind made up, he walked quickly to the front door and went through. A little bell chimed as he did.

"Leave right now or I will kill her!" Steve couldn't see anyone but could tell they were behind the counter.

"I think it's time we meet face-to-face, Watcher."

He heard Rosalyn's sob but didn't know if it was from pain or relief.

"Who are you?"

"You sent someone to kill me today. That didn't work out."

"Steve Drackett? How did you find me?" His tone was incredulous.

Steve took another step closer. He needed to draw the man out. "The same way you've been finding Rosalyn all these months. And the other women. We know about the transmitters in the teeth. It's over."

"Do you know what you've done?" He stood up now but kept Rosalyn right in front of him, his gun to her head. No one would be able to get a clean shot.

And Rosalyn was glassy-eyed, pale and covered in blood. The Watcher seemed to be half propping her up.

Steve forced himself to stay focused.

"You've ruined my research. My life's work! You have no idea what good I was doing for the world." He was frantic, voice high-pitched, hysterical.

"All I want is Rosalyn." Steve kept his arms out in front of him but shifted his weight to the balls of his feet. He was going to make a move that would draw the Watcher's attention and gun to him.

"No. She's already promised me her baby. She understands my research and knows how important it is."

Now. He had to do it now.

But Rosalyn beat him to it. Her eyes rolled up in the back of her head and she slid to the floor.

The Watcher couldn't hold her up and turned his gun on Steve.

Glass shattered all around him and the Watcher flew back and onto the ground, dead, shot six times. Every single member of the SWAT team had taken him out.

Steve jumped over the desk counter and picked up Rosalyn's still form. There was more blood on her now. Had she been shot? His hands were so shaky he couldn't get a pulse.

Derek and Lillian made their way to him first. He was rocking Rosalyn in his arms but couldn't get her to wake up.

"She's bleeding," he told Derek. "She's hurt."

Lillian put two fingers at Rosalyn's throat. "She's alive, Steve. I think she's been drugged."

All he could see was the blood. "But she's bleeding."

He felt Derek's hand on his shoulder, pressing hard.

"You're bleeding, boss. Bastard got a shot off at you before we took him down."

Steve didn't care. As long as Rosalyn was alive, the baby was okay, Steve didn't care about himself. He pulled her close to him, uncaring of the pain, certain he was never going to let her go ever again.

Chapter Twenty-Six

"You're going to get fired if you keep taking all this time off work, you know," Rosalyn told Steve as they walked through the sands of Pensacola beach a month later.

He smiled at her and pulled her closer to his side. "I have ten years' worth of vacation time saved up. I'm not going to get fired."

"So you brought me back here to the scene of the crime, literally and figuratively."

She was glad. The drugs Zenger had given her had slowed both her and the baby's heart rates to dangerously low levels. She'd been unconscious for two days. But that had probably been for the best since Steve had been shot while rescuing her.

He'd gone into surgery and they'd removed the bullet, but there had been some pretty significant damage done to his shoulder. It would require quite a bit of rehab to get it back to full motion again.

While she was unconscious, since the drug Zenger gave her worked similarly to a general anesthetic, Steve had convinced the doctor of the medical necessity of having the crown with the transmitter removed and replaced with just a plain old regular crown.

Rosalyn had been thrilled to hear it, even though the Watcher was dead and it didn't matter anymore.

The Watcher was truly gone. Rosalyn had explained

who he was, and with the technology Molly had cracked, they had let the other women know what had happened to them so they could get the transmitters removed.

Of course, it was too late for the four women they knew of who had committed suicide and a fifth one whose case they hadn't discovered yet.

But Rosalyn had made it. She was still so thankful she'd met Steve at this beach—now seven months ago—because otherwise she wasn't sure that she would've.

He was everything to her.

Rosalyn had been alone most of her life, even when she'd been surrounded by her family. This past month she'd been shown what a family was really meant to be. People willing to stand with you, protect you, put their lives on the line for you.

Family was something that had nothing to do with blood and DNA and everything to do with love. She knew no matter what happened between her and Steve, the baby she carried would have a family who loved him. The people in Omega already did.

She knew Steve loved the baby. She just wished she knew how he felt about *her*. Even though she'd lived in his house the last month, they still hadn't talked about the future.

"I'm not really good at romance," he murmured.

She shook her head. "Says the man taking me on a stroll on the beach as the sun is setting. I think you're doing okay."

"There's something I've been wanting to ask you since the first night we met."

"Oh yeah, what's that?"

"Will you have dinner with me?"

"What?" She laughed.

"I want to take you out to dinner and on dates. I want to court you and show you how much you mean to me. I want to show you that you can trust me with your secrets. You can trust me with your heart."

"Steve, if this is about the baby…"

"No." He turned so they were face-to-face. "All of that has nothing to do with the baby. It's what I've wanted to say to you since the first minute you walked into that tiki bar when I could tell you were capital-*T* trouble."

He smiled at her. "I'm excited and terrified about the baby, as all new fathers should be. But you're the one I want, Rosalyn. Always. I will ask you to marry me tomorrow. But today, I just want to take you out. Will you have dinner with me?"

She reached her arms around his waist and pulled him to her.

"Yes. To both."

And right there in the sand where everything had almost ended, her new life began.

* * * * *

Look for more Omega stories
from Janie Crouch in 2017.

You'll find them wherever
Mills & Boon Intrigue books are sold!

MILLS & BOON®

INTRIGUE
Romantic Suspense

A SEDUCTIVE COMBINATION OF DANGER AND DESIRE

A sneak peek at next month's titles...

In stores from 12th January 2017:

- **Law and Disorder** – Heather Graham *and*
  Hot Combat – Elle James
- **Texas-Sized Trouble** – Barb Han *and*
  Mountain Witness – Lena Diaz
- **Eagle Warrior** – Jenna Kernan *and*
  Wild Montana – Danica Winters

Romantic Suspense

- **Cavanaugh in the Rough** – Marie Ferrarella
- **Her Alpha Marine** – Karen Anders

Just can't wait?
Buy our books online a month before they hit the shops!
www.millsandboon.co.uk

Also available as eBooks.

MILLS & BOON®

Why shop at millsandboon.co.uk?

Each year, thousands of romance readers find their perfect read at millsandboon.co.uk. That's because we're passionate about bringing you the very best romantic fiction. Here are some of the advantages of shopping at www.millsandboon.co.uk:

* **Get new books first**—you'll be able to buy your favourite books one month before they hit the shops

* **Get exclusive discounts**—you'll also be able to buy our specially created monthly collections, with up to 50% off the RRP

* **Find your favourite authors**—latest news, interviews and new releases for all your favourite authors and series on our website, plus ideas for what to try next

* **Join in**—once you've bought your favourite books, don't forget to register with us to rate, review and join in the discussions

Visit **www.millsandboon.co.uk**
for all this and more today!

MILLS_WEB